Twenty Years a Stranger

Deborah Twelves

Fortis Publishing
Kemp House
160 City Road
London
EC1V 2NX

Although this story is based on real events, is is a work of fiction. Some characters and events have been added for creative purposes and are entirely a product of the author's imagination.

About the author

Deborah Twelves was born in Sheffield, but raised in Ponteland, Northumberland. She studied French and Spanish at Edinburgh University and taught languages for some years while living in France, Spain and Northern Quebec. She now divides her time between her home in Pwllheli, on the Llyn Peninsula of North Wales and her family home in Northumberland but often travels abroad. She has a black Labrador called Nala and a black Lusitano horse called Recurso (Ric), who take up a lot of her spare time, although yacht racing, which she began at an early age with her father, remains her great passion.

Deborah has written many articles for the sailing press over the years and **Twenty Years a Stranger** is her debut novel, based on true events in her life.
It is the first book in the **Stranger Trilogy**. The other two books, **Ghost of a Stranger** and **The Boy Stranger** will follow soon.

For Dad

There is a special place in Heaven for a father who teaches his daughter to sail

For Mum

I am a strong woman today because a strong woman raised me

Thank you both for always being on my side and for teaching me that giving up is never an option.

Acknowledgements

My heartfelt thanks go to the following people:

Ken Scott, my amazing book coach and mentor, for believing in me from the start, for giving me the confidence to write this book and for guiding me through the whole process.

My editor Joan Elliott and the team at Fortis Publishing.

My friend, Michael Oliver, who shot the cover photo on Marsden Grotto beach at sunrise.

I consider myself very lucky and am eternally grateful to have such a loving family and so many wonderful friends in my life, who supported me, not only through the process of writing this book, but through some of the worst times of my life. Sadly, I cannot name you all here, or the book would be twice as long, but I hope you know who you are and that your friendship means the world to me. Whether you gave me a place to sleep, fed me, plied me with wine, made me laugh, gave me a shoulder to cry on, listened to my rants, came to my rescue or gave me a kick up the backside when I needed it, know that I would never have got through the last few years without you. Thank you for believing in my ability to write this book, for encouraging me when I faltered or doubted myself and for inspiring some of my characters.

You are the people who understood my past, believed in my future, accepted me as I am and helped turn my dreams into reality. I love you all.

Prologue

The Gaslight effect is a form of emotional abuse that causes a person to lose their sense of identity, perception and self-worth. It may ultimately cause them to doubt their sanity. The Gaslighter feels compelled to dominate and control.

Julia

The woman who opened the gate to the small terraced house was unremarkable. Loose strands of her mid-length, mousy brown hair blew across her face in the breeze and she squinted slightly in the bright May sunshine. A perfect English summer's day in the sleepy little village on the edge of the Derbyshire Dales, where she had lived throughout her whole life.

She glanced nervously back up the lane as she let herself into the house, but she needn't have worried. Nobody noticed her. Not the teenager from next door walking his dog, nor the young couple strolling hand in hand, totally engrossed in each other and oblivious to the outside world. She had perfected the art of melting into the background and it suited her perfectly.

She didn't much care for social interaction these days. She no longer even noticed how overgrown the garden had become, or how grubby the windows were, or how the paint was peeling off the window frames. The chipped fingernails of her hand that would once have been perfectly manicured went similarly unnoticed.

None of it mattered.

She stepped inside, closed the door behind her and hung her jacket on the hook in the hallway, pausing as she caught sight of herself in the full-length mirror. She was not unattractive, but her flat, black shoes and unfashionably straight jeans, together with her slightly scruffy, navy blue jumper and total lack of makeup, gave the impression that she was older than her thirty-two years. Everything about the woman staring back at her from the mirror screamed: Anonymous. Forgettable. Invisible.

It had not always been like that, but little by little she had seen the happy, carefree, fun version of herself slipping quietly away without a backward glance and she could do nothing to stop it happening.

She remembered one particular evening, as clearly as if it were yesterday, because she knew without a doubt that it marked the point of no return for her. It was three months ago, give or take a few days. She had tried so hard, cooking his favourite meal of Chilli con Carne and even dressing up for dinner, just as he liked her to do. No leggings and baggy top for her that night. He had told her repeatedly, in no uncertain terms, that she was letting herself go and she was determined to show him he was wrong, daring to dream that maybe things could work out for them after all.

Staring at her reflection in the hallway mirror, her insides twisted uncomfortably as she relived in her head the crushing humiliation she had felt that night. She could almost feel the buttons of the red, lacy suspender belt she had worn to seduce him digging painfully into her thighs.

She knew it had been a mistake to suggest trying for another baby, even before the words had left her mouth, but she just hadn't been

7

able to help herself. In her mind's eye, she saw herself take an involuntary step backward, recoiling in horror at the look on his face. She cursed her stupidity and wished that she could somehow stop her life unravelling before her very eyes but, before she knew it, she was speaking again and the bitter words of accusation were spilling out like overflowing bathwater, never to be taken back.

'You're glad she died, aren't you? You never wanted her anyway! Admit it!' she had sobbed.

Two years and seventeen days had somehow slipped by since she lost baby Ava. Two years and seventeen days since the unspeakable horror of that day, when she had endured the torture of childbirth. The indescribable pain of pushing out a baby whose cries she would never hear. A baby who would never draw breath. Packed off to a cold hospital morgue and eventually cremated, her ashes scattered on the wind. She had cuddled and rocked the lifeless little bundle, utterly and completely alone in her desolation.

He should have been by her side. He should have held her close and sobbed with her, sharing the grief and the pain, but he had barely even looked into the face of their beautiful, angelic little daughter. He had remained on the other side of the room, looking uncomfortable as he fidgeted and paced the tiled floor, unable or unwilling to connect. He had abandoned her when she needed him the most. She had looked into his eyes, silently pleading for some comfort, searching for a unity of some sort, but she had seen only a cold detachment on his face and that was what had shaken her the most.

'Don't be too hard on him,' one of the nurses had said to her afterwards, trying to be kind. 'People grieve in different ways. The important thing is that you are both there for each other as you move forward.'

The same nurse had sat with her for the rest of the day, even when she had finally been forced to let Ava go. *Let Ava go?* The other nurses had had to almost prise the dead baby from her mother's arms. When they were the only two people in the small room, the same, kind nurse had held her hand, stroked her head and passed her paper tissues when the inevitable tears flowed.

He was nowhere to be seen.

In those early days she could not begin to imagine ever being able to 'move forward', but little by little, she dragged herself back into the land of the living and forced herself to carry on. She knew she would never be able to get over the agony of her loss, but she had learned to live with it and was ready to try again, despite the heartache she had experienced. She was desperate to become a mother and she had convinced herself that he wanted it too.

She had been wrong.

Her thoughts returned to that evening three months ago, when everything changed, when she finally found the courage to speak out and say what she was thinking. Her words of blame hung in the air, and for a moment he said nothing but the look of contempt was enough to silence her. When he eventually spoke, his words came out in a venomous sneer and she realised in growing despair that things were most definitely not going to be okay. There would be no fairy tale ending to her story.

'You're pathetic. How many times have I told you I don't want children?' he snarled. 'How much clearer can I make it? Seriously, are you completely brain dead? I don't want children now and I didn't want children then. Get it through your thick head.'

She searched for some words of defiance, of reason. She found none.

She jumped as he slammed his fist on the table and continued to berate her.

'It was your responsibility to take the pill every day but you couldn't even get that right, could you? I wouldn't mind betting you actually 'forgot' to take it deliberately. I am sick and tired of you and your constant whining about kids. You're just no fun anymore. It's boring. *You* are boring. You're not the only one who ever lost a baby for fuck's sake. Stop making such a drama out of everything and get over yourself.'

She stared at him in silence. His face was ugly and contorted as he spat the words at her. Her bottom lip trembled and the tears welled up in her eyes. But he was not done yet.

'And if you really want the truth, then yes, I was relieved. I mean, look at the state of you. Can you honestly imagine looking after a baby? You can't even look after yourself. You're an embarrassment and I have absolutely no idea anymore what I ever saw in you. You make my skin crawl. And what was this all about tonight? Some sort of desperate attempt to seduce me? Was I supposed to pounce on you and ravish you?' he mocked, looking her up and down with disdain.

She shrank from the spiteful words, which seemed to anger him even more.

He stood up abruptly and shoved the table into her stomach, causing her to gasp in shock. He delivered his parting shot as he was half-way through the door.

'I need to get out of here. I can hardly bear to look at you. You suck the life out of everything and everyone. Why don't you do us all a favour and just fuck off permanently? Seriously, would anyone even notice? Or care? I for one have had a bellyful of your shit. And do not for one second think I will let you drag me down with you, you pathetic, snivelling bitch!'

She flinched as the door slammed and she heard his footsteps on the gravel, heading for his car. She had wanted so desperately to please him, to feel sexy and desirable again, but she knew that he no longer looked at her that way and he had certainly dispelled any lingering doubts she may have been harbouring that evening.

She had tried her best, she really had, but he had barely touched her since baby Ava. She had been prepared to do whatever he wanted, like in the old days, but no matter what she did it was never enough. He despised her and he no longer made even the slightest attempt to disguise it. She looked at herself in the mirror and felt like a cheap tart.

If she was being honest the rot had set in the day she told him she was pregnant. It was true he had said he didn't want children, but she had always believed he would come around. Who was she kidding? They had just grown further apart and she knew for a fact he was sleeping with other women behind her back. She had chosen to ignore that, just so long as he always came home to her and she could maintain her illusion of the happy family life she had always craved, a life that would one day include a child.

She had realised that night, as she tried desperately to reconnect with her husband that her dream was never going to come true. For years she had held onto a fantasy future that would never translate into reality. She had finally acknowledged to herself that their marriage was over and with that acceptance, despite all the hurt, she felt a strange sense of calm wash over her.

It was time to take control of her own life again. Time to move on.

She turned away from the mirror in the hall, no longer able to ignore the frantic whining of her beloved black Labrador Ted, who had been with her from a tiny pup, through thick and thin. He was almost twelve years old now but still acted like a puppy. He leapt on her as she opened the kitchen door, unable to contain himself. He stood tall on his hind legs, front paws up on her chest, tail wagging and tongue licking any exposed flesh he could find. He was desperate to show how much he had missed her and how much he loved her.

She spoke in a whisper and ruffled the soft fur behind his ears.

'Gorgeous boy, yes, I love you too.'

She noticed a few more grey hairs, another two or three white whiskers and he wasn't as agile as he had once been. She felt a fleeting pang of guilt, but she pushed it to the back of her mind.

She was quite proud of herself, feeling that at last there was some kind of order in her life. She was in control and it was a long time since she had felt like that. She had even remembered to post a birthday card to her mother and it would arrive in good time for once, instead of the usual two days late.

There had also been a long and difficult phone conversation with her older sister, but she knew it had to be done and was glad they had made up after the horrendous row of the previous week. The argument had been about money as usual, or rather her lack of it, and her sister had said some awful, hurtful things, accusing her of continually sponging off their mother. The conversation had then turned inevitably to him and she retaliated angrily, jumping to his defence as she always seemed to do, with things that would have been better left unsaid.

Someone once told her that saying sorry is like trying to repair a smashed plate. You can glue it back together but it will never be quite the same again.

She hoped that wasn't true.

She paused for a moment to look at the picture of Amber, the chestnut mare she adored, before lifting it off the wall, reaching into the small hole behind it and removing the thousand pounds in cash she had got from selling her. She put the money carefully into an envelope and wrote simply: *Mum xxx*. Then she placed it on the hall table.

It was too little too late, but what could she do? Things had been tough for her since he left and she could barely make ends meet most months. She was doing her best to make amends for what she had put them all through. She hoped they would understand one day.

She replaced the picture, adjusting it to make sure it was hanging straight. Patting her thigh encouragingly, she walked into the kitchen with Ted trotting eagerly at her heels. She put a generous scoop of food into his bowl and placed it on the floor in its usual place. A smile crossed her face as she watched him pounce excitedly on the bowl, tail wagging as he started to devour its contents.

She looked down at the floor. A dog's life. If only everything were that simple. He remained engrossed in his food and didn't look up as she walked away and closed the kitchen door quietly behind her.

If only things could have happened differently; if only she could turn back the clock.

If only, if only....

She walked calmly up the stairs. By the time she reached the top, the dog had finished his food and was whining and pawing at the door. She ignored him. It was for the best.

On the landing at the top of the stairs, she could see Amber's lunge line with her head collar attached to it. The other end was tied securely to the hand-rail with a bow line. She smiled to herself, remembering how he had taught her to tie knots, recalling happier times on the boat with him, but she was not about to waver now. There could be no room for error and she had been meticulous in her preparation, measuring the rope out carefully.

Without hesitation she picked up the head collar in one hand and stepped over the bannister, standing with her back to the rails. A shaft of sunlight streamed through the window and, as its gentle warmth washed over her face, she felt an overwhelming sense of peace and relief at the inevitability of it all. This was her destiny now and soon she would be free.

She surprised herself at just how calm she was, as she fastened the head collar around her slender neck. She could still hear the dog downstairs, but she did not falter.

'Goodbye my darling boy,' she whispered. 'I'm so sorry, but you'll be ok, I promise.'

She heard his hurtful words again in her head....

Why don't you just fuck off, permanently?

She stepped into the sunlight and she was finally free.

PART I

The Game

Nar·cis·sist

A narcissist, by definition, is someone with a pervasive pattern of grandiosity, need for admiration, and lack of empathy, whose symptoms begin in early adulthood. Narcissists often don't believe the rules apply to them.[1]

---

[1] Cory Newman PhD, Professor of Psychology at the University of Pennsylvania, USA.

The Awakening

Do you ever miss yourself? The person you were before Life changed everything...?

Present Day

Grace

I know now from bitter experience that it is impossible to ever truly know another person. Deceit is two-faced and those who practise the art of deception have two versions of themselves: the idealised, sugar-coated version that they want the world to see, and the other less desirable version, the one that represents who they really are, crouching in the shadows, hidden from view.

Everyone has secrets and everyone tells lies, sometimes for the best of reasons, or so we convince ourselves, but the real danger comes when we have told a lie so often that it becomes an integral part of our lives, no longer distinguishable from the truth. It becomes the truth, or at least our version of it.

I always thought I hated lies, believing I valued honesty above everything else but, then, I never realised just how destructive the truth could be. Ask yourself whether or not you would tell a friend that you knew her husband was cheating on her. Then ask yourself the same question, if you were the one her husband was having the affair with. Life is never simple and things are never black and white but, when it comes down to it, lies never hurt anyone. It's always the truth that hurts. Truth holds all the cards and has the power to shatter dreams, to humiliate and ultimately to destroy, but only if we let it.

When I was jolted rudely awake one day, and forced to confront a much less palatable version of the truth than the one I had been enjoying up to that point, my life as I knew it went very spectacularly and irrevocably down the pan. Suddenly, everything I knew was being challenged and I was left dazed and reeling from the aftershock of all the different twists and turns in the new and revised story of my life, a story I would never willingly have chosen to be the protagonist in.

Since that day I have often found myself thinking about Fate and how the course of our lives can be changed by one split-second action or decision. How does it feel to know you cheated death, like the people who missed their flight on the day of the Twin Towers attack, or the sick children whose parents kept them off school the day of the Dunblane School massacre?

Surely we can all look back at some pivotal point in our lives and wonder - What if...? Like the film Sliding Doors, where two completely different life scenarios are played out, with everything depending on whether or not Gwyneth Paltrow catches the subway train she is running for.

I can pinpoint my Sliding Doors moment exactly. It is etched in my memory forever and, although I have often wished that I could step back in time and play out the parallel version of my life, I'll never have the luxury of being able to rewrite history.

Nor can I blame everything on Fate. We all have choices to make in life and, in the end, we must live by our decisions, take responsibility and accept the consequences of our actions, whether good or bad.

No excuses. No regrets.

I confess I am no angel and there is no escaping the things I have done, but I learned the hard way that none of us can ever know what we are truly capable of until we are pushed to our limits.

Everyone has a breaking point.

In my defence, I do not believe anyone will ultimately condemn me or blame me for what I did.

The Promise

23 years earlier

Grace

The seatbelt sign flashed on above me as the captain announced that we would shortly be entering an area of turbulence. The plane shuddered gently as if to confirm his warning. I looked at my husband sleeping beside me and smiled happily, slipping my arm through his. 'My husband' would take some getting used to, but I liked it already. We were thirty-three thousand feet in the air, bound for the Seychelles, where we would pick up the luxury cruising boat Daniel had chartered for our honeymoon, ready to spend a blissful two weeks away from it all in Paradise. The business class seats had been his extra little surprise present to me, revealed at the airport check-in desk. I downed the rest of my Champagne, snuggled closer to him and closed my eyes, but I was too excited to sleep. The last six months had gone by in a whirlwind and I still found it hard to believe that this was really my life now. After several relationship disasters, involving more than my fair share of tears and heartache, I knew without a doubt that I had found The One and I was deliriously happy.

Alone with my thoughts on the long haul flight, I finally had the time to pause for breath and reflect on everything that had happened over the last few months.

It came as no surprise to anyone that I met the man who would become my husband at a sailing event, having grown up racing on the North East coast of England with my dad since the age of seven. As a child, I was what you might call a bit of a handful: fiery-tempered, headstrong and fiercely determined in the face of any new challenge. Amazing Grace, my dad called me, having named me after Grace Darling, the heroine of shipwrecked sailors off the Farne Islands in Northumberland. Dad was Commodore of his beloved Sunderland Yacht Club and he used to take me and my older brother Jeremy out sailing every weekend in all weathers. Daddy's girl and a tomboy, nothing fazed me and I was always determined to show I was as good if not better than the boys (especially Jeremy), having inherited my dad's competitive spirit. After all, girls had more to prove in those days. When it was rough, I remember being wedged in the companionway with a rope around my waist and told to hold on and keep my head down. I loved every minute of it, but I learned fast to look after myself and to respect the sea.

One hand for the boat and one hand for yourself.

I could still hear my dad's voice so clearly. On calmer days, I was given jobs to do in the race to keep my interest alive and I absorbed it all like a sponge. Dad and his friends called me their 'little mascot' and I had fond memories of how they patiently taught me to tie knots and trim the sails for the different wind angles. As I grew older and stronger, I gradually worked my way through all the different positions on the boat, starting with packing the spinnaker after every downwind leg. It was the job nobody on the crew ever wanted to do, but fortunately, I never suffered from sea-sickness (unlike poor Jeremy) and I was happy to do it, as it earned me the right to be a proper member of the team. By the time I was eighteen I was able to do most jobs on the boat, but I loved either doing the bow or helming. It didn't matter that I got soaked most weekends and came off the water physically exhausted; to me, they were halcyon days with my dad and I smiled to myself at the memories.

I didn't know it then of course, but the Sliding Doors moment that changed the course of my life came shortly after my twenty-fifth birthday when some friends from home chartered a J35 for The Scottish Series, a sailing event based in Tarbert on Loch Fyne, Scotland, and asked me to do the bow for them. Every race boat needs a reliable bowman on the team and I was forever grateful to my dad for the skills he taught me, knowing that, thanks to him, I could be a useful member of any crew. As bowman, my job, in a nutshell, was to ensure that the sails at the front of the boat went up and down as they should, quickly and efficiently. There was quite a bit more to it than that of course, but getting around the marks with perfect spinnaker hoists and drops could gain valuable time and we all knew that races could be won and lost by seconds.

I jumped at the chance to race at Tarbert, such an iconic event in the UK sailing world, and I was even more excited as I knew the J35 was a very competitive boat. Fate had already set a collision course for Daniel and I, and he showed up at the regatta in his brand new, state of the art race boat, Mistress. Everyone was talking about his J125, the new, forty-one foot, high-performance yacht from J Boats, with its carbon bowsprit and huge asymmetric, neon green spinnaker. The guys on the J35 were no exception.

Throughout the regatta, which ran over a long weekend, I engineered every possible opportunity for myself to meet up with Daniel and his crew but, in the end, it was not until I stopped for petrol on the long, four-hour drive home from the event that I finally got to speak to him. Our chance meeting in a service station on the outskirts of Glasgow would be the subject of many a joke for years to come and naturally featured in the best man's speech at our wedding. Finding myself in a long queue waiting to pay for fuel, I had no difficulty recognising the tall, fair-haired man next to me or the boat name and unmistakable logo of a woman in bondage gear on his sweatshirt. I knew Daniel Callaghan was the boat owner, from all the press coverage of the new yacht throughout the week. No time to be shy, I decided quickly.

'How did you do at the Scottish Series?' I ventured. 'I was there as well with some friends. We were watching you guys on the water. The boat is stunning. You must be over the moon with her.'

I could not help sounding just a bit star-struck and was conscious of the fact I was talking faster than normal.

'A couple of great wins, but not so good overall, I'm afraid.' Daniel shrugged his shoulders. 'Two of the crew let us down, so we were a bit shorthanded for the conditions yesterday.'

His voice was soft and low, with an unmistakable Irish lilt that I found particularly sexy. I wanted to keep him talking and bombarded him with questions as we waited to get served. To my delight, he appeared only too happy to talk boats with me and suggested we grab a coffee before carrying on with our journeys. He lived a couple of hours further south than me, in a small village in 'God's own country' of Yorkshire, which was actually where my parents came from, so it felt like there was an instant connection. We chatted easily, having loads in common, and soon I was telling him all about my sailing background and what I had been racing on at Tarbert. He bought me a cappuccino and seemed in no hurry to end our conversation.

'Well, it sounds to me like we could do with you on the crew. Honestly, you'd be welcome on my boat any time. There's always room for a good bowman and the *craic* is good, as we Irish say.'

My stomach flipped as he winked and handed me his business card. I realised he was flirting with me and inwardly cursed my grubby, boat sweatshirt and the state of my hair, that I had been unable to tame, despite my hurried best efforts in the toilets before joining him in the café.

'Seriously,' he continued, 'why don't you come out sailing with us? Just give me a ring if you're free one weekend. I mean it. I keep the boat in Liverpool, which is about three hours away from you, I guess. Plenty of hotels and B&Bs nearby.'

I struggled to hide my excitement and had to force myself to at least attempt to sound casual.

'I would love to take you up on that if you're sure. I'll give you my number if you're ever short of crew.'

I quickly borrowed a pen from behind the bar and scribbled my number down on a beermat.

When he rang the next day, it was to invite me out to dinner and my Fate was sealed. My Sliding Doors moment.

Two months later, we were engaged. Three months after that, we were married. What you might call a whirlwind romance.

The plane jolted and shuddered violently, dragging me back to the present as I remembered the equally turbulent events of the previous day. Our wedding. To say that it did not entirely go as planned was a bit of an understatement.

Daniel had told me early on in our relationship that he did not get on well with his family and stated categorically that he did not want to invite any of them to our wedding. He never talked much about them and the few snippets I had picked up had been either dragged out of him, much like trying to get blood out of a stone, or gleaned from conversations with friends. He grew up in a coastal town called Ardglass, in Northern Ireland with his parents and younger brother Kieran, but the family moved to the UK when he was seven, to escape The Troubles. They stayed in Liverpool for a couple of years, before moving again and settling in Fellside, a small village in Yorkshire, where they lived in the house Daniel now owned. His father was not one for being tied down and had several affairs over the years, finally moving out to go and live with one of his women. His mother left not long after the split, leaving a nineteen-year-old Daniel to look after himself, the house and his loose cannon of a brother, just two years his junior. They had never heard from her again and he had not spoken to, or seen, his father in years. There were no photos of Daniel as a child as all the family photos had, apparently, been destroyed several years ago in a fire started by his brother one night after a riotous party involving an excess of drugs and booze. The fire almost destroyed the house we were about to start our new life in, the family home Daniel had finally bought from his father after the fire.

To be honest, Kieran sounded like a total nightmare but, nevertheless, I decided to make it my mission to mend the rift in the family, imagining how grateful everyone would be to me for doing so. Daniel did not share my enthusiasm for a reunion and told me categorically that it was best not to open up old wounds but I was intrigued by the whole thing and felt compelled to find out more about his mysterious past. To my irritation, the more I probed, the more stubborn Daniel became in refusing to talk about it. In fact, he pretty much refused to talk about his family, full stop. It was as if he wanted to completely erase his past. My own family was a close-knit unit and I was determined to do my best to fix his, convinced he would thank me for it in the end. To my way of thinking, our wedding was the perfect opportunity to build bridges.

I handed him a rum and coke one evening and took a deep breath, preparing to confront the elephant in the room.

'I really think we should invite your father and your brother to the wedding and I'd like to try to track down your mother. They are your family at the end of the day and I think it's time you sorted out your differences.'

Daniel's face hardened.

'Not a good idea, I can assure you.'

'Oh come on, a lot of water has flowed under the bridge, surely? You've told me a bit about what happened, but it was all a long time ago…maybe it's time to forgive and forget?'

I waited. He sighed and rubbed his hand over his face.

'Not this again. I told you already, we're just not close and we don't get on. There's no big mystery, despite what you seem to imagine. We simply have nothing in common any more...we never really did. I don't understand why you're so obsessed about it. Why can't you just leave the past in the past? It's the future, our future together, that I'm interested in now and I don't want anything spoiling our day.'

'Well, if that's really all it is, I don't get why they can't come,' I persisted. 'What harm can it do? I just think it's sad to let the rift between you get worse and worse. You'll regret it if anything happens to one of them and you haven't made your peace.'

I immediately cursed my lack of tact as I remembered he had told me he lost his first wife in a car crash a few years earlier. The last time he saw her alive, they had argued and he had never forgiven himself. He had confided in me about that on our second date, keen to make sure there were no secrets between us, no hidden skeletons in closets. Honesty was everything in a relationship, he had said.

'You're determined to keep pushing this, aren't you? You always think you know best. So go on then, invite them. Just don't blame me when it backfires on you,' he snapped.

His tone was challenging, daring me to do it, to go against his wishes so, naturally, I did exactly that.

Unfortunately, as it turned out, he was proved right, much as I hated to admit it. His father did not reply to the wedding invitation and refused to answer phone calls. There was no card and no message to wish us well. He was clearly not about to engage in any bridge-building activities and I began to sympathise with Daniel's less than positive attitude towards him. His mother seemed to have disappeared off the face of the earth and clearly did not want to be found, so reluctantly I had to give up on that one too.

Only his brother Kieran deigned to honour the occasion with his presence, although it was obvious from the start that he did not come in peace. He glowered at me sullenly as he entered the reception venue, a beautiful country house in the Northumberland village of Dunstanford, refusing to shake Daniel's hand or kiss me. I had an uncomfortable feeling that I had made a terrible mistake and quite possibly unleashed a monster.

Kieran was indeed a ticking time bomb, choosing to bide his time until we were halfway through the main course before standing up, tapping his knife ceremoniously on his glass and declaring that he wanted to make a speech. My heart leapt as he launched in without any preamble.

'I just wanted to tell you all what an absolute fucking wanker my brother is!'

As opening lines go, that one was certainly an attention grabber and not by any stretch of the imagination what you might expect the brother of the groom to come out with. A ripple of surprise ran round the room as people fell silent and turned their heads to look at him, unsure how to react and wondering if they had heard him correctly. He paused for a moment to give that little gem time to sink in, obviously planning to make the most of his time in the spotlight.

'Yes, that's him!' he continued, unabashed, his harsh Northern Irish accent much more pronounced than Daniel's. 'My brother, the great guy over there.'

He staggered slightly and waved his arm theatrically in Daniel's general direction.

'Where do I start to tell you about him, eh? Let me see now, has he told you how he tormented his first wife so much she killed herself?'

A collective gasp ran around the room. Kieran smirked and nodded his head meaningfully, knowing he had everyone's full attention with that one.

'Oh yes, it's true. He drove her to it. Just ask him! Ask him why Julia did it!'

He continued quickly, shoving away the people who had suddenly appeared on either side of him and were desperately trying to shut him down.

'What about the fire? I mean the *truth* about the fire? Oh yes…and don't even get me started about our Mam. Whatever happened to her, eh?'

He laughed, without a trace of humour in his expression. He stared straight at me and raised his eyebrows.

'What Jackanory version of events did he give you about all that, I wonder? I'd run for the hills if I were you, love…while you still can.'

He was swaying and slurring his words, clearly off his face with alcohol and I had a horrible feeling he might actually throw up all over the table. This was supposed to be my perfect wedding day and Kieran was out of control, hell-bent on ruining it. Daniel was on his feet next to me, shaking with fury.

'Someone get him out of here!'

Three of my friends were already on the case, half pushing, half dragging the loose cannon out of the room, before he could say any more. Daniel tried to bluff it out and recover the situation, realising from the horrified stares and murmurings of our guests that we were in desperate need of damage limitation.

'I can only apologise for my brother. He still suffers from delusional behaviour, due to a long history of drug and alcohol abuse. Grace generously wanted to include him in our special day and I'm afraid this is how he has repaid her kindness. Now please, let's not give him any more air time. Fill up your glasses, enjoy the wonderful food and don't let him spoil this day for my beautiful wife.'

He raised his glass in my direction as a toast and sat down. There was much enthusiastic clinking of glasses as everyone returned to their meal and a ripple of voices ran around the room, with no prizes for guessing the new topic of conversation.

'Now do you believe me?' Daniel hissed in my ear, a strained smile plastered on his face.

I believed him alright, but Kieran's little outburst had raised questions in my mind that needed answering. I was confused, but I had to wait until after the more conventional speeches finished and the dancing started before I had an opportunity to speak to my husband alone.

'What did he mean about your first wife killing herself? And what was all that about the fire? You told me your wife died in a car crash…and you…you said Kieran started that fire,' I stammered.

'Kieran talks a load of shit. You cannot believe a word that comes out of his mouth. I'm telling you his brain is scrambled from years of taking God knows what. I knew he would pull a stunt like this, which is why I told you not to invite him. Maybe you'll listen to me next time. He's jealous of me, always has been and he'll do anything to wreck things for me, as he proved today. Why the hell are you letting his poison affect what we've got? I've had enough of his lies and trouble-causing to last me a lifetime. In fact, I don't even know why we're having this conversation. I can't believe you're actually prepared to believe him over me.'

Daniel paused for breath, suddenly deflated. He looked hurt. Worse than that, he looked disappointed that I was questioning him. I was suddenly ashamed of myself. We were supposed to be a team. I looked into his eyes and knew that I had to let it go. He was right. The past belonged in the past and Kieran and his lies most definitely had no place in our future. What did I care about all that stuff? It certainly didn't define the man I had married a mere few hours ago.

'I'm sorry. Of course I don't believe him over you. You were right. I should have listened to you about your family. I just wish you'd talked to me more openly about it all, so I could have understood properly. I only wanted to help. I certainly don't want to argue with you, today of all days.'

I took hold of his hand in a gesture of solidarity.

'Well, please believe me now when I tell you that you know all you need to know. I'm not exactly proud of my family and I don't like talking about all that shit from the past, especially about Julia dying. Yes, if you must know, she killed herself, but I didn't want to upset you by telling you that. Have you any idea how painful it was for me? I loved her and could never understand why she did what she did. The poor girl was clearly psychologically disturbed.'

I felt worse than ever as he continued, looking me straight in the eye.

'I prefer to make my own way in life now and I certainly don't need any of my family interfering. God forgive me, but it would honestly have been better for everyone if Kieran had died in that fire he started. He's poison.'

His voice softened.

'Let's make a pact. I don't care about anything that happened in your past. I don't even want to know about it, certainly not about any of your past relationships. But the same has to apply to *my* past. It's all irrelevant. From now on it's just you and me against the world.'

He took my face in his hands and kissed me tenderly on the lips. I put my arms around his neck and hugged him tightly. I could see the pain and heartache his family, especially his brother, had obviously caused him and I just wanted to make it go away. We were a team now and nothing could break us.

'No more secrets though,' I said sternly, holding his gaze. 'I mean it.'

'No more secrets. I promise.'

He kissed me again and the doubts melted away.

'Now let's get back to the party.'

A couple of the guys had managed to bundle Kieran into a taxi back to his hotel and I had a feeling that would be the last I ever saw of him. I also had a feeling that it was no great loss. The rest of the evening passed in a blur of dancing, drinking Champagne and valiant efforts to spend time with every guest who had made the effort to come and celebrate with us. The reception finally ended in the early hours of the morning with a very drunken version of Swing Low, Sweet Chariot from Daniel and his boat crew, accompanied by full rugby club actions, to the bewilderment of some of the older guests.

I smiled to myself and shook my head. It already seemed so long ago and I felt sure we would be dining out on the Kieran story for many years to come, but right now we had our honeymoon to look forward to. The start of our new life together. Daniel's family and all that they represented belonged firmly in the past.

I was his future now, as he was mine. Bound together by the vows we had made. To love, cherish and obey. Till death do us part.

The Dating Game

Lorraine

The familiar rattle of the letterbox alerted Lorraine to the arrival of the day's post and she hurried into the hallway to collect it.

'Probably just more bills,' she said to herself as she scooped up the little pile of papers and envelopes from the floor and discarded at least half of them straight into the recycling bin.

There was just one that merited her immediate attention and that was the envelope with the hallmark of Wainright and Sons LLP. Her divorce lawyer.

She had been waiting for this for weeks and yet now that she was finally holding the Decree Absolute in her hands, the document that effectively severed all ties with the man she had once been so desperately in love with, she felt strangely numb.

She remembered her wedding day and the way he had made her feel as he undressed her tenderly on the first night of their honeymoon. It was not their first time of course, but it had felt like it; a happy young couple with all the promise of a wonderful future together....

'Sentimental bullshit,' she said out loud to herself, as her mind was jolted sharply back to the present by the ping of a message on her phone. Harriet, her best friend, wanted to meet up that evening.

She hesitated a moment, then texted back decisively:

7.30 fizz and supper at mine – celebrating!

Harriet's reply was brief.
Perfect! See you later xx

The piece of paper in front of her served as a sharp reminder of the reality of her situation. She needed to get a grip and sort her life out, as her mother never tired of pointing out. She sighed bitterly as she remembered what a spineless, devious, little creep her now ex-husband had turned out to be, such a far cry from the man she had thought she was marrying.

Time after time he had emptied their joint bank account to feed his gambling habit. When that particular cash cow ran out, he had taken to sponging off friends and family to pay his mounting debts. As if that wasn't bad enough, she knew for a fact he had been playing away and the cheating bastard had not even bothered to deny it when she challenged him. Harriet had seen him with his tongue down the throat of one of his tarts and reported back immediately of course. The brazen, little slapper from the local Co-op, no less. Talk about shitting on your own doorstep.

Not for the first time she thanked God for her overbearing and controlling older brother, Gerald, who had insisted she open a bank account in her own name after she confided in him about her husband's gambling. Thanks to him she had at least been able to hang onto her house in the divorce. It was in a reasonable, desirable location in Oxfordshire, within easy reach of London, which meant she was now saddled with a massive mortgage and the savings she had tried so hard to build up had been pretty much wiped out.

'Life isn't fucking fair,' she concluded bitterly, but she also knew that no amount of self-pity was going to change things and, sooner or later, she would have to move on and rebuild her life.

She had made a start already and had managed to land herself a new position in the HR department of the Santander bank. Since leaving school with a half-decent set of results, she had worked her way through the ranks at the offices of Kellman & Associates, an accountancy firm in nearby Millingford, but she had felt undervalued there for a long time. The new job was going to mean more hours and more responsibility, but also more money than she had previously been earning, so maybe this was the turning point. She was going to need to smarten her act up though. It was high time she got herself a new image, she had told herself, full of enthusiasm.

By the time it was 7 pm, Lorraine found herself standing in front of the full-length mirror in her bedroom, her earlier optimism having evaporated. She did not like what she saw. She was only thirty-five years old, but the face staring back at her seemed older somehow and the rolls of fat around her middle and thighs were definitely doing her no favours. She was tall for a woman at 5 foot 10 and she had been quite a striking figure in her early twenties, although she had never been what people considered naturally pretty. Her blond hair was cut in an unflattering bob with a messy fringe and it was in desperate need of colouring. Several outfits lay discarded on the floor, mostly because they seemed to have shrunk a couple of sizes since she had bought them. She finally settled on a plain green, tunic-style dress in a forgiving, stretchy fabric, with black, opaque tights and ankle boots that had seen better days. It was not a particularly flattering choice and screamed 'frumpy' if she was honest, but at least it fitted and she would be able to enjoy her food without feeling like she had been laced into a straitjacket. It was only Harriet after all. She turned sideways on to the mirror, sighing loudly as she realised she was viewing herself from an even less encouraging angle. Things needed to change if she was ever going to get herself another man. She reminded herself sharply that that was not the highest on her list of priorities, but still…she didn't want to be alone forever. Note to self:

Start diet tomorrow
Hairdresser appointment
New wardrobe

Positive thinking. Always a good start. Her diet was long overdue, as was her appointment at the hairdresser and the last time she had taken a good look in her wardrobe it was like something from the 90s. She sucked in her tummy and attempted some pouty faces in the mirror to boost her morale, but she merely succeeded in looking like an exaggerated caricature of herself. Disheartened, she left the pile of clothes on the floor and clomped down the stairs in the direction of the alcohol.

Harriet arrived in usual Harriet time, half an hour late and apologizing profusely, but Lorraine didn't mind at all. They had known each other since school days and nothing was going to change her best friend now. She was every bit as bad herself if truth be told.

They sat in the kitchen on the breakfast bar stools, as they often did on their catch-up evenings. Lorraine had kept the food simple, being realistic about her limitations as a cook but, in the end, she had managed to make quite a passable attempt at a lasagne and had splashed out on a few bottles of Waitrose Prosecco to make up for any potential failings with the food.

As they clinked glasses, Harriet raised a toast to her best friend:

'Here's to you and your new life. It starts today.'

An hour later they had polished off the first bottle and were well on the way to finishing a second. Harriet giggled and put her glass down.

'Okay, that's it. Time to hit Match.com I think,' she announced.

Lorraine groaned. It was a familiar story after copious amounts of alcohol.

'First we need to sort your profile out,' Harriet stated decisively. 'You have to sell yourself, girl. Now, let's start with the photos....'

Lorraine groaned in protest but, half an hour later, as she stared appreciatively at the profile they had concocted between them, she had to admit that she came across as very presentable indeed. Admittedly, the photos were not exactly the most recent and she did not entirely recognise herself in the drink-fuelled descriptions they had come up with, but they decided it was acceptable to allow themselves a bit of poetic license. She was pretty sure that was the case with most people on those dating sites anyway, so why should she put herself at a disadvantage?

It did not take long for her optimism to fade yet again, as they waded through the profiles of all the men in the age bracket she had specified and who lived within a fifty-mile radius of her. They decided with a certain amount of desperation to widen the search to two hundred miles and begin again. Before long they had thrown caution to the wind and were searching the length and breadth of the country.

Lorraine laughed and stood up.

'You carry on with this while I get us another drink. Judging by these men we're going to need it.'

Alone in the kitchen, she cursed her marriage and cursed her ex under her breath. She thought the fun-filled evening, the alcohol and the dating sites would have taken it all away, but it was still there, bubbling under the surface. She had to control herself, not do anything too hasty. Maybe take a few months out and review the situation. But the voices in her head were still there. After all this time. They weren't going away and if anything they were shouting even louder. It just wasn't fair. She should not have to be subjecting herself to this humiliation.

When she returned with a third bottle, she no longer cared that she was going to have the mother of all hangovers in the morning. Harriet was hunched closer over the computer, looking intrigued.

'Take a look at this one,' she said moving over so that Lorraine could get a better view. Harriet's tongue was practically hanging out.

'Well hello, *John*,' Lorraine slurred, in what she thought was a sexy voice, gawping at the photo on the screen and giggling like a teenager. 'Now, he definitely has potential.'

The stranger smiling out at her from his profile photo seemed so natural and genuine; he sat on a wall somewhere in the countryside,

35

dressed casually in jeans and a sweater. There was a red sports car in the background. As they delved into his profile, she instantly had misgivings about the distance; she lived in Oxfordshire and he was based up north, somewhere in Derbyshire she had never heard of, but she decided, nevertheless, to keep an open mind and see what happened. She did at least make the effort to locate Derbyshire on a map and worked out that he was around a two and a half-hour drive away.

After a couple of days of flirty messaging, John suggested they meet for dinner at a restaurant near her home. The travelling wasn't a problem he said, as he had business clients down that way and was not averse to mixing a little business with pleasure. She did not really understand what his business was, although he had told her it was something to do with packaging. The long-winded explanation he had started to give sounded pretty boring to be honest, and she had decided very quickly as her eyes glazed over that she didn't need to know the details.

Whatever it was that he did, he was clearly successful at it and made plenty of money, judging by the red Porsche 911 he turned up to meet her in. She recognised it as the one in his dating profile photo.

John certainly knew how to treat a girl, she had thought to herself as he presented her with a big bouquet on arrival and insisted on paying for everything that evening. The conversation flowed easily, almost as easily as the wine, and bit by bit he encouraged her to open up to him and tell him all sorts of intimate details about her life. He wanted to know everything about her, he said, and every time he topped up her glass, she became a little bit more loose-lipped.

She was not good at flirting, but with John, she felt sexy and interesting for the first time in a long while. He was confident and oozed charm. She was beginning to feel like she had won the lottery and for once, the violent thoughts she harboured for her ex-husband faded away in the smoke from the two, small candles on the table. Maybe she really could put all the bad stuff behind her and move on.

'You are a very sexy lady you know. I can't believe you're still single,' he drawled, shaking his head to reinforce his amazement.

'You're not so bad yourself,' she replied playfully. 'Believe me there are a lot of very undesirable characters out there in the internet dating world.'

He laughed and raised his glass to hers. 'Well, here's to us then…two of the good ones.'

She took a small sip from her wine glass before speaking again, leaning in towards him and thrusting her best assets forward, courtesy of the daringly low cut top she had bought specially for the occasion.

'It's weird…I feel like I've known you forever. You're so easy to talk to. I've already told you things I normally wouldn't dream of telling anyone on a first date.'

'I know exactly what you mean. We have a real connection I think,' he replied, holding eye contact until she blushed.

She hadn't planned for it to happen, or so she told herself, but by the time they were onto the main course in the restaurant, she knew she would be having sex with him that night. She was glad she had at least had the foresight to put on matching underwear 'just in case', but she was still self-conscious about her weight and was already stressing about removing the Spanx she had put on over her knickers at the last minute.

As it turned out, she needn't have worried, as John was quick to put her at ease when she tentatively broached the subject, by refusing a pudding and telling him she was starting a diet.

'I'm just not into skinny, bony women. I can assure you I prefer real women with curves in all the right places and some flesh on their bones.'

He winked suggestively, looking her up and down.

'Hmm, well I'll take that as a compliment, I think…,' she joked, secretly relieved.

As she led him into the bedroom later, in eager anticipation of a long-awaited night of unbridled passion, she could hardly believe her luck. Here was a guy who was into 'larger ladies', looked presentable and was clearly loaded. All boxes ticked as far as she was concerned. She had no intention of letting this one slip through her fingers.

The following morning, John left early for a business meeting with a client in Northampton, he kissed her lightly on the lips and assured her he would call soon.

She lay in bed alone for a long time, not quite sure how she felt about the previous night's activities. His approach had been unusual, to say the least, not at all what she had expected, but, emboldened by the wine, she had been desperate to please him and prepared to do whatever it took to make him want to see her again. The morning's sober version of herself was a little more uneasy about it all and she squirmed uncomfortably as a vision came into her mind.

A vision of herself, naked and spread-eagled on the bed, arms and legs stretched wide and secured to the metal frame with the silk scarves he had calmly produced from the bottom of his briefcase.

Fortified by the wine, it had not bothered her in the slightest at the time. In fact, she had found it all highly erotic and had proved to be an extremely enthusiastic participant in the role play. John had taken on a very different persona in the bedroom, making it clear who was in charge of the evening's entertainment as he stood back and took his time to scrutinise every inch of her body. She recalled his face as he smirked down at her, probing insistently between her thighs with the fingers of one hand while massaging her breasts roughly with the other. Several times he brought her to the brink of orgasm and then stopped abruptly, leaving her desperate for more. She recalled how he had suddenly straddled her, seizing both arms in a grip that was a little too tight.

'You're gagging for it, aren't you? Lying there, hoping I'll give you a proper seeing to, fuck you good and hard, just the way you like it.'

The tone of his voice took her by surprise and had a raw, steely edge to it. When she did not answer immediately, he had used one hand to lift her hip roughly and slapped her hard across the backside with the other. She let out a startled little scream, feeling like she had somehow been transported onto the set of a low budget porn movie.

'Answer me, bitch. If you want it, you're going to have to beg me for it.'

He slapped her twice more, harder each time, which she was slightly ashamed to find she thoroughly enjoyed.

She wanted it alright and, despite it all being new to her and the uncertainty of what she was supposed to say, she was more than ready to enter into the spirit of things and give it her best shot.

'Oh God, yes, I want you, I *really* want you. Don't make me wait any longer... please....' The raspy sound of her own voice took her by surprise. She did not recognise herself or the words coming out of her mouth, but she was encouraged by his reaction.

'That's more like it...come on now; you can do better than that. Tell me *exactly* what you want.'

She remembered the words of some of the characters in the trashy novels she liked to read and proceeded to regurgitate them, hoping she sounded convincing.

'I want to feel you inside me right now. I can't wait anymore, I'm begging you...,' she gasped, writhing around in what she hoped was a seductive manner, arching her pelvis upwards to offer herself to him.

She felt like every nerve in her body was tingling with desire. He smiled triumphantly, apparently pleased with her performance, and entered her roughly. It was all over disappointingly quickly and he came almost immediately, leaving her feeling frustrated and confused. Afterwards, he had silently untied the scarves to release her and kissed her chastely on the forehead, before rolling over contentedly and falling asleep, snoring loudly.

Wide awake and alone with her thoughts, as she pleasured herself absent-mindedly, she came to the conclusion that she was not averse to more experimentation in the field of bondage and role play if that was what did it for him. She hoped fervently that he would come back for more because, in her humble opinion, he was most definitely a catch.

Four days later, she had heard nothing from him and she was going frantic, convinced she had blown it somehow. She did not want to appear needy, but could not resist the temptation to try his mobile number on three separate occasions, instantly regretting it when it went straight to answer-phone.

When he finally turned up at the house he was armed with more flowers and apologized profusely for not having been in touch earlier. Apparently, he had been visiting a customer, whose factory was in the middle of nowhere and phone reception was atrocious.

'Of course I tried to call you…several times actually… but I just kept getting cut off.'

He smiled lasciviously at her. 'How could I not want to see you again? I had to hide the massive stiffy I kept getting when I had sex flashbacks….'

She surprised herself at how easily she was won over and blushed at her own flashbacks.

'Don't worry, I understand, really I do. Sorry for being such a nag.'

'You're not a nag, but I do need you to understand that I'm just not a 24/7 kind of guy. My work gets in the way too much. I even have to work over Christmas this year, which is a real pain, but I guess that's the joy of owning your own business,' he sighed resignedly.

'I can live with that,' she assured him quickly, anxious to appear relaxed about the whole thing and get away from the subject.

They skipped the preamble of dinner that night and went straight to the bedroom, where, having had four days to research and prepare, she was keen to show him she could be a much more confident participant.

The following day, when he had gone off again to see another customer back up in Derbyshire, she looked at her reflection in the mirror and noted the red marks on her arms and inner thighs.

It was just a bit of fun and experimentation between two consenting adults behind closed doors, right?

It would be years later and a lot of water would have flowed under the bridge before she answered that question.

The Good Life

Never compare yourself with others and never compromise your dreams for others.

Grace

'**Make** sure you're at the airport for nine, Grace. We don't want to miss our slot.' Charles looked at me meaningfully; he knew I was notoriously late for everything as was his wife Samantha, who was also my best friend.

'Roger, Captain.'

I gave him a mock salute and laughed. There was no way I would be arriving late for this. Our fourth Christmas together as a married couple, Daniel and I were flying out to spend it in the beautiful Austrian ski resort of Lech. Not only that, but we were also going to be travelling in Charles' private jet. I already felt like a film star. Charles smiled and kissed me on both cheeks.

'I know you, remember. See you on Friday.'

I hugged Samantha as Daniel and I left.

The four of us met at a sailing regatta on the Isle of Wight shortly after we were married. Charles owned a Corel 45 and we all got talking in the bar after sailing one day, dissecting the race and analysing where things had gone brilliantly well and spectacularly wrong for us. Samantha was not really a sailor, but she and I hit it off instantly. We soon became firm friends, catching up regularly on the racing circuit and enjoying many wonderful holidays together, either cruising in the summer on Charles' Swan 80 in Monaco or skiing somewhere in the Alps in the winter. Charles had built up a highly successful property development business and had recently added a private jet to his portfolio of toys. Our trip to Lech was its first time out.

Charles' passion for flying was shared by Daniel who had recently attained his helicopter pilot's licence. He was looking to buy a machine of his own (Charles already had one) and intended to build a landing pad in one of the fields outside our house. There was always an undercurrent of competition between the two men that could easily turn a discussion into a heated and volatile argument. Samantha and I became experts over the years at diffusing the situation so that our friendship could remain on an even keel, but I knew Daniel was jealous of the fact that Charles had more disposable income than he did and that his business was more successful. He could not stand to be the underdog and constantly acted as if he had something to prove. Sam and I decided it was a macho thing, boys will be boys and all that, but, given our lifestyle and everything we had, I found it hard to understand why Daniel was never satisfied. Charles and Sam lived about two hours away from us, on the North Wales border near Chester, so Sam and I didn't see as much of each other as we would have liked, but we made the most of the holidays together.

New Year's Eve at the Petersboden Hotel above Lech was magical. The seven-course meal, washed down with free-flowing Champagne and red wine was incredible, although I was so full after it I could barely move. We all headed outside for the fireworks at midnight and I felt strangely detached from reality as we looked across the valley at the sparkling lights of the town below. Samantha and I dressed alike, in black fur coats and white fur hats.

'You two look like a pair of Russian princesses,' Daniel commented, laughing. The photo he took of us huddled together in the winter wonderland and laughing as the snowflakes fell all around us, would take pride of place on the kitchen wall at home.

Later that night I lay contentedly beside my husband, looking up at the stars through the little skylight in the ceiling. It seemed the perfect moment to broach the subject:

'Let's have a baby,' I whispered.

Silence.

'Did you hear me?' I waited for a response.

'Yes, I heard you, but I don't quite know what you want me to say. You know I don't want kids. I always told you that.'

'Well actually, you always said we would have them one day, just not straight away.'

This was not the way I had anticipated the conversation going.

'I don't remember ever saying that. Anyway, the fact remains that I don't want them. I thought you understood that. Come on Grace, kids just wouldn't fit in with our lifestyle. We certainly wouldn't be able to do all the things we do now, like sailing the boat together or going on holidays whenever we feel like it if we had a kid in tow.'

'I suppose not, but you just adapt, don't you? It doesn't have to mean the end of all life as we know it.'

'Oh really?' His voice had a hard edge to it. 'I think you're being a bit naïve there. I think you'd find it would most definitely mean the end of all life as *you* know it because *you* would be the one left at home with the baby, not me.'

'I suppose…I don't know. Other people seem to manage,' I added lamely, thinking of our friends Frieda and James, whose two young children went everywhere with them.

'I'm tired. Let's talk about it another time when we're home. Don't ruin a great holiday with an argument as usual. Jesus Grace, nobody has the ability to wind me up like you. Anyway, I'd be a terrible father. Look at my own dysfunctional family. I don't want to bring a child into the world and end up like that. Just drop it. Please.'

So that was that. Conversation over. I was not exactly happy about his dictatorial attitude, but I decided I would leave it for another year or so. Thirty was hardly old. I had time.

As I lay there, turning things over in my mind, I decided I needed to find out more about Daniel's past. What had happened in his own family to make him feel so negative about us starting one of our own? I needed to understand and he refused to give me the answers I craved, so I decided to look elsewhere.

Once we were home, I arranged to go out for dinner with Frieda. She had known Daniel since they were kids, ever since he and his family had moved over to England. She had also been friends with Julia, his first wife, and because of that I had kept her a bit at arm's length I suppose, but it was time for all that to change. I needed to know what made him tick.

Frieda was easy going, chatty and fun and I immediately regretted not having made the effort to get to know her better earlier. I decided it was time to get to the point.

'I really need your help, Frieda. Daniel won't talk to me about the rift between him and his family. I don't want to put you in an awkward position obviously, but it would be nice to understand a bit more about it and why they don't have anything to do with each other.'

I looked at her and waited, hoping she would shed some light on the matter. She took a sip of her wine and shook her head, sighing.

'Daniel's always played his cards very close to his chest, but he didn't have a particularly bad upbringing as far as I know. His parents were in the sailing club and used to bring the boys down with them, which is how we all got friendly. The boys were always arguing and his mother would try to intervene, but Daniel was vicious towards her and it was almost like she was scared of him. I remember the family going off on camping holidays abroad, but they were never close by anyone's standards. There were a lot of rumours about affairs on both sides and stories going round that his parents were part of the local swingers' crowd.... I don't know for sure if any of that is true, but they were certainly a bit weird. I remember one time when his parents suddenly disappeared on holiday by themselves and just left the boys to fend for themselves at home. There were some seriously wild parties that week. When his parents split up, his father went to live with his new partner and his mother had some sort of breakdown I think. She just walked out of the house one day to get milk and never came back. Nobody ever heard from her again.'

'Daniel told me she went back to Ireland,' I protested.

'Truth is, nobody knows. They reported her as missing, but even the police couldn't find her. There were all sorts of rumours flying around about domestic violence and various theories from amateur detectives as to her fate, but as I say, nobody knows.'

'Wow. No wonder he doesn't like talking about it.'

'Daniel and his brother were left to their own devices in the house after she left and there always seemed to be an ever-changing assortment of random hangers-on, who used the place like a squat. There was all sort of stuff going on: car ringing, petty theft, drugs and bad behaviour. The police were always up there. Daniel moved out when he married Julia, of course, but Kieran was never far removed from trouble.'

She paused and sighed at the mention of Julia, before continuing.

'Daniel was a bit of a loner, to be honest, and he always seemed to be embarrassed by his parents, especially after one of his mates was staying there and came face to face with his mother, wandering around the house completely starkers. When we were younger, he used to tell people who didn't know him that his whole family died in a car crash and he was the only one left.'

'Oh my God, that's awful.'

'Yes...When you and Daniel first got together, he told me the story he had given you about Julia dying in a car crash and I said he was asking for trouble. He said he found the truth too upsetting and didn't want to have to relive all the pain. He begged me not to say anything and I agreed, against my better judgement. I think he was scared of how you would react. It was a terrible time for everyone who knew her. And such a violent, senseless death….'

Frieda's voice tailed off and I could see she was close to tears. I shivered slightly and realised I had never actually asked how Julia took her own life.

'Frieda…how *did* Julia kill herself?' I asked quietly, not entirely sure I wanted to hear the answer.

Frieda looked at me strangely.

'She hanged herself. With her own horse's head collar. I assumed Daniel would have told you everything after Kieran's outburst at the wedding.'

I could not help a little gasp of shock. I had imagined her taking an overdose and somehow drifting away peacefully and painlessly into sleep. Not the brutal version of events I had just been given.

'The thing is, Grace, they were really not in a good place when she did it. It was never the same after she lost the baby and she was living on a knife-edge, terrified he was going to leave her. She called the poor little thing Ava. I'll never forget the sight of that tiny white coffin….'

'Wait a minute, they had a baby?'

'Yes, but she was stillborn. It was a terrible tragedy, with no real explanation. It destroyed Julia, but Daniel just seemed relieved if I'm honest. But there was more to it than that. He was cheating on her with at least two women I knew about and her sister was convinced he was knocking her around. I don't know if that was true…she certainly never said anything to me, but I guess people don't, do they? A lot of people blamed him for pushing her over the edge. He certainly didn't treat her very well and I think he blamed himself too in the end for what she did.'

I was lost for words. It wasn't Frieda's fault of course, but I felt foolish and betrayed by my husband. Trust was everything in a marriage and we had promised each other there would be no secrets between us. That didn't last long - I thought furiously, as I began to wonder how much more he was hiding from me.

Daniel did not react well when I confronted him about what Frieda had told me and predictably turned the tables on me about snooping behind his back.

'Why the hell are you always trying to dig up dirt from the past?' he shouted, clearly furious.

'I'm not!' I replied indignantly. 'I just wanted to understand your family history a bit better, but I guess I found out more than I bargained for.'

'Well, I hope you're happy now. I had a shit childhood, end of story. But then to lose Julia like that...it was devastating. It was a fucking awful time in my life and I just wanted to forget about it, simple as that. Just because we're married it doesn't mean you have to know every detail about my past. I don't ask you about yours, do I? That's because the past belongs in the past, as I keep telling you. It has no relevance to our future together. I thought you finally got that, but apparently not.'

He stormed out of the room and slammed the door hard, bringing the argument to an abrupt end.

I was left consumed with guilt again for hounding him and dredging up secrets that were better left buried. And yet, I couldn't help wondering about Julia. He had told me how much he loved her and how devastated he had been when she died, but Frieda said he had treated her badly and had been cheating on her. With at least two other women. It just didn't add up to me, but I had a feeling I would never really know the truth and tried hard to push the thoughts of my husband's dead wife to the back of my mind. I told myself firmly that there are two sides to every story and nobody really knows what goes on behind closed doors.

Maybe he's right - I thought to myself as I slipped into bed beside him later that night and snuggled close, not wanting to go to sleep on an argument. As he said, the past belonged in the past and no good could come from raking up such painful memories but, at the same time, I had no intention of allowing the memories and ghosts from Daniel's past to destroy my happiness and crush my dreams.

I hoped and prayed there were no more skeletons hidden in the closet but, as I lay there, turning things over in my head, a verse from a poem by Francis Duggan came into my head:

One lie leads to another lie a wise one once did say, 'And you must tell another lie tomorrow for the lie you told today'.

Life after Brian

Jane

Jane stared blankly at the rows of sympathy cards cluttering up the windowsill and gathering dust. They had flooded in from well-meaning friends after the untimely death of her husband. A tragic car accident. Killed outright the police had told her, having encouraged her to sit down before delivering the shocking news.

Naturally, she played the part expected of her, but if she was being brutally honest, it was no great loss as far as she was concerned. Brian didn't have a shred of ambition and would have been content to live in a mediocre house in suburbia for the rest of his boring, little life. That was not how she saw her own future panning out and, if he thought she was going to settle for the occasional pub meal with a glass of cheap plonk as a treat, he had another think coming. Boring Brian had also been desperate to produce the standard quota of 2.4 children, but there was no way she was being lumbered with screaming brats and had taken the necessary precautions while lying to her overly trusting husband.

Jane put on a good show when the police came to the door to deliver the news about the accident, with tears and just the right amount of hysteria, but the fact of the matter was that things had worked out perfectly for her. She had already been planning to leave Brian before the accident, but this way she got to play the grieving young widow *and* inherit the house without a fight. There was also the matter of the life insurance policy they'd taken out on each other at her insistence twelve months earlier.

Result.

Jane had respectfully waited three whole weeks after Brian's funeral before she threw herself into the fray of internet dating. There was no time to waste, and it seemed as good a way as any to meet people in this day and age. This time, she was leaving nothing to chance and would make sure she picked a more suitable partner, one who, at the very least, had enough money to give her the lifestyle she craved and deserved. She enlisted the help of her best friend, Tracy, and together they concocted a dazzling, if not entirely accurate, profile aided and abetted by a couple of bottles of Cava and a large box of chocolates. Tracy had gotten it right; she had married a short, ugly but extremely rich, property tycoon a few years ago. She did not judge Jane about the Brian situation. Time to move on. No point in hanging around. Brutal but honest.

Unfortunately, four months down the line and numerous monumental disappointments later, the internet had failed spectacularly to deliver up the man of her dreams, or even someone vaguely acceptable to be honest. Jane was getting a bit disheartened. She was sick of logging into the various sites she had joined, only to be confronted by the leering photos of men a good twenty years older than her. She had even seen one who called himself Bobby Ninetoes!

Seriously? Did he actually expect to get a response from anything with a pulse using a profile name like that?

True, she had a few body image issues of her own and could do with losing a couple of stone, but even so, she intended to keep some standards.

She invariably deleted all new matches for the day in disgust, without even bothering to read the blurb they had cobbled together. There was no point, as none of them had any understanding of even the most basic concepts of English grammar.

Where, oh where, were all the decent single men?

And then, all of a sudden one evening, there was Matthew, delivered up from the gods and straight into her inbox. No wonder he stood out, with his easy natural pose for the camera and an engaging, mischievous smile that reached all the way to his eyes. The fact that the About Me section of his profile was grammatically accurate and he had actually managed to use capital letters and correct punctuation was another massive tick in his favour.

Matthew was as different from Brian as was possible. He had his own business, flew a helicopter and, apparently had a collection of sports cars (*if* he was telling the truth of course). On this occasion, she decided not to allow her natural cynicism to spoil things and when he suggested they meet in person after a few flirty messaging sessions, she thought all her birthdays and Christmases had come at once, especially as he was keen enough to drive more than two hours from where he lived, somewhere near Sheffield.

Their first date was dinner in a wine bar in her home town of Willowmede, near Birmingham and she approved wholeheartedly of his choice, knowing it to be expensive. He insisted that it would be his treat and she warmed to him even more. He was confident, tall and charismatic, although not exactly what you would call good looking. Jane decided quickly that she could overlook that, given all the other points in his favour.

Two bottles of wine later, she found herself inviting him back to her house, where one thing inevitably led to another, just as she had intended it to. Jane loved sex and had never had any reservations about putting out on a first date. Sex with poor old Brian had been dull, to say the least, and she felt she was long overdue a bit more excitement in that department. Matthew was more than happy to oblige and she was delighted to report to Tracy the next day that they had gone at it like rabbits all over the house: on the kitchen worktop, up against the wall in the hallway, in the bath. She had seen the little pack of blue pills he was trying to keep hidden but, it made no odds to her, so long as it meant he could perform.

When he suggested filming her after a couple of weeks of rampant sex hook-ups, she was flattered and keen to show him she was game for anything.

'It's just a little thing I like to do. It really turns me on, but we don't have to if you don't feel comfortable about it,' he said, almost apologetically.

'Oh no, it's fine,' she assured him quickly. 'It's just that I've never been filmed before, but I'm more than happy to try new things with the right person.'

Jane lowered her eyes in an attempt to look demure, then promptly stripped off, throwing inhibition to the wind and discarding her clothes on the floor.

'Great. Let's start with just a few poses of you, like a glamour model.'

His tone was encouraging. No one had ever accused her of being 'like a glamour model' and she embraced her new persona with gusto, even when Matthew got her to kneel on all fours with her arse in the air and took her by surprise as he moved in behind for a close-up.

Things began to progress after that night and she was delighted when Matthew agreed it would make sense if he moved some of his personal stuff to her house, given the strain of the whole long-distance relationship thing. He made it clear, however, that he would be there as often as possible, but not every night and certainly not every weekend, as his work involved a lot of travelling and he needed to keep his base near the factory. She was happy with that. She was reeling him in and that was all that mattered for the moment.

Filming became a regular part of their sex life and soon there were spy cameras installed all over the house, the results of which were numerous home porn movies and thousands of stills stored on Matthew's computer.

Over time, she learned to contort herself into positions she would never previously have thought possible, none of them particularly flattering, but it certainly got him going. In fact, he almost liked to give explicit instructions and each session brought new surprises. She squirmed; feeling aroused as she remembered the charity fancy-dress party in a pub out of town, where they had both gone dressed as school kids. At his suggestion, she had not worn knickers and had shaved down there to please him. With the party in full swing, he had suddenly taken her by the hand and led her to a secluded room away from the main function and out of sight of prying eyes, but only just. As usual, she had not held back on the alcohol front and giggled drunkenly as Matthew pushed her down onto the banquette. He liked to be in charge and she obediently sat back and opened her legs wide for him, knowing the drill.

'Oh yes, that's lovely,' he murmured as he settled himself on the bench opposite her with his camera and licked his lips lecherously. He proceeded to video her, muttering encouragingly as she used the fingers of both hands to pleasure herself. She uttered a low moan and writhed around on the rough material of the banquette, quickly warming to her task. An expert at doing the job herself, having been married to Brian for years, she brought herself noisily to orgasm, made all the more exciting by the fact that one of the other party-goers could have come around the corner at any moment and discovered them at it. When she had finished, Matthew unzipped his schoolboy shorts, signalling to her to kneel in front of him. Jane was only too happy for the opportunity to perform one of her favourite acts for a close-up action video and prided herself on her technique, perfected over the years. Not with Brian though. Not with that useless prick, who had been so woefully lacking in imagination and was quite content with the occasional shag in the good old missionary position. Brian had taken his marital duties seriously and was more than happy to perform around once a month on a special Saturday night. No wonder she was prepared to jump through all the hoops for Matthew, she thought to herself with a sneer.

Jane had even taken to allowing Matthew to wear her underwear on occasions, which was always a sure way of getting him aroused without any need for pills. Admittedly, even *she* thought that kind of stuff was all a bit weird, but needs must. *Sharing is caring.* Wasn't that the saying?

In a nutshell, she was determined to deliver whatever Matthew required to satisfy his sexual appetite, however deviant. That way, she ensured he kept coming back for more and she remained in control of the situation.

Or so she thought.

The Camera Never Lies

Jane

Jane found out Matthew was married early on in their relationship. He was evasive from day one when questioned on pretty much any aspect of his life and gave very little away. She knew nothing about his family or friends and had no idea where he was or what he was up to when he wasn't with her. She decided to opt for the direct approach one evening as they sat at the kitchen table sharing a bottle of red wine.

'Are you married?' The question hung menacingly in the air.

He looked at her and sighed, rubbing his hand over his face. That was all the answer she needed.

'You fucking bastard!' she screamed and followed up immediately by spitting out all the insults she could think of, as she hurled her glass of red wine in his face.

Tears of fury rolled down her cheeks as he walked behind her to get the kitchen towel. He said nothing and calmly began wiping his face and shirt front.

Far too calmly - she thought.

'How could you do this to me? I really believed you loved me,' she snivelled pathetically, changing tack and going for the sympathy vote.

Quite the actress when she put her mind to it.

'Please calm down and let me explain.'

He looked her straight in the eyes with a sincere and slightly hurt expression on his face.

'I do love you,' he wheedled. 'Yes, it's true that I'm married, but please believe me, my marriage has been over for years and we live completely separate lives. She means nothing to me. We're married in name only.'

That old chestnut.

'Fine, so why don't you divorce her then? Now that you're with me,' she said petulantly, narrowing her eyes.

'I suppose I should have done that a long time ago, but it really didn't seem necessary. We have just been drifting along for the last few years, each doing our own thing. I promise you there is nothing between us anymore, but I really can't divorce her at the moment. It's partly because it doesn't make any sense financially, but also for the sake of her parents who are getting on a bit and not in very good health. I honestly think the shock of our divorce would kill them.'

'So fucking what? I have to think about myself for once,' she screamed, forgetting herself.

'Don't be like that, it doesn't suit you. You always knew I wasn't a 24/7 kind of guy. To be honest, I thought you'd guessed I was married and weren't that bothered.'

'Not bothered? Are you for fucking real? Why the hell would I not be bothered? I want a proper relationship and I want to be number one in your life. You moved in with me, for fuck's sake. I don't want you pissing about spending time and money on anyone else!'

'That's not very nice, is it? You need to calm down. And please stop swearing,' he added sanctimoniously.

Matthew had not raised his voice. Jane realised she was not helping her cause and decided to back off as he began again, in his annoyingly reasonable voice.

'Look, my wife is actually pretty unstable, if you really want to know the truth. A bit of a bunny boiler. No telling what she'd do to herself if I left her. She's tried to take her own life before now.

Thank God I found her in time. I didn't tell you about her, because she just isn't important.'

'All well and good, but where does that leave me?'

She glared at him defiantly, having tried and failed to look sympathetic. She decided to lay her cards on the table and call a spade a spade.

'Look, Matthew, to be honest, I don't give a flying fuck about your nutcase wife or her parents.'

Matthew sighed dramatically before resuming his efforts to manipulate her.

'The thing is, I don't think me being married needs to change anything as far as we are concerned and it certainly doesn't have to come between us. It's just a bit of paper at the end of the day. We don't have to be conventional, do we?'

Jane said nothing and waited for him to continue.

'I love you. You know that. You are one hundred percent the only woman I'm interested in having sex with.'

He hesitated for a moment, before continuing his persuasive rhetoric, realising that flattery was having the desired effect on her, as it always did.

'Come on, you know we have great sex. I've never done all that kinky stuff with anyone else. I'm pretty sure you haven't either,' he said, winking and giving her a playful nudge. 'We're definitely on the same wavelength in the bedroom department.'

He paused for dramatic effect and smirked conspiratorially. Jane had a sex flashback to their previous weekend together and felt the familiar stirrings of arousal as she remembered what they had got up to. She remembered a very drunk Matthew down on all fours, wearing nothing but *her* French knickers, stockings and suspender belt. Herself, equally drunk and stark naked, except for the strap on dick he had produced for her to wear, together with a large tube of Sliquid commercial lube. She could not resist a snigger, as she thought spitefully to herself how much his wife would love that one. Maybe it was time to pay her a visit to share some of their photos.

She knew Matthew was telling her what she wanted to hear to get around her but decided to stop fighting her corner for now. She was a great believer in picking her battles in order to win the war.

'You'd better be telling me the truth about all this. Because if I find out you've been messing me around....'

He put his arms around her from behind and kissed her on the neck, sliding his hands under her top and squeezing her breasts hard, the way she liked it. He clearly thought he had won, but Jane was no fool and she knew when she was being played. Matthew would find out to his cost that she was not the pushover he took her for.

If she was brutally honest, Jane couldn't give a shit that Matthew was married, so long as she got what she wanted out of the situation. She knew that the reason most married men went looking for other women was sex and she was more than happy to put out. If his stupid cow of a wife had taken her eye off the ball in that department, it could hardly be deemed Jane's fault, could it? Nevertheless, she decided she needed to do some digging and find out a bit more about 'the wife'.

Know thine enemy.

Jane smiled to herself at the thought of his wife's face if she should see one of the 'special' photos of the two of them at it. Better still a video, starring Jane herself, glamour model extraordinaire. All those filming sessions Matthew loved so much could prove to be very useful in the future, she decided, making a mental note to get some copies as insurance.

Soon after that conversation, Jane spent an evening alone with a bottle of wine, going through the photos and information the Private Investigator (PI) had handed over to her in exchange for a ridiculous amount of cash. It did not take long for her to realise that Matthew's portrayal of his wife had not been entirely truthful and that she was clearly going to be a more serious threat than Jane had initially thought. She appeared to be obsessed with horses, and there was picture after picture of her at various events, some in white jodhpurs and top hat for dressage, others in some kind of fancy dress riding costume that Jane later discovered was a traditional Portuguese riding habit. The PI she had hired had been thorough and when Jane found out how much the impressive-looking black stallion in the pictures was worth she practically choked. Matthew was certainly not spending that kind of money on her. Her fury was further heightened by the tactless comments from Tracy's lecherous husband, Rodney, when she showed them the pictures the following evening.

'I think somebody's been telling you porkies,' he laughed, practically drooling at the photos.

'You know what they say about horsey women, don't you?'

'No, but feel free to enlighten us,' Jane said sarcastically, staring venomously at him and thinking what a stupid prick he really was.

'They ride with the hands of a lady, the posture of a queen and the hips of a whore!'

He guffawed at his own joke, clearly finding himself hilarious.

Jane did not find him remotely amusing and vowed to drop him right in it with Tracy if the opportunity ever arose, which she felt certain it would.

The most irritating thing for her, however, was the number of photos of Matthew and his wife together, that the resourceful PI had managed to dig up: on a boat, round a table having dinner with friends, at a black-tie event, at a family Christmas.... It looked very much to Jane as if Matthew was enjoying a full life with his 'bunny boiler wife' while she, Jane, remained his dirty little secret for two or three nights each week and occasional weekends. The more she thought about it, the more she realised that, when they went out, it was always just the two of them and always to some obscure place, well away from anyone they might know. Jane had no intention of giving up, but she knew she would need to box clever in order to secure her future; the one with Matthew that suited her so perfectly.

As Jane stared at one of the photos she reminded herself that everyone has their Achilles heel; it was just a question of finding his wife's.

Tick Tock

The room called childlessness has many doors, not just the ones marked 'didn't want' or 'couldn't have'.

Grace

'**Oh** my God!' I shrieked with excitement as I opened the envelope and saw the burgundy coloured horse passport with the Lusitano Breed Society name emblazoned on it.

'Have you really bought him for me?'

'Yep. He's all yours.' Daniel smiled, obviously pleased with himself.

Valentino was my dream horse. I had fallen in love with him the day he arrived at the yard and now he was up for sale, it was a once in a lifetime opportunity. He stood tall for a Luso at 16.3 hands and he knew just how handsome he was. Imported from Brazil when he was four years old by the drummer of a rock band no less, he came from an impressive bloodline and I honestly thought he was the most beautiful horse I had ever seen, with his glossy black coat and long mane and tail. I never imagined I would be able to own him one day.

'Can we go and see him today?' I begged, hardly able to contain myself.

'That's the plan. I've booked you a lesson with Simone this afternoon.'

I was already used to riding Valentino and regularly had private lessons on him with Simone, the talented dressage rider and trainer who owned the yard where he was kept. Valentino was not only stunning to look at, he was also extremely talented and I was dying to start taking him out to shows, now that he was mine. Obviously, I would have to work around the race schedule for the boat, not to mention my part-time teaching job, but I was determined to show him off as much as possible. To be fair, we were not campaigning the boat as seriously as we had done a few years earlier and were sticking to a few key events each year. Daniel was run ragged at work and any spare time he did get seemed to be spent enjoying the new challenge of flying his beloved Schweizer 300c helicopter around the country. To compensate for the lack of sailing, I had taken up riding again and was learning classical dressage at the Lusitano stud and training centre, owned and run by Simone, her twin sister and her mother, near our second home in North Wales. I loved it down there and spent as much time as possible in our little cottage overlooking the water in the village of Llandovey, near Conway. We bought the house the year after we were married, as it made sense to have a base near to the marina where we kept the boat. It was in my name and I paid the mortgage, as Daniel said it would be protected that way if ever the business went under, not that that seemed likely. Most weekends, I headed for the coast and Daniel joined me as often as work permitted. The location was stunning and it was a great bolt hole to get away from the rat race of normal life. I imagined us retiring there one day, hopefully in the not too distant future. The constant travelling around, both in the UK and abroad, was taking its toll on my workaholic husband and I worried how long he could sustain the frenetic pace without making himself ill. He was permanently exhausted and sometimes even ended up working over the weekend. According to him, it was the price you had to pay for running your own business and having the lifestyle that goes with it, but I was beginning to wonder if the price was just too high. I needed to get him to slow down, but it would not be easy.

The main events I wanted to get straight in the calendar were the Lusitano Breed Show, Warrington Show and Royal Windsor. Being a Lusitano, I would be able to show Valentino in the Parade classes in his ornate Portuguese tack. He had a gorgeous bullfighting saddle with intricate patterns embossed in the black leather flaps and a contrasting beige suede seat, which set off the colour of his coat beautifully. His black leather bridle and breastplate were adorned with gold ornaments and, even better, I would get to dress up in my traditional Portuguese riding costume and hat, reminiscent of a bullfighter's outfit. A friend of mine had made me the outfit a couple of years ago when Valentino's previous owner had generously allowed me to take him out to shows. She was living abroad and knew the special relationship I had built up with him.

Later that afternoon, Daniel and I stood side by side, admiring my beautiful boy as he munched on treats in his stable.

'This one's going to keep you on your toes,' he began, with a knowing laugh. 'You're going to need to put in some serious hours of practice if you're going to take him out to the big shows and do well. Aren't you glad now that we don't have children? Like I said to you before, you just wouldn't be able to do all this stuff with a kid in tow.'

And there it was. The real reason for the sudden extravagant gesture. Why did he always have to spoil it? Of course I knew I was being manipulated but, at the same time, how could I be cross with him when he had just made my dream come true? I chose my words carefully.

'You're right about him needing a lot of attention, but owning Valentino doesn't mean I don't ever want children. I haven't changed my mind on that,' I stated firmly.

I was not ready to sell out completely just yet and he needed to know that.

'Well neither have I,' he retorted sharply. 'You know my feelings. We're fine as we are, just the two of us. We have a fantastic lifestyle that most of your friends are extremely envious of. It's about time you began to appreciate what you've got and accept that the baby route is not for everyone. I honestly don't think you realise just how lucky you are.'

'That's a bit unfair, don't you think? It's just…well, I'm not getting any younger and we have been married eight years now….'

I thought back to the day two years ago, when Daniel had walked through the door at home and presented me with an adorable eight-week-old black Labrador puppy. It was as if he could hear the tick-tock of my biological clock loud and clear and was intent on filling the void in my life with an assortment of fur babies. Of course, I adored Hero the black Labrador, who followed me loyally everywhere, and naturally, I was besotted with my new boy Valentino. I just didn't think the two things were mutually exclusive and I had more than enough love in my heart to welcome a human baby into our lives. I could not dispel the feeling that Daniel was being incredibly selfish. He was ten years older than me, but as a man, he would be able to father children until a ripe old age. It is a different story for us women of course.

There was no doubt in my mind that God did not create men and women equally and it was becoming increasingly obvious to me that women got the short straw, some shorter than others.

The Dream House

Lorraine

Lorraine screamed and giggled like a little girl as John scooped her up in his arms and bundled her through the door, across the threshold of their new home in the picture-postcard Oxfordshire village of Hazeldene. She felt like a child in a sweet shop as they walked through the cottage together, taking in every detail. Her favourite room was the kitchen. They had created a large, farmhouse style room with French windows opening onto a little, south-facing courtyard with a bistro table and chairs. She could already imagine them sitting there together, enjoying a lazy breakfast or a glass of wine in the evening. A massive Aga range cooker set in a stone fireplace dominated the room, and to the side of it was a wine rack made from clay pipes. She looked appreciatively at the traditional style, cream-painted, wooden units with their black, ceramic knobs and ran her hand over the cool, black granite of the work surfaces. The gold flecks in the granite sparkled under the down-lighters in the ceiling and the stone flags on the floor matched the ones on the patio, perfect for coming in wearing wellies after a muddy dog walk. There was even a space in the units for the basket of her beloved black Labrador Dexter, near the Aga so he would be toasty and warm in the winter. A sturdy, oak table with six chairs around it stood in the centre of the room. This would be the heart of the house - she thought to herself with a smile. The kitchen design was all John's work, which she had been nervous about at first but, she had to admit, it had turned out to be absolutely perfect. He had apparently got all the ideas from a friend of his, who was in construction and had recently renovated a similar property somewhere in the north of England, near where he lived. John had been so impressed with the kitchen in that house, he had decided to recreate it for her and she was delighted to see that it lived up to her highest expectations.

This was everything Lorraine had ever dreamed of. A beautiful, seventeenth-century, stone cottage in the heart of rural Oxfordshire and the man she loved by her side. She still couldn't quite believe it. Her father had died suddenly the previous year, leaving her a share of the family home. When everything was sorted, she received a relatively modest amount from the proceeds, as everything had to be divided up and shared between her and her two brothers of course, but once she had sold her own house as well and paid off the remainder of the debts her ex-husband had saddled her with, she found she had enough left to put down a healthy deposit on her dream house with John. She had had to borrow some money as well, but the hefty, monthly payments she had signed up for were only a temporary measure. John was just waiting to be paid for a really important and very lucrative job that was currently being finished over in America and once that money came through, the plan was that he would pay off the mortgage in full.

When her father died, and Lorraine first broached the subject of buying a property together, she had offered to move further north to be nearer to John's work and try to cut down on some of the travelling he had to do. He was, of course, grateful to her for being so thoughtful, but he explained that he did not think it was a good idea for several reasons, which ultimately made sense to her. Oxfordshire was a much nicer area in his opinion with a lot more going on and he was more than happy for them to be based there. He pointed out that it would not make any difference to the amount of time he spent at home with her as he had to travel around so much anyway. That was why he didn't want to have a big house up in Derbyshire. He preferred to just use the bedsit he had rented there, which doubled up as his office when he needed to be near work. He explained to her that he had been looking for a long time to buy a nice property in the country as a bolt hole to escape to but just hadn't found the right place or the right person to do it with. Until now.

Lorraine and John had searched for months before deciding on the picturesque cottage in Hazeldene, just outside the lively, market town of Marchfield. It needed fully renovating, but that was part of its attraction, as they felt they wanted somewhere they could put their own stamp on. The cottage came with nearly four acres of land and, as part of the renovations, they had been granted planning permission to build a set of garages to house some of John's growing collection of cars and motorcycles. It was an exciting project, but a costly one. The plan was originally for her to rent a flat while the bulk of the building work was being done, but John suddenly came up with the brilliant idea of buying a canal boat with some of the money from her dad's estate and her own house sale. Lorraine loved the romantic notion of living on a longboat and was only too happy to go along with the new plan. She imagined herself taking in the early evening sun with a glass of wine as she waited for John to join her, maybe reading a book on her little deck, crammed with colourful pot plants.

John volunteered to do all the hard work to find the right boat and sort out all the paperwork, as he had contacts through one of his customers. All Lorraine had to do was transfer the money and they would be the proud owners of the perfect boat for the two of them. He explained he was having a few cash flow problems, but promised that as soon as he was paid for the American job he would put the money straight back in her account. She knew there was nothing to worry about. Just the normal ups and downs of running your own business.

John confided to her that he had always wanted a canal boat, but had never found anyone to share his dream with until he met her. She was his soul mate.

After a lot of research, they decided to keep their boat on the Oxford Canal at Cranburgh, a medieval market town about half an hour away, bustling with quaint little pubs. The plan was to sell the boat once the house was completed but, when the time came, neither of them could bear to part with it. As John pointed out, the money was spent and forgotten, so they might as well continue to get pleasure from it. She did not take much persuading, having loved her time on the boat and also feeling it was something of a status symbol in the eyes of her friends and family.

Lorraine's only reservation was that she didn't know how they were ever going to find the time to enjoy both their gorgeous new home and the canal boat. John seemed to be working longer hours than ever and she was worried about how stressed he was getting. He was travelling a lot, all over the country and also abroad, but she supposed that was the nature of his work and she had to admit she had known that from the beginning. It didn't stop her feeling lonely though and she wished he could be with her more often.

She consoled herself with the fact that at least she had Dexter. John had turned up with the gorgeous little bundle of fur when he was just three months old, placing him in her arms as he stepped onto the boat one evening. He said he would be able to keep her company on the nights when he couldn't be with her. Dexter had taken to the canal boat surprisingly well and he was a firm favourite with all the regulars, wandering around on the hunt for treats in his red, doggy life vest. Lorraine knew he was happy to be anywhere so long as he was with her. He was going to love his new home in the country with all that space to explore.

As soon as they were properly installed, Lorraine was desperate to show off their new home, knowing it symbolised a new stage in their relationship and would finally silence the doubters, namely her brother and her best friend Harriet. John was not a big socialiser and certainly not a fan of parties, so she picked her moment carefully to broach the subject with him.

'Let's have a bit of a get-together, a sort of house-warming party. Fairly low key. Just Harriet and Keith, Gerald and his family. I'll ask Mark and Susan as well, but I doubt they'll be able to make it,' she began, breezily.

Lorraine's younger brother Mark worked in the oil industry and he and his partner lived up in Aberdeen, Scotland so she rarely saw him these days. She looked at John cautiously to gauge his reaction as he replied.

'I suppose so if you want to. I have to say though, they're not really my kind of people and, to be honest, I didn't think they were yours either,' he said, pulling a face. 'Didn't you fall out with Harriet after that big row you had a while back?'

He looked at her questioningly, before adding:

'And I'm sorry, but you have to admit your brother is a pompous arse.'

'Oh come on John, he's still my brother for God's sake. I know you both have had your differences, but if you could maybe relax with him and get to know him a bit better, I'm sure you'd like him. He's just over-protective where I'm concerned, after all the shit I went through with Bernard. Try to get on with him, for my sake. As for Harriet, I've known her forever. Anyway, they'll all have to change their tune now that we've got the house together. We're a proper couple now,' she finished, brightly.

'As I said, they're just not my kind of people and I don't really get the whole 'family thing'. If you feel you have to do it, then go ahead, but I draw the line at Gerald's kids. They're out of control at the best of times and I don't want them breaking anything. Anyway, I've got to go into town for a couple of things now, so I'll see you a bit later.'

With that, he kissed her and left, obviously keen to get away and avoid any further discussion on the subject.

Lorraine was disappointed by his lack of enthusiasm for her party idea, but she was determined to improve their joint social life. She and John had been together now for over seven years and she was devoted to him, but she was aware that she had gradually drifted further apart from her family and even her close friends. John always said he preferred to have her all to himself, but she needed other people when he wasn't there.

Despite her enthusiasm, she knew the party would not be without its challenges. Gerald, her over-cautious and over-protective older brother did not approve of her and John buying a house together, making it clear he felt she was stretching herself beyond her means. For some unknown reason, he had taken a dislike to John from day one and, because of that their relationship had become strained. She loved him dearly, but he just couldn't resist sticking his nose in and trying to spoil things for her. She was certain it was a jealousy thing. Her brother was an accountant, who admittedly made a decent living and had a nice house on the outskirts of Peterborough, but he was never going to set the world on fire or be able to afford the lifestyle that she and John now enjoyed. To put it bluntly, he was Mister Average, with two kids and a primary school teacher for a wife. He drove a Volvo estate and his wife a Ford Fiesta. John always said you could tell a lot about people from the cars they drove, and it was certainly not meant as a compliment in her brother's case. Gerald, on the other hand, thought John's Porsche was far too showy, labelling him an arrogant braggart who was not to be trusted. It was clear to Lorraine from the start that they would never be best buddies and she put it all down to envy on her brother's part.

Then there was Harriet. Her best friend. Somehow they had fallen out a year or so earlier and things had never been quite the same since. Lorraine still remembered the occasion vividly and cringed at the harsh words they had both hurled at each other. The trouble was that once hurtful things are thrown out there, they can never be taken back and they are rarely truly forgotten.

She had planned to see John the weekend of the argument, but he rang to cancel at the last minute as there was a major problem at work. 'The joys of owning your own business,' he had said, with a troubled sigh. Lorraine wondered how many times she had heard that phrase, but she knew the score and, as usual, he had promised to make it up to her the following weekend by taking her away to her favourite hotel in Kent for a mini-break. Lorraine had hung up, looked miserably at all the food and wine she had bought in for their weekend together and decided to call Harriet on the off chance that she was free. A few hours later they were sitting together with a large glass of Prosecco, just like old times, although there had been a couple of barbed jibes from Harriet about always being the stand-in dinner date.

She was quick to start quizzing Lorraine on her relationship with John.

'So I take it things are still going well with you and John? I hardly ever see you these days, now you're all loved up.'

She laughed as she said it, but there was a hint of awkwardness between them that had never been there before.

'I really love him, Harriet. He makes me happy. He spoils me whenever I see him and between you and me, the sex is out of this world,' she giggled.

Lorraine knew she sounded smug, but couldn't help herself.

'Whoa, too much information thanks. I'm glad for you, I really am, it's just….'

She did not finish the sentence.

'Just what?' Lorraine snapped, immediately on the defensive.

'Okay, so where is he this time then? Let me guess…another problem at work? I just think…well, he does seem to let you down an awful lot.'

Harriet stopped and looked at her friend with a concerned expression, but Lorraine leapt to John's defence as usual.

'Yes actually, it is another problem at work. It's called *owning your own business* Harriet, not something you and Keith would understand anything about.'

Harriet bristled at the condescending tone of her friend but decided to let it go.

'We know plenty about hard work, thank you very much. I just don't want to see you get hurt. If I'm honest, you've been together what...six years now isn't it? Well then, I don't get why you haven't moved in together properly, or why you've never met any of his family. You haven't even been to visit him to see where he lives, have you? Don't you think that's weird? He seems to just turn up randomly at your place whenever he feels like sex.'

Lorraine felt the familiar anger bubbling up inside her.

'That shows how much you know then,' she retorted. 'And for your information, we are looking for a place to buy together right now. Why are you always so down on him anyway? You just can't bring yourself to be happy for me, can you? Do you know what I think? I think you're jealous. You've never really given him a chance. You've got a massive chip on your shoulder just because you're stuck with a boring, predictable husband who's never likely to make more than forty grand a year if he's lucky.'

Lorraine recalled the conversation in the pub a while ago; when John had rather tactlessly said to Harriet that he couldn't understand how anyone could possibly survive these days on less than a hundred grand a year. She had not been impressed with him at the time and could not believe she had just said such a crass thing to Harriet, but there was no taking it back now.

'You snotty bitch!' her friend retaliated. 'When did you get to be so up yourself? It wasn't so long ago you were on the bones of your arse with no idea how you were going to make ends meet and snivelling to me about it. You've got a short memory, haven't you? I've always been there for you and always tried to support you, but it seems that I'm surplus to requirements, now you've got your precious John. I just hope for your sake he doesn't drop you from a great height, because the way you're going, you'll be left high and dry with no-one to pick up the pieces.'

'Well, that's fine by me, because I trust him and I know he *won't* let me down. In fact, the more I think about it, the more I think you prefer it when I'm unhappy and things are going wrong for me.

73

That way you get to play Saint Harriet, don't you? There's nothing you enjoy better than a drama at someone else's expense,' Lorraine spat, unable to stop herself.

'Oh my God, you're certainly showing your true colours now, aren't you? I've stood by you and put up with your vile temper and mood swings over the years. And don't forget I've seen what you're really capable of. I always gave you the benefit of the doubt, but it just goes to show how wrong you can be. Friendship clearly means nothing to you. You're just out for number one, always have been.'

'Yeah, right. It's not like I didn't have to put up with more than my fair share of you whining about your boring marital problems over the years. I think we're quits on that score, don't you? Anyway, I think we'd better change the subject and agree to differ before we both say things we regret.'

'I think it's a bit late for that, don't you? The pair of you deserve each other.'

On that note, Harriet stood up, reached for her coat and flounced out, fighting back the tears.

They had barely seen each other since.

Lorraine looked around her at her shiny, new kitchen and realised how much she missed her best friend. She regretted the argument and knew it was up to her to bury the hatchet once and for all and get their friendship back on track, before it was too late.

She sent out messages inviting the select little crowd to dinner, adults-only, of course, to keep John happy. To her delight, Harriet graciously accepted the olive branch. Lorraine made a mental note to remind her not to put anything on Facebook. John hated all social media and refused to engage with any of it, declaring that in his opinion it robbed people of both time and privacy. He liked to keep his social life private and was paranoid about his customers knowing anything about him. Lorraine kind of got that and respected his wishes. She was seldom on Facebook herself these days anyway, but Harriet was a different kettle of fish. She was prolific on social media and regularly posted updates on every insignificant event in her life, including pictures of what she was having for dinner, tagging friends right left and centre. John would do his nut if she put anything on about him or their new house.

By the time the night of the party arrived, Lorraine had the house looking exactly as she wanted, with scented candles and scatter cushions everywhere, just like she had seen in the magazines she read. She had cooked a Beef Stroganoff in her new Aga, which was one of John's favourite dishes and also happened to be one of only two things she could pull off with any degree of success. It was just the six of them in the end, and she was pleased to note that John and Gerald seemed to be on their best behaviour with each other. John was an expert at ensuring everyone's glass was always full, although there was an awkward moment when he picked up the bottle of Cabernet Sauvignon Gerald had brought as an offering, he did not attempt to hide his disdain for what he considered to be cheap plonk. She knew he fancied himself as a bit of a wine buff, but she cringed as he raised his eyebrows, shoved it in the cupboard and opened a bottle of Barolo from his own stock in the wine rack. Fortunately, Gerald had already had a fair amount to drink and did not appear to notice.

Once the meal was finished, everyone retired to the lounge, leaving Lorraine to clear away with the help of Gerald, who was obviously looking for an opportunity to catch her alone.

'The place is lovely. I have to admit, you've done a great job of doing it up.'

He nodded appreciatively as he surveyed his surroundings.

'Thanks so much. I *knew* you'd love it.'

Lorraine beamed happily at him, grateful for his approval.

'You must come back soon and bring the kids. They'll have such fun exploring in the garden.'

'Hmm,' he murmured, thoughtfully. 'I'm not so sure John would approve of that idea. Who's actually paying for all this if you don't mind me asking?'

Gerald had changed the subject abruptly, always one for getting straight to the point. Lorraine felt her hackles rise, as she realised where the conversation was heading.

'You know perfectly well the mortgage is in my name for the moment. John intends to pay it off in full just as soon as the money comes in from the job he's working on.'

'Ah, right,' Gerald laughed wryly, not one for keeping his thoughts to himself.

'To be honest, Lorraine, I think the man is full of shit. I don't trust him further than I can throw him.'

'Well I *do* trust him,' she hissed. 'And I'm warning you, I will not have you speaking about John like that in *our* home. Get back in there with the others and leave me to sort this lot out. You just can't help yourself, can you?'

Lorraine was furious with her brother, who had the unfailing ability to make her feel about five years old. What was it with him? Why did he always have to piss on her bonfire? She clattered around in the kitchen for a bit, trying to calm herself down before making coffee and going through to salvage what was left of the evening.

At least things seemed to be back to normal with Harriet now. She had come into the kitchen earlier to help serve dinner and they had both ended up blurting out how sorry they were at the same time. Prosecco always helped in those situations and after a few tears, they had hugged each other tightly, promising to get together more regularly.

By the time everyone left, Lorraine felt drained, mainly from having to play peacekeeper most of the night and prevent John from lording it too much over her brother. She sighed and put her arms around his neck.

'See, that wasn't so bad, was it?'

'I suppose not,' he said grudgingly, then suddenly cheered up as he remembered something.

'Did you see your brother's face when I told him how much the home gym had cost? And when I showed him the pictures of my cars and told him what they were worth, I thought he was going to explode.'

Lorraine sighed and frowned.

'I just wish you wouldn't wind him up so much all the time.'

'Sorry, but he deserves it. Now come to bed. I've waited long enough to get you all to myself.'

He thrust himself suggestively against her hip, clearly turned on by the evening's bragging.

Later that night Lorraine lay awake in bed, as John snored drunkenly beside her, having fallen asleep before she got anywhere near the bedroom. Gerald's words had got to her, despite her protestations. She had mortgaged herself up to the hilt, knowing it was only temporary but, if she was being honest, things had not entirely gone to plan. John had told her there were some temporary problems and unforeseen complications with the job in America. They were behind schedule with it, it was still not finished and they were now being sued by the 'totally unreasonable customers'. John was having to plough more and more of his own money into the company to finance lawyers and keep everything going, but the long and short of it was that he was not in any position to pay off the mortgage or return the money for the canal boat at the moment. John was confident he would win the lawsuit and get substantial damages and costs in the end as the customer was completely in the wrong but, as he pointed out to her, these things have a habit of dragging on before they are finally resolved, sometimes for years.

No matter. They were a team now and her job was to support him through this in any way she could.

The Acceptance

When faced with a difficult situation there are only three choices: leave it, change it or accept it.

Grace

The red Porsche Boxter in Champney's car park had its hood down and there was a massive gold bow attached to the windscreen. Daniel had taken me away for the weekend to the luxury spa hotel near London to celebrate my thirty-fifth birthday and the car caught my eye as we walked through the grounds of the hotel on our way to dinner. Daniel said nothing, but as he turned to me he held up a car key attached to a red leather Porsche key ring.

'Oh my God, you are kidding me!' I shrieked in excitement.

'Nope. It's all yours.' He dropped the keys into my hand and grinned at my reaction.

'Happy birthday, Hun.'

'*Hun!* That's a bit American, isn't it?' I laughed, as I took the keys and ran over to the car, unable to believe it was really mine. Daniel was fond of grand gestures and always seemed to be able to pull something out of the bag when things were a bit sticky between us. It was as if he felt the need to prove how much he loved me by spoiling me with an extravagant present. Or maybe he just wanted to distract me. I already had a dog and a horse. And now I had a brand new sports car.

What I did *not* have was a baby.

I still didn't understand why Daniel was so against the idea of us starting a family. We had plenty of money most of the time, although admittedly there were a few problems with the business at the moment. Nevertheless, I was sure things would work themselves out and I was certain we could give a child a great life. I had always imagined I would have children and it left a huge void that just couldn't be filled with anything else. I was also sick of fielding all the questions from friends and family about it and became defensive as soon as the subject was broached. Strangers were just as bad.

So do you have children then?

It seemed like people were obsessed with that question as a conversation starter, yet totally incapable of coping with the 'wrong' answer. My curt reply in the negative inevitably resulted in an uncomfortable silence and a patronisingly sympathetic expression, which fuelled my irritation even further.

Most of the time I managed to convince myself that it was not what I wanted either, but periodically the subject would bubble back to the surface, resulting in the inevitable argument. Daniel was resolute in his stance on the matter. His way of dealing with it was usually to shout, storm off and then come up with a distraction. Hence the puppy, the horse, the car and some extravagant holidays abroad.

Of course, I loved being spoilt and I loved the presents, but I was always left with a gnawing feeling that I was somehow selling my soul to the highest bidder and giving up on my own hopes and dreams. There was a time when I thought about just going ahead and getting pregnant against his wishes, but somehow that didn't seem right either. For me, it was about more than simply having a child. It was about us being a proper family and, old-fashioned and naïve as I perhaps was, in my eyes, it had to be something we both wanted.

I remembered the heated words of the previous evening and looked at my shiny new car.

The trade-off. He had done it again.

Daniel looked pleased with himself as we sat at the dinner table and the waiter poured us a glass of the Laurent Perrier that had been ordered.

'How do you fancy ten days holiday with all the beautiful people in St Barths?' he asked, knowing how much I loved the place.

'What? That's a bit out of the blue, isn't it? Of course I'd love to go back there. It's just….' I hesitated, remembering a heated exchange about money the previous week.

'I thought you said there were some problems with the business at the moment. The customer that's threatening to sue you? Are you sure we can afford to go right now?'

I looked at him for reassurance. I worried about the money we spent sometimes, especially as I knew Daniel had re-mortgaged our house to secure a business loan recently. I had been very uneasy about compromising our home like that, but he had insisted I sign the paperwork as the business needed the injection of cash.

He laughed and shook his head.

'You worry too much. Of course we can afford it. It's okay for me to spoil my wife, isn't it? I got a last-minute deal, but if you don't want to go, I suppose I can always cancel…take the car back….'

He was mocking me and I giggled, relieved. Apparently, he was on a roll and his excitement was infectious.

'Can we stay at The Eden Rock?' I asked.

'Of course. I've already booked the Captain's Cabin, the same room we had last time.'

'Oh my God, fantastic! I love that place so much.'

St Barths was an idyllic little island in the Caribbean, playground of the rich and famous, just off the larger island of St Martin. I remembered the short flight over from St Martin in a light aircraft the last time we had been there. Hair raising to say the least. The pilot had to come in low over the trees on top of the mountain, seeming to almost touch them, then dive sharply down to make the scarily short landing strip, which finished just before the beach met the sea. Occasionally a plane failed to stop in time and ended up crashed on the beach. The photos of such incidents added interest to the walls of the fashionable Eden Rock Hotel perched as its name suggested on a large rock near the landing strip.

We had been to the tiny island twice before; the first time we stayed at the Eden Rock, the second time we were cruising with Charles and Samantha on their Swan 80. Like so many of the larger cruising yachts, theirs spent the summer in the Mediterranean, based in Monaco, and the winter in the Caribbean. The four of us could easily handle the boat for cruising with its furling sails and electric winches.

Daniel was not joking when he said he got a last-minute deal. Two weeks after Champneys we were walking along the sandy pathway to the Eden Rock Hotel, with the sunset providing a spectacular backdrop for our arrival. We were sure to have a wonderful ten days in Paradise, but I somehow couldn't quite get rid of the niggling little worry in the back of my mind that the money from the re-mortgage was paying for the holiday and we were living on borrowed time.

I had spent a frantic couple of days going back and forth between hairdresser and beauty salon, endeavouring to ensure that my body prepping was up to standard for the chic French island.

'No fatties allowed in here!' Daniel quipped as we arrived. 'Good job you keep yourself nice and trim or you'd find yourself back on the plane, rejected by the customs police.'

Daniel hated women being overweight and I was always paranoid to make sure I did not fall into that trap. I liked the compliments he always gave me about my figure and, like most women, I was not averse to flattery. At thirty-five years old, I knew I could scrub up well with a bit of effort, but I had to work at it. I told myself that was one of the advantages of not having had children; my body had not been subjected to the ravages of childbirth.

Every cloud….

Throughout our marriage, Daniel had remained vehemently against the idea of having children and, as the years rolled by, I wrestled with my own feelings and tried desperately to accept the situation. I could have left him of course, in the hope of meeting someone else who wanted me to be the mother of his children, but what if that had never happened? I knew there were no guarantees and I was not prepared to take the risk of losing what I had. At the end of the day, I loved him and did not want to throw away the life I had by chasing after an elusive dream that may or may not have come true.

And yet, despite what I told myself, I still clung to a little glimmer of hope that Daniel would change his mind before it was too late for me.

The Trap

Jane

Men were uncomplicated creatures in Jane's opinion and easy to manipulate. It came down to sex, simple as that. Matthew had unconventional tastes in the bedroom department and she always made sure she pulled out all the stops, especially after a row, just to remind him what he would potentially be missing. Sex was always the key. Jane knew when she was onto a good thing and never pushed too far in an argument. As a result, eight years down the line, she was still hanging on in there.

Jane had a strong suspicion that Matthew was still sleeping with his wife, but she also knew he kept on coming back to her for the more 'alternative' option. She made sure she indulged him and was always quick to massage his ego. In return, he paid a regular sum of two grand into her account each month for 'services she provided to his business'. To be fair, she did actually get involved in some of the accounting for his company as she had quickly realised it gave her the perfect opportunity to snoop and gather potential ammunition, just in case he ever got any ideas about leaving her in the lurch.

In reality, she was forced to admit that things had not progressed as planned and the status quo after all this time remained the same. To all intents and purposes, they were like a proper couple. They went for walks in the country with the dog he had suddenly presented her with one day, went on holidays and had occasional weekends away.

Like a proper couple - she thought to herself - but not quite.

His wife was still there in the background, somewhere on the other side of the country, spoiling everything. If Matthew didn't buck his ideas up soon she was going to have to take matters into her own hands. Jane was still 'the other woman' and she was getting mightily sick of it. She had one last trick up her sleeve, but if that didn't work…. Well, let's just say she knew there were people out there who had made a career out of 'problem-solving'. Tracy's pervy husband, Rodney, was not as squeaky clean as he liked to make out and Tracy had been less than discreet about his dealings on several occasions. Jane was pretty confident he knew the right people to talk to if necessary. She was certainly not ruling that option out, but it could get very complicated, not to mention dangerous. Before she went down that route, she intended to try a change of tactic.

Jane had mistakenly believed that, sooner or later, Matthew would leave his wife for her, but he seemed more than happy to jog along with things as they were which did not bode well for the future in her opinion. She had no intention of being a glorified shag buddy for the rest of her life, nor did she have any intention of letting her meal ticket slip through her fingers. She worked on him for months to take her on holiday to South Africa, until he finally caved in; actually believing it was his idea.

'That sounds amazing,' she said eagerly, then jumped to her feet and hugged him, before slipping her hand deftly down the front of his trousers to reward him.

Martini girl, that's me - she thought wryly to herself - Any time, any place, anywhere and always up for a quick shag.

What the heck. She enjoyed it most of the time. On the balance of things she felt she had made the right decision over the last few years to put up and shut up about his wife. Until now. South Africa was her opportunity to put her well and truly in her box.

They flew into Cape Town on the overnight flight from London and had breakfast at the top of glorious Table Mountain, with its spectacular views of the sea and the city. The plan was to take their time and drive towards Durban along the Garden Route via the Transkei in their hired 4x4, stopping off several times along the way. Jane had planned the journey meticulously and was accepting nothing less than five-star luxury wherever possible. He needed to realise she did not come cheap. It took nearly six hours to reach the Outeniqua Mountains, where they were spending a couple of nights in the exclusive Teniqua Treetops Hotel, in a hand-carved treehouse in the middle of the protected forest. It was truly breath-taking, although the atmosphere was somewhat spoiled by the fact that Matthew was infinitely more interested in whether or not he could get a mobile phone signal. Jane couldn't work out what he was up to, but she was pretty sure it wasn't for work reasons.

On the edge of the Wild Coast, not far from Durban, was the five-star Prana Lodge, with its own Thai spa, nestled in the middle of a deep forest. It promised 'ultimate relaxation for body and soul', but Jane's temper was becoming increasingly frayed by Matthew's lack of enthusiasm in bed. He was going through the motions but was permanently distracted. He actually fell asleep on the job one night and when she challenged him about it, he gave the feeble explanation that he was worried about work. Jane had recognised all the signs recently back at home, but if he thought he was going to get away with pushing her to one side after all the effort she had put in, he had another think coming.

Jane knew exactly how she was going to play this and decided it was time to use her trump card. She opened her toiletry bag and took out the strip of little white contraceptive pills, wrapping them in tissue paper and throwing them in the bin with a satisfied smirk.

'You're not getting rid of me that easily mate,' she said to no one in particular.

When Matthew announced a few days later that they would have to cut their holiday short, due to a crisis with the business back at home, she didn't really care.

Two months later, on a minibreak in the Cotswolds, she dropped the bombshell, after a particularly energetic sex session.

'I'm pregnant.' Short and to the point.

He nearly choked on his Mount Gay and coke and Jane felt an immediate rush of power and control. She liked the feeling.

'You're what? But you're supposed to be on the pill! How the hell did that happen?'

He stopped talking, apparently lost for words.

'Well, it happens when a man and a woman…,'

He cut her short.

'Don't be so fucking smart. It's hardly a laughing matter, is it? This was not part of the deal. I always told you I didn't want kids and you said you didn't either?'

Yes, but that was before you started to lose interest – she thought to herself.

'I know and that was true, but now that it's happened by accident, it's not such a disaster, is it?' she asked, trying her best to look tearful.

'Well no, I don't suppose…Christ, I don't know.'

He was red in the face and beads of sweat had formed on his forehead.

'I need some air. I'll be back in a minute.'

He pulled on a dressing gown and disappeared onto the terrace. Jane took a sip of her orange juice and waited patiently.

She knew it was a risky strategy, but she was confident it would work.

A child is born

Jane

A baby had never been part of her original plan and, as her face contorted with the indescribable pain of another contraction, she cursed her change of heart. The lights in the delivery room were too bright and her annoyance was turning rapidly to fear. This was not how it was supposed to be. She liked to be in control and this was unfamiliar territory for her.

Up until the moment when the midwife felt the need to call in the doctor, things had been progressing well. The announcement that the baby was showing signs of distress changed everything, and the staff all seemed to go into emergency overdrive. They were now preparing to perform a caesarean on her and there was still no sign of Matthew. Jane was furious with him for letting her down yet again, but just as she had given up on him, a smiling nurse burst in with perfect theatrical timing to deliver the triumphant news that her husband had finally arrived.

Someone else's husband actually - Jane did not bother to correct the young nurse.

'Talk about leaving it until the eleventh hour,' she spat, making her displeasure clear.

'I know, I know, but I'm here now. That's all that matters, isn't it? I got here as quickly as I could.'

He kissed her on the forehead.

'Come on now. Let's do this. Let's meet our son.'

God, he is so cheesy sometimes – she thought - Always one to put on a good show.

She was not convinced about his sincerity, but what she did know was that everything was about to change. She would no longer be 'the other woman'. Very soon her status would be elevated to 'mother of his child'. That poor cow of a wife wouldn't know what had hit her. Jane almost felt sorry for her.

Almost.

Smug and elated despite the pain, she was secure in the knowledge that all her scheming would finally be worth it. The plan was coming to fruition.

As she drifted into a semi-conscious state, courtesy of the drugs they gave her, she told herself that this was no more than she deserved. She had invested everything in this relationship and she had no intention of allowing herself to be cast aside. She had simply taken the necessary steps to protect her investment, insurance in the shape of a child.

From somewhere nearby, she heard the words:

'Congratulations, you have a beautiful baby boy!'

The nurse in the delivery room was speaking quickly. 'He's having a bit of trouble breathing, so we're taking him straight to the special baby unit. It's nothing to worry about. You'll be able to see him very soon. We need to look after you both now.'

Jane opened her mouth to say something, but the nurse was already disappearing into the corridor with her baby.

Jane felt as if she was in some kind of parallel universe. Things were happening all around her and to her, but she had no control over anything. It was six hours before she was allowed to hold her baby, but in those six hours, she was delighted to note that things had most definitely changed. The two of them were in this together now, united as parents. Matthew, who had never wanted children, seemed utterly smitten. This little baby was the one that would finally get rid of his wife once and for all. She could not help gloating that, at last, she would be number one. They were a proper family now and there was no way 'horsewoman' could compete with that.

Jane suddenly remembered Matthew had told her his wife couldn't have children, which was partly why she was so unhinged.

Shame.

Five years later, as Jane sat alone at her son's school play, in which he had a starring role as Old Macdonald, she realised to her consternation that she was still 'the other woman'. Matthew had been called away on business at the last minute, so sadly couldn't be there, or at least that was what he told her. She didn't believe that cock and bull story for a second. In the drawer of her bedside table was a photo of Matthew's wife she had childishly defaced with a black moustache and beard. She thought of all the other photos she had on her back up device and decided she had had enough. It was time for action.

Unfortunately for Jane, what she did not know then was that Matthew's wife was not the only one she needed to worry about.

The Conversation

'**It** won't be cheap and you know there's always the chance that we might be found out.'

'How big a chance?'

The man took a long drag on his Marlboro Light and blew the smoke residue high into the air, despite the no-smoking sign by the window of the hotel room. He shook his head from side to side. The movement was barely noticeable.

'Not much,' he said, 'everything will more or less be destroyed.'

'Are you sure?'

He nodded.

'Full tank of fuel, everything will be vaporised.'

He flicked his ash into the overfull ashtray.

'So who's your client.'

'That's not your concern,' she said, reaching into her handbag and pulling out a manila padded envelope. 'Here's what you asked for. You'll get the rest after the accident.'

The man reached out for the envelope and took it. He couldn't help but smile. The woman was already describing it as an 'accident'. It was going to be no accident. He looked up. 'You realise there are no guarantees?'

'Yes.'

I can bring it down but the rest is in the lap of the gods. Your client is aware of that?'

'Yes.'

'Miracles do happen,' he said as he leafed through the bundle of fifty-pound notes he had pulled from the envelope.

She looked on for a good minute until the man was satisfied that the money was all there.

And then he looked up. 'The tracker has been fitted?'

'Yes.'

'Good.'

'The helicopter will be on The Isle of Wight in precisely seven days from now.'

'Good.'

He was a man of few words. Another half-minute passed. He looked up at the woman,

who lingered uncomfortably. He pointed over to the door.

'That's our business concluded. You may go.'

The Calm Before the Storm

When you can't control what is happening to you,
you must try to control the way you respond to it.
That is where your strength lies.

Grace

I wound the window down in the car and sang along loudly with Bruce Springsteen on the radio. I was struggling to keep awake, despite the fact it was early afternoon. It had been a tough couple of weeks with very little sleep, but I was on a high. I could still hardly believe it, but we had actually won Cowes Week, one of the most iconic regattas in the UK sailing world, and I was about an hour from home, having driven for almost five hours solid.

On the water, the racing had been tough, in a fleet of over 60 boats. The weather had thrown everything at us, from howling gales and big seas to flat calm with virtually no wind. I did my usual job of bowman on the boat, with my friend Maria on mast. The two of us had sailed together for a long time and our teamwork was solid, both of us being fiercely competitive. A few of my old friends from home, all super talented sailors, had joined us for the event. We had also got ourselves a local navigator, who turned out to be a bit of a secret weapon, with his knowledge of the notoriously tricky tides in the Solent. Daniel liked to win but had enjoyed little success himself with the boat recently and had suddenly decided to pay a professional helm for Cowes, assuring me with a wink that he would be able to put it through the company books. In the end, it proved to be a good decision and we won the regatta with a day to spare.

There was no feeling on earth as good as being part of a winning team, so naturally, we were all up for one hell of a crew celebration after the prize-giving ceremony in the Royal Squadron. Daniel and I had flown down to the Isle of Wight in the helicopter and were supposed to be leaving together a couple of days after the event finished, but immediately after the prize-giving, he took me to one side. I had a feeling I would not like what was coming.

'I've just had a message from work. There's been a breakdown on one of our machines. The customer is kicking off massively about it, as they're losing production hand over fist. The lads have been down there all day but they can't sort it, so I have to go and fix it myself. I'm so sorry to spoil the celebrations Hun, but I have no choice. I've clearly got a bunch of incompetent wankers working for me.'

'Shit, that sounds bad. Don't worry, I'm sure the guys will manage to party without us.'

I resigned myself to leaving immediately.

'No, no,' said Daniel hastily. 'There's no need for you to leave. You might as well stay here as planned and come home in a couple of days. It's better if one of us is here anyway. I feel awful ruining the party and, to be honest, I'd feel happier if you were around to make sure everything is okay with the boat. You're the only one I can always rely on where the boat is concerned.'

'I don't suppose I've got many choices as usual,' I said, sulkily. 'You've obviously got it all planned out. How am I supposed to get home then?'

He knew I was miffed.

'I'm sure one of the guys will give you a lift, or just get a one-way car hire if you prefer and charge it to the company.'

I sensed the impatience in his voice.

'Look, I really have to go now and I will be quicker on my own. You know you always take ages to pack.'

'Okay, fine. Just go then and I'll see you at home in a couple of days.'

I scowled at him, knowing there was no point arguing. It was becoming an all too familiar scenario, leaving me in the lurch.

'Great. Have fun.'

He kissed me briefly on the lips and disappeared, leaving me to explain to the others.

I was annoyed of course, but I knew I would have a great night with the rest of the crew and, at the end of the day; the business had to come first. Daniel never tired of reminding me that the company paid for the house, the holidays, the lifestyle, the boat…. He had to look after it or we would have nothing. He always seemed to forget that I worked too.

I jumped as my mobile phone interrupted The Boss on the radio and I could see from the caller display it was Frieda. I picked up enthusiastically, assuming she was ringing to congratulate us.

'Hi, how are you? I assume you've seen the results?'

I was dying to tell her all about it.

'Yes, I have. Well done.'

She paused and sounded a bit odd, kind of distracted and flat. Strange reaction - I thought as she continued.

'Have you spoken to Daniel?'

'No, not since yesterday. He left straight after the prize giving to sort out a machine break down. Why? What's wrong?'

Something in her tone told me I needed to be worried. She did not answer straight away.

'Frieda? What's happened? You're worrying me now. Whatever it is, just tell me.'

'Shit, I'm sorry, I thought you would know already. I didn't expect to be the one telling you this. It's Daniel. He's had an accident.'

'Oh Christ, what do you mean, an accident? Is he okay?'

Silence.

'Oh fuck, not the helicopter....'

'Yes, there's been some sort of crash, but try not to panic. I don't really know any details, but I think he's okay. As far as I can gather, he was taken to hospital in the air ambulance with no serious injuries, but I can't be sure....' she tailed off.

'Try not to panic! Oh my God, I can't believe this is happening. Why has nobody been in touch with me?'

I realised I was screaming down the phone and could hardly see the road through my tears of panic. I pulled over into a layby.

'They couldn't find any next of kin information. I gave the police your mobile.'

The phone showed an unknown caller was trying to get through to me as we talked.

'Frieda, I have to go. This may be them now.'

I cut her off and accepted the new call. The policewoman at the end of the phone spoke calmly and impassively, informing me that my husband had been in a helicopter accident and had been taken to Chesterfield Royal near our home in Derbyshire. I was to get there as quickly as possible. She wouldn't tell me the extent of his injuries. Wouldn't even tell me if he was dead or alive. She just kept repeating that I needed to get myself to the hospital urgently. My head felt like it was about to explode. This was the sort of thing that happened to other people. Not to me.

Half an hour later, as I was being led into a little side room in A&E to wait for the doctor, I still had no idea of the extent of Daniel's injuries or, indeed, whether he was alive. It seemed to take an age for the doctor to arrive, but when he did he was smiling and I grasped that little bit of positivity with both hands.

'You can come in and see your husband now, but you need to be prepared for how he looks. We're still assessing his injuries and he's hooked up to a lot of monitors while we do tests. He's in quite a bit of pain, so he's had morphine, which will make him behave a bit strangely and maybe say odd things.'

He paused, allowing me to take in the information.

'What are his actual injuries?' I asked tentatively, terrified of the answer.

'The X-rays show that he has broken his pelvis, hip and ankle. Also his neck and collar bone.'

'His neck?'

This was far more serious than I had hoped.

'You can fix him up though, can't you? He will be able to walk again, won't he?'

'I'm sorry, I really can't tell you any more at the moment. His injuries are very serious. To be honest, he's lucky to be alive. We need to operate as soon as possible and check for any internal bleeding. There will have to be an extensive period of rehabilitation before we will know the level of recovery he will make. Let's just take things one step at a time. Would you like to see him now?'

I could see he was keen to end the conversation and avoid any further questions.

'Yes please,' I answered flatly.

Numb shock replaced hysteria and I moved as if I was in a dream.

Daniel was laid out practically naked on the trolley in a neck brace, wires everywhere, just as the doctor had warned. His legs were bruised and swollen and seemed to be set at strange angles to his body. He was breathing rapidly through an oxygen mask and was sweating profusely.

To my amazement, he greeted me cheerily, as if I had just walked through the kitchen door. I assumed that was down to the drugs.

'Hiya, Hun.'

Don't call me 'Hun' - I wanted to scream but decided to cut him some slack.

I took hold of his hand and plonked myself down in the chair they gave me.

My voice came out in a whisper.

'Oh my God, what have you done to yourself?'

'I know. Turns out helicopters don't glide so well,' he laughed, probably on account of the morphine.

I tried to rally myself and attempted to sound positive, for his sake.

'The doctor says you're going to be okay. They're going to operate on you soon and put you back together. Everything's going to be fine.'

I didn't entirely believe my own words but felt I should reassure him. I didn't know what else to say. The doctor had implied to me that it was highly unlikely he would ever walk again. How could I tell him that?

I was glad when a nurse came in a few moments later and said that they really needed to get him down to theatre and I should go back to the waiting room. I was more than happy to escape out of there. I didn't want to look at him like that; I didn't want it all to be real.

When I finally left the hospital at 10.30 pm, I was physically and mentally exhausted. They had said that the operation on his pelvis had been a success, although he was probably going to need further surgery. I had passed the time in the waiting room ringing around family and friends to tell them what had happened. Many of them knew already, as the crash had been plastered all over the news that evening. The helicopter was in pieces, strewn across a field about three miles from our house. I shuddered as I remembered the pictures of the shattered remains on the TV screen and found it difficult to believe that anyone could have come out of that twisted wreckage alive. Something had obviously gone horribly wrong, but now was not the time to look for answers.

Despite my exhaustion, I could not sleep that night, tormented by unwelcome thoughts that kept running away with me. How the hell was I going to cope with a husband in a wheelchair? I would have to become his carer. My life would change beyond recognition and I wasn't sure I was ready for that.

I immediately hated myself for being so selfish. Clearly I was a terrible person. Daniel needed me now and I would have to step up and be there to help him through this. He was the most strong-willed and downright bloody-minded man I knew and if anyone could beat the doctors' doom and gloom predictions, he could. In any case, being in a wheelchair was not the end of the world and, if that happened, we would simply adapt to the situation. I would have his back, no matter what.

As I arrived in the ward the following morning, it was clear that Daniel was not going to be an easy patient. He was already demanding to be discharged, although that was clearly not an option the day after surgery. Despite my earlier optimism, all positive thoughts vanished and I felt physically sick as the reality of his situation, our situation, began to sink in. He could do virtually nothing for himself, could feel nothing from the waist down and would probably never walk again. He had zero control over what was happening with his bowels and the nurses were wiping his backside for him.

Would I be expected to do that? How did people come to terms with that? - I wondered.

My mind continued to work overtime. Given the nature of his injuries and going on the internet research I had done, I deduced we were unlikely to ever have sex again and he would in all probability be left impotent. I hated myself for being so shallow, but I was still a relatively young woman. One who had been hanging onto the vague hope that we would have a family one day.

My sympathy turned abruptly to anger. How could Daniel have played so fast and loose with his life? Why did he always have to show off? He had insisted on buying a helicopter, largely because Charles had one and he wasn't going to be outdone. He was cocky and always quick to trot out the famous quote by R.J. Childerhose:

There are old pilots and there are bold pilots, but there are no old, bold pilots.

He should undoubtedly have heeded that quote, but his undoing was always going to be his arrogant streak. I knew he took too many risks, without having the flying hours behind him to support his overly strong self-belief. I rarely flew with him and even Charles made sure he always had an excuse to avoid it.

He had cheated death this time, but at what price? I couldn't stop thinking that he had ruined my life as well as his own. Bitterness and resentment were eating away at me, but I also knew I had to stop thinking like that for the sake of my own sanity. I was not the only person to be dealt a shit hand in life and I had no choice now but to look to the future and deal with it.

Daniel seemed to go straight into some sort of weird acceptance phase after the accident and began talking almost immediately about motability cars, motorised wheelchairs, lifts in the house and a whole load of other things, as calmly as if he were buying a new TV. He was also completely obsessed about getting his mobile phone and laptop back from the police. He would not stop banging on about it and was furious with me for failing to get either of them out of the clutches of the local constabulary.

I stared at him blankly, having endured yet another tirade about my lack of effort and understanding.

'The police won't release your phone yet. I already spoke to them before I came in today.'

I decided I could make allowances and was determined to remain calm with him, despite his unreasonable behaviour.

'I tried my best, but they were having none of it. In any case, I think you've got bigger fish to fry right now. And don't you think it's a bit early for all that other stuff? You don't know how much movement you will get back in your legs or how good a recovery you will make yet. You might not need any of it if you just give yourself time. You need to slow down a bit and take one day at a time.'

I was taken aback by his aggressive tone as he barked at me in retaliation, 'What the fuck would you know? Shit happens and I need to deal with it in my own way. I need to accept the way things are now and move on. If I can do it, I don't see why you're finding it so fucking difficult. At the end of the day, it's not you it's happened to. The bottom line is I can't run my business from a hospital. I need to get out of here and you need to help me sort it out.'

He was shouting, but I kept my voice low, conscious of the other patients and staff on the ward who were looking disapprovingly in our direction.

'Well, that's all very well, but how the hell do you think I'm going to cope with you at home in this state? Our house is not exactly suitable, is it?'

Tears of frustration and anxiety sprang to my eyes. He was being so bloody unfair.

'Charming! Because it's all about *you* as usual.'

His sharp words did not change the fact of how vulnerable he looked lying there in the hospital bed and I softened, knowing he was simply lashing out in frustration. I did not want an argument in front of everyone.

This was not the Daniel I was used to seeing. After nearly seventeen years of marriage, I felt I knew him pretty well. My husband was usually the one giving the orders and liked to be in control. This was torture for him. I just couldn't understand why he was so desperate to go against the doctors' advice and get out of hospital so urgently. How the hell did he think he was going to function in our three-story house? It could not possibly have been worse equipped for someone in a wheelchair. Surely he could see how ridiculous he was being? Maybe further down the line we could look at adaptations or even consider moving house to somewhere more suitable, but none of that was going to happen overnight. The immediate priority surely had to be getting the best possible treatment and at least giving himself a chance of a full recovery. Obviously, that meant staying in the hospital. Why couldn't he accept that?

Days went by and, little by little, despite his constant complaining to the doctors and nurses as well as me, Daniel had no choice but to accept that he was going nowhere fast. Inexplicably, he refused point-blank to allow any of our friends to visit him in hospital, insisting that he didn't want people to see him like that and begging me to keep people away. He didn't even want me hanging around there and seemed determined to deal with it all on his own. I didn't agree with his logic, but the nurses said I should respect his wishes and so my time away from the hospital was spent fielding calls from people who couldn't understand why they were being shut out when all they wanted to do was to offer support to a friend.

At Daniel's insistence, I endured pointless visits to the house from occupational therapists, whose remit was to assess the suitability of the property for a disabled person. They went through the motions of discussing things such as altering the height of the toilet seat in our en suite on the third floor, to make it easier for him to transfer from a wheelchair. I looked at the woman in disbelief, realising that she actually believed she had just made a helpful suggestion.

'And just how do you think I'm going to get him to the en suite in the first place?' I asked sarcastically. 'I think the height of the toilet seat is the least of our problems, don't you?'

'Well yes, I take your point,' she said, somewhat sheepishly, then concluded swiftly: 'To be honest, I really don't think this is a suitable environment for someone with a disability such as your husband's, certainly not at this early stage of his recovery.'

I thought - No shit Sherlock. I never would have guessed. Now maybe you can stop wasting my time.

Just over two weeks after further surgery on his pelvis, ankle and neck, which left him with a substantial amount of metal holding him together, Daniel announced that they were moving him to a specialist spinal injuries unit near Birmingham, a good two hours' drive from our home. I was obviously concerned about the distance for visiting, but it was apparently the best place for him to get the support he needed and would mean a proper rehabilitation programme with an expert team. No more wearing adult incontinence nappies and festering in a hospital bed. They would teach him to manage everything in the best possible way and they would help him to make the best possible recovery. Whether or not that would mean being able to walk again, only time would tell. It was a relief to see that he was positive for the first time in a couple of weeks and he reassured me that he really wanted to do this for the sake of our future. Being apart for a while was a small price to pay, he said. Apparently, the specialists at the unit discouraged too much visiting anyway, as they wanted their patients to focus fully on their recovery, without distractions.

Things were looking up at last. While he was away at the unit, I could spend time getting everything ready for when he was able to come home properly.

I would stay strong and do whatever it took to support him through this.

The Miracle

The knock on the door was quiet, almost imperceptible. The waiter stood patiently, knowing better than to knock again. Employees at the five star Hillcrest Hotel were trained to be discreet. The man who opened the door was clean-shaven and dressed smartly in chinos and a Lacoste shirt, despite the fact it was barely 7 am.

'Room service, Sir.'

The man stood aside, allowing him to place the tray on the table in the room.

'Thank you,' he said curtly, pressing a couple of coins into the waiter's hand. There was no need for small talk.

The man did not sit down immediately, but walked to the window and looked down at the city below him. His face was impassive and only the tightly clenched fist of his right hand betrayed his inner fury. He looked at the page of newspaper cuttings and headlines he had saved.

Local businessman makes miraculous escape from helicopter crash
Miracle of helicopter crash survivor

There were two big problems as far as he was concerned:
The 'miraculous escape'.
The man had been alone in the helicopter.

He had foreseen very different headlines in his mind's eye. Something along the lines of:

Local businessman and wife die in tragic helicopter crash

The client would not be happy. People came to him when they were desperate, and desperate people tended to pay him a lot of money to make their problems disappear. His most recent client had been no exception. The brief had been very specific and the client had given him detailed information to work with. It needed to be made to look like a tragic accident.

He was as shocked as the journalists that anyone had come out of the mangled wreckage of the helicopter alive. Now, he had a whole new problem to deal with in the form of an angry client who would no doubt be looking for a refund. His T&Cs covered all that of course and he always insisted on a big payment upfront but, nevertheless, he could do without all the hassle. Worse than that, he hated failure. But, at the end of the day, he had done his bit, even if the outcome had not been the desired one. The client would just have to come up with a better plan, a more fool-proof one with fewer variables. Or maybe let him do things the way he wanted.

The man sighed and sat down at the table. He remembered he had been more than a little surprised when he met the client in person. Not the usual type he dealt with at all, but what did he care, so long as he got his money. In all honesty, he was not entirely sure his client had the stomach for all this.

Would they want him to finish the job, or would it be called off?

He thought it could go either way, although in his humble opinion, from what he had been told, the client had a very good reason for wanting both the targets dead.

A Diagnosis

*Life is a storm. One minute you are bathed in
sunshine, the next you are picked up by the waves
as the clouds roll in, and dashed on the rocks.*

Grace

They say bad news comes in threes. Bombshell number two was
just around the corner and nothing could have prepared me for it.

The day after Daniel was transferred to the spinal injuries unit, I
spoke to my mum on the phone. She sounded preoccupied.

'I'm so sorry to tell you this now love, but we've had a bit of bad
news ourselves. Your dad's not well.'

Her words hung in the air and I felt the panic rising in me.

'What do you mean, 'not well'?' I was scared.

'There's no easy way to say this.' Her voice sounded shaky. 'He's
got cancer of the oesophagus. We've got a meeting in two weeks'
time to decide what they can do for him.' There was a long silence
while I processed this. Then the voice of reason kicked in.

'Well, obviously they'll operate and get rid of the tumour. Won't
they?'

I waited hopefully for reassurance, but there was none.

'I just don't know love. They won't say anything for sure yet. Apparently, it's very advanced.'

My world imploded all over again. Not my dad. Please God, not my dad. He had never smoked in his life, didn't drink to excess and was as fit and strong as any man I knew. His affectionate nickname among his many friends at the sailing club, where he had been President for the last ten years, was Turbo Wellies, because of the boundless energy he expounded in everything he did.

This couldn't be right. It had to be a mistake.

Dad had been one of the top road cyclists of his day, racing hundreds of miles all over the Yorkshire Dales and hills of Derbyshire and he still kept himself super fit. The photos, medals and trophies in the house were a testament to his success. He was fiercely determined and competitive, striving to be the best at whatever he did. I always told myself I would be happy if I had inherited even a little bit of that fighting spirit of his. Dad was never ill. He was always there for me and I needed him so badly right now. This couldn't be happening. It just didn't make any sense. It was so bloody unfair!

But it wasn't a mistake.

The GP, who worked in the same practice as my brother Jeremy back home in Northumberland, had listened to his symptoms of heartburn and difficulty swallowing and referred him immediately to an oesophagogastric consultant. Scans showed there was a 12-centimetre tumour in his gullet and it was marginal as to whether or not it was operable. The one big thing in his favour apparently was that he had the heart rate and fitness level of a much younger man. Jeremy made sure he was seen by Professor Garrett, the top man in the department. He was world-renowned and I put all my faith in him, certain that he would come through for us and fix Dad.

The meeting to decide on a plan of action was held in the Professor's small office at the end of Ward 36 of the Queen Alexandra hospital. I sat beside my brother and parents, staring intently at the man I had already placed firmly on a pedestal, as he explained to us that Dad would need six months of chemotherapy to try to shrink the tumour, followed by an operation just before Christmas if all went well. That was all I needed to hear. He was telling me they could do something. They were not giving up on him. They would operate at Christmas and my dad would be ok again.

Daniel had only just been moved to the spinal injuries unit and I did not want to pile any more problems onto him of course, but I had to tell him about Dad's illness. He was wonderfully supportive, despite his own problems and I loved him all the more for it.

'Don't worry about me,' he said stoically. 'I'm in a great place here, with the best possible chance of a good recovery. I just need to concentrate on working hard in the gym and do my physio sessions. Your dad needs you now, much more than I do. Go and spend as much time as you can with him and your mum.'

'But I want to be there for you as well. I'm not just going to abandon you,' I said, determinedly.

I had never felt so torn.

'Don't be silly. Besides, the last thing any of us needs is the added worry of you driving up and down the motorway, completely exhausting yourself and risking having an accident. You need to stay strong and look after yourself through all this if you're going to be any use to your mum and dad.'

He took my hand and looked concerned as he continued.

'Seriously, I'm fine. I have plenty of support here. Everyone is great. It really helps to be with other people in the same situation as me and see how much progress some of them have made. The doctors here have said there is every chance I will recover movement in my legs, as my spinal cord wasn't severed in the accident. They can't promise I'll be able to walk again, but I've decided one hundred percent I *will*. Positive mental attitude counts for a lot you know.'

I felt so proud of my husband at that moment. His dogged determination and optimism convinced me that, if anyone could come through this, he could. We would all be okay.

By the time December came, Daniel was making truly miraculous progress and had exceeded the expectations and predictions of all the doctors. Despite his protestations, I had made the arduous three and a half hour journey from my parents' house to see him religiously every two weeks. He was ready to be discharged from the spinal injuries unit and amazingly, although he was still on crutches, he was actually able to walk a few steps. It was not yet possible for him to manage at home, but the wonderful staff at the unit had arranged a place at a half-way house nearby, where he could complete his rehabilitation. It was a kind of assisted living place apparently, with a fully equipped gym and physiotherapists on hand, so he would be able to continue all his exercises and keep checking in regularly at the unit.

It seemed he really was going to come through this and there was light at the end of the tunnel.

So far as my dad was concerned, the six months of gruelling chemo took its toll on him, but he was a fighter and at the end of it the doctors declared him fit enough to undergo the major surgery he needed.

He was admitted to hospital ironically on Friday 13th December. Mum and I took him in, kissed him and told him we would see him in the recovery room. We both refused to say goodbye. Although the wait seemed interminable, we were finally given the news that he was out of theatre and the operation had been a success, but a mere six hours later, elation turned to despair, when Dad suffered a massive haemorrhage and was rushed back into theatre for more surgery.

The hours and days that followed were some of the worst of my life, as we seemed to crash from one life and death crisis to another. Christmas Day was spent holding vigil at Dad's bedside in the intensive care unit. He was not expected to make it. It broke my heart to look at my mum's face, as she held his hand and chatted to him as though everything were normal. She would never give up on him and neither could I. Three days later, he was still hanging on in there. The doctors had not counted on his incredible strength of character and will to live. He was not ready to leave us and was determined to fight with every ounce of strength he had left.

The next few months were a roller coaster of highs and lows. One day Dad was making good progress, the next he was being rushed back into intensive care. The pressure was destroying my mum, who was not in the best of health herself. Daniel and I discussed it and agreed that I should continue to stay with her while things were so unpredictable. It seemed the most practical solution to an impossible situation.

Daniel was getting stronger all the time and was able to walk longer and longer distances, although he still needed the aid of a stick. He was even able to drive an automatic car with no adaptations and had bought himself a white Range Rover Overfinch, pimped to within an inch of its life by the prestigious Leeds based company, as it would be more practical than the Porsche. Charles drove a Range Rover so, of course, Daniel had always coveted one, but naturally, he felt obliged to try to upstage Charles by opting for the flashy Overfinch version. He promised to visit as often as possible, now that he was mobile again with his new 'toy', but I was not keen on him driving such a long distance so soon and made sure he understood there was no pressure from me. It was not an ideal situation, but our marriage was solid and we both knew it was not going to be forever.

Six months later, when Dad was finally given his reprieve and allowed home from hospital, I began to look forward to getting back to some kind of normality, totally unaware of the third bombshell lurking in the shadows, biding its time. And of course, I had no idea then just how convenient Dad's cancer had been for Daniel.

A Dish best served cold

Lorraine

John sat on the balcony of the pretty little white-washed villa in the Algarve region of Portugal, reading his book. The late October sun still had lovely warmth to it and they would be able to sit outside there for at least another couple of hours. Lorraine padded barefoot across the cool tiles and silently handed him a drink, before sitting down opposite him, smiling. He was wearing the Panama hat she had bought him, knee-length chino shorts and a polo shirt. His skin was tanned and he looked relaxed, with his feet stretched out on the little table.

'Thanks, Hun. I love the way you look after me.'

He blew her a kiss across the table and she smiled back at him.

'Well, you deserve it. You've been so stressed about work recently. I've been worried about you especially after all you went through with the accident. Let's just enjoy spending some quality time together. We both needed this little break. I might even give you a special massage later....'

'Ooh, now you're talking.... Why wait until later?' he asked, sniggering in anticipation.

'Because it'll be so much better if you have to wait for it,' she purred.

Lorraine was toying with him, like a cat with a mouse. The best part was he had absolutely no idea. He was bumbling along in blissful ignorance and when the apocalypse finally came, he would have no clue what had hit him.

She had known about John's betrayal and lies for nearly nine weeks. He had got up one morning to go into town after a particularly exhausting session the night before. He had left her in bed, but more importantly, and very unusually, he had also left his iPad on the bedside table. After half an hour she could no longer ignore the incessant pings of incoming messages that were tormenting her and making her headache worse. She reached across to silence the tablet, but the partial messages that appeared on the screen caused her to sit up abruptly, all thoughts of her hangover forgotten. The messages of irritation, some of them in capitals, left no room for doubt in her mind. The sender of the messages was becoming increasingly frustrated at his lack of response, referring in particular to the fact that his nine-year-old son was ill.

What the fuck was all that about?

The messages were all signed off with kisses, despite the obvious annoyance of the sender.

Lorraine clenched her fist tightly and fought hard against her impulse to smash the place up. Instead, she messaged John with a shopping list to keep him out of the house for a while longer. Then she called her brother's friend, Marcus, who was a genius with computers and bragged that he could hack into pretty much anything. She was going to need his expertise. John was obviously cheating on her but, with the help of Marcus, she would be able to join up all the dots.

Her mind drifted back to her Secondary School days and the same humiliation and rage she had felt when she found out her boyfriend, Theo, was cheating on her. She recalled the feeling as the red mist descended and she realised she was losing control. She had flown into a blind fury and rushed at him, screaming, when they were alone in his house one afternoon.

It was true that he had been shocked and stumbled backwards, falling and hitting his head on the hard kitchen tiles. It was also true that she had seized the opportunity to grab him by a fistful of his hair while he was still dazed, lifting his head as high as she could and smashing it back down hard onto the unforgiving tiles, but she left that bit out when the ambulance and the police arrived. Poor Theo regained consciousness after several weeks, but never recovered sufficiently to tell anyone the full story. The damage to his brain was permanent, they told her, as she collapsed in floods of tears.

She learned that day that she was actually very good at lying. She had initially anticipated serious repercussions for her part in the incident, but there were none. Everyone believed her tearful version of events and she was even referred to a counsellor to help her cope with the trauma of what she had experienced.

She snapped her thoughts back to the present. That was all in the past and she was not like that anymore. She had learned a few more subtle tricks since those days.

Nine long, torturous weeks she had had to keep up the pretence with John, carrying on as if nothing were wrong. She had been determined to get all her ducks in a row before letting the cat out of the bag, so she had painstakingly maintained a façade of normality, while tirelessly plotting and scheming behind the scenes. She had been meticulous in her scrutiny of all the information she could lay her hands on and Marcus had proved to be a very useful ally indeed. Thanks to him, she had gained access to pretty much everything on John's computer, iPhone and iPad and it had all been painstakingly copied to a backup device of her own. She had gone through everything with a fine-tooth comb, realising with mounting anger what a fool she had been. In a file named Rosalie, she found the paperwork for their narrow boat, all in his name, although it was her money that had paid for it. Furious at the discovery, she immediately produced a new bill of sale, transferring it to her name with a forged signature and then promptly sold it from under him. The deal was all done through word of mouth. A reduced price of twenty-five grand for a quick cash sale.

Next, she emptied the business account he had set up in her name with the intention of confusing HMRC and put the forty grand into a personal account he knew nothing about. She was irritated there wasn't more in there but, it didn't really surprise her, as she suspected he had numerous accounts both in the UK and abroad and was always moving money around to make it more difficult to trace.

Lastly, just before they went away, she had arranged for the locks on their 'dream house' to be changed. She couldn't wait for him to find out that the two cars from his prized collection that he had put in her name and stashed in her double garage, in a further attempt to bamboozle the taxman, were no longer there.

All in all, she was proud of what she had achieved, but the best was yet to come. She found the sense of power intoxicating and quite a turn on in fact. She was not sure yet just how far she would be able to go with this. Ironically, their sex life had been given a whole new lease of life since she found out about his infidelity and she thought with a tinge of sadness that she would miss their little games. She had embarked on a personal mission to pull out all the stops where sex was concerned and make sure he couldn't get enough of her. She wanted him to have a vivid memory of all that he would never have again, to feel the same searing pain of betrayal she had felt. She also found it hugely satisfying to know that, as she was shagging him senseless, she was at the same time plotting to screw him over royally.

That night in the villa, after two bottles of wine and several rum and cokes, she decided to up the ante in the bedroom department.

'Let's try something a little different tonight,' she said with a suggestive wink.

'Hmm, I'm intrigued. What did you have in mind?'

She despised his lecherous grin as he grabbed her by the hips and ground unsubtly against her pelvis to show her he already had an erection, probably courtesy of the Viagra she knew he always took. No chance of any action without that since the accident.

'I have a little present for you,' she murmured, stepping back from his grip.

He raised his eyebrows as she presented him with a pair of black PVC pants with a built-in butt plug that she had acquired from a sex shop the previous week, knowing his fascination with anal sex.

He was predictably enthusiastic, even when she helped him to get the butt plug into position a little too roughly. She took the lead, straddling him and riding him like a rodeo bull, while at the same time amusing herself by imagining the look on his face if she suddenly pulled out a knife and plunged it into his neck. She made sure she pulled away just in time and finished things off by executing a textbook blow job, giving the performance of her life. When the ordeal was finally over and he had finished grunting and pumping his way to orgasm, he fell over onto his back and began snoring almost immediately. She shuddered in revulsion, almost gagging at what she had just endured. As she lay there beside him, staring at the ceiling, she vowed that he would never touch her again.

She had found out about his treachery quite by chance, but it was remarkable how easily the whole thing had unravelled, like an old woollen jumper, once she had started to do a little digging. It would have been so easy to shout and scream and hurl accusations at him, but where would that have left her? No. She was smarter than that. It was essential to maintain the element of surprise to carry out the plan to her best advantage. So she had taken her time and made sure she missed nothing. Planning and preparation were the keys to success and she knew exactly how she was going to play this.

Not long to wait now - she thought to herself.

Lighting the Fuse

Lorraine

Four days later, back home after the holiday in Portugal, Lorraine sat alone at her kitchen table, laptop open in front of her. She took her time to read, for the hundredth time, the message she had so laboriously composed.

She checked every detail.

She noticed the time. Just before 10 pm on a Saturday.

Taking a deep breath, she pressed *send to all*.

Then she sat back, smiling to herself and waited.

The Explosion

Enjoy what you have today, for you never know what tomorrow may bring, or what it may take away.

Grace

'**Do** you realise next April we'll have been married for twenty years?'

'Jeez, people get less than that for committing murder!' Daniel responded, as he winked at me and laughed.

'Only joking. I think we make a pretty good team, don't you? We've had our fair share of ups and downs, but look at us, still here enjoying life.'

He was right there. We had a great life on the whole and I appreciated it all the more after what we had been through in the last few years. Daniel's recovery after the accident had amazed the doctors and he was now walking around without even needing a stick. He was able to sail again although, due to pressure of work, we only tended to do the small events with friends for crew. The business had suffered after the accident of course, but we finally seemed to be getting back on an even keel. I had done my bit to help by re-mortgaging my little house in Conway and putting eighty grand into the pot. It was only supposed to be a short term loan and the plan was that the business would pay me back with hefty interest, but things had been tougher than we expected. It seemed to cause an argument every time I mentioned it, but Daniel had promised faithfully to try to sort it all out by the end of the financial year, now that the company was doing better. At the end of the day, I told myself it didn't really matter. We were husband and wife after all. What was mine was his. But I still couldn't help worrying.

'Come on, it's a big milestone,' I continued. 'We should do something special to mark the occasion.'

A holiday in the sun was uppermost in my mind.

'Maybe we could go back to the Seychelles again?' I suggested.

'Leave it with me and I'll come up with some ideas. I need to look at the schedule for work. It's pretty busy around that time with a couple of big jobs due to be finished over in the States.'

Daniel had always done a lot of business in America and had recently set up an office in Boston. He spent so much time over there these days it made sense to have a proper base. I had been with him on the odd business trip in the past, but he usually went when I was working and of course, I had Valentino to consider. I did worry that Daniel was pushing himself too hard though and I felt we could both do with a holiday, so I had no intention of giving in on this one.

'Oh, come on. You're already working away over Christmas. Surely you can take some time off in spring?' I persisted.

'You're not going to start going on about Christmas again are you? You know I hate Christmas. I always have done. I've told you a hundred times I'd rather be working. I'll be back for New Year, I promise, and we'll have a great time in Italy with Charles and Samantha.'

'I suppose so,' I muttered, sulkily.

Of course, I was disappointed about Christmas, but I would spend it with my family as usual and look forward to the planned Italy trip. Charles and Samantha had rented a farmhouse in Tuscany for a month and we were going out to spend a week with them over New Year. Daniel couldn't ski any more after his accident, but Samantha and I were hoping to get a few days in the mountains. I just needed to get a move on and sort the flights out, given that it was already November and we had agreed on dates. No harm in looking at deals to the Seychelles as well, I decided.

If I was honest, Christmas no longer held any real charm for me either. My Dad had fought bravely against cancer, but he had finally lost his fight almost a year ago. The funeral was the day after what would have been his eightieth birthday, a few days before Christmas. It hit Mum very hard, of course, and I did my best to support her as much as possible. Daniel was always understanding and said that, in his opinion, it would be better for me to spend quality one on one time with her, especially when he had to work away so much.

I was visiting Mum one weekend shortly after the holiday conversation when Daniel rang from Ireland. He had been visiting a customer and had stayed on for a couple of days to try and fit in a sail on a friend's boat.

'Honey, you need to sit down,' was his opening gambit. I was instantly nervous.

'I've bought a Swan 40!'

It took a few moments for his words to sink in.

'You've done what?'

My voice was shrill. I was literally gobsmacked.

'When did you decide to do that?' I asked, tersely, wondering why I hadn't been party to the decision. 'Can we afford it?'

I knew he was expecting me to be excited, but I couldn't help feeling a niggling resentment at his extravagance. I suppose I would have liked him to have sorted out the money from the re-mortgage first, or at least consulted me about the purchase instead of just presenting it as a 'fait accompli' and making big decisions without me as usual.

Swan was the Rolls Royce of yachts and needless to say, they were not cheap. The company produced boats that were beautifully styled and elegant, with classic lines and timeless luxury below decks. Charles and Samantha had a Swan and so, of course, Daniel had always coveted one.

'Why didn't you tell me you were buying it?' I continued.

His voice took on a sour tone.

'Well, I'm telling you about it now. I wanted it to be a surprise, but you always have to put a damper on things,' he said, accusingly.

'Where have you got the money from all of a sudden?'

'For fuck's sake! Why do you never trust me? I told you, the business is picking up again and I got the deal of the century. It's being sold by a guy who has terminal cancer, which is sad I know, but he basically just wants rid of the boat. I got it for an absolute song, £100,000 if you must know the details.'

'Really? That sounds a bit cheap for a Swan 40 to me,' I said, suspiciously.

'Well I admit it needs a fair bit of work, but it was too good a chance to miss. I thought you'd be happy.'

'Okay, okay. I'm sorry. It was just a shock, that's all.'

Things that are too good to be true usually are.

My brain was working overtime as he continued.

'So now I need you to start thinking about where you want to keep it and do some research into marinas. How do you fancy Spain for starters or maybe Portugal?'

I loved Spain and spoke fluent Spanish. Perhaps I needed to lighten up and trust him a bit more. This could be the start of a whole new chapter for us. Surprisingly, since the accident three years earlier, things had become easier. The doctors had told Daniel he could no longer father children, so the decision to start a family was taken out of our hands and the arguments became irrelevant. Besides, I was already very firmly in the camp of 'geriatric mothers' for whom pregnancy held far greater risks. It was time to let the whole baby thing go.

'Spain. Maybe Valencia, or even Palma,' I added, trying to sound more enthusiastic.

'Well, I'll leave that up to you. The thing is, I'm not going to be able to get away for our wedding anniversary, unfortunately, so I thought a new boat might make up for that. It's in Ireland at the moment, so I'll probably leave it there to get the work done on it and then we can move it to the Med early next summer.'

It was impossible not to get caught up in his enthusiasm, but at the same time, I felt that, if he could afford to buy a Swan and the business was doing so well, he could afford to pay back the money for the re-mortgage on our Conway house. I intended to make sure he dealt with it when he got back home the following week, no arguments. In my opinion, we needed to reduce all our debt as a priority.

I thought about Dad, as I so often did. If only he were still here. I desperately wanted to tell him about the Swan and knew how much he would have loved to be involved. He would almost certainly have done the delivery from Ireland to Spain with me. Just like the old days. Tears sprang to my eyes, as all the memories of sailing with him flooded into my mind. I swallowed hard. He would not want me to be sad and I did not want to cry in front of Mum and upset her.

Later that night, as I was going to bed, I enveloped Mum in a big hug. I looked at Dad's photo on her chest of drawers and blinked back the tears.

'I miss him every day too you know.'

I kissed her goodnight and looked casually at my phone as it pinged to signal an incoming message.

A new email from a name I didn't recognise.

A woman's name. Lorraine Huntley.

The subject of the email was:

The wife, the mothers, the other women and the bits on the side.

PART II

Consequences

So·ci·o·path

/ˈsōsēōˌpaTH/

A person with a psychopathic personality whose behaviour is antisocial, often criminal, and who lacks a sense of moral responsibility or social conscience.[2]

Sociopath is a term used to describe someone who has Antisocial Personality Disorder (ASPD). People with ASPD can't understand others' feelings. They'll often break rules or make impulsive decisions without feeling guilty for the harm they cause.[3]

---

[2] *dictionary.com*

[3] *Medically reviewed by Timothy J. Legg, PhD CRNP on January 11, 2018 — Written by Tim Jewell*

The Email

---

*Lies do not erase the truth, they simply delay its
discovery.*

Grace

It was the following day before I could finally summon up the
courage to read the email in full. Until I did that, I could convince
myself it did not really exist or it was all some terrible mistake. I
concocted all manner of explanations. Someone must have hacked
his computer and sent this malicious nonsense out of spite. You
heard about that sort of thing all the time. I kept on telling myself
that over and over again in the interest of self-preservation, but I
knew it couldn't go on forever. Sooner or later I would have to face
up to it. I had read the first line the previous night:

*I have been in a relationship with a Daniel Matthew John Callaghan for
the last 16 years.*

Then I had immediately turned off my phone, unable to face
reading any further.

I looked at my gorgeous, black Labrador, Lola, and remembered
how Daniel had comforted me when I had to make the heart-
breaking decision to let Hero go. No dog could ever replace him,

but when Daniel came home a couple of weeks later and thrust the chubby little fur ball now known as Lola into my arms, I had fallen in love with her instantly.

Daniel loved me. I knew he did. He was my rock. That email had to be some kind of cruel hoax, it just had to be.

I still couldn't bring myself to say anything to Mum, so I took Lola out for a long walk as if everything was normal, stuffing my phone into my Barbour jacket pocket as I went out. I walked a couple of miles to the park in a weird kind of daze and finally settled myself down on a bench by the river. Staring at the water with Lola lying patiently at my feet chewing a stick, I gathered all my strength to read the poisonous message lurking in my pocket. My hands were shaking and I felt sick to my core as I forced myself with trembling fingers to unlock my phone, open the email and read:

Subject: The wife, the mothers, the other women and the bits on the side.

I have been in a relationship with a Daniel Matthew John Callaghan for the last 16 years, photo attached as I believe he uses an alias. Since finding this out several weeks ago I have been doing some digging and this is what I came up with.

Married to first wife Julia Summers for nine years, until she committed suicide.

Married to second wife Grace King a year later, due to celebrate 20 years together in March. Lives with her in Fellside, Derbyshire.

Partner to Jane Sutcliffe for around 15 years, son Aaron, aged Lives with her in Willowmede, near Birmingham.

Partner to me for 16 years. Lives with me in a village near Oxford. We moved into our dream house a week after Aaron's Christening.

Ex-Partner Niamh Ryan, together around 28 years ago for a number of years, lives in Ireland. Very friendly emails sent back in July, but unable to meet up when he was in Dublin recently, apparently. Very friendly one-off email exchanges with a number of other women.

The rest is some knowledge with some guesswork. John told me previously that he had lived with someone in America who had a child. Not sure when he fitted this in, given his marriages, but there are friendly emails from an Anita Barnes and a Tara Callaghan-Barnes in July and September this year which coincide with his recent visits to the States. I have an email address for Tara but not Anita. They live in Jamestown, Rhode Island and I believe Tara is his daughter, based on her surname. She is approximately 15 years old.

If you were aware of the above, then you truly deserve each other. If you weren't, then I would suggest you read on.

It was the morning after a very heavy night before and he had gone into town, leaving me in bed with his iPad beeping away. Using his pin 0007 it was easy to hack into his emails and find some very revealing photo albums. The rest is history.

Jane was easy to track down, especially after I uncovered her very detailed Twitter and Facebook accounts, which filled in a lot of gaps.

Company checks led me to Grace, with no record of a divorce. For the last few years, John has been squirreling things away into his 'pension fund', worth approx. quarter of a million I believe, maybe more. Not sure if you know about all of his cars and motorcycles or the Vettriano paintings he has recently been investing in. A couple of his cars were stored in my garages. The rest are in a unit somewhere near Jane's house.

It appeared he was trying to turn money into assets in preparation for a divorce, but some of your emails showed you were still together earlier this year, celebrating your 19th wedding anniversary and you still seem to be involved with his business.

I am still not sure how he kept us all apart for so many years, especially in the various hospitals after he had his helicopter accident.

I am also not sure how he keeps us all off his back when he goes 'incommunicado', as we all seem to be chasing him to call us. The following timeline might interest you.

16th 17th September - the weekend I found out he'd been cheating on me.

23rd 23th September - the weekend I found out that I was the other woman.

7th to 14th October - on holiday with me in Portugal. Jane, there was no unexpected software upgrade on his phone; he'd actually used this excuse on me when you went to Disneyland with him at Easter. There was also no traffic warden, he just cut the call short as he was calling you between the starter and main course in the restaurant and the main arrived too promptly.

23th 29th October - unexpected weekend he called it as he was supposed to be in the States. Jane, he didn't go Twickenham to watch the rugby, he just couldn't be arsed to phone his son, even though he was ill.

11th 12th November - just can't keep away. I lied to him about my plans for the weekend, as he was still expecting to come down on Sunday for a duvet day.

For the record, I've bought nearly every piece of M&S clothing he has. I don't know where he goes to at Christmas, but he usually spends Boxing Day with me, starting with a duck race and mulled wine in our local village and often seems to spend New Year's Day at the footie with Jane.

Jane, I know him as John Callaghan (as per his passport, driving licence, gun licence and his blue badge). I believe he is Matthew to you and uses his first name with his wife.

When we first met, he told me he wasn't the marrying kind or a 24/7 type of guy. He also said very recently that I should count myself lucky that he collects cars rather than women, his words not mine. Oh and, to make it easier for him, he calls us 'Honey' or 'Hun'.

Well, it's up to you whether you believe this email or not. I've told him today it's over. Just wondering which one of us he sucks up too, the wife or one of the mothers of his children. I certainly don't think it's going to be me unless he wants to make sure that I don't trash any of his stuff.

Three times I read that email, from start to finish, and yet still I could not bring myself to accept the information it contained. I stubbornly kept telling myself I needed to ring *my husband* so that he could reassure me that it was all a lie.

I did not cry. Nor did I allow myself to panic. Daniel would obviously tell me it was some crazy stalker. A clever hacker. Someone with a vendetta against him because of work.

Anything, other than that it was true.

My capacity for self-delusion was apparently limitless.

I decided to read it all again one more time before ringing him. Just in case I had misunderstood something.

The thing that terrified me most about the email was the amount of detail it contained about Daniel. This woman seemed to know a hell of a lot about the man I was married to and yet most of the stuff she was claiming just couldn't possibly be true. She had to have got her wires crossed. For starters, she said he had children, but I knew that was impossible. He had never wanted children. There was just no way. He wouldn't do that to me. Why was she doing this to us?

Still I didn't cry. In fact, I had absolutely no idea how I felt or how I should react. The enormity of it all overwhelmed me totally. It was too much to take in. Too many dates. Too many places. Too many names of people I did not know. Detail after detail of the everyday lives of women I had never heard of and the relationships they seemingly enjoyed with my husband. I, on the other hand, only merited a small mention in despatches and my apparently unremarkable and insignificant part in his life was summed up in a few paltry lines.

I stared blankly into space as I desperately tried to process what I had just read. I couldn't imagine myself ever being able to get off that bench. It still made no sense. And yet, there was no denying the fact that the man in the photograph was the man I was married to. It was a recently taken picture and he was wearing the chino shorts I had so often seen him in, together with an equally familiar polo shirt.

I've bought nearly every piece of M&S clothing he has.

He was sitting on a balcony somewhere in the sun, sporting a Panama hat and the aviator sunglasses he always wore. He held a copy of Yachting World magazine in his hand and there was a beer on the table. He was looking towards the camera and smiling at whoever was taking the photo. I could see a second bottle of Peroni on the table opposite him, a pair of tortoiseshell-framed, women's sunglasses and a novel lying face down. He looked happy and relaxed. A typical, holiday photo. I suddenly remembered his irritation with me every time I tried to take a picture of him recently. His barked instructions that nothing was to be put on Facebook.

Now that I had actually read the email, of course, even I had to acknowledge that there was no going back. I had to find the strength to confront Daniel, but the thought of doing that terrified me. There remained in my mind a tiny glimmer of hope that he was not that man and I clung to it like a drowning woman clinging to a piece of wreckage.

I took out my phone to ring my husband. He answered uncharacteristically on the second ring and his friendly, chatty manner took me by surprise.

Perhaps I had got it all wrong after all - I thought to myself.

I was clutching at straws.

'Hi Hun, how are you? How was the show with your mum?'

Oh and, to make it easier for him, he calls us 'Honey' or 'Hun'.

I hesitated a moment before answering, unsure how to respond.

'Erm… It was great thanks. She really enjoyed it.'

'Great stuff. What are you up to now?' he asked, a little too enthusiastically.

I paused for a moment to give myself time to adjust to the way the conversation was going.

- What am I up to? What are you up to? More to the point.

This was not what I had expected at all. I answered his question mechanically.

'Walking the dog. Where are you?'

The background noise on the call told me he was driving, but I realised I had no idea where.

'I'm on the way to see another bloody customer. More problems with work,' he sighed, theatrically.

- How many times had he used that lie? Would I ever be able to take anything he said at face value again?

I could no longer carry on with the strange charade of normality we had somehow slipped into.

'Listen...I got a really weird email about you last night,' I began.

He sighed again.

'Yes, I know.'

I was wrong-footed, realising that, for some reason, I hadn't expected him to know about the email. Because if he had known, then surely he would have been on the phone to me immediately, begging forgiveness or something?

'What do you mean, you know?'

'Well, I got a copy of it.'

'Oh, right. So...what's it all about?'

I remained pathetically hopeful. A condemned woman, waiting for a reprieve as she climbs up onto the gallows. Last chance for him to tell me a plausible tale to explain it all away and make everything okay again.

A short silence followed the question and then the final crushing blow.

'It's this girl I've been seeing.'

And that was that. With those six little words, all hope vanished. Game over.

I began to shake uncontrollably with shock and I felt physically sick.

'A girl you've been seeing?'

I repeated his words like an idiot until my brain finally allowed the truth to enter and my mouth went into overdrive.

'Oh my God, are you telling me it's true? Please...tell me it's not true. It can't be true. I love you. How could you do this to me? I don't understand it...all those women she's talking about...and she says you've got kids...but you never wanted kids....'

My voice sounded shrill in my own ears and I was becoming increasingly hysterical, as first reality, then panic, set in.

Daniel remained silent and allowed me to prattle on, incoherently. When I paused for breath, his words cut through me like a knife.

'Look, it's all in the email. Please just read the email. I'm not exactly proud of myself, but I admit it's all true and everything's in there. I really have no idea how I got myself into this mess. Whatever you do, try to calm down and don't do anything rash. Don't say anything to anyone yet. When you've had a chance to come to terms with it, we can talk and decide where we go from here. I'm happy to go along with whatever you want.'

There was no shouting. No screaming. No pleading.

I longed for something that would make it seem like I actually mattered. Like our twenty-year marriage was a thing of some value to him. Anything would have been better than the crushing humiliation of indifference that he was forcing me to endure. It felt like my own inadequacy was staring me in the face, mocking me. I was, quite simply, nothing. A person of no value or importance in the whole, sorry business.

I was stunned into an uncomprehending silence. His tone was so cold and detached. He did not even raise his voice as he ripped my heart in two with his callous, dismissive words. He was talking as if he had just forgotten to pay a bill or post a letter, totally devoid of all feeling or remorse concerning the storm of cataclysmic proportions that he had just brought crashing down on my head.

I realised I had absolutely no idea what to say next, so I opted for saying nothing and simply pressed the red button to end the call, in a futile attempt to make it all go away.

Nothing would ever be the same again. Now that the information in the email had been confirmed as the truth, the life I believed I had been living had just gone up in smoke. I stood up but felt suddenly light-headed and my legs threatened to give way underneath me. I gripped the bench to steady myself, then set off on automatic pilot in the direction of my brother's house, tears of pain streaming down my face.

I asked myself - What had I been expecting from the phone call? Tears of regret as he pleaded with me to forgive him? Tormented sobs as he begged me to take him back? At the very least, maybe a declaration of his love for me, despite what he had done?

There had been none of that.

I was his wife. The woman he was supposed to spend the rest of his life with. Yet apparently I was insignificant, nothing more to him than an annoying irritation he had to deal with, utterly alone in my desolation and humiliation.

The black hole of despair stretched out in front of me and threatened to engulf me.

I had no idea how I would ever be able to come back from this.

Picking up the pieces

Anyone can love you when the sun shines brightly, but only in the darkest storms of your life will you find those who truly care for you.

Grace

There were no cars on the drive at my brother's house and I knew instantly that everyone was out. I sat down on the wall and cried like a baby; heart-wrenching, gasping sobs, not caring who saw me or what they thought of me. In fact, I wanted someone to see me. To come over and ask me what was wrong. To put their arms around me and try to comfort me. But of course, no one did. My isolation was all-consuming and I could feel the panic and hysteria rising in me again. I took out my phone to call Samantha and saw a text from Daniel, short and to the point, composed as always in fully punctuated sentences:

Grace, I know you're upset at the moment, but please don't do anything you will regret. Don't go talking to everyone about this. No one else needs to know at the moment. We need to talk to each other first and, hopefully, we can work things out so that no one comes off too badly. I don't want you to suffer. xxx

I stared at the message incredulously, unable to comprehend how he could be so blasé about everything. He didn't want me to suffer! He was talking about me as if I were an injured dog that needed to be put out of its misery. His brief and succinct message seemed almost farcical in light of the enormity of the recent discovery.

I suddenly realised I had hit the nail on the head with the word 'discovery'. No wonder he wasn't shocked. This was no 'discovery' for him. He had been living this elaborate lie for most of his adult life and was wholly familiar with all the places, events and characters in the drama. He had played a leading role in every scene, whereas I was simply an extra, frantically trying to keep up with all the twists and turns of the intricate plot.

He had written the script, for Christ's sake.

I knew instinctively there was no way on this earth I could deal with the chaos of my newly shattered life alone and no way could I keep it to myself. I had always worn my heart on my sleeve and I needed the support of all my family and friends more than ever if I was going to have any chance of getting through this.

Besides, I wanted to get in first and tell everyone what he had done before he could spin any more lies. A little voice in my head suddenly began to nag at me.

- What if they knew all along? What if everyone was laughing at me for staying with him all these years? Who could I really trust?

I refused to allow myself to dwell on that. Time would tell.

I swiped my phone open and called Samantha, praying she would answer.

'Hi Grace, how are you?'

It was Sunday, and I imagined her and Charles in the kitchen preparing a roast. They loved entertaining and often had friends and family round for Sunday lunch. I knew the garbled message I delivered was totally incomprehensible, but I seemed to have lost the ability to speak in coherent sentences. The words tumbled out of my mouth.

'What am I going to do? What am I going to do? You've got to help me. Please help me.'

I kept repeating the phrases through broken sobs.

'Grace, for God's sake, you're scaring me. You need to stop talking, calm down, take a few deep breaths and tell me what the hell has happened. Whatever it is, of course I'll help you.'

Samantha's voice was stern and decisive. Hers was the clear voice of reason, taking control as I wanted and needed her to do, bringing me out of the tailspin.

'Grace? Tell me what's happened.'

I took a deep breath and tried again.

'It's Daniel…he's been cheating on me. He's got four other women and he has had children with two of them….'

That was all I could manage to blurt out before dissolving into tears again. She spent the next fifteen minutes on the phone with me, alternating between trying to extract key information and offering words of support and comfort, telling me it was all going to be okay. Not surprisingly, she was still struggling to understand what I was saying so, in the end, I forwarded her the email, which seemed the easiest way to explain things, and waited.

She stayed on the phone as she read it then unleashed a torrent of expletives about Daniel. She went silent for a moment, clearly trying to find the right words for the bizarre and totally unexpected situation we suddenly found ourselves in.

'Look, why don't you come down here and stay with us for a bit? Charles will be able to help with everything. I'm going to bring him up to speed about it all now. He'll know what to do. You will be okay, I promise you that. You're strong and you'll get through this. I still can't believe it Grace, but it seems like he has duped us all. He is a total bastard who clearly never deserved you and he is about to realise he has lost the best thing that ever happened to him. He will certainly never walk through *our* door again. I'll make sure of that.'

I hesitated a moment, before asking:

'Samantha, do you think Charles knew anything? I mean…he and Daniel were friends….'

'No Grace, absolutely not. He would definitely have said something to me and he never did, I promise you. He loves you just like I do and he would never have let that arse-hole deceive you and betray you like that. You know what he and Daniel were like. It was always a bit of a love-hate relationship. He only put up with him half the time because of you.'

I knew I could trust Samantha one hundred percent. She was that friend who would always tell you the truth when you tried something on that didn't suit you, let you know discreetly when you had something stuck in your teeth after a meal. She would never have kept a secret like that from me. For the first time, I was grateful for the many occasions that I had her in my camp; I agreed to go down to see them as soon as I could.

I managed to pull myself together and regain enough composure to go home, knowing I could not put it off any longer. At some point, my brother would see the twenty-something missed calls on his phone and get in touch. In the meantime, I had to face Mum, make her a coffee, sit her down and blow her world apart.

Mum was chattering away as I took off my boots in the porch and gave Lola some food. I was lost in my own thoughts, trying to formulate the shortest, least painful version of the story for her in my head, when her words cut through.

'You're obviously not listening to me, so I might as well stop telling you about it.'

She sounded hurt.

'Look, Mum, I'm sorry….' I knew my voice sounded harsh and irritable.

'I've got a lot on my mind at the moment. Can you just sit down for a minute, please? I've got something I need to tell you.'

She sat down abruptly on a stool and looked terrified, steeling herself in anticipation of whatever bad news I was obviously about to deliver. I hated Daniel for what this would do to her. Since we lost my dad, she seemed so much more fragile and vulnerable and I felt fiercely protective of her, but I knew there was no way I could protect her from this.

'The thing is…I got an email last night, from someone I've never heard of. A woman. Look, there's really no easy way to say this Mum. Apparently, Daniel has been cheating on me.'

She gasped in horror and her hand flew to her mouth as I continued.

'Not only with this woman, but with a load of others as well.'

I paused to let that sink in, before delivering the final blow.

'And he's got kids with two of them.'

That just about sums it up - I thought miserably to myself.

The last five words were like daggers in my heart and I collapsed in tears again, despite my resolve to stay strong.

'Oh, Christ, the bastard…the bastard. Oh, love, I'm so sorry, so sorry.'

Mum knew how much I had always wanted kids and I could see she was struggling to take it in, unable to find the words. Infidelity on this scale, or indeed any scale, was totally incomprehensible to her. She stood up, wrapped her arms around me and we sobbed together, clinging to each other as she rocked me from side to side. There is nothing worse for a mother than seeing her child in pain and nothing worse for a child than knowing you have caused your mother so much pain.

'But how could it happen?' she began again. 'I don't understand. Are you sure she's telling the truth?'

'Yes Mum, I'm sure. I already spoke to him and he didn't deny any of it. Just said everything in the email was true….'

My voice tailed off and I slumped despondently onto a stool.

'Show me the email. Let me read it.'

I was desperate to keep the sordid details from her, but she was equally determined to know everything. Her face changed as she read; her mouth hardening into a thin line of anger. As I watched her, I realised I had massively underestimated her. She did not need protection. It was her job to protect me and she would fight for me, like a tiger with its cub. My mother was a far tougher cookie than we all gave her credit for.

I thought of all my mother had had to endure in her life. Born with three holes in her heart and various other health complications, including rheumatic fever as a child and severe, debilitating, migraines; her parents were told she would not live beyond the age of ten. And yet she did, surviving as a young girl during the war in bomb-ravaged Sheffield, spending most of the time in a convalescent home for children, whose strict rules stated that parents were only allowed to visit once a month.

After the war, she continued to defy the doctors' predictions and continued to grow up. As a teenager, she loved the cinema and went to see all the latest musicals with her best friend, Jean. Despite her lack of formal education, she was bright and got herself a good job in the office of an engineering firm, which was where she met my dad, who worked there as a draftsman. They fell in love and, by the time she travelled to London Middlesex hospital at the age of twenty-four to undergo one of the first pioneering operations in open-heart surgery, they were engaged to be married and Dad was by her side. Not only did she live to tell the tale, just three months after coming out of hospital she married my dad, although they were told it was unlikely she would ever be strong enough to have children. Determined to have a family of her own, Mum had other ideas and went on to have first my brother and then me. Her life was blighted by ill health and she endured several further operations as the years rolled by, including open heart surgery for a second time the year I got married. Throughout it all, she remained positive, coping with everything Fate threw at her and living life to the full with the family she had always wanted.

As I looked at her sitting there, my heart was full of admiration. How could I have been so patronising and arrogant to think this remarkable woman needed *my* protection?

'Stop crying now,' she stated decisively.

She held me at arms' length and looked me in the eyes.

'He is not worth your tears or mine. He is nothing but a liar and a cheat and, believe you me, between us we will make sure he gets his comeuppance. Your dad would have killed him. Oh God, I wish he was here to help you, but it would have broken his heart to see what he has done to you….'

Tears began to roll down her cheeks again at the thought of my dad and she dabbed at her eyes with a handkerchief.

'Have you told Jeremy?' she sniffed.

'I tried. He wasn't in and he isn't answering his phone.'

I snivelled pathetically, but a little bit of fire was beginning to smoulder deep inside me. My mother and father had not raised me to be a wimp, wallowing in self-pity. What had happened to me was shit, there was no denying that, but I told myself philosophically that nobody died at the end of the day and so there had to be a way forward, a way to make them proud of me.

I jumped as the front door slammed shut and my brother walked into the kitchen, looking anxious as he took in my tear-stained face.

'What's up? I've just seen all your missed calls and came straight round. What's happened?'

The relief on Mum's face was obvious as she stood up to make coffee. The cavalry had arrived.

'You need to read that.'

I brought up the email and shoved my phone at him with no further explanation.

He looked confused but began to read. When he had finished he did not speak for a moment, just rubbed his hand over his face.

'Oh Christ, Grace, I'm so sorry. I can't believe it. Phoebe and I always thought there was something not quite right with him, but…the scale of the deceit…it's just incredible. The man's a bloody sociopath. I honestly can't take it all in.'

'How do you think I feel?'

I dissolved into tears yet again, forgetting my earlier resolve. I desperately wanted my dad, but Jeremy was the next best thing and I knew he would come through for me and tell me what to do. He was older than me by a couple of years and had always been the sensible, reliable, one; well respected in the community as the local GP, but even he seemed to be at a loss with this one. He enveloped me in a massive bear hug and I clung desperately to him, sobbing uncontrollably.

'Have you spoken to the tosser?' he asked disdainfully.

'Yes. And before you ask, it's all true. He's not even trying to deny it.'

'Okay, okay. Let's think here. We need to be practical and methodical. Mum, have you got some paper?'

He paused to think as Mum scurried off to get paper.

'I'm going to write a timeline of events regarding everything that woman says in the email. You need to write down notes about your life with Daniel, especially the financial side of things. You're going to need a bloody good solicitor. One that will take the bastard to the cleaners. You'll have a fight on your hands though because he's devious and unfortunately he's one step ahead of you. I think you should probably get back to the house as soon as possible, just in case he takes anything important away. Go through all the paperwork and gather any information you can get your hands on that could help your case: bank statements, invoices, account details, literally anything.'

I nodded, relieved. This was what I needed. Clear instructions. Someone else taking charge.

'Will you come back with me and see the solicitor?' I asked, hopefully.

'Come on Grace, I can't just drop everything at work. You know I'll help you with anything I can, but we live two hours away and you should really use a solicitor nearer home. You need to do this bit on your own. I know it's been a horrendous shock, but you're a big girl now and you will get through this, I promise.'

Reality check number one. Of course, he would help me, as would all my friends, but everyone had their own lives and their own problems going on. I couldn't just expect people to suddenly jump to it and run around after me, holding my hand. Everyone would be sympathetic, I was pretty sure of that, but I also knew that sympathy did not have a long shelf life. I had to stand on my own two feet, be brave and accept that this was my mess to clean up. I needed to make sure I only called for back-up when I really needed it because I could not afford to wear out the sympathy card.

An hour or so later, my brother stood up to leave.

'Come round to ours for something to eat this evening and we'll talk it through some more. I don't want you and Mum on your own here tonight.'

A family meeting was assembled that evening: Mum, me, Jeremy, his wife Phoebe and my three beautiful nieces, Felicity, Serena and Amelia. My young nephew Luke was sent to play on his X-box; they could give him a watered-down version of events later.

Phoebe had never really taken to Daniel and I wondered how things would have turned out if I had listened to her earlier. She placed a large gin in my hand and smiled as I walked through the door.

'Come on, I think you need that. What an absolute arse-hole.'

'Understatement of the year,' my brother added, taking Mum's coat.

I was trying desperately not to cry again and focused on the gin, as we all sat down at the kitchen table and Phoebe continued.

'You know what I think about him, Grace. I didn't hide it. I never liked or trusted him. I thought he was an arrogant dick head, always bragging about what he had and how much it cost. He definitely looked down his nose at us, thinking he was so much better than everyone else. It doesn't surprise me at all to find out he's capable of something like this. He's nothing but a con man and a compulsive liar.'

I nodded miserably. That just about summed him up. I had definitely backed the wrong person when I refused to believe what she said about him in the past. She looked at my face and decided to change tack.

'Have you had a look at the other women on Facebook?' she asked, with a glint in her eye.

'No, I haven't dared. I bet they're all younger than me, slimmer, more glamorous…I just can't bear feeling even worse about myself than I already do.'

'Oh don't be ridiculous. He's not exactly George Clooney, no offence. He was always punching above his weight with you. Anyway, you have to know what you're dealing with. Come on girls,' she said, turning to her daughters. 'You try to find them on the laptop. I'll get more gin.'

It did not take them long. Felicity gasped and her hand flew to her mouth in shock.

'Oh my God!' she exclaimed.

All three girls collapsed in laughter and a few moments later I confronted the first of the enemies I never knew I had. To my surprise and undeniable relief, Jane turned out to be none of the things I had feared. She was short and overweight, her round face framed with a medium length, dark bob. She was wearing glasses and was most definitely not what you would call glamorous. Her thin lips were smiling, but the smile did not reach her eyes and there was a cold, calculating edge to it that was particularly unattractive.

Plain Jane was prolific on Facebook and there were numerous posts and photos to look at. Her privacy settings were lax and it was almost as if she wanted me to know all about her, wanted to rub my nose in it. It was frightening how much information we gleaned about her from just a few minutes on social media, including where she lived, somewhere called Willowmede, near Birmingham. My nieces immediately christened her The Whale of Willowmede that night and the name stuck. It had a certain ring to it I felt.

We took great pleasure indulging in a massive bitching session, ripping Jane to pieces for the next half an hour or so, zooming in on every photo and analysing every post from the last two years, to build up a full picture of her character, which we then promptly assassinated without mercy.

The smile was immediately wiped from my face however when I was shown her most recent post, featuring a photo of Daniel, asleep on top of a double bed, wearing his standard uniform of jeans and an M&S polo shirt. He had one arm cradled around a young boy who looked about nine years old and was nestled into him. There was a glass of something dark on the bedside table, presumably his signature drink of Mount Gay and coke. The photo was accompanied with the hashtags:

#family time, #family is strongest bond, #love kids, #daddy and son.

This woman knew what she was doing. It was obvious she was using the child to assert her dominance and to cause me maximum pain. She had succeeded. The physical agony I felt as I looked at that picture of Daniel with his son, the son that should have been mine, was unbearable. No matter what happened in the future in any divorce proceedings, Daniel had won. She had won. There was no magical antidote or cure that could ever fix this for me.

'Oh my God, what a vile bitch!' my niece, Felicity, shrieked. 'You need to keep away from her. I think she could be dangerous. I bet you anything she knew he was married all along. It looks like he's gone and shacked up with her and the kid now. She's obviously desperate.'

'I think we should ignore The Whale now and look for the others,' said Serena tactfully, noticing my face and shoving a box of Ferrero Rocher towards me.

The stalking continued, but Lorraine Huntley, the author of the email, proved to be a more elusive target. She was on Facebook, but it was locked down with tight privacy settings and her profile picture was a photo of a dog; a black Labrador who, disturbingly, looked a lot like Lola. I decided to reserve judgement on her until I had found more evidence. I had not replied to her email and had no intention of doing so for the moment.

'Why don't you go down to see her?' Amelia suggested. 'I'll come with you,' she added excitedly.

'Maybe the two of you could get together against him as they did in that film...what was it called again...?' Serena asked, looked at her sisters questioningly.

'Do you mean The Other Women?' Felicity offered.

'That's the one!'

I laughed despite myself. I remembered watching the film one evening with the girls. Me joining forces with the woman who had been sleeping with my husband behind my back for pretty much my entire marriage was never going to happen, but they might have a point about going to confront her in person.

We spent another hour drinking and trawling the internet, trying to find out about the mysterious Anita in America and her daughter Tara (Daniel's daughter - I reminded myself), but we were finally forced to admit defeat, as she irritatingly appeared to have no social media presence whatsoever. That was for another day. There were so many more pieces of the jigsaw to fit together, but I told myself that at least I had made a start.

Phoebe had cooked a roast dinner and the girls had done an apple crumble for dessert. Perfect comfort food. The conversation eventually turned to other things and, for a little while at least, as we laughed and chatted and Luke showed me his latest Star Wars figures, I forgot my troubles and the world returned to normal.

As I lay in bed at Mum's house that night, unable to sleep, the initial surge of relief I had felt at the photos we found of Jane, aka The Whale of Willowmede, began to turn to self-doubt and then self-loathing.

What the hell was wrong with me? I must be a really terrible person for Daniel to cheat on me with these women, who were neither attractive nor younger than me if Jane was anything to go by. It just didn't make any sense. Clearly, they had something I did not have, though.

They had my husband for a start.

I eventually drifted off into a fitful sleep, steeling myself for the fact that tomorrow I would have to return to the forever home I thought I had made with my husband. The home that I now knew had been built on sand.

The Thief

If you allow the wolf to get away with stealing one of your sheep today, he will come back tomorrow and take the rest of them.

Grace

Alone in the car, as I drove home, I gave myself a pep talk and vowed to be the strong woman that everyone knew would make it through the worst that life could throw at her. The fearless woman who dared to do anything she had to do. The independent woman who did not need a man by her side. Above all, I promised myself I would be the woman who never backed off in the face of adversity and who always got back up when life knocked her down. I was my father's daughter - I told myself.

But the superhero version of myself I had conjured up evaporated the minute I entered the bedroom on the top floor, which Daniel and I used as an office. Apart from the basic furniture and some junk lying around on the windowsills, the room was totally empty.

My eyes darted around the room, desperately searching for the boxes containing business and personal accounts, normally stored under the desk.

Nothing.

I looked at the desk which normally had papers piled high at the side.

Again nothing.

I pulled open the filing cabinet drawers at the side of the desk.

Empty.

The whole room was uncharacteristically tidy. It looked as if we had been burgled by a thief with a conscience, one who had been careful not to make a mess. But I knew the thief who had been here and he was devoid of all conscience. My own little box file of personal documents sat forlornly under the window, looking out of place.

He had certainly been thorough, erasing all traces of himself from the office. The only thing left on the desk was the new twenty-seven-inch monitor he plugged his laptop into when working (or doing whatever else he got up to of course). Everything was stored and backed up on that damn laptop of his and I had about as much chance of getting my hands on that as I had of flying to the moon. Once again I had been caught napping, wrong-footed. I was making this all too easy for Daniel and if I didn't get my act together he was going to trample all over me with his size 11 boots and squash me into the ground like an insect.

I realised as I stared at the space in front of me that there was no point in harbouring any sentimental thoughts I may have had about Daniel and his love for me. This was a blatant declaration of war and I needed to toughen up if I was going to survive, let alone win.

Time was not on my side. My appointment with a solicitor was scheduled in two days. My brother had called a friend of his who was a top divorce lawyer for advice and she had confirmed that I would need to take in as much information about our finances as possible, both joint and individual, so that my solicitor would have something to build my case with. I realised in dismay that I was going to be heading to that initial meeting with nothing but a few vague notes I had scribbled on a piece of paper. I had a horrible feeling I was going to look like a complete idiot, who deserved everything she got.

I couldn't face being alone in the house so, when Frieda called, I jumped at the chance to go round for dinner with her and James and stay the night. James was a great cook, although I decided I had better wear something loose as he was renowned for over-catering and the food was always too good to resist. Tom, their son and my mast man on the boat for the last couple of years (Team Bow we called ourselves), came to pick me up and, without saying anything, enveloped me in a massive bear hug. Tom and the rest of our crew had all walked off the boat in a touching demonstration of loyalty the minute they found out what Daniel had done, vowing never to sail with him again.

'Come on then,' Tom said, opening the car door for me. 'Dad's catered for at least thirty, so I hope you're hungry! You look great, by the way.'

I adored Tom and his younger sister Alexandra, having known them since they were little kids, so I was delighted to find Alex, who lived nearby with her fiancé, was coming round to join us for the evening. Frieda had also invited Neil and Gwen for added moral support. They had all been part of the old crowd from the sailing club when Daniel was with Julia, and the six of them had been great friends. Like Frieda and James, Neil and Gwen had been disgusted to hear the news of Daniel's horrendous betrayal and shunned him immediately, calling me as soon as they found out to offer their support. As the evening progressed, the alcohol was doing a great job of numbing the pain and, to my surprise, I was actually able to find humour in the outrageous absurdity of the whole situation. As I looked around the table at the smiling, laughing faces of the friends who were all rooting for me, I felt incredibly grateful and suddenly felt I would get through this.

That was the night Little Miss Turbine was born. Her main mission was to honey trap Daniel (aka Rotorvator) on the flying forum he was a member of and pump him for information. Daniel had told me about the forum in the past and I remembered how I had laughed at the ridiculous name he had given himself, to his great irritation. Tom and Alex came up with the idea of joining the forum, basically to stalk Daniel and gather information. It was a loosely planned idea, but it seemed as good a way as any to find out what he was up to, given that we all knew how Daniel loved to boast about what he had, how much it cost and what he was doing. The jury was out on just how useful it would ultimately prove to be, but at least we were having some fun playing detectives.

After dinner, the three of us grabbed a laptop and hurriedly set up Little Miss Turbine's account on the forum, going with Alex's inspired suggestion of *Dickhead 1* for the password, which seemed fitting. Little Miss Turbine wasted no time in posting a 'damsel in distress' message, on the pretext of planning a first solo flight into the Oxfordshire area, asking for advice on landing grounds and places to stay nearby. Rotorvator was predictably quick to engage and responded with a lengthy, flirty message, offering to meet up and take our heroine to dinner. Tom, Alex and I looked at each other and burst out laughing, unable to believe how easily he had been reeled in. The problem was we had no idea how to continue Little Miss Turbine's adventures, as the face to face meeting we had suggested was clearly out of the question. Still laughing, I picked up my drink and wandered through to the lounge to join the others, leaving Tom and Alex to ponder that one as they continued trawling through the messages on the forum.

I was actually gobsmacked. The email from Lorraine had been sent just a few days earlier and I had to believe that chaos reigned all around in the world of Daniel, yet there he was, large as life, apparently without a care in the world, looking for the next woman to prey on. Frieda had been a close friend of Daniel's since their teenage days, but as I looked at her face I could see only disgust at his behaviour and the betrayal of their friendship. She shook her head in disbelief.

'Unbelievable. He really is a piece of work. I'm afraid he's pissed on his chips one time too many with me now. I've had it with him. I'm warning you though Grace, there's a ruthless side to him. Remember what I told you years ago about how he treated Julia? I don't know for sure whether he was physically violent, she would never admit it, but all the signs were there. He certainly tormented her relentlessly and messed with her head in a big way.'

'I've always been wary of him,' added Gwen. 'I hated the way he cheated on Julia, flaunting it to all of us, as well as her. She was scared of him, I know that. The police were called out to their house on more than one occasion when neighbours reported a disturbance. I questioned her a few times about the bruises she sometimes had, but she always insisted they were accidental. He treated her appallingly and then turned on the charm with everyone else.'

'Do you think that's why she killed herself?' I asked suddenly. I had never pushed the subject with any of them before.

'We'll never know I guess,' said Frieda, sadly. 'By the way, I noticed Niamh Ryan was mentioned in the email you got. I know for a fact she was one of the women Daniel was having an affair with. It was obvious he didn't want to be with Julia, but he would never let her move on either. He was always ringing her and going round to see her after they split up, so she kept convincing herself they were getting back together, but it was just a control thing with him. When she finally saw the light and realised he was playing her for a fool, she couldn't handle it and went to pieces completely. The worst of it was she was still totally besotted with him.'

'Oh God, that's so awful. The poor woman.'

'Tell me about it. I was stuck in the middle,' Frieda continued. 'We had all been friends with Daniel for a long time, but it was obvious to all of us that he was no good for her. I told her she needed to stay away from him and make a clean break for her own sanity. I tried my best to support her, but I'll never forgive myself for the fact that

I didn't see the suicide coming. Things were obviously worse than any of us realised.'

She paused at the memories of her friend and looked sadly at the picture of Julia on the wall, show jumping on her beloved Amber. I waited for her to continue, feeling uncomfortable and not knowing what to say.

'Daniel stepped back completely after it happened…said it was his way of coping, but I'm not so sure. He just seemed to switch off, like he didn't care…almost like Julia never existed. He took himself off somewhere with Niamh the week of her funeral, which infuriated me. He came back for a couple of hours to show his face after I had a go at him then disappeared again. That's not normal behaviour when your wife is being buried, even if you are technically estranged.'

'Well, he always was a tosser,' said Neil, decisively. 'He pissed off pretty much everyone around here by being such an arrogant twat,' he added. 'We all knew he didn't give a shit about Julia. To be honest, I don't know why any of us put up with him for as long as we did.'

'So, how did he meet Niamh?' I asked, hungry for information now.

'She's an artist,' said Frieda. 'Northern Irish, but moved to the Republic years ago and lives and works in Cork now, I believe. Daniel said he met her on a plane when he was going over to do a job in Ireland. They ended up buying a house together somewhere near Kinsale, I believe, but I assume that was sold before he married you.'

She paused a moment, then added, 'I would maybe check on that if I were you.'

I was already thinking back to a time when we were first married and Daniel went to do a sailing event in Ireland without me, as I had to work. He told me he was staying with 'friends' but, when I asked him about them, he was evasive.

'Oh, you don't know them,' he had said, refusing to elaborate any further.

Did he stay with Niamh? In their house near Kinsale? - There was so much I didn't know.

My 'to-do list' was getting longer by the minute, but I felt that was a good thing. I needed to focus on that list and keep searching for information. The alternative was to go over and over what had happened in my head and to question everything about the life I thought I knew, the life I thought was mine. In a nutshell, I had been married to a stranger. A man I did not know at all. Our life together had been built on lies and deceit. Focusing on that would drag me down into the depths of despair and I was not going to let that happen.

Frieda's was the voice of reason as always, with a cool, calm approach to everything.

'On a practical note, you need to write a little plan each day of what you need to do,' she continued. 'Keep it small and achievable. Slowly, slowly, catchy monkey! We'll do some searching as well and we can all compare notes about what we find out. A team effort!'

I nodded enthusiastically as Tom and Alex came through with a load of print outs of forum chats they thought may be useful. We decided it would be best for Little Miss Turbine to play hard to get and not reply to Daniel's message. She could still be a great asset to the team however, by simply logging on each day and monitoring posts.

'Are you going to be okay at the house by yourself Grace?' asked Gwen, concerned.

'Oh yes, I'll be fine,' I lied.

James looked at me reassuringly as he spoke.

'You know you can stay here as long as you want, but I honestly think you need to get back to the house and stake your claim to it, so to speak.'

'He's got a point,' agreed Neil. 'Don't give Tosser an inch of wiggle room or he'll shaft you with the house. Remember it's your home and you have rights.'

'Just make sure you ring any of us if there's a problem,' added Gwen, as she and Neil left to go home.

They were all right about the house, of course - I thought to myself as I lay curled up on Frieda's sofa later than night but, the truth was, I dreaded having to live there on my own. Daniel appeared to be holed up with The Whale, playing happy families for now, but what if he came back? I was clearly a nuisance factor, the same as Julia had been. What if he just wanted to get rid of me? Make me disappear? The house was isolated….

I laughed out loud at my own stupidity. I told myself firmly that I was being ridiculous, allowing my paranoid thoughts to run away with me, imagining myself in some kind of thriller movie. I needed to get a grip.

Tomorrow I would go home and prepare properly for my meeting with the solicitor.

It was time for me to take charge of the situation.

The mother of his child

Jane

Jane stood in the bedroom doorway and stared at Matthew and her son, asleep on the bed. Words could not describe how livid she felt with him, but she had forced herself to take a step back and think of the bigger picture. That email had been the biggest shock she had ever had in her life. She had always known he was married of course, but she had never for a second imagined there was a whole load of others lurking in the shadows, just waiting to pounce and spoil things for her. Everything she had worked towards for the last fifteen years had been put in jeopardy and she needed to think and act fast. She did not like being caught on the back foot.

She had called Matthew immediately of course and told him in no uncertain terms to get himself home. Home, as in the one where she lived, just to clarify. He had been sheepish and apologetic, but there had been no declaration of undying love for her, no rejection of all the others in favour of family life with her. He was pathetic and appeared to have no idea how to deal with the fallout from his colossal mess. She realised that she needed to take charge.

First, she dealt with the email. A curt reply to put that scheming bitch firmly in her place:

Lorraine,

I have no idea who you are or what kind of hold you think you have on my partner, Matthew. I suspect you are delusional and have created a relationship that does not exist from a stupid fling you once had.

A mistake.

I have a child with the man you are referring to and I can assure you he is wholly committed to us. In fact, he is here with me, the mother of his child, right now.

I would strongly advise you to check your facts more carefully before sending such spiteful nonsense, or you will be hearing from my solicitor regarding libel. Please do not contact me again.

Jane

That should do it, she thought as she pressed send. It was essential to present a united front for now, even though it was fake. Jane was no stranger to lies and deceit.

Next, she needed to deal with finances as a matter of urgency. There was almost certainly going to be a divorce on the cards and Jane did not want that bitch of a wife coming out of this well. She could see things turning into an almighty scrap before much longer and she had no intention of sharing anything if she could help it. She assembled all the paperwork she needed, starting with the Will.

She had insisted Matthew make a Will when Aaron was born and had seen to it that they were both well provided for in the event of his demise. She paused and wondered for a moment, as she often had done, what would have happened if he and the 'bunny boiler' had died as planned in that helicopter crash? It would all have been so much neater than the bun fight that was about to ensue. She needed to keep the Will safe as, in her opinion, Matthew had suddenly acquired a long list of enemies, many of whom would be more than justified in harbouring murderous thoughts towards him.

There was a problem with the Will, however, given that there was apparently another child. An older child. Jane clenched her fist so tightly her nails bit into the flesh of her palm, leaving red lines. She had to force herself to stay calm and think. The American woman Anita, and her kid Tara were thousands of miles away. He could not possibly have the same bond with Tara that he had with Aaron and surely it would be much harder for an American to stake any kind of claim in British courts. Jane was sure she still held the ace card, but there was no harm in taking out additional insurance. She decided after some deliberation to go after his car collection and set about coming up with an argument to convince him to sign at least some of them over to her. Once things were in her name, at least that bitch of a wife would not be able to snatch them in a divorce settlement. To her mind, it was a no-brainer.

So far as his business was concerned, there were more than a few loose ends to tie up there. She had started her own Life Coach company some time ago. Even she didn't know what the fuck that really was when it was at home, but this latest trend seemed like an easy way to fleece people out of some money and she was quick to spot an opportunity and jump on the bandwagon. She was on Matthew's company books as a 'service provider' which suited him as a way of easily transferring money to her for child support and hiding it from both his wife and the taxman. She had also made sure she got involved with his highly creative accounting at an early stage and consequently she now felt in a position to hold a gun to his head if necessary. Now that she knew about the American woman and her daughter though, she was more than a little concerned about the extent of Matthew's state-side business interests and finances and also suspected there may be another Will lurking somewhere.

Jane was satisfied that she had dealt with the basics to salvage at least something from the mess, but there was still a hell of a lot to sort out. For the moment, she wanted Matthew living with her, where she could keep a close eye on his activities and protect her own interests, but she had no intention of that becoming a long term arrangement. She was hell-bent on making that lying bastard pay for humiliating her, but she would wait until the time was right. She was not sure yet exactly how she would make him pay, but one thing she was sure of was that Matthew/Daniel/whatever he chose to call himself had gone way too far this time.

Jane thought to herself that someone should have told him about Icarus. He flew too close to the sun. And look what happened to him.

The waiting game

Lorraine

Lorraine knew she had a massive advantage over all the women she had sent the email to. She was actually feeling pretty pleased with herself as she went about her daily business as normal, waiting for the replies to come in. Secretly, she was revelling in the power she suddenly had.

Predictably, John had been the first to get back to her. She despised him, the pathetic worm that he was. He had cried and snivelled on the phone to her, declaring her to be his soul mate, telling her she was the only one he had ever truly loved. He had begged her to forgive him and take him back so that they could presumably live happily ever after, now that he would be getting a divorce.

When he realised that wasn't happening, he had started to panic about the vintage Bentley and the Porsche 911(the very one he had turned up in for their first date) that he had stashed in her garage, not to mention all the paperwork and other stuff he had in her house. When it finally sank in that she had absolutely no intention of allowing him back in the house, never mind letting him have any of his things back, he predictably turned nasty. In the end, she decided to cut him off completely and block his number to shut him up.

Lorraine had not been particularly surprised by the email she received from Jane. She looked like a hard-faced cow from the photos of her on John's iPad and on social media. Clearly, she was prepared to stand by her man no matter what. More fool her.

The one that had surprised Lorraine the most was the wife, Grace. She had maintained complete radio silence and it was now more than three weeks since the email had been sent. She seemed to have disappeared off the radar completely and Lorraine was a bit unnerved by that. Who knew what she might be plotting now that the cat was well and truly out of the bag.

Lorraine's musings were interrupted by a car drawing upon the gravel outside. She recognised it instantly as John's and felt a little frisson of excitement. He walked up to the door and attempted to open it with his key.

One step ahead of your there, mate - she thought to herself smugly.

He banged on the door in annoyance.

'Lorraine, let me in! We need to talk about this. I've said I'm sorry. I love you, I really do. None of the others mean anything to me. I just want to be with you.'

'Well, I don't want to be with you anymore. You should have thought about how much you loved me before you cheated on me.'

'Please, Lorraine, just let me in,' he pleaded.

'Go away! Did you *really* think I was going to let you in here? From now on you can speak to me through a solicitor.'

'What the fuck are you talking about? We can sort all this out ourselves, but you need to talk to *me*. Surely you don't want to just throw away everything we had together? What about all my things? What about this house? It's half mine...it was our dream home,' he finished pathetically.

'Half yours? We'll see about that. It's my name on the deeds remember.'

'Don't be like that Lorraine.'

He paused for a moment, but when she remained silent he began to lose his temper.

'Open the fucking door or I will kick it in!' he yelled.

At that point, she made a tactical decision to call the police. She wasn't the least bit afraid of John, but she knew it would paint a good picture for the Courts if it came to that in the future. She dialled 999 and prepared to give the performance of her life.

'Emergency services, which service do you require please?'

'Police. It's urgent,' she gasped.

Once they had got the basics out of the way, the officer promised to stay on the line and tried to calm the apparently hysterical Lorraine, as she sobbed down the phone and begged for help.

'Don't worry Lorraine, they're on their way now,' the operator assured her. 'Are the doors locked? Does he have a weapon of any kind?'

'I don't know...Oh God, please hurry...I think he's going to kill me!' she screamed. 'The door's locked, but he's threatening to batter it down if I don't let him in. I can't see if he has a weapon...but he did tell me once he had a gun...Oh God, I'm scared!'

She had no idea if that last bit about the gun was true, but she felt it was a nice touch.

'Right, I've sent that information to the officers. Now try to stay calm. They should be with you in about five minutes. Stay away from the door and go upstairs,' the woman instructed her decisively.

Lorraine was delighted to note that John was furious when they turned up. Typically, he did not help his own cause by being rude and obnoxious to the officers.

'I live here, you fucking jobsworths. I have every right to be here and every right to go into that house. I want my stuff out of there and I want my fucking cars!' he shouted in the senior officer's face.

Lorraine watched the scene unfold from inside the house, as the police became increasingly irritated.

'Back away please, Sir, and calm down. You are not going in there. The lady inside has explained the situation and I would suggest the best thing for you to do is leave and then deal with all this through your respective solicitors.'

'I'm going nowhere. Are you even listening to me? This is my house as much as hers so get out of my way and make her open the door. If you don't, I will,' he threatened, somewhat unwisely.

'We have already checked the house, sir. You are not registered as an owner of this property. Nor are you on the electoral register here. If you continue to refuse to leave, we will have no alternative but to arrest you.'

'Oh fuck off, you tossers. Why can't you see it's her who's in the wrong here? She's stolen my stuff. You lot are all the same. I wouldn't piss on you if you were on fire!'

That was the straw that broke the camel's back. Finally, the patient officers had had enough and, to Lorraine's immense amusement, John was arrested and carted off unceremoniously to spend the night in their cells.

One of the officers stayed behind with Lorraine to reassure her and discuss the option of applying for a restraining order, which would effectively prevent John from coming within a five-mile radius of the house.

'Given his violent behaviour this evening and the historic abuse you have just told me about, I really think you should pursue that avenue,' the concerned officer had said before leaving, assuring her of their full support in the matter.

Lorraine could barely disguise her elation, as she wiped away a tear with a trembling hand, promising to read the leaflets and get in touch with someone who would help her.

The pain that she had in mind for John was only just beginning.

Letting go

Grace

I did not speak to or communicate with Daniel for a whole two weeks. Finally, I found the words and composed an email, determined to keep it both formal and dignified, despite the inner rage I felt.

Dear Daniel,

I remain in a state of utter shock and disbelief at the total devastation and humiliation you have brought crashing down on me.

From the start of our 20-year marriage, you were screwing around, having 'one night stands', several of which you developed into long term relationships with an utter disregard for the consequences of your actions.

The news that you have fathered at least 2 children that we know about is the cruelest blow of all of course. You knew fine well that I always wanted children myself, but you forced me to give up on that dream. I have no words to describe the bitterness and hatred I now feel for you, knowing that you went off and had children with other women. How can you live with yourself, you sick bastard, knowing what you have done to me? You are evil through and through and you have quite literally ruined my life.

I now have to come to terms with the fact that I was married to a total stranger for 20 years and that my whole life with you was built on extravagant lies and deception.

I really hope you will come to regret throwing away the life we could have had as you look at the fat, ugly tramps you chose to betray me with and are now saddled with. I almost feel sorry for you.

You really should have died in that helicopter crash, as the world would have been a much better place.

Obviously, I want a divorce and I want to be rid of you as quickly as possible. I am giving you one chance now to make me an offer of a settlement that properly compensates me for what you have done and it had better be good.

If you do not come up with a suitable figure, I promise I will drag you and all your whores through the Courts.

And I will destroy you.

Grace

My first draft had been a little more strongly worded, containing phrases such as:

I hope you burn long and slow, writhing in agony in the fires of Hell with a red hot poker up your arse…

I curse you and all the hideous trolls you have stuffed your disease-ridden dick into…

But I had deleted those. A bit too dramatic, even for me.

Daniel's response to the more grown-up version he finally received came almost immediately:

Dear Grace,

I am really sorry it has come to this; I don't know quite how it did, but we can't change things.

I have always loved you and you are still the best bowman I have ever had!

I will look into your request but I don't have an awful lot of assets left and I have just had a tax judgement against me for nearly £700,000. It's totally unfair, but they refuse to listen or let it go. Obviously, I have appealed, but they have got it in for me.

This will probably bankrupt me, but I don't think the receivers can touch your Conway house.

November started well but it's really gone pear-shaped!

Hope you're ok.

Love,
Daniel XX

I looked in utter disbelief at the email in front of me. He was clearly not right in the head. How could anyone of sane mind ever contemplate sending something like that? The brief apology, as if he'd left his underpants on the floor or forgotten to unload the dishwasher. The light-hearted banter about me being his 'best bowman'. The flippant tone of the whole thing.

And what the *hell* was all that shit about bankruptcy?

I began to consider the very real possibility that my husband was completely and utterly insane and also potentially extremely dangerous.

The Fallout

It is only when you walk alone that you will discover your true strength. The path is always harder, but that is the walk that makes you strongest.

Grace

The bedroom curtains were parted slightly and I reluctantly opened my eyes, squinting in the pale winter sunlight. Sleep at least provided some respite from all the unwelcome thoughts that dominated my waking hours these days. I pulled the duvet over my head to shut out the light, having absolutely no desire or motivation to get out of bed and face the day.

I refused to let anyone else see just how hard things had become for me but, in truth, I was a mess, unable to accept and come to terms with my new reality. The metaphoric rug had been pulled from beneath my feet. Everything had been snatched away from me in the blink of an eye. Only a few months ago I had inhabited a world of exotic holidays, helicopters and yacht racing, planning a celebratory anniversary trip with my husband of twenty years.

What the hell happened? - I asked myself a hundred times a day.

Everyone said I was perfect for him.

- So why wasn't I enough?

I really didn't see the bombshell coming. One minute I was making holiday plans with our best friends. The next thing I knew, my world was plunged into chaos and I was fighting to keep a roof over my head.

Of course, I was not the only woman who ever found out her husband cheated on her, but surely no one could dispute the fact that my husband had found a way to take cheating to a whole new level.

On top of that, he was now claiming bankruptcy. Was that really true, or was it just part of a grand plan to make sure I came out of our marriage with nothing? I didn't know what to believe anymore. I squeezed my eyes tighter shut, but the thoughts wouldn't stop bouncing around in my head.

The Swan conversation had taken place just a few weeks ago. Why would he ring me and tell me he had bought a new boat for us if our marriage was a sham? We had so many plans and dreams for the future together. It simply didn't add up.

I curled into a ball under the duvet.

- How did I get it all so badly wrong? Why didn't I see this coming?

My brain still struggled to accept the fact that I was now completely alone. It all seemed surreal, as if I was outside in the cold, looking in on my own life through a window, unable to influence or connect with anything.

My husband, who had stood beside me all those years ago in front of our friends and family, promising to love, honour and cherish me till death did us part, had tossed me aside like a piece of rubbish and left me fighting to salvage any scraps I could from my past life, emotionally and financially devastated. He had signed the death warrant on our marriage the first day he betrayed me and his feeble protestations of regret to save his own skin changed nothing. My only communication with the man I had loved and trusted for so long was now through solicitors as we hurtled towards the inevitable divorce.

A loud bark from downstairs brought me sharply back to reality. Lola. Thank God for my gorgeous girl who would not allow me to languish in self-pity all day. I could never let her down. I dragged myself reluctantly out of bed, trudged downstairs in my dressing gown and opened the back door to let her out. She was easily pleased and wolfed down her breakfast, having returned almost immediately from the field to get her food. She was a Labrador, after all, a pure eating machine. As soon as she had devoured her breakfast she immediately lay back down in her basket, head on her paws, staring at me. I sat at the kitchen table and opened my laptop to check my emails. Predictably there was a string of messages from my solicitor, reminding me of the questions she wanted answers to. I steeled myself to read them.

Who is his accountant? Does he have life insurance? How many bank accounts does he have? Do you have any information about his offshore accounts? How many cars does he own? What are the details of his American bank accounts? Does he have a pension? Does he have any shares or other investments? Does he have a Will?

How the fuck should I know, I wanted to scream in response.

I snapped the laptop lid shut and stared blankly through the window, my head already beginning to pound.

How had I let this happen? I was not a stupid woman, but I had to admit I was doing a bloody good impression of one at the moment. Forty-six years old. The best years of my life wasted on a man who didn't give a shit about me. Unless I made some pretty drastic changes, I was going to wind up well and truly on the scrap heap now, in more ways than one.

I studied the kitchen wall that I had completely covered in photographs. There were some of my parents and some of my brother and his family, but mostly the photos were of Daniel and me. Sailing regattas, holidays, black-tie dinners, The Dream Team everyone had said. I was fairly tall at five foot seven, but Daniel was well over six foot and so killer heels were never a problem when I was with him. I smiled as I remembered how Daniel used to tease me about all my shoes, but he knew I loved them, especially the carefully stored Louboutins in the wardrobe upstairs that I had treated myself to. I was dressed to kill in all of the black-tie photos. My hair was down in most of them, long dark curls framing my face. People used to say I had my father's dark brown 'chocolate drop' eyes, always a little sparkle of mischief in them and I worked hard to keep slim and toned, just the way Daniel liked me. He always said being overweight was so aging. I thought of the photos of Jane and realised that even that had been a lie.

Tears sprang to my eyes and I wondered again what the hell I had done wrong.

- What happened to me? Where did that sassy, confident girl in the photos disappear to?

My thoughts returned to the initial, depressing meeting with Eleanor, my solicitor. It dragged on for over three hours and at the end of it, she gave me a pitying look. She predicted that at best I would be able to keep the house in Conway (along with its hefty mortgage) that was in my name. Nothing else in her opinion.

I stared at her in disbelief. That was the best-case scenario? She clearly thought I was an idiot. It was written all over her face.

'Grace, we have to be realistic,' she stated patiently. 'If you can't come up with any evidence or paperwork to support what you have told me about your husband's financial affairs, we are going to have a very difficult time in court. You have a lot of theories, which I wholly believe are correct, but you have no proof.'

She shook her head and sighed, before continuing.

'The thing is Grace, I'm afraid it really doesn't matter who is the wronged party in a divorce. No one cares. It's all about the finances. A mathematical exercise. You have been treated abysmally by

Daniel and I can honestly say I have never before in my career encountered deception on this level, but the harsh fact is that the judge will ultimately divide everything straight down the middle, 50/50. Right now, on paper, we're looking at 50% of not a lot where you're concerned.'

I was astounded by the apparent injustice of our legal system.

- How could he not be punished for what he had done to me? Why should he be treated fairly?

'So what am I supposed to do then? Walk away with nothing, while he just gets away with it all?' I retorted, angrily.

'No, that's not what I'm saying at all, but you're going to have to find a way to help yourself here. Nobody else can do it for you. From what you have told me, your husband is, in all likelihood, a very wealthy man and owns several valuable assets, but he is clearly not planning on sharing any of that with you. You have to face the fact that he's scheming to hide everything from you and probably has been for some time. He's cunning. Worse than that, I'm guessing he's prepared to lie through his back teeth, even under oath.'

'Yes, I'm well aware of that,' I said sulkily as she continued, clearly not about to spare my feelings.

'He basically intends to cut you off and leave you high and dry with nothing to show for your lengthy marriage to him. If we're going to stop that happening, we need evidence. It's as simple as that.'

I burst into tears of frustration and sobbed uncontrollably at the unfairness of it all.

'But he's cleared everything out at home and taken all the paperwork away. There's literally nothing left in the office. How the hell am I supposed to find out all that stuff you're asking me about? It's obvious he's been planning this for ages and as you say, he's devious. To be honest, I have absolutely no idea where to start.'

I was furious with myself as well as with her. The realisation dawned that for years I had allowed myself to be kept in the dark about our finances, fed bite-size pieces of information by Daniel to keep me happy, but never given the full picture.

I had only myself to blame for allowing this to happen.

I remembered what Charles said to me when I went down to see them shortly after receiving the email. Charles was always a straight talker and never one to tell you what you wanted to hear for a quiet life.

'Moping around feeling sorry for yourself is not going to get you anywhere. You're an attractive, intelligent woman and you need to sort yourself out. Start by getting up and getting ready each morning as if it's a Saturday night out. You can't let what's happened with Daniel define you, or it will destroy you. Shit happens, Grace! I've had enough of it in my lifetime. You need to deal with it, then move on and enjoy the rest of your life. As for all the financial stuff, it's not rocket science. My advice is to start digging around, be methodical and think hard about what you do actually know. I'm guessing you know a lot more than you think you do. Hire a Private Investigator if necessary. You need to show what you're really made of and stand up to him. You know I'll help you in any way I can.'

He paused and hugged me before continuing.

'Just one more thing...I don't want to frighten you, Grace, but I know what Daniel's like. He won't be taking any prisoners in this. Whatever was between you in the past, believe me, he doesn't give a shit about you now. He'll be playing hardball. Don't be on your own with him. People become unpredictable when they're backed into a corner. Remember that and be careful.'

Back in my own kitchen, I thought hard about what Charles had said and knew for certain that I did not like this weak, whinging version of myself and I especially hated the pitying looks of people who had already branded me as a victim. I had no intention of being a victim.

I made up my mind there and then to fight and to win, but I needed to be clever and I had a feeling Charles was right when he said that I needed to be careful.

Buoyed up once again, I put on my standard, country, dog-walking gear of jeans, Barbour jacket and wellies and headed out across the fields with Lola to clear my thoughts. I would miss this house, miss being able to walk straight out of the back door and into a scene from James Herriot country. There was not an electricity pylon to be seen here, just rolling hills covered in heather, fields segregated by traditional dry stone walls and beautiful stone farmhouses, like ours, dotted around the place. I clambered over the wooden fence that marked the edge of our land and headed straight up the hill. There were no sheep in the fields, so Lola could have a free run. She never bothered with the sheep to be fair, but the farmers had learned from bitter experience to be angry about dogs running free amongst livestock and a few of them were trigger happy with their shotguns. I couldn't really blame them, so I was always careful to keep Lola on a lead when the sheep were in there. I was out of breath when I got to the top and turned to look back, loving the bird's eye view over the roof of our house and across the valley. It was a harsh place to farm in the winter, but I found the rugged beauty of the landscape uplifting in any season. Lola suddenly lifted her nose in the air and set off at high speed across the field. She had the selective hearing of a Labrador following a scent and totally ignored the whistle, forcing me to chase after her. We had never quite mastered the recall part of dog training and a walk with Lola always ended up being a full workout. I could not help laughing at her face when I finally caught up with her. She had perfected the cute look of innocence, which she knew would get her out of a serious telling off. I ruffled her ears and headed home, ready to face what I had to do.

The fight starts now - I told myself.

An hour later I sat down at the kitchen table with a coffee and spread out all the information I had managed to gather about

Daniel. It was true that he had pretty much emptied the house of all paperwork, but he had missed some stuff in cupboards that he had either not seen or thought was of no importance. 'Be methodical,' Charles had said. My task was to sift through every single scrap of paper and begin piecing together the complex jigsaw that was the picture of my husband's life.

The first lead I came up with was a simple address: 12b Channing Street, Stainsford. The registered office of Daniel's company. It just didn't sit right with me.

- Why would he have a registered office in Stainsford in the Midlands, when his business was in Derbyshire?

- Why would he need another office at all, when he already had a perfectly good one at home?

Thoughts raced through my head and I struggled to make sense of them. I searched the land registry and also one of letting agents in the area. The address was a bedsit.

- Why? Why? Why?

- Why would you have a bedsit, miles away from your business, as its registered office?

I had to get myself to Stainsford. I had to see for myself. It was a very small lead, but it was the only one I had and somehow I felt sure I would find answers there, probably not ones I wanted. I remembered Charles' words about people being unpredictable when backed into a corner and felt a little tingle of fear. If Daniel really was hiding something there, there was no telling how he would react to me poking around the place.

I decided to wait until I knew he was miles away somewhere on 'business', preferably out of the country, but monitoring his movements was going to be very tricky indeed now that he had moved in with The Whale. I would need to look into that and figure out how best to do it. It would possibly involve a stakeout of her house. In the meantime, I was psyching myself up for two other extremely important visits I intended to make. Just over three weeks had slipped by since the email and it was time for me to get moving.

The first visit was to Kieran, Daniel's brother. I had not seen him since our wedding, which seemed a lifetime ago, but I now felt it was time I heard what he had to say.

The second was to Lorraine, the woman who had sent the email.

The Brother

---

*Don't play with fire if you're not prepared to get
your fingers burned.*

Kieran was naturally suspicious and more than a little hostile
when I approached him to see if he would meet me. I couldn't really
blame him. He and his family lived just a few miles away from us in
a neighbouring village, but Daniel and I had cut him off completely
after our wedding all those years ago. I had slagged him off to
anyone who would listen about his impromptu speech at the
reception. In the end, his desire to gloat and say, 'I told you so' must
have got the better of him, because he agreed to meet me in town on
neutral ground, outside Costa so he could smoke.

'So, now you want to talk to me,' he drawled, clearly enjoying my
discomfort at having to eat humble pie. The unmistakeable
Northern Irish accent reminded me instantly of Daniel.

'I heard what happened,' he continued, unable to resist a half-
smile.

Fellside was a small town where everybody knew your business. I
knew the jungle drums had been working overtime with the news
of our dramatic split. To be honest, I couldn't blame them for
gossiping. I would have done the same.

'You could have saved yourself a whole load of heartache and pain if you'd just listened to me all those years ago,' he continued. 'I was trying to help you, not hurt you.'

'Hindsight is a wonderful thing Kieran. I can see that now, but at the time I was obviously going to side with the man I was about to marry and believe what he said. Perhaps if you'd tried a more subtle approach? Anyway, that's all water under the bridge now as far as I'm concerned. I asked you to meet me because it would really help me if I could understand a bit more about the past. Things that happened before I knew Daniel.'

I took a deep breath.

'Like his first wife. Like the fire. And of course your mother.'

Kieran's eyes narrowed and he did not speak immediately.

'Please. I really want to hear your side of things. I promise not to judge,' I continued.

'There's nothing for you to judge because I didn't do anything wrong,' he snapped.

'But Daniel told me you started the fire....'

'Course he did, lying bastard. Everyone believed him, the respectable local businessman, over me. I had form. I had already been in trouble with the police for minor drugs offences, nicking cars, disturbing the peace and stuff like that. It was easy for him to pin it on me. I fucking hate the police....'

'So tell me what really happened then,' I interrupted, keen to stop him going off on a tangent with a rant about the police.

'When Dad pissed off to go and live with his girlfriend, Mam went a bit doolally, though God only knows why she was so surprised...they always had what you might call an 'open relationship'. Daniel and our mother fought like cat and dog and he was vile to her most of the time, calling her every name under the sun and threatening her with all sorts if she dared to stand up to him. She was shit scared of him, I know that for sure. When she left, the house was already pretty run down. Daniel stayed there with me until he got married to Julia. I'm not gonna lie, we had some

176

pretty wild parties in that house and always had a load of mates sleeping over. It was an amazing time and the parties were legendary, mostly alcohol and weed, but occasionally a bit of the harder stuff. Daniel bought a house on the new estate in the town with Julia, but he always wanted to get his hands on the big family house and hated the fact that Dad let me stay there pretty much rent-free. He suddenly seemed to be making quite a lot of money, although the word on the street was that it was not coming from his packaging business.'

'What do you mean?'

'Look, this was all a very long time ago. All I know for sure is that he liked to live life on the edge and a lot of what he got up to was at best borderline legal. You wouldn't want to mess with some of the guys he was dealing with, believe me. It wouldn't surprise me at all if that helicopter crash wasn't engineered by someone he'd got on the wrong side of.'

He paused to let that sink in. I mentally stored the information but did not comment.

'Anyway, as I said, Daniel tried to buy the house from Dad for next to nothing and kick me out, but Dad refused to sell it to him. Daniel came to the house the night of the fire, angry about the state the place was getting into. It was a Friday night and a few of my mates were there. I told him it was none of his fucking business and laughed in his face. He was pretty mad when he left, shouting that I would be sorry I had crossed him. I don't remember how I got to bed that night, but I woke up to smoke and flames all around in the bedroom and my mate Josh screaming at me. If it hadn't been for him waking me up and dragging me out of the house, I'd have died in my bed.'

'Are you saying you think Daniel could have started the fire?'

'I'm not saying anything. How should I know? You work it out. The fire investigation team blamed me for falling asleep with a cigarette, but that would've been tricky, as I ran out of fags that night. All I know is the house wasn't fit for anyone to live in after the fire, so Daniel got what he wanted in the end. He bought it from the insurance company for a song, I was given my marching orders and he rebuilt it.'

'Wow. I had no idea.'

'Yeah well, it's all true. No one would listen to a word against him and I got the blame.'

I looked at the man opposite me and wondered whether I could believe his version of events. I was beginning to realise that there were always two sides to a story, but that didn't necessarily mean that one of them was the truth.

'Why doesn't Daniel get on with your father? I never met him in all the time we were married.'

'Don't know really. We were never a particularly close family. My parents were part of the local swingers' crowd around here for a while.'

He sniggered at the memory before continuing.

'Daniel hated the way everyone took the piss about them at school. He always took it personally, especially after one of his mates was staying here and came down in the morning to be confronted by Mam doing the laundry, stark bollock naked. Daniel went ballistic.'

Kieran laughed and lit a cigarette before carrying on with his story.

'First Dad went, which was no great surprise, and then Mam presumably got fed up with us and left as well. Walked out of the house one morning to get milk and never came back. Just literally disappeared. As far as I know, no one has heard anything from her to this day. Weird, eh? I did warn you.'

He laughed again.

'I suppose our upbringing wasn't entirely conventional and there were always a lot of rumours going around about us. Not much fun at school, as you can imagine. It didn't really fit in with Daniel's image and, to be honest, he always acted like he was better than the rest of us, as if he was ashamed of us. He used to make up names for himself when we were younger and lie about being an orphan. I always thought he had a bit of a screw loose, to be honest, but he had a hell of a temper and a way of storing things up until he could make you pay when you least expected it. Put it this way, I tended to make sure I didn't cross him.'

'What about his first wife, Julia?'

'Julia was lovely, but she should never have been with him; she was far too sensitive. Things seemed okay for a couple of years when they were first married, but he was a bastard to her in the end. She went right off the rails after she lost the baby, but my charming brother just seemed to want to stick the boot in and punish her for getting pregnant in the first place. She was scared of him, just like Mam was. The word on the street was he used to knock Julia about. And I know for a fact he was screwing around behind her back, pretty much all the time they were married. Sound familiar?'

He laughed ironically and took a long drag on his cigarette.

'How do you know all that?' I asked.

'She was friends with Becky, my girlfriend at the time. After their marriage broke up, Becks was pleased, thinking that Julia would be able to move on and get her life together, but it was obvious he wasn't going to let her do that. He had to keep control. He didn't want her, but he wasn't going to let anyone else have her either. Just kept her dangling, like a spider with a fly trapped in its web. In the end, she just couldn't cope anymore. He's got a lot to answer for if you ask me. I'm warning you, you need to watch your back with him. He's dangerous. Toxic.'

With that, he abruptly stubbed out his cigarette and stood up to leave.

'Nice chatting to you, but I think we're done here.'

As I later reflected on all Kieran had told me about Daniel and the past, I realised again that I had never really known the man I had been married to. It was as if he were talking about a complete stranger, not the man I had shared my life and my bed with.

It seemed to me that Daniel created chaos, then simply walked away from it and started all over again. His life's motto of leaving the past in the past and never looking back was simply a way for him to do exactly what he wanted and avoid the consequences.

Well, not this time. This time he would be made to take responsibility for what he had done. He did not get to walk away from *me* scot-free.

The Other Woman

You cannot defeat your enemies if you do not know who they are. Know your enemy and know yourself. Then you need not fear the battle.

Grace

My first visit to the 'dream house' in Hazeldene to confront the face behind the email did not entirely go to plan. My friend Sylvie refused point-blank to let me go to visit the mystery woman alone, so we set off together in her Land Rover with Lola on a blanket in the back for moral support. Sylvie was originally from South Africa but had been in Yorkshire for years. She and her husband, Andrew, together with their son, Adam, and his gorgeous wife, Melissa, ran the hotel and bar just up the road from our house in Fellside. The hotel had become my refuge and second home since the nightmare began and I headed over there pretty much every morning for a coffee and a chat.

I had still not replied to the email from Lorraine, but I had done some extensive searching of the electoral roll, the land registry and Linkedin. I was becoming quite the amateur detective. I knew where Lorraine lived and where she worked, but, despite my best efforts, not much beyond that. At least I had retained the element of surprise for my visit.

The house was tucked away on the edge of the village of Hazeldene, near Oxford, and we had to do quite a bit of driving around and asking for directions before we eventually found it, despite having put the postcode into the satnav. The pretty stone cottage was at the end of a farm lane and we drove past it several times before parking up on the verge a little way away from the house. It was getting dusk, which suited me fine as I got out of the car and crept down to the house in stealth mode with my phone, keen to gather important photographic evidence. As I stood in the ditch and parted the hedge, trying to get a better view, I recoiled in horror. Daniel's car was there. I could see him clearly on the other side of the yard, arguing with a tall blonde woman who was shouting at him from inside the house. I took a quick picture, just as a large black Labrador ran towards me from around the back somewhere, barking excitedly. I almost fell over in my panic and legged it as fast as possible back up the lane towards the car, feeling more like I was in a Carry On film than a spy thriller.

'What happened? What could you see?' Sylvie asked excitedly.

'Just drive, quick. Daniel's there and I think they might have seen me. We need to get out of here. There's no way I'm confronting the pair of them together.'

'I need a pee first, I'm desperate,' she announced.

'Can't you wait?' I asked, looking at her incredulously as she opened the car door.

'No, honestly, I'll be quick.'

Lola immediately struck up a frantic whining to show her support for the idea, so two minutes later all three of us were squatting behind the Land Rover to relieve ourselves and silently praying that there was no CCTV anywhere near.

As I hastily bundled Lola back into the car, Sylvie started the engine, but the Land Rover had sunk into the muddy ditch and the wheels were spinning wildly, splattering mud everywhere as it listed over onto its side. Sylvie began to giggle.

'Christ, we're stuck. This place is in the middle of nowhere and Daniel is probably the only one around who can tow us out,' she announced through her laughter.

I failed to see the humour in the situation at first, but her laughter was infectious and I soon joined in.

'This is a Land Rover for fuck's sake. Doesn't it have diff lock or something?' I asked, laughing hysterically as the tears rolled down my cheeks.

'I don't know. I've never had to use it.'

She tried again and again to move, but the wheels just sank further into the mud.

I was close to full-on panic mode. I had no idea what Daniel would do if he caught us down there spying on him. The whole thing suddenly seemed ridiculous.

What had we been thinking? What the hell had we hoped to achieve there?

Five minutes later, after a desperate phone call to Adam at home and a lot of swearing as we tried frantically to get the right combination of gears, the trusty Land Rover began to move slowly forwards, dragging itself effortlessly out of the ditch and onto the tarmac.

No one emerged from the house and I finally breathed a sigh of relief. It appeared they were too busy with their own arguments to notice what the dog was barking at and the slapstick comedy sketch being acted out by us a few metres up the lane.

I realised, that day, that there was more to this Private Investigator lark than met the eye. I had a lot to learn and I would have to learn fast.

Sylvie was disappointed that we had driven four hours to get down there and effectively achieved nothing. She was determined to salvage something from our flawed plan.

'You need to get a tracker on that car of his and find out where he is going when he moves. It might lead you to where he is hiding things,' she said, excitedly.

'And how am I supposed to do that?'

'I'm pretty sure there are PI companies that do it for you. Ring Adam, he's bound to know. Or he'll find out for you.'

Half an hour later, after a couple of desperate phone calls, I had engaged the services of Night Owl Investigations. They promised to go to the address I gave them, fit a tracker to Daniel's car and monitor it for one week.

They coolly relieved me of a thousand pounds, payable upfront, for the privilege, but I told myself it was worth it. At least I was actually doing something. I answered their phone call the following day with eager anticipation of an update but, of course, it was not that simple.

'I'm afraid we couldn't fit the tracker,' said a woman's voice, in a neutral tone.

That was not what I had been expecting.

'What do you mean? I paid you a thousand pounds to do exactly that!'

'The car wasn't there when our agent got to the property.'

'Well, you need to go back and try again.'

'That's not the way it works. You paid for one visit, at very short notice and, as I explained to you last night, it is your responsibility to ensure the vehicle is where you tell us it will be.'

I tried to argue some more, tried to convince them to give me some money back, but I quickly realised I was dealing with nothing more than glorified thugs, who made a living out of ripping off gullible people like me.

That was the first time I got my fingers burned. It wouldn't be the last.

I sat at home licking my wounds for the next few days and feeling miserable. It felt like every time I took a step forwards I got shoved at least two steps back.

I knew I had to go back to see Lorraine and confront her about the email. She was a vital piece of the puzzle. Much as I hated to admit it, she would know things I didn't about Daniel and could potentially be very useful to me. I tried to remain detached, but I also needed to see the woman my husband had been sleeping with for the last however many years. The woman he apparently preferred to me (or at least one of them - I reminded myself).

The second time I visited I decided to go it alone, apart from Lola of course, and I told no one. We set off around lunchtime and by 5 pm I was parked up in a strategic surveillance position a little way from the house, watching and waiting to pounce when Lorraine got home from work.

I saw her car arrive at the house, instantly recognising the silver Freelander Daniel had turned up with a while back for me to use when my Porsche was in for repairs. It seemed our lives were more interlinked than I thought. A blonde woman got out of the car and went into the house. I could not see her face, but she appeared tall and well built. I was sure she was the one I had seen in the house arguing with him the other night. The lights went on upstairs and I couldn't help torturing myself with thoughts of what the bedroom was like and what she and Daniel used to get up to in there. I waited until the lights upstairs went off before driving up to the house.

I did not allow myself any hesitation. Switching off the engine and leaving the window open slightly for Lola, I got out of the car, walked straight up to the front door and rang the bell. The blonde woman appeared after a few moments and half-opened the door.

'Lorraine?' I asked confidently, despite my churning insides.

'Yes.' She looked at me suspiciously, waiting for me to elaborate further.

'I'm Grace. Daniel's wife.'

I don't know what I expected really, but it suddenly all felt very weird and my heart was thumping hard in my chest. Her face softened into a vague smile and she stepped back as if she had been expecting me, opening the door wider.

'Oh right. You'd better come in.'

I had half expected her to slam the door in my face, but she was actually quite welcoming and was acting like it was the most normal thing in the world to invite me in.

Yet we both knew there was nothing normal about this.

'Would you like a coffee?' she asked, seemingly friendly.

'Yes please, just black.'

I couldn't help letting out a little gasp of surprise as I tentatively followed her into the kitchen and she gestured to me to sit down. I could have been walking into my own kitchen. Everything was identical. The stone flags on the floor were the same as the ones outside on the patio. I had come up with that idea as a practical feature when coming in from muddy dog walks. I looked around incredulously at the cream-painted, wooden units with the black ceramic knobs. The Aga range cooker set in the stone fireplace. The wine rack made out of clay pipes. The oak dining table in the centre of the room with six chairs around it. The deep Belfast sink under the window. The exposed oak beams creating a vaulted ceiling. She even had a black Labrador for God's sake! This was all too weird.

'Oh my God, this could be my kitchen,' I exclaimed.

'I know,' she stated calmly. 'I've seen the photos. John told me it was a property developer friend of his who had renovated an old farmhouse. He was so impressed with the kitchen he wanted to replicate it here. Obviously, he left out a few pertinent details.'

I felt indignant and instantly defensive.

'I designed that kitchen myself and my dad fitted it for us,' I snapped.

She did not comment as she handed me the coffee.

I assessed her appearance slyly as we weirdly began to chat like old friends. She was taller than me by a good few inches and I guessed bitchily about three stone heavier, but she was not really what you would call fat. Not like The Whale. Her clothes were drab, although to be fair I had caught her on the hop and she was clearly dressed for a night in front of the TV with the dog, rather than a night on the town. Nevertheless, I was glad I had been to the hairdresser last week and had chosen to wear my black, quilted Barbour and Ralph Lauren jeans and sweater, with dark grey, suede ankle boots. Understated chic.

I reminded myself sharply that I was not there to judge her but to see if she could be any sort of ally against Daniel, aka John. She certainly seemed keen to get me on her side and was quick to assure me that she had not known he was married.

'I was married to a cheat once myself and I promise you I would never knowingly get involved with a married man. I know how it feels and I just wouldn't do that to another woman,' she declared, with a pained expression on her face.

Did I believe her? I wasn't convinced. I didn't trust anyone anymore. I decided I needed to stop pussyfooting around and get down to business.

'So how did you meet then?'

'Match.com. I thought you knew that. He failed to tick the box that said 'married' of course.'

A dating website. Fuck. So there had been no chance meetings, no accidental encounters. The treacherous bastard had actually gone out of his way to look for women.

'Yes, I found out he's on several different sites,' she added casually. 'Some of them are purely for hook-ups and one night stands. I found it all when I hacked his iPad. There's Uberhorny, Shagbuddy, New Honey, Grindr, Tinder...he's on them all. One of them even uses the strapline *Life's too short; have an affair.* He knew exactly what he was doing.'

'I get the idea,' I interrupted, then thought of something. 'But I thought Grindr was a gay dating site? I can't see why he would have been on that.'

Lorraine simply shrugged her shoulders in a 'draw your own conclusions' kind of way, which irritated me.

I had to admit though, I felt a certain degree of admiration for this woman and the way she had been able to find out so much by hacking into Daniel's phone and iPad, even if some of her information was a bit off target. In the early years, he must have been able to operate covertly and with almost total anonymity, but the social media boom had put paid to that in latter years and, with camera phones everywhere nowadays, there was simply no hiding anymore. Technology had been Daniel's downfall and the irony of that was not lost on me, given that he was the man who always bragged about having every new gadget the moment it came out.

My thoughts turned to business again and I began to quiz her as subtly as I could about anything of Daniel's that she might be harbouring in the house. What it really boiled down to, as far as I was concerned, was that I was his wife and therefore, what was his was mine. She had no right to anything in my opinion, but I was already getting the distinct impression that I was going to have to play nicely if I was to get anywhere with her.

'Do you have any of the paperwork for his cars here by any chance? Or the paintings you mentioned in the email?' I asked politely, trying to look at the walls around me without turning my head.

She looked pleased with herself and opened the lid of a big trunk in the corner.

'I certainly do. It's all in there. The files and documents for all his cars and motorbikes are in there, but I have no idea where he stashed the paintings. They were only bought fairly recently at an auction. He came down last week demanding that I let him have that stuff and a load of other crap he left here. I didn't let him in of course.'

I blushed slightly, as I remembered scrambling around in the hedge and the argument I had witnessed the last time I was there. I leaned forward to get a better look, but she closed the lid down immediately, narrowly missing my fingers.

'He ended up being arrested and taken away by the police. I called them when he refused to go away and became abusive towards me. I had no idea whether he was going to turn violent. They advised me to apply for a restraining order against him through the Courts, which I have already seen a solicitor about. I don't want anything further to do with him at all. To be honest with you, I just want to get on with my life, but he won't stop pestering me, telling me he loves me and wants to be with me....'

She saw the expression on my face and tailed off, suddenly realising what she was saying and who she was saying it to.

Or maybe she was saying it deliberately, to twist the knife.

'Sorry,' she said innocently, but not entirely sincerely.

'It's okay. I guess in the end we're both victims,' I said, graciously.

I did not believe for a second that she was really a victim, but I needed to get more information out of her.

There was a long silence and the atmosphere was becoming increasingly tense. I tentatively began to ask her about the holidays they had been on and the things they had done together. It hurt like hell to hear the details, but I couldn't stop myself asking for more and more. I learned that he had taken her to the Seychelles *six times*. They had chartered a boat each time, even though she didn't sail and had no real interest in it. I was close to tears, realising I had not anticipated just how difficult it would be to hear all that personal stuff. The Seychelles was *our* special place. It was where we had spent our honeymoon. He had never taken me back there and I thought bitterly how much I would have enjoyed those sailing holidays, how it should have been me, not her. It felt as though she had stolen my life but, of course, Lorraine was not the only thief in all this.

I decided to focus on what was really important in an attempt to salvage some dignity.

'Can I take that paperwork with me?' I asked bluntly.

'Sorry, but my solicitor has advised me to keep everything here for now until things are a bit clearer,' she replied, smiling sweetly.

I briefly entertained the idea of punching her hard in the stomach and simply taking what I wanted, but I reluctantly decided against it. Apart from anything else, she was bigger than me and there was no guarantee I would come off best. One thing was for certain, she was no ally of mine. Quite the opposite in fact.

'Just one more thing before I go,' I said casually, trying to hide my contempt.

'Have you ever been to Daniel's office in Stainsford?'

'No, I haven't. But I'm pretty sure something is going on there that's not above board. He would never take me to the office, even when I did some work for his company. He was always very cagey about it. I'd like to know what he's got in there that he needs to be so secretive about. Maybe you could find out and let me know?' she suggested, throwing down the gauntlet.

She mumbled something about having seen receipts and invoices on his computer for a lot of personal things being sent there, but she didn't give details. I got the distinct impression she was drip-feeding me information, telling me only what she wanted me to know, just like Daniel had done for years. I needed to be on my guard and take care to do the same.

I looked at her in silence, making sure my face gave nothing away, but I made a mental note to bump Channing Street up to the top of my list of priorities.

- As soon as Daniel goes away, I'll be getting into that office. And I'm damn sure I won't be telling you what I find in there, you manipulative cow.

As I stood up to leave, she hit me with one last gem of information.

'Oh and…I suppose I should tell you. I have an STI.'

'Oh for fuck's sake,' I blurted out, shocked.

My mind immediately thought HIV and I sat back down abruptly. She really was the gift that kept on giving.

'What is it?' I demanded, not sure I wanted to hear the answer.

'I've got Herpes.'

Marvellous. To cap it all, I now had to go through the humiliation of attending the STI clinic to get myself tested. I should have thought of that before, of course. It should have been blindingly obvious to me from the outset that someone as promiscuous as my husband apparently was could have infected me with any number of filthy diseases.

As I drove home I went over and over our meeting in my head, trying to decide what the worst thing I had discovered was: the holidays in the Seychelles, the kitchen she 'stole' from me, the Herpes...?

One thing was for certain, I was beginning to toughen up at last. In fact, that was the night I began to fantasise about doing my husband some serious harm.

A turning point

There is twice as much pleasure to be gained from deceiving a deceiver.

Grace

I had to admit the tracker was a stroke of genius, although when Adam first suggested it, during one of my 'therapy sessions' at the hotel, I was sceptical.

'Bit like shutting the stable door after the horse has bolted, isn't it?'

'Yes, I agree you probably should have done it years ago, but I still think it will be useful for you now. How else are you going to find out where he's squirrelled everything away?'

'I suppose you're right, but I have absolutely no idea how to fit a tracker. I don't even know where to get one from. And I'm certainly not getting any private investigation companies involved after what happened last time.'

This was an alien world to me. Suspicion did not come naturally. I trusted people to tell me the truth. It had never occurred to me to have Daniel followed or to hack into his phone or computer. Clearly things had to change because twenty years of trusting the man I had married had not exactly ended well for me.

'Come here and look at this...,' Adam said, beckoning me over to show me a picture on the screen of his laptop.

'Eighty quid, that's all they are. I can get you one delivered here tomorrow and I've got a mate who will fit it for you, no problem.'

I thought to myself with some amusement that Adam was better connected than Don Corleone in Derbyshire. I concentrated as he filled me in on more important details.

'Actually, I think you should get two of them, as it says the battery life on them is only about a week. That way, you can always have one on charge and you just keep swapping them over.'

He paused, looking at me expectantly, but I was still reticent.

'Are you sure about getting involved? You'd really do all that for me?' I asked hesitantly.

'Hundred percent. It's not a problem at all.'

'Is it legal?'

'Bit of a grey area. The point is it goes on all the time with husbands and wives trying to catch each other out for cheating. I've done a bit of research on the subject and so far as I can see, no one's ever been prosecuted for it. There's nothing to worry about, honestly. Just make sure you keep it to yourself.'

I was nervous about this. I was crossing into a world I knew nothing about, but I had to admit that what Adam was saying made sense. He certainly had my attention, as he leaned against the bar with his arms folded, studying me and undoubtedly wondering whether I was up to all this.

'Only snag is, you'd have to get Daniel to come to the house on some pretext so they can fit the tracker. Maybe tell him you're ready to talk things through or something.'

Pretty big snag - I thought to myself; and immediately opened my mouth in horror to object, but closed it again just as fast, as he continued, raising a hand to silence me.

'Just hear me out on this. You won't like what I'm going to say, but I honestly think you're going about things the wrong way. Daniel is streets ahead of you at the moment. Let's face it, he's been

193

conning you for years and you can bet your life he's got some kind of escape plan in place. He must have known it would all go tits up someday. All his assets and his money will be protected somehow and you're going to get nowhere by locking horns with him. You've gone in there all guns blazing with the divorce, but all that legal shit takes forever and he knows that. He will be using his time wisely, to hide things, move money around…it's obvious. The bankruptcy crap is all part of the plan if you ask me. And who's to say he won't just do a runner to the States and leave you high and dry to face the taxman with all his debts here? My bet is on most of his money being over there anyway.'

He stopped and waited for my reaction. I stared at him, deflated.

'Thanks for that. That's really cheered me up. In reality, I can't stop him from doing any of what you've just said, can I?'

'Maybe not, but you can be clever and play him at his own game. Make him think there's still a chance for the two of you to stay together. Make him believe you could forgive him and take him back.'

I thought I was hearing things.

'Are you kidding me? Why the hell would I do that? I can barely look at him. I haven't spoken a word to him since the day after the email.'

'You need to brush up on your acting skills then.'

'It's not just that, Adam,' I added, despondently. 'It won't work, because I don't even think he wants me back. According to Lorraine, he's running around after her, declaring his undying love and begging her to forgive him. He hasn't done any of that with me. It's as if he doesn't care about me at all,' I said, close to tears again.

'I think the problem is you've backed him into a corner. You just need to show him a way out and I bet you anything, he'll snap your hand off. Financially, the divorce is still a big risk for him. He stands to lose a lot if you can find the right evidence and, if what he says is true, he's also got the taxman breathing down his neck. That email has taken him by surprise and caught him on the hop. Believe me, he'll jump at the chance to make the divorce go away and regain some element of control over everything. You need to make him think he can trust you. Make him think you're on the same side, like Bonny and Clyde, fighting to save everything from HMRC. Remind him about all the Irish businessmen who signed everything over to their wives to avoid taxes and try to get him to do that with you. It's been in the news recently. Trust me on this. It's the only way you're going to find out what he's up to and where he's hiding stuff.'

'I get what you're saying, really I do. I just don't think I could go through with it in all honesty. And don't forget, he may be an arrogant arse-hole, but he's not stupid. I'm pretty sure he'll smell a rat if I suddenly do an about-turn and start being all reasonable with him.'

'It's worth a try though, isn't it? From where I'm standing you don't have a lot of options. We can sort the tracker for you, but *you* need to start speaking to him and drawing him in. Con him, just like he conned you all these years.'

I tried to think beyond my loathing of Daniel.

'I have to admit it would be amazing to be able to see exactly where he went every time I logged into the computer. I could bust all his secret hidey holes and he wouldn't have a clue how I was doing it.'

Melissa came in to do my gel nails for me as a treat and sat down, catching the end of the conversation.

'Adam's right Grace. Play the bastard at his own game. Imagine the satisfaction you'll get out of conning him. If anyone can do it, you can,' she said with a wink and a little smile.

I began to wonder if this crazy plan could actually work. Finally, I would have the upper hand. Surely I could pull it off if I set my mind to it. I just had to believe in myself.

'All you need to do is get him to come over to the house and then go out for dinner with him, in your car obviously,' Adam continued. 'While you're out, I'll arrange for a couple of the guys I know to slip over to your place and do the business. He'll be none the wiser.'

I finally decided to take a risk and back myself, and it felt good.

'Go on then. Let's do this,' I said, impulsively.

The balance of power was about to shift.

'Just one word of caution though, sweetheart. Always remember who you're dealing with and be on your guard. Don't let him in the house when you're alone.'

'I'm not scared of him,' I retorted.

'Well, maybe you should be. None of us know for sure what he's really capable of. Don't forget, I grew up with him and his brother in this village. A lot of people around here thought he was a wrong 'un and the rumours were rife when his mother suddenly disappeared without a trace. Very strange business, that was. Then there was the fire. Kieran was the scapegoat for that but, in reality, I think he got off lightly when he walked out of there alive. At least he's here to tell the tale, unlike poor Julia of course. Did she really commit suicide or was she pushed?'

He held up his hands as I pulled a face.

'Hey, I'm just playing Devil's advocate here.'

I laughed out loud.

'Oh come on, Adam. Daniel is many things, none of them good, but do you honestly think he's capable of murder?'

'I think any one of us is capable of murder if we're pushed too far. Just be careful is all I'm saying. And remember you can call us here any time of the day or night if you're scared or there's any kind of problem.'

'I will, I promise. And thank you for being so totally amazing, all of you. I have no idea what I'd do without you guys.'

He gave me a quick kiss on the cheek and left me enjoying some girlie pamper time and chat with Melissa.

The hardest part of the tracker plan was obviously having to engage with Daniel again. I had to make him believe I wanted to talk about things 'like grown-ups'. The story was that I wanted us to try to agree, without solicitors interfering and bleeding us both dry. I practised my dialogue over and over again before making the dreaded phone call to tell my treacherous husband I was prepared to extend an olive branch of sorts. My words sounded false to my own ears, but I persevered, laying down clear ground rules from the start.

'We need to go out for dinner so we can talk on neutral territory. You're paying by the way and it won't be cheap,' I sniped.

I struggled to be polite, let alone nice. I told myself sternly that I needed to try harder if this was going to work, but to my amazement, Adam was right. Daniel seized the wilting, half-dead olive branch eagerly with both hands and apparently could not believe his luck.

'Of course, no problem. That's the least I can do. Glad you're seeing sense about all this at last.'

He had been emailing and pestering me regularly about there being no point in using solicitors when we could sort things out by ourselves. He promised to see me right and settle fairly if I would just call off the dogs and wait two or three years. Of course, he only had my best interests at heart.

Not.

Up until then, I had ignored all communication on the advice of my solicitor, simply passing everything on to her, but Daniel was obviously arrogant enough to believe in his own powers of persuasion in winning me round.

Our first meeting was scheduled for a Tuesday at 6.30 pm. I was taking no chances and was already half way up the steps to the driveway of the house by the time he switched off the engine. Adam's words had rattled me despite my bravado and I had no intention of allowing Daniel to set so much as a foot inside my home territory.

'Let's go to The Ram's Head. I've booked a table. I'll drive.' I had no desire to waste time with small talk, but I forced myself to calm down and remember the bigger picture. He had to believe I was serious about this because Adam had told me that changing the trackers over would need to be a weekly event in the diary.

The waiter gave us a cosy little table for two in the window, clearly assuming this was some sort of romantic date night. How wrong he was.

As soon as we were seated, I excused myself and went to the Ladies to call Adam, as planned.

'Adam, it's me,' I whispered furtively into the phone. 'I did it. We're in The Ram's Head now. We came in my car as you said, so his car is on the drive. There's no CCTV at the house, but remember I told you the security light will come on. Text me when it's done.'

'Okay sweetheart, well done. I'll text. Remember your poker face and be careful.'

'Will do.'

I ended the call and checked my face in the mirror, feeling like a spy in a James Bond movie. I adjusted my expression to get what I thought was the right balance of sadness and vulnerability for the 'tragic heroine' I needed to play when I returned to our table.

I looked at my husband, the stranger, and objectively studied every inch of his face. He looked noticeably older and more tired than I remembered. Not surprising really. I tried not to show my anger, but it was harder than I had anticipated keeping my temper as he tried to wheedle his way around me.

'We don't have to go through with the divorce you know,' he began, pausing to gauge my reaction. 'The only winners in all this are the lawyers.'

'I know that, I'm not completely stupid. So what do you suggest we do then?'

I could hardly wait to hear his master plan.

'The thing is, I'm in real trouble financially.'

'Oh do me a favour,' I interrupted, sarcastically.

'No really, they're trying to make me bankrupt. The truth is Grace, I'm just not in a position to give you anything right now, but what I suggest is that we agree on a settlement between us, even get it drafted by a solicitor if you want and I'll be able to get you your money in the next three years…five at the most.'

He paused again, before continuing with what he presumably thought was a convincing argument.

'Who knows, maybe by then we'll have changed our minds and decided to stay together.'

I wanted to spit in his face and tell him that Hell would freeze over first. Inside I was raging at the audacity of the man, but I forced myself to keep my temper.

'I had no idea things were that bad. You should have told me. We were supposed to be a team.'

'I know, I'm sorry. I suppose I was ashamed. I didn't want to lose you.'

He paused again, waiting for a reaction, but I remained silent.

'You're the best bowman I ever had…,' he added, in a poor attempt at humour. It was the same old line he always trotted out when he wanted to get around me.

'We've been through so much together,' he persisted. 'Surely you don't want to throw all that away?'

Priceless!

'I'm pretty sure you're the one who threw everything away,' I retorted.

As I waited for that to sink in, I had to admit that Adam's theory was right. Daniel was clutching at straws for damage limitation. Maybe this would be easier than I had thought. I offered him the tiniest glimmer of hope.

'I'll think about what you've said and we'll talk about it again next week. Let's not get ahead of ourselves. That's all I can give you at the moment. Let's enjoy our meal at least.'

I put on my best-injured expression.

'Are you still in contact with the woman who sent the email?' I asked slyly, unable to resist.

He shuffled uncomfortably on his chair, pondering his response.

'Not really. Only for the legal stuff about the house and my personal belongings that she refuses to give back. I don't know what I was thinking when I got involved with her, to be honest. I was confused. When I look at her now, I've got no idea what I saw in her. I've already told her it's over between us.'

- Really? That's not what she said.

'Did she accept that?' I asked innocently.

'Well, she's got no choice. Look, I know I don't deserve a second chance, but if you could find any way for us to move forward and stay together...I'd be the luckiest man in the world.'

'Yes, you would. But like I said, let's not get ahead of ourselves here.'

Somehow I managed to get through the next couple of hours without screaming or stabbing him, although his steak knife did look particularly attractive to me on several occasions.

I made it clear that the evening was over as I parked on the drive next to his car, then I stood and watched him drive away, having agreed to meet again the following Tuesday.

The second his car had disappeared off down the road, I raced excitedly down the steps and in through the back door of the house. I grabbed my laptop, typed in the login details Adam had given me and waited. Sure enough, there it was. A little green cursor called *Daniel 1* flashed on the map. It showed him heading off in what looked to be the direction of Stainsford or The Whale's house. I sat back and stamped my feet on the floor in excitement like a little girl. The first part of my comeback plan had worked.

Fuck you, tosser!

Over the next few weeks, I watched his movements avidly, making copious notes for myself and recording the various locations he visited. A pattern was emerging and I had several places marked down as 'key locations' to be followed up on.

As I suspected, there were regular visits to 12b Channing Street. I was pretty sure the visits had nothing to do with legitimate business, so as soon as an opportunity arose I headed down there for a proper recce.'

I had planned it all carefully, waiting until the tracker told me Daniel was well out of the way somewhere near Aberdeen, Scotland. What he was doing there was anybody's guess. Business? Another woman? Drug running? I didn't know and I didn't care. The important thing was that I knew exactly where he was because I was now monitoring his every move on my computer screen.

Daniel had not chosen the most salubrious area of Stainsford for his secret hideaway and my red Porsche looked ridiculously out of place in the seedy little street of shops with flats above them. I made a mental note to borrow a less conspicuous car for any future visits.

There was a little hardware shop on the corner and I decided that was as good a place as any to start my investigations. A tall, ginger-haired man who looked about twenty-five was cutting a key with his back to me. He stopped what he was doing as I entered and turned to serve me. I could see an older man busy doing something in the back.

'Can I help you?'

That was the first problem. I hadn't really planned any pretext for going into the shop. Rookie error.

'Erm, have you got any superglue, please?'

I asked for the first thing that came into my head.

As I paid for the unwanted glue, I attempted to ask casually about number 12a, making up my story as I went along. I told him I understood it to be the office of a packaging company that owed my boss money and I had been sent to speak to the director. He looked at me strangely and I knew I sounded dodgy as hell, not to mention a highly unlikely debt collector, but he seemed happy enough to part with information.

'It's a private flat, as far as I know, not an office. The guy who lets it comes in here quite a bit to pick up parcels I've taken in for him. He's a tall bloke, oldish, grey hair. He gets a lot of parcels, but the address on them is always to him personally, rather than a business address, so I think your information might be wrong.'

I smirked at the description of Daniel, but I had no idea what to say in response to that. What happened next could only be put down to some sort of sudden rush of blood to the head. I lowered my voice conspiratorially and leaned closer over the counter to confide in him. It was a well-known technique on the TV crime dramas I watched: tell your suspect a bit of a secret to draw them in and then they will immediately tell you something in return. Not that the lanky, ginger guy was a suspect exactly, but he was certainly a potential source of further important information. I pressed on with my part of the bargain.

'Look, I'm going to level with you here because you look like a decent guy. The man you were talking about, he's my husband and he's been cheating on me with loads of different women. And he's hiding money from me. There's lots of other stuff as well, so I really need to find out what's going on,' I blurted.

The older man emerged from the back.

'Is everything okay?'

He looked at me suspiciously and I was brought sharply to my senses. The only sensible option was to leave immediately before I could do any more damage to my cover. I couldn't risk either of them saying anything to Daniel before I got the chance to go back there or my whole plan would be ruined, thanks to my own stupidity.

'Yes, great thanks. Just came in for some glue,' I said, in a voice that was far too jolly and an expression that may well have placed me firmly in the camp of the criminally insane. I was reminded of Baby's infamous and cringe-worthy line in Dirty Dancing:

I carried a watermelon.

I held up my purchase to prove I was telling the truth as I backed away.

'Bye then. Have a good day,' I said cheerily.

I was mortified as I hurried back to my car to escape, but as I opened the door, I was startled to see my new found confidante running after me.

'Listen, I didn't want to say anything back there in front of Steve, but I'm really sorry for what's happened to you. You seem like a nice person. I can't tell you much, unfortunately, but I just wanted to say…I would never have put you and him together.'

'Really? Why is that?'

I expected him to say something about Daniel being too old for me or maybe punching above his weight, given his earlier description of him. I prepared myself to accept the compliment gracefully and drive away, but I found myself staring at him in stunned silence as I heard the words:

'I thought he was gay.'

The Liar

*It does not matter how many times a snake sheds
its skin; it will never be anything but a snake.*

Grace

I was becoming braver.

After five times of the dinner/tracker ritual, I decided to learn to do the dirty deed myself. I didn't want the other guys to be involved any more than they had to be.

There was another more pressing reason. I wanted to get into Daniel's car and to do that, I needed to be more in control.

It had not escaped my notice that Daniel always made sure he locked his briefcase in the car when we went out, so it did not take a genius to work out that there was stuff in there he didn't want me to see. I suspected he could trust none of his women anymore, including me of course, so it seemed logical that his entire life was now being stored either in the mysterious 12b Channing Street or in his car, aka mobile office.

The downside of this new part of the plan was that I would have to allow him back into the house and I was even intending to allow him to spend the night there, although obviously not in my bed. My solicitor had annoyingly informed me that, until things were decided in the divorce, I had no right to change the locks or prevent Daniel from staying in the house if he wanted to, so I decided it might as well be on my terms. With him in the house overnight, I would be able to find a way to get my hands on his keys, sneak out in the middle of the night to the car park, fit the tracker and generally have a good old rummage around in the car.

First I needed to build on my skills as a Private Eye. Tom, Adam's mechanic friend, who was particularly knowledgeable about Range Rovers apparently, was only too happy to give me a crash course in tracker fitting using a friend's car in a quiet corner of the hotel staff car park. The process was surprisingly easy, just a bit awkward. I had to lie on my back at right angles to the car on the passenger side, about halfway along and wriggle underneath. Once I had a close-up view of the chassis, Tom pointed out the steel U-section bar running across the underside of the vehicle. As luck would have it, it was a perfect fit for the tracking device, which turned out to be not much bigger than the size of a box of matches. Tom had thought of everything, even putting the tracker in a little vacuum bag so that it stayed dry. Fitting it was a simple matter of pushing it up and over into the U-section, before finally securing it with a cable tie to be sure it couldn't move or bounce out.

I could do that.

I emerged from under the car just as Adam arrived to see how my lesson was going.

'So, Nancy Drew, are we letting you fly solo this week?'

'Yep. Piece of cake. In fact, I might start doing this for a living,' I joked as we walked back into the hotel.

'Did Sylvie tell you what the guy from the hardware shop said when I went down to check out Channing Street? About Daniel being gay?'

'Yeah, she did.'

Adam laughed.

'I'm betting that's not an image he would be overly keen to portray,' he said with raised eyebrows.

'I know, but I wonder why he said that. Do you think Daniel looks gay? Because I've never seen that in him or thought that about him. He's always been a real man's man, I thought. Borderline homophobic to be honest. Shit, I don't know what to think anymore,' I laughed.

'Well, maybe he's still in the closet and that's why he did what he did to you. Maybe he's actually a woman-hater and can never be satisfied with any woman.'

'Maybe. Funnily enough, that's exactly what my sister-in-law said. I just don't get it though. That guy must have seen something to make him think Daniel's gay. It's not really the sort of thing you just come out with is it?'

'I honestly don't know sweetheart. I guess you'll find out more if you do manage to find a way of getting into the flat. Nothing would surprise me about him anymore.'

The 'gay' thing prayed on my mind. I had only just come to terms with Daniel's promiscuity with other women. Now a whole new dimension had been introduced and I did not find it a particularly appealing one. It wasn't that I was homophobic. I just didn't like being lied to. Confident that I was now fully proficient in tracker-fitting, I gathered up my little bag of chargers and leads and headed home to secrete them carefully in the house until it was time to use them a week or so later. I had been a bit lax with the tracker information lately, as Daniel had become fairly predictable in his movements, but I could not afford to be complacent and as soon as I had hidden everything properly, I set about the task of going through the log, noting times and locations again to see if any new patterns had emerged.

An hour or so later, I was kicking myself for taking my eye off the ball. A new address had indeed cropped up and Daniel appeared to be going there quite regularly.

He was also staying there overnight.

I was starting to learn my craft and it was not difficult to join the dots once the tracker pointed me in the right direction. In fact, it was frighteningly easy to find out someone's personal details. From the house address, I moved to the Land Registry, then a search of the electoral roll, then various social media sites.

Boom.

In a matter of a few minutes, I had a woman's name, a full address, where she worked, email address, phone number and numerous photos. In her profile picture, she had fair hair, taken up in a messy bun. She was definitely on the chubby side, but (I had to admit) not fat, at least not by Daniel's usual standards. I concluded that her non-descript, pink tee shirt and jeans did nothing for her and put her probably around fifty.

I sat back and looked at my scribbled notes, shell shocked. This was a new character in the plot. She had only recently been introduced. There was no mention of her in the email and it felt as if I had been punched in the stomach. All the feelings I had when I first read the email, and learned of Daniel's betrayal, came flooding back. I began to cry. Then my tears turned to anger and I slammed my fist down hard on the table.

How could he do this to me all over again? Just a few nights ago, we had been out to dinner and he had been telling me how he wanted to give things another go. He wanted me to think about taking him back. Said he would do anything to turn back the clock....

I realised in horror that I had been playing a dangerous game, one that had backfired on me. All the time I was thinking I had the upper hand and was laying a trap for Daniel, he was actually playing me for a fool.

He had lied to me again and I had fallen for it again, believing he really did love me.

I shut the lid of my laptop and hid it as I always did these days whenever I went out, between the mattress and the bed frame in my room, before heading out to see Sylvie and the guys at the hotel. I wanted a shoulder to cry on about this latest development.

'You're not going to believe what he's done now,' I sniffed, as I sat down at the bar.

'Go on then, what?' asked Andrew, in the process of cleaning the coffee machine.

'He's actually got another one on the go. Can you believe it? He's only gone and picked up *another* slapper. Presumably from one of the internet dating sites he's such a fan of. Like fucking internet shopping!'

Adam and Andrew laughed out loud.

'It's not exactly a laughing matter. He's lied to me *again*,' I said indignantly.

'I'm sorry, I just don't get why you're so surprised,' Andrew said as he handed me a large glass of wine. 'Let's face it, we all know that the way to tell whether Daniel's lying or not is to see if his lips are moving.'

'Yeah, I know that, but…I don't know. I thought maybe he was regretting it all. I really thought he was telling the truth about loving me and wanting to win me round. Even though I don't want him back…obviously,' I added quickly.

Adam raised his eyebrows questioningly.

'Are you sure about that?' he asked.

'Don't be ridiculous! I do have a modicum of self-respect left you know.'

'Well, it sounds to me like you were considering it. I know what you women are like. You like to win. Maybe there's a bit of you that just wants him to choose *you* over all the others?' he teased.

I forced a tight little laugh.

'I can assure you, that's not the case at all. I'm telling you now, I'm going to make him pay for this.'

'That's more like it. *That's* the attitude you need to keep.'

I could be as indignant as I liked, but I had to admit Adam was right. I had lost sight of what I was really trying to do and had begun to actually listen to Daniel's manipulative lies. I had let him inside my head.

I could not afford to make that mistake again.

Sylvie had her laptop open and there was concern in her voice when she spoke.

'I honestly think you need to warn this new woman. At the end of the day, Daniel will be lying to her too and he shouldn't be allowed to get away with this. He's preying on women and it's obviously starting all over again, like history repeating itself.'

She was right. I had to remain objective. The new woman in his life, Stephanie Barton, would have no clue about what she was getting into. She needed a wake-up call and there would, of course, be the added bonus of bursting Daniel's bubble.

'I think you should forward her the email,' continued Sylvie.

'I bet she hasn't got a clue and that'll certainly put her straight about him.'

'Well yes, I could send it, but I have to be careful. I don't want Daniel to know where all this is coming from. And I especially don't want any questions raised about how I found out she even exists. He *can't* find out about the tracker.'

It didn't take long for our combined imaginations to come up with the perfect solution in the form of the fictitious persona of Gloria Stanton. It took just a few moments for the ghost of Gloria, who was actually Andrew's late mother, to set up her own email account on Sylvie's laptop and send a message to Stephanie Barton. The message contained a slightly edited, copied and pasted version of the email, omitting the original sender's address. It had to be completely anonymous. All we had to do next was sit tight, have another drink and wait for the outcome of our meddling.

When the reply came, just half an hour later, it was formal, to the point and not at all what I had expected.

Lorraine,

I have no idea how you got my details. What I do know is that it constitutes a serious breach of my privacy and I will be taking legal advice regarding how best to proceed.

I am fully aware of your relationship with my new partner Daniel and how you have stalked him since he split up with you a short while ago. You are clearly a bitter ex who will stop at nothing to cause trouble and prevent Daniel from moving on with his life.

Do not contact me again.
Ms Stephanie Barton

'*Lorraine?!*' I shrieked. 'Oh shit, she thinks Lorraine sent the email.'

I began to laugh at the absurd situation. I laughed until the tears rolled down my cheeks as I realised that this was even better than I had planned. Not only was I sure I had managed to sow the seeds of doubt in the woman's mind, despite what she said in the email, but even better, Lorraine had got the blame for it all! I really hadn't intended for that to happen, but the more I thought about it, the more it was obvious Daniel would assume it was from her. An unexpected added bonus.

My phone pinged and there was an email to me from Daniel. I quickly knocked back the rest of my wine, before opening it with some trepidation and reading it out loud to the others, in a mocking attempt at an Irish accent.

Dear Grace,

Don't be scared, but I need you to be on your guard. Lorraine has hacked the email account of a female friend of mine and sent her the same spiteful email she sent you. She has clearly not bothered to check her facts and is on some kind of vigilante mission to ruin my life. I have told my friend not to respond, but I am taking this to the police as there is no telling what she might do next. She is clearly unhinged and may come after you.
Please be careful and ring me if she tries to contact you.
I think she could be dangerous.

Love, Daniel xx

I reminded myself Daniel had no idea I had already met with Lorraine and clearly he had no idea his 'female friend' had ignored his instructions and already responded to the email herself. I was no longer quite so pleased with myself however and was beginning to feel a bit uneasy at the mention of the police. Suddenly, it didn't all seem quite so funny.

'Oh shit, what do we do now?' I asked, looking to the others for advice.

My first thought was that I had done everything on Sylvie's computer and the police would easily be able to trace the IP address of that if they chose to. I had recently learned all about IP addresses, as part of my career development as a detective. I had disturbing visions in my mind of the police breaking the door down and rushing in to arrest poor Sylvie, so I frantically set about erasing all traces of Gloria Stanton's brief existence, deleting her account and all messages from it. I was sorry to say goodbye to her so soon but, hopefully, I had done enough to keep the police at bay and we would get away with it. At least I had the satisfaction of knowing I had caused a hassle for Daniel and hopefully put a spanner in the works where his new relationship was concerned, but the incident with Gloria highlighted the fact that I was still an amateur in the dark world of espionage and deception. A bit of a loose cannon, to be honest, blundering around and only really succeeding in causing more trouble for myself.

As I lay in bed that night, I thought to myself that maybe my naivety, occasionally bordering on total incompetence, wasn't such a bad thing after all. In fact, maybe it was the perfect cover, because who would ever believe I was capable of pulling off the acts of treachery I had in mind?

The Investigator

You will never know how strong you are until being strong is the only choice you have left.

Grace

I stood nervously outside the door of 12b Channing Street.

Again.

I had timed my second visit to the office carefully, waiting until Daniel was away 'on business' in America. I had watched the little green cursor drive all the way from Jane's house in Willowmede to Birmingham International airport. To make absolutely sure, I had driven into the airport car park and physically saw his car in the Meet and Greet section, waiting to be driven away to one of the off-site storage areas. Only then did I drive to Stainsford in the black Ford Focus I had borrowed from Tom, secure in the knowledge that I had days rather than hours of safety to do whatever I wanted.

This was my big chance.

I turned to the man in the Hi-vis jacket behind me and thanked him profusely, as I pushed open the door to the bedsit. I tried my best to look confident, as though this was an action I performed several times every day. There was something large and soft behind the door, which prevented it from opening fully. I shoved harder, careful not to show surprise. He needed to think I belonged there.

'God, it's such a mess in here. We're still moving stuff in. I can't believe I've lost my keys.' I laughed apologetically and rolled my eyes, flashing him my best 'helpless woman' face to distract him.

'Thank goodness I left a spare set in the kitchen,' I added for good measure.

I almost believed my own lies. I was definitely getting better at this.

The man behind me smiled with an understanding but slightly weary look on his face.

'Don't worry love. You're not the first and you won't be the last.'

I had no wish to enter into a conversation with him and was more than a little anxious to get rid of him and his Hi-vis jacket before they started attracting too much unwelcome attention from the other residents. I felt conspicuous and exposed. A young woman entered one of the adjacent flats with a small child in tow, giving me a curious look as she passed.

I needed to be careful. I needed to be invisible.

'Hadn't you better switch the alarm off?' asked Hi-vis Man.

He was looking patiently at the fob in my hand, clearly wondering why I was just standing there vacantly in the doorway. I was pretty sure he was also thinking it was a bit odd that I had one of the two-door keys needed in my possession, but had mysteriously lost the second one.

'Oh yes, of course.'

I laughed nervously and reached inside, wondering where the hell the alarm was located. I could see a box at the top of the stairs that appeared to be a likely candidate and waved the fob in that general direction, hoping to God it worked. I had to assume it did as no alarm went off. I turned back to the man with what I thought was a confident smile, eager to take charge of the situation. Time he was off.

'Thank you so much, you're a lifesaver. Here's the eighty pounds then.'

I pressed the little bundle of cash into his hand. I had, of course, made sure there was no paper trail to link me to anything there, running through the streets like a woman possessed in search of a cash machine just ten minutes earlier.

I was quite proud of myself for thinking of that at the last moment, knowing I was going to have to provide twelve months of bank statements to the divorce court as proof of my financial situation. Daniel and his lawyer would be able to study them, and I had no wish to answer awkward questions about why I had randomly engaged the services of a locksmith in Stainsford. A fleeting thought crossed my mind and I hoped I was not starring on CCTV anywhere. I reminded myself that I was not exactly in the league of criminal masterminds wanted by Interpol and produced an extra fiver for Hi-vis Man to encourage him to leave with a bit more urgency.

'Right then. If you're sure you're ok now, I'll get off and leave you to it. Have a good day,' he said cheerily.

I felt a surge of relief as he drove away and I was left alone. Suddenly the pressure was off and I had all the time in the world to find the answers I needed.

I already knew far more than Daniel thought I did, but I still needed the evidence to back it up. I was essentially looking for files and paperwork, but I had a creeping suspicion that there was something else going on there and that the bedsit was merely masquerading as the company office. I could not get rid of the ominous feeling of some deeper, darker secret lurking in the background and I felt a sudden frisson of fear at what I might find inside. There could be Eastern European girls kept hidden in there for all I knew. My imagination conjured up unwelcome images of wanton debauchery and for a moment I regretted going there alone.

I hastily put all that to the back of my mind and took a moment to congratulate myself on my own ingenuity and deviousness in finally gaining entry to the flat. I was becoming more inventive and resourceful all the time, but I had to admit it had proved to be a lot trickier than I had initially anticipated.

First, there was the visit to the letting agents to get the key, which should in all fairness have been the end of the matter. I rocked up to the office, wearing my glasses instead of my contact lenses and my hair scraped into a tight bun in a half-hearted attempt to disguise my appearance. I launched immediately into the pre-prepared cover story I had concocted, explaining that my husband and I rented the bedsit but he was abroad and I needed to get in urgently to deal with important company business. I punctuated my story with lots of hand gestures and rolling of the eyes, to emphasise my frustration with the situation. As I spoke I was half expecting the woman in the office to call the police immediately, so it really wasn't difficult to look genuinely stressed as I explained that I had mislaid my own set of keys.

I needn't have bothered. She showed no interest whatsoever in my story and was more than happy to hand over the keys to number 12b, together with the alarm fob, in return for my passport (which conveniently still bore my husband's name of course) and a signature. In fact, she couldn't wait to get me out of there and get back to her coffee and chat with her colleague which I had so rudely interrupted. I felt very uneasy about leaving my passport behind, not to mention signing my name, but I had to bite the bullet and do it as there was no way around it. I did at least have the presence of mind to make sure my signature was completely illegible and bore no resemblance to the real thing.

Back in bedsit land, I eagerly put the key in the lock, delighted that it actually fitted, turned it and pushed. Nothing. As I shoved harder at the door to no avail, I realised in dismay that it had been fitted with an additional lock, one that the letting agents clearly did not know about and did not have a key for.

Disappointment and frustration hit me again.

Why did Daniel always manage to be one step ahead of me?

I retreated to the car and tried to remain calm as I pondered my next course of action, feeling more determined than ever. Clearly, he was hiding something in there if he had gone to the lengths of putting an extra lock on the door. He was obviously not prepared to risk the letting agents going in without warning, so there was absolutely no way I could leave without getting in there. Failure at the last hurdle was simply not an option.

Fate intervened on my side for once and I remembered an evening the previous week when I arrived at my friend Bethany's house to find her sitting on the doorstep, locked out. We called the emergency locksmith who turned up looking highly suspect in jeans and a hoodie and, worryingly, took less than two minutes to break in with a tool that looked exactly like a credit card. He turned and looked triumphantly at us, pocketed his fee of £120 and was off without having asked at any point in the process for identification or proof that Bethany actually owned the house.

Thanks to my friend's carelessness, I knew exactly how easy it was to get into a locked house without a key and Hi-vis Man performed exactly as I expected him to. Ten minutes to pick the lock. No questions asked. A simple cash transaction and he was gone.

Standing in the doorway of the bedsit, I reached into the pocket of my black hoodie, purchased specially for the occasion from Decathlon on the way down to Stainsford, and pulled out a pair of latex gloves, struggling to get them on over my sweaty palms. I was taking no chances. I forced the door open against the squashy blockage and squeezed in through the gap, before closing it firmly behind me to stop prying eyes and allowing myself time to take stock of my surroundings. The tiny hallway was cramped and dingy and I could finally see that the cause of the problem was fortunately not a dead body, but a pile of four large bin bags jammed in between the door and the foot of the stairs.

I opened one of the bags and immediately recognised some of Daniel's signature M&S polo shirts and a load of other clothes belonging to him. It looked like someone was having a charity shop clear-out. The first shirt I took out of the bag had *Knob* scrawled on it in black marker and had been ripped or cut with scissors. The next one had *Tosser* written on one side and *Dickhead* on the other. There was definitely a theme here.

I remembered what Lorraine had told me about chucking all his stuff out of the 'dream house'.

Serves him right - I thought to myself with a smug smile, taking inspiration from the untidy pile and making a mental note to get creative myself with the contents of his wardrobe at home later.

I replaced the shirts in the bag, exactly as I had found them. Further analysis of the clothes could wait until later. I was anxious to get on with my real mission and the bin bags were nothing more than a mildly amusing distraction.

I looked up at the two doors leading off the landing at the top of the stairs, took a deep breath and stepped over the pile of bin bags.

As I began to climb the stairs, I could not shake off the undeniable feeling of dread that I was about to open Pandora's box.

The Mistake

Lorraine

Lorraine was fuming. She sat alone in her kitchen and vowed that John would learn the hard way what happened to people who crossed her.

Up until now, she had played her part well and everyone seemed convinced by her performance. She was the vulnerable woman in an abusive, controlling relationship. The

woman who was afraid of her lying, cheating partner and who simply wanted to be free of him to move on with her life. The police and lawyers had certainly bought into it and a court date was scheduled for the harassment case she had brought against John. A restraining order would almost certainly be put in place, they had confidently told her, and he would no longer be allowed anywhere near her or their 'dream house'.

That would teach him to mess with her.

He was already starting to turn nasty, now that he realised he was not going to get his own way and was making noises about instigating a claim against her for the house. Lorraine's solicitor had told her categorically that he hadn't got a cat in Hell's chance of getting anywhere with it, as it was Lorraine's sole name on the deeds. John had ploughed the best part of £200k into the extensive renovations one way or another, but she had been careful to destroy the file of receipts and invoices they had kept for the house, making sure there was no evidence of his contributions, which were mostly cash transactions. She had no intention of him seeing anything from his investment. It would be his word against hers at the end of the day. And where was his credibility after this fiasco?

When the police turned up unexpectedly at her house one day she reasonably assumed it was to give her an update about the harassment case.

Not so.

They had the audacity to accuse *her* of sending an email to some woman she had never even heard of.

They had used the words *stalking* and *hacking.*

They had warned her to be very careful about doing anything that might jeopardise her case against John.

Lorraine did not want to be portrayed as the slightly unhinged, crazy woman, hell-bent on stalking her ex. That didn't fit her desired image at all. She did not know for certain who had sent the email, but she could hazard a pretty good guess. Her money was on the wife. The cheeky bitch had not even bothered to reply to her email, and then just turned up one night on her doorstep, large as life. Lorraine still didn't know quite what to make of her, but she had a sneaking suspicion she could turn out to be more of a problem than she had originally imagined. She had made a mistake in trying to frame Lorraine with her own email though, and she would do well to watch her back from now on.

As Lorraine looked around her she began to calm down as she realised she had pretty much got rid of all traces of John from the cottage. His clothes and any other personal effects had all been placed in bin bags and put outside for him to collect. She had allowed herself to have some fun modifying them first of course. The numerous M&S polo shirts he loved now had terms of endearment such as Wanker, Dickhead, Knob, Cheat or Tosser scribbled on them in black marker pen. Other items had pieces cut out of them or buttons removed. It had been quite an enjoyable way to spend a couple of hours when she was bored one afternoon and she hoped he would appreciate the effort she had gone to.

Her eyes alighted on the box chest containing all his car documentation, the certificates of authenticity for the Vettriano paintings he had recently invested in and a load of other personal stuff of his. She thought about burning the lot, imagining his face when he found out and knowing that would really hit him where it hurt. On a practical note, however, she decided it could be worth money to her. His wife was clearly after it all for starters. She decided against burning it for the moment.

Besides, Lorraine had other ideas for making John pay.

The American Connection

Jane

Jane could not believe her ears. Matthew was clearly far more delusional than she had at first thought. They were sitting on the sofa in her living room, sharing a bottle of Rioja and discussing the 'situation'.

'I'd really like the two kids to meet,' he was saying, with a straight face. 'I'm going over to America in a week or so and I want to discuss it with Anita then. I want to arrange something soon. What do you think?'

What Jane actually thought was that it was a bloody good job she did not have a knife in her hand at that particular moment, especially when she heard him mention the name *Anita* out loud. She inhaled deeply and closed her eyes to dispel the murderous thoughts from her brain, reminding herself that their son was asleep upstairs. She had to hold it together for both their sakes, at least until after the divorce.

'I suppose it has to be done,' she conceded. 'I certainly don't want Aaron finding out about his long lost sister from anyone else. I don't trust that tart Lorraine or your bitch wife further than I can throw them. The pair of them are out to cause trouble.'

'I know. They're both so bitter and jealous. I don't understand why they can't just accept what's happened as you have so that we can all move on with our lives. What's done is done and, quite frankly, I'm actually relieved it's all out in the open now. We can't change the past, so we need to look to the future, I say,' he concluded, rather too chirpily for her liking.

'Hmm. The meeting has to be on my terms though,' Jane added, thoughtfully. 'Anita and her daughter will have to stay in a hotel nowhere near here and you must have no contact with them at all unless I'm there. You need to make it very clear to her that we are together, as a family, and all meetings happen on neutral ground. This is hard enough for me as it is.'

Matthew seemed happy enough to allow her to dictate terms, given that his negotiating position had been somewhat undermined by recent events.

'That sounds reasonable to me. And thank you for doing this. You've been amazing. You are literally the only person I can trust.'

Trust. That was exactly what Jane wanted to hear. She had made the snap decision when she first received the email from Lorraine that she would stand by Matthew, at least so far as the others were concerned, and stake her claim from the start. She had made sure she left Lorraine under no illusions as to where she came in the pecking order.

No child. No wedding ring. Bottom of the pile.

Of course, Jane did not really buy into all that nonsense Matthew had tried to feed her to keep her on his side, but it suited her to go along with it for the moment. She had been invoicing him regularly for 'work' done through her own company for several years now. It had proved to be a useful way for both of them to syphon off money from his company and far more lucrative, as far as she was concerned, than any conventional child maintenance payments. He had created a new umbrella company, Jupiter Holdings LLC, based in Delaware and large sums of money made their way over there regularly, via several other subsidiary companies, to avoid the taxman in the UK. The subsidiaries were all named predictably after the planets, but avoiding Uranus for obvious reasons, she thought with a snigger. Money circulated round them all as fast as a game of pass the parcel. Jane helped him with the company accounts and reminded herself that she had plenty of stuff she could hold him to ransom with if he did not play ball, although she had a strong suspicion there was also an awful lot she did *not* know about.

Before the email from Lorraine, Jane believed she was holding all the cards, smugly laughing at his wife behind her back, believing her to be as thick as two short planks. Jane had known all along she was 'the other woman', but she was working on that. What she hadn't bargained for was that she was not the only one with that particular job description. Matthew had played her for a fool and he would not be getting off lightly.

Jane had never heard any mention of an American woman with a child prior to the email and she was now faced with a massive problem, given that the American daughter was five or six years older than Aaron. This gave the girl seniority in status as well as age. The American partner had clearly been on the scene for a long time and Jane was concerned about how much money she may already have managed to get her hands on. She worried about the American bank accounts and this woman's access to them. It certainly appeared, from the bits she had managed to find out, that Matthew had carved out a very nice little life for himself over there with her on Rhode Island.

Rhode Island, for fuck's sake. Not exactly slumming it - she thought angrily.

Whatever else may be going on over there, she had no idea, but she needed to find out and that was why she agreed to the meeting.

'I'm doing this for Aaron, Matthew. He's confused enough as it is since he found out about *Daddy* being married to someone other than *Mummy*,' she said sarcastically.

The divorce papers had been served on him at Jane's house on Christmas Eve, which had triggered a load of questions from Aaron, given that the visitor was most definitely not dressed like Santa.

Christmas fucking Eve! That bitch!

The gloves were off now after that little stunt. If his wife (Jane could not bring herself to call her by her name) wanted a fight, she had picked the right person.

'I know, I know,' Matthew whined. 'I've said I'm sorry about all that. I had no idea she was going to do that. I will make sure you and Aaron are okay, don't worry.'

'Well, you say that, but we need to get things put in place properly. And fast. Now that the divorce is underway, everything you own will come under scrutiny. Your wife will be aiming to clean you out, you can bet on that.'

'Don't worry about her. I'm making progress with her. I reckon I can persuade her to hold off on the divorce, which will buy us some time to sort everything out.'

'I'll believe that when I see it.'

'I can assure you, she's the least of our worries. The real problem is that most of my assets are owned by the company, not me personally, and I've got the sodding taxman breathing down my neck. I'm not lying about HMRC you know. They've really got it in for me this time and they're threatening to bankrupt me. Not just the company, me personally. I'm trying to do a deal with them, but they just won't accept it, so God knows what's going to happen with that.'

'Bullshit!' she screamed. 'Do not lie to me Matthew, or I may just decide to hand over everything I have to HMRC in a gift-wrapped package. There's enough there for them to put you away behind bars for the merry dance you've been leading them all these years, never mind bankrupt you. You and I both know that you and The Company are very much one and the same thing and you have never been one for sticking to the usual rules of business practice, shall we say?'

Matthew stood up abruptly and began pacing around in irritation.

'Look, Jane, I don't know what the hell you want from me. I've told you I'll see you right, and I will. I don't need any more fucking pressure.'

He was clearly riled. He deserved to be. Jane was not letting him off the hook that easily.

'You have a collection of several high end and very collectable cars, not to mention the motorcycles and the artwork. I *know* how much all that is worth. Between HMRC and your wife, the vultures are circling and you need to think about providing for your son. You need to transfer as many things as possible into *my* name and you need to do it fast because from where I'm standing, it looks to me like I'm your only chance of hanging onto anything at all. Surely you would prefer *me* to have things rather than have them snatched by the taxman or your wife? Keep it in the family, so to speak?'

Matthew looked at the woman in front of him with barely disguised revulsion. He needed her to stop banging on at him. What the hell had he been thinking, allowing her to know so much about his business? She was just another one in the growing list of people trying to bleed him dry. He didn't deserve any of this, he thought bitterly to himself, but he couldn't get away from the fact that the money-grabbing bitch had his balls in a vice.

By the end of the evening, they had forged and backdated several documents, resulting in Jane 'owning' (she failed to spot the get-out clause in the small print) a Ferrari, a BMW convertible and a VW Beetle, which she thought would potentially be quite a cool first car for Aaron in the future. Not a bad few hours work as far as she was concerned. She had rented a storage facility nearby for her new cars and taken out insurance on them in her name only. That should ensure it all stood up in court if it ever came to that. She gave herself a pat on the back for her thoroughness. Jane had no intention of scrabbling around for the scraps of whatever was left after the scavengers of divorce and bankruptcy had picked everything over.

She turned the conversation to the numerous bank accounts she knew he had on the go. It was imperative to get as much money as possible abroad and to be creative with the invoicing. 'You need to move money around and close accounts wherever possible. Once the money has disappeared, it will be virtually impossible to do anything about it from the UK, especially given the secrecy and high levels of security surrounding Delaware.'

Matthew agreed with her in principle and liked the idea of thwarting both the taxman and his wife. What he did not agree with was letting Jane get her hands on too much or know too much about what he was doing. Who did she think she was anyway, talking to him as though he was some sort of clueless idiot? He informed her in no uncertain terms that he would deal with the bank accounts himself, as he saw fit.

Pushy cow.

She had already squeezed more than enough out of him in his opinion. Mother of his child or not, she had let herself go in the last few years and there was no way he was going to be saddled with *her* on a long term basis.

Jane was playing a dangerous game and, as he listened to her incessant nagging, he thought she would do well not to push him too far if she knew what was good for her.

The surprise

Everything you see is real, but not everyone you know is true.

Grace

The room immediately in front of me as I reached the top of the stairs in Daniel's Channing Street 'office' was the kitchen. I glanced to the left and saw a door leading into what appeared to be the lounge, another set of stairs up to the top floor and a door leading into the bathroom. I peeked cautiously into the bathroom and, hanging from the bathroom mirror, was some sort of fancy dress, red devil's horns on a headband, a cat's mask and a long black cat's tail. I screwed my face up as an unwelcome image of Lorraine or Jane wearing them came into my mind, but I quickly reminded myself that Lorraine at least claimed never to have set foot in there.

Interesting.

I forced myself to be methodical and decided to start with the kitchen. It was a compact, square-shaped room and was surprisingly clean and tidy. There was an iron in the corner on the work surface and my first thought was that I had never known Daniel to iron anything, or indeed to do any other form of housework, in his life. The units were a bog-standard, pale grey colour, cheap-looking, and the room was equipped with the basics of a washing machine, fridge and dishwasher. I opened the fridge door and inspected the contents, but there was not much in there except half a dozen bottles of Oyster Bay, Sauvignon Blanc, Daniel's favourite white wine.

I turned my attention to the units, pulled open one of the drawers with my latex-gloved hand and rummaged around furtively. There was a torn, brown envelope full of smiley-faced condoms in assorted colours, with some of them spilled out in the bottom of the drawer. They looked like kids' balloons and I curled my lip with distaste as I remembered how Daniel had always said he hated wearing condoms.

Right at the back of the drawer, just as I had hoped, was a spare set of keys to the flat. I snatched them out of the drawer and went straight back downstairs to check them in the door. Bingo!

My next job was to get them copied. I had no idea what I would find in the flat or whether I would need to go back there, so I had decided in advance that I needed my own set of keys if at all possible. I had of course planned to have the key from the letting agent copied, but that idea was down the pan thanks to the unexpected problem of the second lock.

There was another very important consideration. I needed to make absolutely sure that Daniel had no idea I had been in there, for my own safety, so that meant locking up properly when I left. Whatever I did or did not find, he had gone to great pains to hide something and I was pretty sure he would not take kindly to me snooping around in there. The hardware shop on the corner did key cutting, but it was out of the question to go there, especially after my previous visit. I did a quick Google search and, minutes later, I left the flat locking the door carefully behind me and headed up into the little shopping centre to find Timpsons.

Half an hour later, I had my own shiny new set of keys in my hand and I began to relax. I would now be able to lock the door properly behind me and come and go as I pleased, invisibly, at least until Daniel came back from America. I checked that the keys worked, and then drove back to the letting agent to return their key and retrieve my passport.

It was a long-winded and tedious process, but an essential one and, once I had covered the basics, I could get back on track with my mission.

As soon as I was safely in the flat, I locked myself in and left the key in the lock. No harm in being extra cautious. I returned to the kitchen and began systematically going through everything, starting with the bin, thankful I had had the foresight to buy the box of latex gloves. Satisfied there was nothing of interest in there, having carefully analysed the various dirty food containers, old receipts and wrappers, I moved on to the washing machine. Reaching inside I pulled out a crumpled item of clothing and it took me a few moments to work out what exactly it was. I could not help laughing out loud as I realised I was holding a very large pair of pale pink bloomers, the ones old ladies used to wear, probably still do. Elasticated waist and down to the knee with a little lace frill around each leg. I held them up in front of me, pulling on the elastic to see the full expansion potential and spluttering with laughter at the vision that popped into my head. These must have been worn by Jane in some weird kind of role play, I decided, thinking they would be a perfect fit, judging from the size of her in the photos I had seen. The bloomers were enormous. I remembered the general hilarity at Adam's comment in the hotel when we first began stalking Jane on Facebook.

'Wow! So Daniel is, in fact, a closet chubby chaser. No wonder he left you.'

At least I had the satisfaction of knowing I would always compare favourably there. Not that the bar was set very high.

Another thought crossed my mind that maybe Daniel had developed some kind of weird granny fetish. I had heard jokes about the various websites that existed to cater for all tastes these days, and told myself that just about anything was possible where he was concerned.

I laid out the bloomers on the worktop and photographed them. In fact, I set about photographing pretty much everything in there, including the contents of the drawers, the bin and the fridge. I was pretty sure that was what any PI or SOCO worth their salt would do. I planned to document it all so that I would have a detailed record in case I forgot anything later. I could not help a little snigger, thinking to myself that there was no way I would be forgetting those bloomers anytime soon.

Ready to move on, I bundled the bloomers back into the washing machine and made sure everything was replaced just as I had found it, including the original keys at the back of the drawer. I had the bit between my teeth and was eager to see what other surprises the flat would offer up in my quest for the increasingly elusive truth.

I headed into the lounge. Despite the fact I was alone and not likely to be disturbed, I felt the need to tiptoe around in my stocking feet like a cat burglar. I stopped and took a moment to assess my surroundings.

There were two small sofas arranged in an L shape and a desk in one corner under the window, covered with messy piles of papers as if someone had been rummaging around looking for something. I wondered for a moment whether someone could have got there before me and ransacked the place, but decided on reflection that it was pretty typical of Daniel's generally chaotic approach to filing and paperwork. In the other corner of the room was a smaller desk with a computer and more papers piled up on it. There were boxes and bags all over the place, some containing files and others containing assorted personal effects. I assumed it was more of the stuff Lorraine had told me she had thrown out of her house for Daniel to collect. I was leaving no stone unturned and everything would have to be carefully sifted through and photographed. The task I had set myself was already beginning to overwhelm me, but I had to press on. I reminded myself that I could always come back, as I casually picked up a card on the small desk. It was from Stephanie, the 'friend' Daniel had told me about.

Some friend - I thought to myself as I read it.

My darling Dan,

Thank you so much for the wonderful few days in Venice and for spoiling me rotten. Can't wait to see you again.

Love and hugs,
Stephi xx

Unbelievable.

He had taken her away to Venice on some sort of a dirty weekend, somewhere in between declaring undying love for Lorraine, spending time with Jane and his son and starting to make overtures to me again. Oh and, of course, going bankrupt.

Liar, liar, pants on fire. He just couldn't help himself.

And what was with *Dan?* He hated his name being shortened and always insisted on people calling him *Daniel.* I was not sure why I felt so affronted on his behalf.

I photographed the card and replaced it where I had found it. Then, on an impulse, I changed my mind, ripped it angrily into pieces and shoved the bits into the bottom of my bag.

There were other older cards piled together in a bag: a Valentine card from Jane and a Father's Day card from Aaron.

For a few moments, I was lost in my thoughts, as I imagined Jane helping her son to choose all the cards over the years and write the messages to his daddy in his scrawling child's handwriting. I wondered what it felt like to have a little person in your life who depended on you for everything, came to you for comfort when they were hurting, spontaneously hugged you, just for being Mummy....

He had robbed me of the chance to know that feeling and I would never ever be able to forgive him for it. I snapped my mind back to the present, knowing that if I went down that particular rabbit hole I would never get out.

I looked inside one of the boxes near the desk and moved the contents around, then pulled my hand back sharply as if I had been bitten. I wrinkled my nose in disgust as I realised what was in there and began to remove the items one by one for photographing, holding them at arm's length, as if I might catch something from them. Underneath a layer of innocuous stationery items, there was a collection of dildos of varying sizes and colours, a pair of black PVC pants with a butt plug attached on the inside (I knew all about such things since reading Fifty Shades of Grey), a lime green mini butt plug still in its packaging, some sort of paddle thing, presumably for smacking, a feather tickling thing that made me think of Ken Dodd, and a heavy-duty black leather collar covered in metal spikes with a chain attached. Further in-depth rummaging revealed *more* butt plugs, an assortment of masks, nipple clamps and clitoris clamps, the very thought of which made my eyes water. I was repulsed and yet strangely fascinated by this new insight into the secret life of my husband (lives plural, I reminded myself).

I felt increasingly like a pathologist as I neatly laid out my evidence and took my photos. Pretending I was here to do a job was the only way I could get through this. My eye was drawn back to the sofa and a couple of gift bags with Disney images on them. I carefully pulled out some boy's T-shirts, blue and red, with superhero motifs on the front. I read the messages on the label and was powerless to stop an overwhelming sadness invading my mind.

To Munchkin, with lots of love from Daddy xxxx

Bitter tears sprang to my eyes at the unfairness of it all. These were the things that could bring me to my knees and drag me down into the darkest of places. Not the boxes of sex toys. Not his trips to Venice or anywhere else with other women. Not his pathetic attempts to hide his money from me. Just something as simple as that little message and a father's affectionate nickname for his child.

I wiped away the tears roughly with my sleeve and hurriedly shoved everything back where it belonged, determined to stay strong.

Slowly I moved over to the large desk by the window. Time for something a bit less personal. The first thing I picked up was a bill of sale for a Ferrari. I knew Daniel had recently imported that particular car from the US as he had told me all about it when we were out for dinner one night with Frieda and James. He had been showing off to them as usual with the photos of all his cars and I remembered thinking it actually looked a bit tacky with its red leather interior. He had said it was due to come into the country just before Christmas, which would have been just after the email sent everything into turmoil.

I felt the fury rising in me like the rumbling of a volcano, as I stared at the names and signatures on the bill of sale. Jane Sutcliffe's name and paw print were all over it, with no mention of Daniel anywhere. I had to fight to stop my temper getting the better of me as I realised what was going on. Smashing the place up would get me nowhere. I had to be smarter than that. Clearly, they were in this together, beavering away behind the scenes, transferring assets to her name to put them out of my reach in the divorce court.

They were obviously trying to stitch me up and I was pretty sure the Court took a dim view of that sort of behaviour, but I needed proof of what they were doing if I was going to have any chance of stopping them getting away with it. I realised the bill of sale was only a tiny part of the jigsaw and meant nothing unless I could find the original one in Daniel's name, which would prove they were trying to pull a fast one. Nevertheless, I had to believe the rest of the pieces would come together if I did not give up. The shipping documents and the insurance certificate were all there with the bill of sale. All in her name. They clearly thought they were so incredibly clever, but both of them were going to learn the hard way that they had massively underestimated me.

Despite my earlier resolve to be methodical I was too angry about this latest discovery to think clearly and stepped back from the desk. Suddenly, I felt a compelling and overwhelming desire to see what was going on in the bedroom upstairs, the room I had subconsciously been avoiding.

I marched up the stairs, and then stopped dead in the doorway, looking around, unwilling to go in straight away. I stared at a full-length mirror opposite the entrance, which had several long women's nighties draped over it and a couple of long whips leaning against it that looked remarkably like my dressage whips. I could see two tall chests of drawers to one side in a little alcove and a double bed in the middle of the room. The walls were painted a non-descript, magnolia colour like the rest of the flat and there were net curtains at the window. It all looked dated and more than a little grubby. I wrinkled my nose as I stepped inside and detected a slightly unpleasant, musty smell.

The double bed was made up with white satin bed linen.

Tacky.

I immediately recognised Daniel's small holdall on top of the bed. There was no mistaking it because I had made it myself from one of our old racing sails and had given it to him for Christmas the year before. Beside the holdall on the bed were a couple of car magazines and an old fashioned, large-sized woman's corset that would have looked more at home in Queen Victoria's era, with red stockings attached to the suspenders.

Who the hell wears red stockings? More to the point, who wears a corset-like that these days?

I tentatively peeled back a corner of the duvet to reveal more stockings stuffed down the bed, black this time, screwed up in a ball as if they had been taken off in a hurry. The bed looked like it hadn't been changed in a while and I noticed a bottle of water and a half-empty wine glass on the bedside table. I pulled the duvet back up towards the pillow, glad once again of my latex gloves, and went over to the chests of drawers in the corner, carefully avoiding the suspicious stain on the carpet.

One by one I opened the drawers and found them all in the same jumbled and messy state. They were crammed full of oversized, women's underwear and a load of extra-large stockings, still in their packs. The material of the underwear looked cheap, involving a lot of lace, net and nylon and it struck me how random the selection was, from heavy-duty, old fashioned corsets and bloomers to crotchless pants and peephole bras. The colours were garish and there were a lot of bright reds and shocking pinks, mingled with animal print. No self-respecting woman would have been seen dead in any of it unless she was working the streets, I decided disdainfully. I thought, with a certain amount of smugness, of my own underwear drawer, with its neatly arranged, matching sets from Agent Provocateur and La Perla. At least I could hold my head high if anyone decided to go rummaging through *my* knicker drawers.

I turned my attention back to Daniel's sex den. All the stuff I found was massive, clearly pointing to his apparent penchant for larger ladies.

Jane. Had to be.

One of the top drawers was packed full of G-strings, several of them with rows of large beads attached to the string at the back. I could not imagine that was particularly comfortable but, then again, I decided that probably wasn't the point.

Some of the stuff was just plain weird, like the white lacy, sequinned tutu skirt I found amongst the corsets. I imagined Jane cavorting around the room in it like a baby elephant, which cheered me up no end.

My amusement was cut short, however, when I opened the third drawer down of the second chest, expecting more of the same.

Not so. The contents were very different indeed. Once again Daniel had managed to pull a rabbit out of the hat, even in his absence.

I stared in stunned silence, trying to make sense of the neatly arranged pairs of silicone breasts I saw in front of me, all different sizes and assorted colours.

Nothing could have prepared me for that.

Slowly I poked one with my finger and watched the indent disappear from the soft tissue. I picked one up, bouncing it in my hand, and was surprised at the weight of it. I squeezed it and it felt almost real. I dropped it like a hot potato, suddenly repulsed, but my eyes remained fixed on the contents of that drawer.

I was confused at the thoughts racing around in my head.

Why the hell would Jane need silicone breasts? From the pictures I had seen, she was not exactly behind the door when tits were handed out.

More to the point, why would any woman need such a large and varied assortment of false boobs? I had counted ten pairs.

Slowly the penny began to drop.

What if it wasn't a woman who was wearing them or, in fact, any of the other gear in there?

What if it were a man?

What if it were Daniel?

I banged the drawer shut abruptly and sank onto the floor, leaning against the wall with my hands over my face. I was starting to feel like I really couldn't cope with any more. I took out my phone, suddenly remembering I had forgotten to take photos, and decided to call Sylvie. I had not told anyone I was visiting Stainsford, so she had no idea where I was when she answered.

'Hi darling, are you okay?'

'Hi, yes I'm fine, but listen…I'm in Stainsford. I'm in Daniel's office.'

'On your own? Why didn't you tell me? It's too dangerous! You know I would have come with you,' she cried, clearly horrified.

'I know, I know. Don't panic, I'm fine, really I am. I just needed to do this by myself.'

She was reassured for the moment and continued in an excited voice:

'So come on then, don't keep me in suspense. What have you found?'

'Well, I've found quite a lot actually, a lot more than I bargained for in fact. Listen, Sylvie. You're just not going to believe it….'

I paused briefly, deciding to leave out the earlier details and skip straight to the juicy bit.

'There's a bedroom upstairs and I swear there's enough women's outsize underwear in it to sink a battleship. Really gross, tacky stuff.'

'Oh my God. Do you think he's got more women living there?'

'No, I do not. I think he's wearing the stuff himself.'

'What? Are you serious? Why do you think that?'

I paused, trying to process things and make some sense of the confusion in my own head, desperately trying to come to terms with the enormity of what I was saying.

'In one of the drawers, I found about ten pairs of false boobs. Christ, Sylvie, I honestly don't know what to think anymore. Daniel has always acted so macho, a real man's man….'

Sylvie gasped in surprise, but her words when she eventually spoke made me thank God yet again for my amazing friends.

'Right, stay there, I'm coming over. You shouldn't be on your own there. I don't know what the hell's going on, but I'm coming down there now,' she informed me decisively.

'I'm okay, I promise. It's just a massive shock. Daniel's in America, so I'm not in any danger from him. You really don't need to drive all the way over here.'

'I don't care. I'm coming down. Keep the door locked and stay where you are. I'll be there in about an hour.'

Despite my protestations, I was relieved she was coming to meet me. I desperately needed someone to confirm what I had seen and what I thought was the latest twist in the plot.

My husband, the cross-dresser. Who knew? I no longer had any idea where the hell I had ever fitted into his complex story.

I stayed where I was on the floor and closed my eyes.

My mind drifted back to an evening many years ago, when Daniel and I were first married. We had been out celebrating something or other and we were both a bit the worse for wear. As I undressed in the bedroom he lay on the bed watching me. He whistled appreciatively at the leopard print satin bra and knickers he had bought me, together with matching suspender belt and fishnet stockings of course. Suspenders and stockings were always his thing.

'Very sexy,' he slurred.

I did an exaggerated model's pose and pouted my lips at him. He was looking at me strangely and I giggled.

'What does it feel like to wear all that stuff?' he asked. 'I bet the satin feels good against your skin.'

He licked his lips and paused before continuing.

'Maybe I should try it, just to see?'

I laughed, putting it down to the drink.

'I don't think my stuff would fit you, do you? We're not exactly the same size!'

I discarded the underwear on the floor, thinking to myself as I disappeared into the en suite that I had only worn it to humour him and it would not be seeing the light of day again. He had even got my bra size wrong, for God's sake. When I came out, I was greeted by the somewhat surreal and bizarre vision of Daniel, who had squeezed himself into my knickers and suspender belt, testing the lycra to its limit. He had even managed to fasten the bra himself, which on reflection suggested a worrying degree of familiarity with a notoriously tricky garment. He was imitating my pose from before. At six foot two, weighing just under a hundred kilos and nurturing a beer belly, he was not the most convincing glamour model.

I exploded with laughter at the spectacle before me, assuming that was the point.

'Oh my God, hilarious. Not your best look to be honest,' I mocked.

Not to be deterred, he insisted on wearing his new get up to make love to me that night. It had all seemed hilariously funny at the time.

I shuddered at the memory of how aroused he had been. It had never happened again and had all been forgotten in the cold light of day when we were sober again, but maybe I should have seen the writing on the wall. The clues were there but, once again, I had seen only what I wanted to see.

True to her word, Sylvie arrived at the flat after about an hour and a half. To my amazement, I had fallen asleep on the floor, mentally exhausted. I was shocked back into reality by the shrill ring of my mobile and Sylvie's voice when I picked up.

'Hi, it's me. I'm parked up on the street outside the hardware shop like you said. Where do I go now?'

'Okay, leave the car there and walk along the street until you come to a little alleyway leading round the back of the flats. Turn left and you'll see me.'

A couple of minutes later I was showing her around the flat like an over-enthusiastic estate agent, saving the best until last of course. She wanted to see everything. We looked in the boxes in the lounge, marvelling at the huge variety of dildos and butt plugs that seemed to be available on the market and trying to work out what some of the more obscure stuff would actually be used for. We looked at some of the papers and took more photos, but I was exhausted and decided I would need to come back the following day with someone a bit more tech-savvy to really get to grips with all that. We agreed that Adam's friend Liam, who did all the IT stuff for the hotel, was probably the man for the job. Once again, Adam seemed to know a man for everything. Memory sticks were lying around that needed investigating and copying, together with a go-pro camera on a shelf and an SLR camera in a cupboard. I was more than slightly nervous about what I would find stored on those, but I had to be 'professional'. Liam would also be able to scan all the documents I wanted, rather than just take photos.

I could contain myself no longer as I turned to Sylvie and said in a conspiratorial tone:

'Come on, shall we go up to the bedroom now?'

I led the way to the stairs, feeling much braver now that I had an ally.

Back in the bedroom, I showed Sylvie everything I had found already, but two pairs of eyes were always better than one and together we were able to conduct a more in-depth search of the room. It was already starting to go dark and the dingy light from the overhead lamp made the room look even worse. I went through the laundry basket, looked under and behind the chests of drawers, under the bed, in the bed, literally everywhere. I had no idea what I was looking for anymore, but I felt sure I would know when I found it.

'Did you look inside the base of the bed?' Sylvie asked.

'What?'

I followed where she was pointing and, at the end of the bed, I could clearly see tabs sticking out.

'Oh my God, this bed lifts up. How the hell did I miss that? Let's see what's in there.'

Together we yanked the mattress up on its gas struts and peered inside. Sylvie immediately let out a high pitched scream and jumped back, turning her head away. Startled by her reaction as well as what I saw in there, I screamed even louder and stumbled backwards, falling over her foot and clutching at her arm in fear.

'Fuck! It's a body!' I shrieked, as my hand flew instinctively to my mouth.

The grotesque, headless body of a woman was lying there in state, dressed in a long red satin nightie and surrounded by untidy piles of more cheap and tacky underwear, just like all the other stuff in the drawers.

Sylvie suddenly began to giggle uncontrollably, as she always did when she was nervous. I remembered the Land Rover incident when we first went to see Lorraine. I forced myself to look again and slumped against Sylvie in relief.

'Jesus, I really thought that was a dead body!'

My heart was still thumping hard against my ribs, but I could now see for sure that the 'body' was actually a life-size mannequin and not a decapitated murder victim, as we had initially thought.

I edged forward, knelt by the bed and gently lifted her nightie to see what she had on underneath. It felt like a violation of her privacy, but it had to be done. I wanted to know everything. She was wearing white bloomers, similar to the pink ones lurking in the washing machine, a suspender belt and black fishnet stockings. I refrained from pulling down her bloomers, feeling pretty sure she would have orifices in all the right places. A black, lacy peephole bra held her buxom silicone breasts in place. I pulled down the nightie to preserve what little dignity she had left.

'That's gross! Why is there no head, for God's sake? Christ, Sylvie, this is just horrendous. I can't believe I was actually married to Daniel for all that time and yet I had no idea who he really was. How the hell could this all have been going on behind my back? How could I not know? How is that possible?'

Suddenly it was too much to handle and I began to sob uncontrollably at the enormity of it all. Tears of anger at all the lies and deceit. Tears of frustration at all the wasted years. Tears of mourning for my babies that would never be. Tears of bitterness at the way I had unknowingly provided a respectable 'front' for Daniel to hide behind, only to be tossed aside like rubbish as soon as I was no longer of use.

I thought then that I had reached rock bottom. I thought that was as bad as it could get.

I was wrong.

The worst of times

*If you seek to destroy someone's life with a lie,
remember that yours could so easily be destroyed
with the truth.*

Grace

After the discovery of the 'body in the bed' and my subsequent meltdown, we decided to call it a day and get the hell out of 12b Channing Street. That address would haunt me for the rest of my life. Sylvie insisted I went back to the hotel with her for something to eat and, of course, to dissect all of this new information with Adam, Andrew and Melissa.

Adam listened, enthralled, then thumped his fist down hard on the table and laughed out loud.

'Ha! What did I tell you? I always knew there was something not right about him. What do you reckon Dad?'

Andrew nodded sagely.

'I've always said there are only two things in this world that make you any serious money: drugs and sex. With what you've just told me, I think Daniel's money is coming from the sex industry. My betting is he's got himself into quite a niche market down there and is doing very nicely thank you. It would certainly explain the wad of cash he always has on him.'

I didn't know what to say to that. I was busy struggling to come to terms with the fact that most of my adult life had been built around an elaborate lie, never mind the fact that my husband was quite possibly making dirty money out of some pervy sex scene he had going on.

'I don't know what to think anymore. I still keep thinking about that guy in the key shop near his flat. You know the one who said he thought Daniel was gay? Do you think he's seen him with other men? There's that seedy-looking hotel on the corner opposite the shop that looks like it rents rooms by the hour. Maybe Daniel's been going in there with men. What do you think?'

Adam laughed again.

'Anything's possible. Daniel the rent boy in his spare time. Fucking hilarious.'

I was not quite ready to see the funny side of it all.

Sylvie looked at me sympathetically as she spoke.

'Look, darling, this must be so difficult for you. We're joking about it, but it's your actual life.'

She flashed a warning look at her husband and son.

'I don't think we need to analyse it all too much tonight. At the end of the day, it takes all sorts in this world. To be honest, I don't have a problem with him cross-dressing. I actually feel sorry for him if he really is trapped in the wrong body. What I *do* have a problem with is him lying to you all these years. Using you. Stopping you having children and then having them himself with other women. All that stuff is unforgivable and just plain cruel in my opinion,' she said gently.

Andrew saw that I was close to tears again and took hold of my hand.

'She's right. He's treated you abysmally and you have to remember you didn't deserve any of it. None of this is your fault. At the end of the day, he should have just let you go a long time ago so you could get on with your life. Or, at the very least, he should have been honest with you. I have no respect for him at all for the way he has conducted himself. The fact that he is now trying to leave you with nothing financially makes me despise him even more but, at the end of the day, like we keep telling you, it's time for you to toughen up and stop the tears. It's time to accept what's happened and hit back hard. Crying will get you nowhere. He sure as hell doesn't care about you so you need to box clever now.'

Adam nodded his head in agreement, but he was no longer laughing.

'I agree with Dad, no more tears. But all joking apart, I think this whole cross-dressing business changes the goalposts. I'm not happy about you being at the house alone with Daniel anymore. Are you absolutely sure he won't know you've been in the flat?'

I thought for a moment before replying.

'As sure as I can be. I covered my tracks carefully and made sure I replaced everything exactly as I found it. The only slight worry is the alarm. I used the fob from the letting agent to turn it off when I first went in, but I don't know whether it links somehow to his phone, or if there was a camera on it…I couldn't see one, but I can't be certain.'

Adam continued, his face deadly serious, 'Liam will check that tomorrow. The point I'm making is that Daniel has gone to great lengths to keep this part of his life a secret from you. If he finds out you've busted him, there's no telling what he might do. I've told you before, I think the man's a psychopath. He's dangerous and he's unpredictable.'

'Oh come on, Adam, 'psychopath' is a bit strong isn't it?' I said, pulling a face.

'No, I don't think it is. Melissa and I were watching this programme on TV the other night called Meet the Psychopaths and it was scary, I'm telling you. There's apparently no real clinical difference between a sociopath and a psychopath. They both have what you call an Antisocial Personality Disorder. They don't care who they hurt. They show no empathy towards other people. They constantly lie and deceive others. They feel no guilt; show no remorse…recognise anyone?'

Adam paused to let that sink in before continuing, clearly fascinated by the topic.

'Apparently, not all psychopaths are violent, but that doesn't mean they won't *become* violent if pushed too far. Seriously, it was a hell of an eye-opener. If you ask me, you need to be very careful from now on. Go home tonight and do your own research. You'll be shocked.'

'Christ Adam, you're really freaking me out. I'm going to be terrified in that house on my own now, never mind when Daniel is there.'

'Look, sweetheart, I'm not trying to scare you. I just want to be sure you understand what you're dealing with here. Daniel's psyche is clearly very complex indeed and I just don't think you should underestimate how he might react. I mean it. The two main rules are: don't believe a word he says and watch your back. He has built up this 'respectable' version of himself and that's what he wants people to see. All the other stuff happens behind closed doors and in secret. I'm betting he will do literally *anything* to protect that secret.'

Later that night I lay in bed in the spare room that I had made my own since the split. I stared at the ceiling, wide awake, mulling over the events of the day that had rocked my world all over again.

Lola lay in her basket on the floor by the bed, snoring loudly. I smiled to myself, thinking that she was almost worse than Daniel. I wondered briefly why, when it was the dog snoring somehow it didn't matter, but when Daniel started, I immediately had an urge to put a pillow over his face and press down hard until he stopped breathing altogether.

I had taken to allowing Lola to sleep in my bedroom these days, as it felt safer for both of us. Not that she would ever have made the grade as a guard dog. I pushed my hand under the pillow and felt the comforting handle of the serrated-edge diver's knife I now kept there permanently. I had bought it as a spare for the boat a while ago. We always kept one strapped to the boom, as all race boats tend to do, to be used as a get out of jail free card and cut ropes if we really got into trouble. It was razor-sharp and more than man enough for the job, should I need to use it in self-defence against my husband.

My wandering thoughts turned to where I would stab him if I had to and I decided it would most probably be in the neck. There would be a lot of blood though. I would be covered in it. Did I really have the stomach for that? The jury was out on that one.

Maybe I should be thinking outside the box. I always seemed to be on the defensive, always reacting to something that might happen to me. Maybe it was time I took charge and got rid of Daniel before he tried to get rid of me. I knew my imagination was running away with me, but I couldn't stop this new train of thought, which was rapidly gaining momentum. I began to rack my brains for a cleaner way of killing my husband. A way that did not involve a lot of messy blood and, more importantly, a way that would not mean I ended up rotting in prison for murder. Obviously, I couldn't let that happen.

It was freezing cold outside and I remembered how I had slipped earlier on the ice on our uneven, stone steps. Daniel was not particularly good with steps since the helicopter crash and ours were lethal at the best of times. What if I poured water on the steps in time for it to freeze before he came to visit on one of our special Tuesday dates? The plan was not fool-proof of course, as there was no guarantee he would actually slip and no guarantee he would die from the fall, even if he did slip. It was certainly worth considering though. I could always be lurking in the shadows, ready to give him a helpful shove in the right direction, which would be downwards of course. I smiled to myself as I conjured up an image of him lying at the bottom of the steps, limbs broken and twisted, writhing in agony and pleading with me to help him. I imagined myself bending over him, seeing the look of relief on his face as he thought I was rushing to his aid, and then savouring the moment his look turned to despair as he realised I was no good Samaritan. I saw myself smiling sweetly, as I gently took his mobile out of his pocket to drop it on the floor near his car, well out of his reach, before simply driving away and leaving him to freeze to death overnight. Hopefully slowly. And in excruciating pain. A perfect crime.

I came abruptly to my senses and shuddered at my own callousness.

- What the hell happened to me?

- What sort of a monster had I become?

I woke up the following morning with a splitting headache. Lola was whining to go out, so I was forced to drag myself out of bed and downstairs. Business as usual. I made coffee and downed some painkillers before heading over to the hotel to meet Liam. Today was an important day of espionage and I needed to sharpen my mind.

A quick check of the tracker before I left reassured me that Daniel was not going to be posing a threat to my plans. What I hadn't banked on was an unforeseen problem with Liam's pregnant wife, which meant that we had to put off our visit until the following day. I tried not to panic, but I was desperate to get back to the flat as quickly as possible and do what needed to be done, in case Daniel's US visit proved to be a fleeting one. You never could tell with him.

I had no choice but to wait.

The following day we set off early, having checked the tracker again. Still no movement on *Daniel 1*, but I made a mental note to keep looking at regular intervals. I could not afford any slip-ups. There was none of the drama of the previous visit and it felt good to be able to turn up at the flat and let myself in with my own keys this time.

Liam laughed as I insisted he removed his shoes and put on the old pair of Daniel's slippers I had brought with me for him to wear.

'This is not CSI Miami you know,' he said, humouring me by putting them on anyway.

'No harm in being careful,' I retorted, removing my own shoes and handing him a pair of latex gloves.

The first thing on the agenda to tackle was the alarm. I had not re-set it when I left, having returned the only fob to the letting agent, but I was anxious for Liam to take a look at it. To my immense relief, he seemed confident it was not a problem.

'Nothing to worry about there as far as I can see. It looks a pretty basic affair, certainly no camera.'

'Great, I thought so.'

'Won't he wonder why the alarm isn't set though?'

'Maybe. I'm just banking on there being so much going on in his life at the moment that he will assume he forgot, or think it's faulty. There's nothing I can do about it in any case. I searched everywhere and I couldn't find a spare fob.'

'Okay, forget it then. Where shall we start?'

Two hours later, Liam was still systematically scanning documents and copying various USB sticks and camera memory cards onto the Maxtor disk drive attached to my laptop. Meanwhile, I busied myself rummaging through more boxes and cupboards, making sure I missed nothing. I was beginning to wonder just how much women's underwear one man needed in his life. There were dozens of unopened packages around and I noticed to my great indignation that many of them were actually addressed to *me*. I ripped a few of them open and noticed that the underwear was second hand, probably from eBay sellers. I had heard about people selling used underwear, unwashed even, but would never have imagined in a million years that my husband was buying stuff like that behind my back. Especially not in my bloody name! I shoved the packages back where they belonged. There were so many of them that I was confident Daniel would never know whether he had opened them himself or not.

Liam interrupted my rummaging.

'Do you want all these photos copied? There're thousands of them and I'm not sure they're any real use to you.'

'Yes, I want everything. I'll go through it all in my own time at home and decide for myself what I need to keep.'

'I'm just not sure it will do you any good looking at some of these. There are a lot of family photos that I think will be hurtful,' he persisted.

It was sweet that he was trying to protect me, but it was far too late for that.

'Liam, I'm tougher than I look and I promise you I want to see it all. I *need* to see it all.'

I walked over to where he was sitting, hunched over my laptop. I understood what he meant as I looked at the thumbnails on the screen. Photos of a Christening, with Daniel holding a baby and smiling proudly. Family holiday snaps. Eating ice cream on a beach. Children's parties. Disney World….

I looked away. My husband. The one who never wanted children. The one who always insisted he would be a terrible father. That was not what it looked like to me. It looked to me like he was going for the Daddy of the Year title.

'Please Liam, just do it. I don't need protection from this. I need to know who my husband really is,' I said firmly.

It was another hour at least before he finished. I knew he would be curious about the other stuff Sylvie and I had found and I was keen to give him the full tour. In fact, I could hardly contain myself.

'Do you want to see in the bedroom then?'

Of course he did.

I led the way, showing him the highlights and building up to the glorious finale with a certain amount of dramatic effect. I pointed to the third drawer in the chest.

'Open that.'

I folded my arms and stood back, waiting in silence for his reaction. Liam's face remained impassive, eyebrows raised.

'Well, there's something you don't see every day,' he announced, candidly.

His voice was so calm and matter of fact, I burst out laughing.

'Talk about stating the obvious! I can always count on you to lighten the mood.'

'Always glad to be of service. What's in the bag there?'

He gestured towards the holdall on the bed.

'Don't know. I got distracted with the 'body in the bed' situation last night.'

I laughed again and opened the sailing bag I had painstakingly made for Daniel, remembering how much effort it had taken and how I had persevered time and again when the needle kept breaking, all because I wanted to do something special for him. Inside was a random selection of underwear, including a couple of the beaded G-strings, a pair of false 'travel boobs' and a pair of black patent court shoes. I picked up one of the shoes and looked at the sole. Size 11.

I found myself feeling ridiculously insulted by what he was using the bag for. As if that were the biggest thing to worry about here.

I closed the zip and looked more carefully around the bed. On the floor, I could see another pair of shoes. These were peep toe, with a medium heel and covered in a bronze sparkly material. Also size 11. Daniel's shoe size. I was no longer shocked by anything I found. This was my new normal.

I suddenly realised we had been there over four hours and felt instantly unnerved.

'I need to check the tracker.'

My heart was racing as I ran downstairs and opened my laptop. I typed in the password and waited for the GPS to update. To my utter horror and disbelief, *Daniel 1* was flashing green, which meant it was on the move. I began to panic.

'Shit Liam, we need to get out of here, fast.'

Liam looked over my shoulder at the map on the screen and the little green cursor.

'Right, well first of all stop panicking. He is obviously back in the country and it looks like he's driving towards here, but looking at where he is on the road it will take him an hour to get here, at least. We've got plenty of time.'

'You've copied everything, right?'

'Everything I could, yes.'

'And I've still got my keys if I need to come back.'

'You don't need to come back, trust me. You need to stay well away from here now. It's far too risky to come back. Remember we can't be one hundred percent sure he won't know you've been here.'

I knew he was right, but in my own mind I did not rule out the possibility of a return visit. We took one last look around in each room to make sure we had left no trace of our presence, before going down the stairs, stepping carefully over the bin bags still piled in the doorway and locking the front door. I hoped no nosey neighbours were watching our comings and goings, but I was also pretty sure this was the sort of area where people kept themselves to themselves and didn't ask questions.

Outside the sun was shining and it felt strangely normal to be there. I smiled to myself and felt happy that at least I had something to work with now. I had a lot more pieces of the jigsaw in my possession and hopefully, some of them would turn out to be key pieces.

A couple of hours later, Liam dropped me off at the house and I sat down at the kitchen table with Lola watching me curiously from her basket. I opened my laptop, keen to begin the mammoth task of sifting through all the material Liam had saved for me.

I began with the photo albums. It was like picking at a scab. I knew it would hurt me, but I still did it. The worst ones were obviously the pictures of Daniel with his children. There were just so many of them. I recognised The Whale as she stood by his side in church for Aaron's christening, Daniel smiling and cradling the baby in a white lacy blanket. Birthday parties with Daniel helping

Aaron to blow out the candles on the cake. A whole album of a holiday in Disney World, when Aaron must have been about six.

- Just two or three years ago. What was I doing, I wonder?

Typical family photos of the three of them. I sniggered, in spite of myself, at one of them in front of a giant model of a killer whale and considered framing it with a 'spot the difference' caption.

Then there were the photos of another woman with a girl who looked about twelve, at what appeared to be her First Communion. Proud Daddy had clearly enjoyed taking dozens of snaps. The woman was thin and blonde with sharp angular features and my first impression was that she looked like the child's grandmother. It was the first time I had seen her, but I knew immediately she had to be the American woman. Daniel had deviated from his usual type with her, I noted. There was another album of the American family on holiday in Wales. I recognised Caernarfon Castle, wondering for a horrible moment whether he had actually dared to take them to stay at my house in Conway. I forced myself to look at every photo, despite the pain they caused me. Every twist of the knife only served to strengthen my resolve.

When I had eventually finished, I closed the laptop and stared into space. An overwhelming sense of sadness flooded into my soul and I was powerless to keep out the thoughts that it should have been me in those photos with Daniel and the children.

Not for the first time, or the last, I told myself that those women had stolen my life.

The First Born

Anita

Tara was upstairs in her room when she heard the car on the drive outside. She had a quick look out of the window to check it was him and then raced down the stairs to open the front door. She ran to the car as he got out and flung her arms around his neck.

'Dad, you made it, you made it!' she shouted excitedly.

It was her fifteenth birthday and he noticed how much she had grown. She was going to be tall like him. He laughed and disentangled himself from her embrace. He wasn't particularly fond of physical displays of emotion at the best of times.

'Of course I made it. I promised you didn't I? When have I ever let you down?'

He looked towards the house and saw Anita, mother of his daughter, standing in the doorway of the porch with her eyebrows raised at that last comment. She had a strained half-smile on her face. She was clearly not going to make this easy. He laughed and tried to appear relaxed, for Tara's sake.

'Let me get in the house at least,' he said to the girl, who was tugging at his arm.

'Wait to you see what Mom got me!'

She was already racing back upstairs. Daniel walked up to Anita and bent to kiss her. She turned her head and frostily presented him with her cheek.

'Have you told her?' he whispered before Tara came back down.

'No. I most certainly have not. I thought I'd leave that pleasure for you.'

'Great. I thought you would have found a way to explain the situation to her by now. You're her mother after all.'

'And you're her father. Or had you forgotten that with all your other families in England now?' she snapped.

Tara came in before the argument could escalate, proudly brandishing the latest iPhone.

'It's the best present *ever*. No one else I know has this one yet.'

Daniel smiled at her. He had paid for the phone of course and in his bag were the new iPad mini and a Bluetooth portable speaker to go with it. He had decided it was only fair to spoil her a bit before delivering the blow that would shatter her world.

The house in Jamestown, Rhode Island, was built in the traditional clapboard style, painted pale green with a white picket fence and in an enviable location, overlooking the water. Anita had inherited the house when her parents died some years ago and Daniel liked living there. He thought to himself that, if things did not improve in the UK, he would maybe go and live there full time, at least for a while. He had to admit, the thought of just walking away and leaving all that shit behind had a certain appeal.

Later that evening, when Tara had gone to bed after a meal at The Lobster Pot, her favourite seafood restaurant in the busy little town, Daniel sat down with Anita.

'I'll talk to her tomorrow. I wasn't going to ruin her birthday,' he stated, in a matter of fact way.

'Make sure you do, first thing. I don't want any more secrets and lies.'

Daniel really couldn't be bothered with her hurt face and reprimands. He looked at her skinny body and lined face and wondered yet again how he had got himself into all this. She wasn't even his type, for fuck's sake.

'Seriously Anita, what did you think was going on here? You knew I had a life in England. I never lied about that. You always knew I was married.'

'Married, yes, but you didn't exactly tell me the whole truth, did you?' she hissed, pointedly. 'In fact, you told me your wife had terminal brain cancer. You told me it was all over between the two of you years ago, but you couldn't leave a dying woman, because you would never be able to forgive yourself. How could you tell such a wicked lie?'

'Oh, don't be so fucking dramatic. She got better. What can I say? The treatments worked, despite what the doctors said. She's now in remission. Would you have preferred she died?' Daniel goaded her, lies dripping from his tongue with alarming ease.

'I don't believe your wife even has cancer. There was no mention of that in the email I got from that other woman. *Lorraine,*' she drawled.

'Well, I suppose what it comes down to is whether you believe what I tell you or what some deranged woman you have never met tells you in a random email.'

His tone was sharp and he appeared detached and cold. Anita was close to tears but had learned over the years that he despised women crying. She had lived for years under the illusion that one day, when his poor sick wife died, Daniel would come and live permanently with her and Tara in Jamestown and they would be a proper family. Now here she was, suddenly having to try and come to terms with his latest suggestion that she should travel to England so that Tara could meet her younger half-brother. The one she didn't even know existed yet.

Anita felt as though she was trapped in some horrendous nightmare, unable to wake up. Daniel was further irritated to find himself consigned to the uncomfortable sofa bed in the spare room, but Anita refused to budge on that one.

The following morning, when Tara came down to breakfast, the teenager learned about her brother from her Dad, whom she idolised. He made little attempt to sugar coat the news.

'Sit down Tara. I have a surprise for you. It's quite exciting news actually.'

The girl looked at him with eager anticipation. More birthday presents, she supposed, hanging on his every word.

'The thing is Tara, a little while ago I got involved with someone else, a lady, over in England. One thing led to another and...well, the long and short of it is, you have a little brother. He's called Aaron,' he announced, proudly.

Her face fell and she stared at her father incredulously.

'What are you talking about? What do you mean? How can I have a little brother? You're with Mom....'

Her voice tailed off and she looked at her mother accusingly as he began again.

'Yes, I'm with your Mom. But I'm also with this other lady. Things get complicated sometimes with grown-ups.'

'What am I, five years old?' she snapped. 'Mom...? Did you know about this?'

'I found out a short while ago honey. But we decided it was best that your dad to come over and tell you in person,' she said gently.

'And you're *okay* with this?' the girl screamed at her mother.

'Well not really, but....'

'God, I hate you both!' she shouted, running out of the room and slamming the door, tears streaming down her face.

She had always been the apple of her father's eye. His pride and joy. The little girl he doted on. His only child.

Except now, apparently she wasn't.

Daniel remained in the kitchen and immediately opened his laptop, glad that the conversation was over and done with. He felt she had taken the news reasonably well, all things considered.

'She'll come round,' he called out as Anita disappeared to console her daughter.

'Kids are more resilient and more adaptable than people often give them credit for,' he added, sagely.

He had already lost interest and was absorbed in checking his emails.

Tara sulked in her bedroom for most of the day but, eventually, her curiosity began to get the better of her and her father was proved right. By the time he left for the airport later that evening she was starting to get excited about the promised trip to England and she knew the story of her new-found, little brother would make her the centre of attention amongst her friends at school. She asked questions about Aaron and looked at photos of him, surprised to see how alike the two of them actually were. The plan was that they would start by Skyping each other to break the ice before they met face to face. The trip to England was scheduled for the middle of summer and her dad was going to book a lodge in Scotland for all of them to stay in together. They would be able to ride bikes and swim, visit real castles, maybe even go horse riding.

Tara decided it could be fun after all and began to make plans for milking the situation to her best advantage.

Daniel sat alone in business class on the plane home. He had only been away for a couple of days, but it had been an essential exercise in damage limitation to visit Anita in person and make sure she wasn't planning to do anything stupid. He couldn't risk her going off-piste in the middle of everything else. The house in Jamestown was his base in the US and he used that address for all his American bank accounts. He didn't want any hiccups with that side of things. He had also found time to make a quick visit to the car dealer who had sold him the Ferrari and tie up any loose ends with the revised paperwork he had requested from them in Jane's name. Best Anita knew nothing about that.

All in all, it had been a successful trip, but he didn't dare stay away from the UK for any longer than he had to. Grace was a ticking time bomb, despite all that crap she kept churning out about being prepared to think about taking him back. He didn't buy that for a second. It just wasn't her style.

He was also pretty sure the conniving bitch was tracking him somehow or having him followed maybe. She suddenly knew far too much about where he was all the time and he didn't like that at all. He had been used to operating under the radar for so many years. Now all of a sudden she was poking her nose into everything and she was hell-bent on getting considerably more out of him in a settlement than he thought she deserved. He was not sure exactly what game she was playing, but he intended to find out and stop her in her tracks.

He laughed quietly to himself as he remembered a saying he had once heard.

If you poke the bear, don't be surprised when he turns around and bites you.

His wife would find out just how hard he could bite if she kept on pushing her luck.

The Spreadsheet

*On the darkest days, when I feel inadequate,
unloved and worthless, I remember whose
daughter I am and I straighten my crown.*

Grace

Daniel was back from America, although of course I was not supposed to know he had been there.

Welcome to his world of lies and chaos - I thought to myself.

I was quickly beginning to realise that a good memory was essential in order to be a good liar. The tracker battery was dead and so I had arranged 'date night' again, supposedly to discuss progress regarding a settlement out of court. It was becoming increasingly difficult to maintain that particular charade, with a court date for the divorce hearing already set for the end of June, just seven months after I received the email. It was now April and time was running out.

Daniel arrived at the house early, trying to catch me off guard as usual. We were deviating from the usual plan and I had offered to cook dinner for him in the house. I was also allowing him to stay overnight so that I could change the tracker while he slept upstairs. At last, this was my opportunity to get into his car and find out what golden nuggets of information he kept concealed in that bloody briefcase of his.

Making himself at home, to my intense annoyance, Daniel sat back in his chair with a glass of wine in his hand and looked at me, clearly wanting to say something. Whatever it was, I was pretty sure it was unlikely to please me. I looked back at him challengingly and waited.

'So…,' he began.

I said nothing.

There was a long pause while Daniel stared at me, trying to gauge my mood while seemingly wary of my volatile temper. I remained silent and stared back at him, a fake smile plastered on my face like a mask. I wondered uneasily what was coming next and braced myself as he continued, more decisively this time, apparently encouraged by my non-committal demeanour.

'So…I did a spreadsheet on all my women and you came out top!' he announced, proudly.

I had no words. Not in my most vivid imaginings could I have predicted that one.

There was a further pause, as he searched my face for a reaction, or more likely any sign of an imminent explosion. I assumed I was supposed to look pleased about this latest revelation, but inside I was screaming with rage.

ALL MY WOMEN!

How could that arrogant, egotistical, psychopathic bastard stand there and actually say those words to me?

My eyes darted around, lighting on the various heavy objects on the kitchen surfaces, as I fantasised about smashing them down on his head, over and over again, but I knew I had to remember the bigger picture. I had to remember why I allowed him to come to the house at all, why I was even entertaining the idea of a conversation with him. I inhaled deeply, telling myself it was simply a means to an end.

'Yes. You scored 75%,' he continued, completely oblivious to the effect his utterly abhorrent words were having on me.

I managed to regain my composure, ensuring my smile did not slip and attempted to reply in a light-hearted tone.

'Seriously? Only 75%? What happened to the other 25%?'

He laughed, clearly buoyed up by my reaction.

'Come on, you should be pleased with that. Nobody scored 100%. Honestly, Grace, I have no idea how I got myself into this mess and how I ever let things go so far. I should have just stayed with you. You were always the best one for me. This spreadsheet just proves it.'

I really had no idea why I was engaging with him on the subject of his spreadsheet, but I suddenly seemed unable to help myself.

'So, what were the categories?' I asked as if we were discussing TV awards or something. I hated myself for it, but the truth was I actually wanted to know why I was top of the class. I needed to know where I had lost marks, in the interests of future self-improvement.

'Well…intelligence, attractiveness, weight, personal hygiene, how often you wear stockings and suspenders, how good you are in bed, cooking, laundry…,'

I homed in on the last one and interrupted his flow.

'Sorry…what? Did you say laundry?'

I stared at him incredulously. It was so utterly ludicrous that I genuinely had to suppress the urge to laugh. Properly laugh.

'Yes,' he continued, apparently unperturbed. 'That's where you lost most of your marks.'

I realised he was deadly serious as he continued the bizarre dialogue.

'Lorraine was like the magic laundry basket. I used to put my dirty clothes in the basket in the morning and they came out washed and ironed the same night! You, on the other hand...,' he chuckled, warming to his subject.

My expression darkened. I utterly despised the smug, self-satisfied leer on his face and I felt a renewed urge to stab him. Repeatedly. I was really beginning to understand how a person could commit the crime of murder when pushed beyond breaking point and it had to be said that he was dangerously close to finding my breaking point.

I took a deep breath and forced myself to stay calm before responding, choosing my words carefully.

'Do you know what? I'll take that. I have no ambitions to be top of the class for laundry.'

My tone was measured and I glared at him defiantly.

I had to admit though that I was secretly pleased I had not lost marks for being rubbish in bed. My stupid female pride and competitiveness came to the fore every time.

I looked Daniel in the eye and knew I had to give an Oscar-winning performance if I was to have any chance of convincing him I was considering allowing him back into my life. Adam had persuaded me that it was the only way of getting him to let his guard down, the only way to find out what I needed to know about his various underhand dealings to avoid my own financial ruin. The unexpected flaw in the plan was that I actually had fleeting moments where I believed my own lies and found myself beginning to soften towards him. I could not deny the fact that there was still a little piece of me that just wanted all this to go away, to be able to wind back the clock and carry on with our life as it had been pre-email.

I reminded myself of what he had just said and abruptly pushed those ridiculous thoughts to the back of my mind, concentrating on the task in hand.

I stood with my back to the stranger in my kitchen, making him a drink, and wondering yet again how we came to this point. He was blissfully unaware that there had been a shift of power in the last few weeks, ever since I acquired the trackers. I now knew his every movement and, best of all; he hadn't got a clue about it.

I asked him where he had been the last few days, as a kind of test. I so desperately wanted him to tell the truth, just once, so I could believe there was some hope of eternal salvation for him. But, of course, it didn't happen. Apparently, he had been fixing a machine up in Scotland.

I knew the tracker did not lie to me and I knew he had been nowhere near Scotland. The lying, cheating, manipulative piece of shit I had married was not to be trusted an inch and it was high time I faced up to that fact.

I returned to the task in hand.

Pouring far too much Mount Gay into his glass, I surreptitiously added a crushed sleeping tablet to the mix, for good measure. For myself, just a hint of rum, lots of ice and a full glass of coke. I could not afford to be anything less than fully alert. The sleeping tablets made me slightly uneasy, in case I accidentally killed him, but I justified it by telling myself it was insurance necessary for my own safety.

I found out a while back that the doctor had prescribed Daniel with Amitriptyline, an anti-depressant/sleeping drug. I didn't want him playing the 'depressed' card in the divorce court and getting one over on me, so I had taken myself off to the doctor with all the right symptoms (thank you Google) and, lo and behold, came out with my very own prescription for Amitriptyline. I had no intention of ever taking it myself, but it was certainly coming in useful that night.

As I watched the powder dissolve and disappear without a trace into the dark liquid, I felt satisfied that, should anything go wrong, it wouldn't be the end of the world and I could certainly not be accused of murder. A court would surely rule that he had taken his own life, or simply got confused and taken too many of his own drugs by mistake. After all, who could blame him for being confused, depressed and suicidal; living with the damage he had done to so many lives? Some darker thoughts crossed my mind fleetingly.

- What if I just put some extra in his drink? As in, quite a lot extra?
- It would be so easy.
- Wouldn't I just be doing the world a favour?
- There would be no mess, no blood, just an end to the nightmare.

I felt a sudden empathy with vigilantes and all that they stood for. I understood completely, but my conscience got the better of me and I refrained for the time being.

I handed Daniel his drink and sat down opposite him, careful to keep the kitchen table between us. I did not trust him and had no idea what he was ultimately capable of if he got wind of what I was up to.

He took a large gulp, then suddenly lurched forward across the table and grabbed my hand before I could react.

'They should have been yours!' he blurted out, a sob catching in his throat.

He looked genuinely distraught and for a moment I was completely wrong-footed.

'The children,' he clarified. 'They should have been yours. I'm so, so sorry.'

To my horror, he actually looked like he meant it. He hung his head in shame and clutched my hand tightly, pressing it between both of his. I hated him more than words could ever express at that moment but, despite the hatred, I could not stop the tears. Nor did I pull my hand away.

Children. That was always my Achilles heel and he knew it. In a split second, I went from a position of strength and power, a feeling of being in total control, to a feeling of utter desolation and despair, as the pain flooded in once again and I felt as if I was going mad.

All of our married life, he insisted he did not want children. He liked our life the way it was, he always said, just the two of us (and the rest of his harem of course). Eventually, I had been forced to choose and make a decision, possibly the worst of my life, because

265

that decision meant giving up on my own dreams of a family in favour of my husband.

If ever there was a case of misplaced loyalty and dedication to a marriage that was surely it. I broke down, unable to stop the tears.

'How could you do it? How could you betray me like that? How could you be so cruel?' I implored him piteously. 'How could you go on telling me all those years that you didn't want children and then go off and have them with other women behind my back?'

He had no answer to that and eventually just shrugged his shoulders awkwardly.

'I suppose you should have just got pregnant if you wanted kids so badly. It's true I never really wanted them, but when it happened I just had to deal with it. It seemed to turn out ok in the end and it wasn't as bad as I thought to be honest. Ironically, I quite like being a dad.'

And there it was. The real Daniel was back in the room. His words cut through me like a knife, as he undoubtedly knew they would. The moment of weakness and vulnerability was over and I snatched my hand away. There was no place for this kind of emotion and sentimentality, especially not in front of him. I needed to toughen up and remember what this was all about. Operation car search.

I noted with satisfaction that my special cocktail of rum and Amitriptyline was beginning to have the desired effect and, after listening to a final, ludicrous gem about how he wanted me to meet his children so that I could teach them to ride, sail and ski, he blundered his way up the two flights of stairs to the top floor and into our former marital bedroom.

My new bedroom on the middle floor was now fully and permanently equipped with a knife under the pillow and a dining chair in the corner, which I could wedge under the door handle to prevent uninvited guests. If faced with the worst-case scenario and things turned nasty, I had no intention of coming off worst.

I listened to him undressing and clumping around on the wooden floor of the bedroom then, as soon as I heard him go into the bathroom, I sprinted up the stairs two at a time and slipped silently into the bedroom to retrieve his car keys. My heart was thumping and I knew I only had a couple of minutes before he was done. He always kept the keys in his trouser pocket, but a quick rummage through all the pockets revealed nothing.

Where the hell were they?

I frantically opened the bedside drawers and my scrabbling fingers finally located them, buried under a couple of pairs of his silk boxers, stuffed towards the back of the middle drawer.

BASTARD! He had actually hidden them from me.

I knew that meant he was suspicious of me, despite his claims of wanting us to get back together. Apparently, we were *both* playing games, but only one of us could win and I intended to do everything I could to make sure it was me.

I snatched the keys out and straightened the boxers before closing the drawer and creeping, Pink Panther style, out of the bedroom and down to my own room. It was not long before I heard him stagger back into the bedroom and collapse on the bed, no longer able to fight off the effects of the drugs and alcohol.

I lay in bed for a while longer, fuming.

- How dare he hide his keys from me.

I played through his words in my head, again and again, delivered earlier that evening with his best 'sincere' face.

'We don't have to be conventional. If you hadn't told all our friends and your family about it…well, I'm sure we could have worked things out between us.'

Then the best bit, the icing on the cake:

'I really want you to consider something. I've hired a lodge for a week in the summer, up in Scotland near Pitlochry. I want the children to meet each other. There are three bedrooms: one for Anita and Tara, one for Jane and Aaron and there's a spare one for you and me if you'll come with me.'

I felt as if I was actually going crazy. Did he really just present that to me as a reasonable suggestion? Did he plan to bed hop his way around us all, making sure we each got a fair turn with him? Who the hell did he think he was?

I came to the conclusion that Adam was right. Daniel was not of sound mind and was, in fact, displaying all the traits of a full-blown psychopath.

I listened for him snoring, my signal to move. I slipped on the leggings and black hoodie I had bought for my covert operations in Stainsford, pulled on my trainers, headed out of the kitchen and up the stone steps to the car park. The security light immediately flooded the whole area with light, illuminating me and everything else around with alarming clarity. I felt a frisson of fear as I lost the cover of darkness, but reminded myself that the car park was on the opposite side of the house to the bedroom and besides, there was no way Daniel was going to be waking up from his drug-induced coma any time soon.

First things first. I lay on my back at right angles to the car, with my head by the passenger door. I shuffled back underneath, commando-style, and felt above my head for the metal U-shaped section running across the chassis. I wiggled the little black box out of its position and squeezed it over the top of the metal bar, just as I had been shown, replacing it with its fully charged twin which I carefully secured with a cable tie. I thought again how good a fit it was, practically made for the purpose. I wriggled out from under the car, stood up and stretched, feeling pleased with myself. It had been surprisingly easy. Now for the interesting bit.

I pulled on my latex gloves, staple equipment for the amateur PI I had become, and opened the car, making a beeline for the briefcase. I had watched enough crime TV and learned enough over the past few weeks to know I had to be careful to leave no fingerprints and to make sure everything was left just as I had found it so that Daniel did not suspect I had been there, or if he did, he couldn't prove it. The first thing I came across was his passport and I had to fight my initial impulse to steal it and cut it up into little pieces.

- That would scupper his next trip to see that bitch and his daughter in America.

No. I was quickly learning the value of self-control and keeping my powder dry. My cool, calm Investigator head took over and I refrained from doing that, proud of my restraint. Destroying his passport would simply alert him to my nocturnal antics and would ultimately serve no useful purpose, other than to annoy him in the short term.

I continued sifting through the papers and had my first breakthrough: the file for the Ferrari I knew he had bought and imported from America. The one he was trying to make out belonged to The Whale of Willowmede, aka Jane Sutcliffe, mother of child number two.

The second find of not insignificant interest was the insurance schedule for all of his cars and bikes, stating their value and clearly showing Daniel personally as the owner. I couldn't resist getting comfortable in the back seat for a few minutes and looking down the list:

1973 Ducati 250 SCR	£8,000
1938 Nimbus Model C	£10,000
2018 Norton Commando 961 Mk11	£15,000
1969 VW Beetle	£10,000
1985 Mercedes-Benz 500SL	£18,000
1977 E-type Jaguar 4.2 Challenger	£50,000
1978 Mercedes-Benz 450 SLC	£14,000
1963 Ford Thunderbird	£25,000
1968 Daimler V8 250	£20,000
2001 BMW Ci Convertible	£5,000
1933 Talbot AW75	£25,000
1972 Chevrolet Corvette	£30,000
1990 Ferrari Mondial Cabriolet	£30,000

There it was! The Ferrari, insured and owned by Daniel M J Callaghan. Finally, I was getting somewhere. More vital pieces of the jigsaw. I briefly considered trying to copy the documents but, in the end, I just couldn't be bothered and settled for the easier route of simply taking them.

What's his is mine and all that - I thought bitterly.

He would, of course, notice they were missing, but I was banking on the fact that he was by now so confused and muddled with all his shenanigans and stories that he would simply believe he put them somewhere else or misplaced them.

Or maybe Lorraine has stolen them - I said to myself with a little snort of laughter, as I remembered the fraudulent email incident she had been blamed for.

I left the briefcase exactly as it was, except for the two missing items of course and moved on to the boot. I took my time and had a good snoop around, looking in particular for the ten thousand euros emergency stash he once told me he always left in the car. No luck on that score unfortunately, but on the whole I was pretty happy with my booty and decided to settle at that for the first night, confident that there would be many more opportunities now I knew what I was doing.

I locked the car and crept back into the house, securing myself in the bedroom with the chair under the door handle. I could hear him snoring loudly.

- Still alive then.

I set the alarm for 5.30 am. Daniel was not an early riser, especially after what I had given him to drink, but I needed to be on the ball and ready to get the keys back in place among the boxer shorts at the back of the drawer as soon as I heard him go into the bathroom.

I felt strangely elated and powerful in the knowledge that I was finally taking back control of my life.

My dad would be proud of me.

My final thought as I drifted into a fitful sleep was that perhaps it was Daniel who should be worrying about what *I* was really capable of, rather than the other way round.

The fear

There are two options when confronted with fear:
forget everything and run or rise up and face it.
You always have a choice.

Grace

I heard the crack of a twig somewhere behind me and instinctively quickened my pace, suddenly fearful. Someone was there. I knew it, despite trying to convince myself otherwise. I cursed my own stupidity and wondered what on earth had possessed me to walk Lola down the secluded, tree-lined, bridle path in the dark. It was a route I took most days and, to be fair, the light was only just beginning to fade when I set off but there was no moon that night and, after half an hour, it was difficult to make out anything beyond my immediate surroundings. Lola stopped to sniff something and then turned to look back down the path, her ears pricked and her tail wagging. I tugged on her lead and she reluctantly came with me. I broke into a slow jog, my heart thumping hard in my chest, but Lola was having none of it. She stopped again and tried to pull me back the way we had just come. I strained my eyes, trying to make out anything at all, but to no avail.

Without warning, the shape of a large man loomed out of the darkness. I was startled and opened my mouth to scream, but no sound came out. I took a step backwards as he moved towards me and I prepared to turn and run away as fast as I could, but as I did so my foot caught on a raised tree root at the edge of the path, causing me to stumble and fall amongst the damp leaves and thorns in the undergrowth. My fingers scrabbled desperately for something I could use as a weapon, but I found nothing.

I could not see his face, but there was no doubt in my mind that it was my husband. Panic and fear shot through my body like an electric shock and the metallic taste of blood filled my mouth where I had bitten my lip as I fell. Still I could not scream.

Oh God, he knows I know - was my first thought - He will kill me for this, I know he will. Nobody knows I'm out here. How could I have been so stupid?

I tried desperately to scramble to my feet, but I was too late. He was already upon me and shoved me so hard in the chest with the heel of his hand that I fell straight back to the ground. I shuffled backwards as quickly as I could in an attempt to get away from him, but he laughed quietly and moved with me, clearly enjoying the game, like a cat playing with its prey. I could smell his sour breath on my face as he leaned closer and, although it was impossible to make out his features, I knew it was him. He spoke quietly, his tone menacing.

'What the hell did you think you were doing, snooping around in my private affairs? Did you really think I didn't know what you were up to? You're even dumber than I thought,' he sneered. 'Did you honestly think you were going to get away with your stupid little games, trying to ruin my life? Believe me; you have no idea who you're messing with. You never could just do as you were told, could you? You're pathetic. *Exactly* like Julia.'

I searched in desperation for a way to escape, but I was helpless, my arm pinned to the floor by his boot. I considered pleading for my life but knew instantly there was no point. He had no conscience, no empathy for his fellow human beings, especially not me. I watched in silent terror as he raised one arm high in the air and noticed he was holding something long and thick, cylinder-shaped, in his hand. Maybe a torch? A baseball bat? I instinctively threw my free arm across my face and brought my knees up to my chest in an attempt to protect the most vulnerable areas of my body.

I tensed every muscle, waiting for the blow, but there was nothing.

No pain. No noise.

I moved my arm away from my eyes and stared into the darkness, straining to see what lay beyond.

Gradually I began to make out the shapes as my eyes adjusted. My brain fought to make sense of what I was seeing as the random objects slowly drifted into focus.

A chest of drawers.

A dining chair tipped backwards by a door.

I sat up abruptly in bed, my brain finally allowing me to understand that I was in my own bedroom. Safe in my own house. I listened to the rhythmic snoring from upstairs and felt a surge of relief. The man upstairs, at least while he was in his drugged stupor, was a far cry from the monster my nightmares had given life to.

None of it had been real, except the fear. The fear was very real indeed. My hair was stuck to my neck with sweat and my hands were clammy. My heart was still beating far too fast. I realised that, no matter how brave I tried to appear on the outside, I was actually terrified of Daniel and what he might do.

I looked at my phone, 4.15 am. I lay awake, waiting for sounds of movement as he got up so that I could get his keys back to where he had left them in the drawer, praying he had not already noticed they were missing. I made the decision there and then that I could not carry on with the elaborate charade anymore. It was time to stop the games before they destroyed me. I was worried that Daniel was the one playing me rather than the other way around and I knew I needed to put distance between us again.

No more overnight visits or 'friendly' chats. If we carried on, at least one of us was going to end up dead and I was beginning to think the odds were not in my favour.

Fate was on my side for once and I was offered a helping hand the next day in the shape of Tom, Adam's mechanic friend, the one who had educated me in the art of tracker fitting. All that seemed a lifetime ago already. I had met him several times in the hotel and was not surprised to see him in the bar when I went up there for a drink that evening. Tom was tall, good looking and charismatic and, as he came over and kissed me on the cheek, I felt a guilty little twinge of sadness that he was happily married.

'How's it going Ace Ventura?' he teased.

I laughed, loving my new nickname and impressed by the fact that everyone seemed to see me as some kind of Lara Croft heroine. I knew Tom was up to speed with most of what was happening in my world, courtesy of Adam.

'Okay I guess, but I must admit I'm getting a bit fed up with having to meet up with Daniel and pretend I actually *like* him. You should hear some of the shit that comes out of his mouth. It's really freaking me out now, having to sleep under the same roof as him, even if it is only once a week. The more I learn about him, the more nervous I get and I'm definitely beginning to think Adam might have a point about him being a psycho.'

'Well, I have come here tonight on my white horse in answer to all your problems,' Tom

said, pausing for dramatic effect.

'Really?'

I was not convinced.

'Seriously, I've got an idea. Adam tells me you managed to get into Daniel's car. If you can get me his keys for an hour or so, I can hardwire the tracker in for you. That means it would work off the car battery, so it would never run out and there would be no need for all the nonsense of changing it over every week.'

'Oh my God, that would be amazing! But what if he found out about it? Wouldn't you get into trouble?'

'Well, I'm assuming I can trust you and you're not going to tell anyone I put it there, so how am I going to get into trouble? No one could ever prove anything and besides, the thing will be buried so deep in the bowels of the car, it'll never be found. Trust me, it's no big deal. I'll be happy to help make sure that bastard gets what's coming to him. I never liked him.'

Once again I marvelled at the generosity of so many people and their willingness to help me. I was also beginning to realise just how many people disliked Daniel and had only tolerated him for my sake.

I supposed what it really came down to was the age-old battle between Good and Evil. People were choosing to stand with me because they ultimately wanted to see Good triumph over Evil. I allowed myself to feel optimistic again.

'When could we do it then?' I asked eagerly.

'Name the day. Any evening next week is good for me. I'll wait up at the hotel and come over to you as soon as you text to give me the all clear.'

Of course it meant one more sleepover for Daniel, but I could handle that. It was different now. The end was in sight.

And so, a week later, Daniel was unwittingly doped up once again and sleeping like a baby on the top floor, oblivious to the feverish activity going on in the car park. Tom worked his magic as promised. It took him a little over an hour to do it, while I stood guard, just in case. When he had finished, I hugged him, unable to hide my excitement.

'Thank you so much again for doing this. You have no idea how much this means to me. I owe you big time.'

'Just buy me a beer next time we're in the bar,' he laughed.

'Deal.'

With that, he disappeared down the drive and I went back into the house, creeping up the stairs and barricading myself in the bedroom as usual. I held my breath and listened for any sign of movement upstairs, but there was nothing, except the loud snoring that had grated on me and deprived me of sleep for so many years.

Not anymore - I thought to myself happily.

The following morning, I could hardly contain myself when Daniel came downstairs into the kitchen, looking decidedly groggy and rubbing his hands across his face.

'Daniel, I need to tell you something,' I began, determinedly. 'I've thought long and hard about everything and I've decided there's simply no way I can ever come to terms with what you've done. I'm definitely going ahead with the divorce and so I don't want you around here anymore.'

I was delighted to see the shock on his face as I calmly delivered the death blow.

'Whoa...what? What's changed all of a sudden?' he asked, bewildered.

'Nothing really. I've just come to my senses. Basically, I can't believe a word you say and I know you're not being straight with me. You're totally refusing to sign anything over to me, and yet you're happy to put things in that fat, bush-pig Jane's name,' I said, deciding to let rip with my true feelings. 'You're also lying about who owns the cars and bikes. I know for a fact they're all yours.'

'Where the hell did this come from since last night? I thought we were getting on better, possibly even planning a future together...Grace, I'm not lying, I promise you. I *can't* sign the cars over to you because they don't belong to me,' he lied. 'I don't want you to come out of this badly, I really don't,' he lied again. 'I'm trying to help you. You just need to do what I tell you and stop messing around because this is getting serious. We need to do a deal that will work for both of us and we need to stick to it, not go changing our minds every five minutes. If I'm made bankrupt, we'll lose the house but they can't take it if you're living here because you have rights to the marital home. I'm happy for you to stay in the house for another three to five years and I promise after that I should be able to pay you a decent settlement. Who knows, maybe by then we'll have decided to stay together after all. I'll obviously need to live here as well, but we can have separate rooms if you prefer.'

He was prattling and beginning to sound desperate, but this time I was having none of it.

'You're *happy* for me to stay in the house? Nice,' I said, sarcastically. 'Well, let me explain something to you. My solicitor says I'll get to keep the house, all to myself, or else you will have to buy me out. So I don't actually need *your* permission for anything. Do you honestly think I'm going to live under the same roof as you and wait *five years* before I get any money out of you? There's no way on this earth I'm staying with you. Hell will freeze over first,' I spat, contemptuously.

'Well, you're really showing your true colours now, aren't you? What happened to all that stuff about wanting to find a way through this? What about not wanting to throw away everything we had together?'

'Don't even go there! You have no right to act like the victim here. You are the one who threw everything away the day you slept with the first of your ugly, fat slappers behind my back.'

The sudden look of menace on his face made me shudder and I deftly moved to within reach of the kitchen knives, as he took a step towards me and spoke in a low growl.

'You really are as hard as nails, aren't you? You conniving, manipulative, little bitch. You've been lying all along. Go ahead and take this to court then, but I'm telling you now, you'll come out of it with nothing, same as the taxman. I've tried to help you, but you seem to be on some kind of self-destruct course, egged on by that cow of a solicitor you've hooked up with.'

'Oh, just piss off and leave me alone. You don't scare me,' I lied, determined to tough it out. 'I'll see you in court. Oh, and from now on you can deal directly with my solicitor for everything.'

'You're a fucking lying psycho with your stupid mind games,' he yelled in my face.

'Ha! Says you.'

'Don't think for one second I'll let you get away with this. And for your information, this is *my* house and I'll sleep here whenever I feel like it. See you soon, Grace,' he mocked, in his Irish accent I had once found so sexy, but which now merely grated on me.

On that note, he stormed out and slammed the door.

I was shaking, despite my bravado and suddenly felt terrified that I had done the wrong thing in showing him my hand so openly.

- What happened to keeping my powder dry?

I sat down at the kitchen table and opened my laptop. There he was, *Daniel 1*, a little green cursor heading off down the drive in the direction of who knew where. At least I would now know whenever he was on his way back to the house and could prepare myself.

Still furious with him and feeling braver now that I knew for sure the tracker was permanently fitted and working, I grabbed a pair of kitchen scissors and ran upstairs into his bedroom, ready to unleash my inner creative genius. Opening his wardrobe, I snatched out a plastic suit carrier containing his tux, dinner shirt and evening trousers. First I removed the trousers and laid them out on the bed, before roughly cutting a huge circle out of the crotch. Next I unpicked the buttons from the tux and the shirt, leaving them hanging on by a thread and cut through the armpit seams of the shirt. Finally, I replaced everything neatly back in the suit carrier, zipped it up and replaced it in the wardrobe. It took a mere five minutes. I was particularly proud of my skills in making it all look perfectly normal at first glance. Only when Daniel wanted to wear it to some black-tie dinner with one of his slappers would he realise the little trick I had played on him.

I felt sure he would see the funny side of it.

I thought to myself with disdain that Lorraine's childish scrawling over everything in marker pen was not for me. I preferred a more grown-up, subtle approach.

Back downstairs in the kitchen, I picked up the phone and rang my solicitor to tell her that there would be no more messing around. No more talk of settlements out of court. I was ready to throw myself at the mercy of the British judicial system, trusting that the law of the land would protect me as the innocent party in all this.

I had to believe that justice would be done, but given that life is full of surprises, not all of them good, I suppose I really should have known better.

PART III

The Reckoning

Kar·ma

/ˈkärmə/ noun

The definition of karma is the destiny that you earn through your actions and behaviour.[4]

Karma is an ancient concept. The law of karma teaches us that all of our thoughts, words and actions begin a chain of cause and effect and that we will personally experience the effects of everything we cause. [5]

---

[4] yourdictionary.com

[5] Spiritual-encyclopedia.com

The funeral

True friends aren't always the ones you've known the longest. They're the ones who walked into your life, said, 'I'm here for you,' and proved it.

Grace

Charles' death came as a devastating shock to us all. A bolt out of the blue that put everything else sharply into perspective. He suffered a massive stroke that cruelly snuffed out his life and in a matter of seconds, he was gone forever.

He and Sam had recently returned from a four-month trip touring around South America and only a couple of weeks earlier I had spent the weekend with them, hearing about their adventures and talking about my still uncertain future once the divorce was finally over. Daniel was still refusing to cooperate, which came as no great surprise to anyone. He had failed to produce any of the required documents concerning his finances and was still bizarrely insisting that he did not even want a divorce. Nobody, least of all the judge, cared what he wanted and the hearing was scheduled for the following month, at the end of June. It was expected to be a two-day contested hearing, which would not be pretty (or cheap) and Daniel was apparently intending to represent himself, which promised to be entertaining.

Charles had been on great form and I realised just how much I had missed him and Sam with all the dramas of the past few months. The three of us had put the world to rights over a few stiff gins and some very good red wine from his impressive collection in the cellar. It was almost like old times, as we reminisced about some of the fantastic holidays the four of us had enjoyed. Charles spoke a lot of sense as usual.

'The thing is Grace, you have to remember that those were the good times we had, even though Daniel was part of the memories. You knew nothing of his other lives or his deceit then and I honestly believe that he lived in the moment, almost like a different person. with whoever he was with at the time. All of that stuff we did together was real and no one can take the great memories away from you. Don't let him destroy your past and everything that was good about it and remember, if you hadn't got together with him, we would probably never have met.'

He paused briefly before adding, with a mischievous wink,

'On the other hand, if *he* hadn't been with *you*, I would almost certainly never have had anything to do with him as a friend.'

I laughed, feeling suddenly more positive.

'You're right. Do you know, I hadn't really thought of it like that. I've just been obsessing about the fact that my whole life has been built on a lie. I guess I need to remember that there were a hell of a lot of good times along the way.'

'That's it exactly. Cherish the good times and look forward to the future, 'cos it's going to be amazing. Cheers! To new beginnings!'

He raised his glass and we all clinked in accordance.

I could hardly believe he was gone.

At sixty-eight, he was a good few years older than Samantha and I, but we never thought of him as any different in age to us. He was always so full of life and energy and he was most definitely not ready to leave this mortal coil. He and Sam both loved travelling and had already begun planning their next trip, a five-week 4x4 car rally round Madagascar in two years' time. So much to look forward to. The house felt empty and hollow without him and Samantha was bereft without her soul mate. She wore his wedding ring on a chain around her neck, inscribed on the inside with the words they had said in their marriage vows: *Together in love, life and beyond.*

They just hadn't expected the 'beyond' part to come so soon.

The day before the funeral, Samantha and I were alone in the kitchen.

'Thanks, Grace,' she said, flatly, 'for being here. I don't know how I'd have got through this last week without you.'

'Don't be ridiculous. You know I'll always be here for you. But you are stronger than anyone I know. You will get through this and you will enjoy the rest of your life, just as you know Charles would have wanted you to. He lived his best life with you and he will be with us forever in our hearts.'

We both burst into tears as the finality of it all hit us. We hugged for a long time, both alone now, but for very different reasons. We vowed to support each other and have each other's backs, whatever life threw at us. Our bond of friendship was stronger than ever.

'They'll be bringing Charles home any time now. I wanted a bit of time with him on my own before the others all arrive this evening. I've told people to come any time after 6 pm,' Samantha stated, beginning to think of the practicalities.

'You take as long as you need. Don't worry about anyone else. I'll look after everything.'

We had made a massive pot of Chilli to feed everyone that evening and intended to make the occasion as happy as possible. A chance for people to swap stories about a great friend, a father, a grandfather and a husband. A lot of friends were travelling from other parts of the UK or abroad to pay their final respects and every room in the house was full.

That was the night I met Phili, a close friend of Samantha's from childhood and my roommate for a couple of nights. We immediately got on like a house on fire and, as the evening progressed and the alcohol flowed freely, I opened up to her about my own situation. To tell the truth, I actually got a bit of a kick out of seeing people's shocked faces these days, taking every opportunity to hone my story-telling skills and entertain at Daniel's expense. At around midnight that night, as we raised a toast to Charles before heading up to bed, I almost found myself looking around for him in the little crowd. It just somehow felt like his spirit was there with us, no longer in need of the still, lifeless body he had left behind in the coffin.

I was tormented by an ominous feeling that Daniel would turn up at the funeral, although Sam had made it clear he was most definitely persona non grata. I had not seen him for several weeks, since the evening of the tracker being hardwired into his car, but his recent exchanges with my solicitor had been less than friendly.

At 6.30 am, before the alarm went off, Phili suddenly sat bolt upright in bed and announced excitedly:

'I know what we need to do if your vile husband dares to show his face today.'

I groaned, still half asleep and not quite ready to cope with my bubbly new friend, who was speaking and acting like a woman possessed.

'Do you know what time it is? The alarm hasn't even gone off yet.'

I snuggled under the duvet and yawned.

'Never mind about that. Seriously, I've been thinking about it and I've come up with a great idea. Just hear me out. You'll love it.'

'Okay, go on then,' I said, laughing at her over-zealous enthusiasm. Sleep was clearly not an option anymore and I had to concentrate as she outlined her plan, speaking rapidly.

'First of all, we need to drug him. Then we kidnap him, drive his car into the woods near here, strip him naked and superglue him to the bonnet on his hands and knees with his arse in the air. We put a sign on the windscreen saying, *All welcome,* and we leave him there until somebody finds him. Or he dies. Either way works for me,' she finished triumphantly, waiting for my reaction.

She had clearly put a lot of thought into this. I laughed hysterically at the image she had conjured up, but at the same time, I found myself subconsciously wondering where I could get some superglue from. Just in case.

'I have to say I like your style,' I admitted. 'I just think it might be a *bit* tricky to pull that one off today. Maybe with a bit more planning.'

'Well I'm up for it whenever you want,' she said animatedly.

And I was pretty sure she genuinely meant it.

Naturally, I was right about Daniel turning up, but it was not difficult to ignore him and I steadfastly avoided all eye contact with him as I stood outside the church a few hours later, surrounded by loyal friends. I tried not to make it all about me, but I couldn't help being pleased that he was treated like a pariah and nobody wanted to be seen speaking more than a few cursory words to him. The church was packed inside and there was a further crowd of people outside, come to pay their respects to a much-loved man, who had made a huge impact on so many lives. The local Welsh male voice choir he loved to hear were singing as he was brought into church and the service was perfect, with lovingly spoken tributes from friends and family, carefully chosen words to capture the true essence of his life and character.

Charles had wanted to be cremated and, as Phili and I arrived at the Crematorium, I noticed Daniel's car was already parked up there. He obviously intended to stick it out to the bitter end. Glancing around furtively, I could not resist walking down the side of his car and dragging my key surreptitiously along the full length of the paintwork in an act of rebellious defiance. It was an opportunist crime and I hoped there was no hidden CCTV to incriminate me.

Finally, it seemed even Daniel knew where he was not wanted and he had the good grace not to bother making an appearance at the wake. I stood and watched him kiss Samantha outside the Crem as she visibly recoiled, watched him offer her his sincerest condolences, get into his car and drive away. I realised with satisfaction that he had not noticed the deep scratch on the passenger side of the car. That would be a nice surprise for later.

The wake was exactly as Charles would have wanted it, except he would, of course, have preferred to be at the party in person. People were laughing, talking about their favourite memories of him, reminiscing about scrapes they had got into together and the fun they had had over the years.

There were people there from all walks of his life: people he had worked with, people he had grown up with, friends from the sailing scene, friends from his car rallying adventures, friends from the flying world, employees and colleagues.

Samantha had done him proud and he would definitely have approved - I thought sadly.

- God, I'm going to miss him.

I fell in naturally with the sailing crowd of course and immediately started on the rum and cokes with Rob, Ben and Spike, so-called because of the marlin spike tool he carried on his harness as bowman on the boat. They had been part of Charles' team on the Corel 45 back in the early days when we had all been on the race circuit together. Spike was a top bowman and I had learned a lot from him over the years. Naturally, they had all heard about Daniel and me and were hungry for the gossip.

'I swear you lot are worse than a bunch of women,' I teased.

Fuelled by alcohol, I was more than happy to indulge them and spilled the beans about everything in glorious, technicolour detail. I felt a burning desire to humiliate Daniel and shatter the macho image of himself he had always been so keen to promote. Why should I protect his dignity? He hadn't cared about mine for all those years. I had done nothing wrong in all this and I owed him no loyalty.

I was, in fact, becoming a bit of a professional storyteller and took great delight in making them all laugh at Daniel's expense. Rob disappeared to the bar again and Ben began talking to Will, another one of the old crew, leaving Spike and me on our own. He leaned towards me and lowered his voice.

'You know we're all on your side, right? He really is the scum of the earth and I don't know anyone decent who'll sail with him after this. I know you're making light of it all now, but a betrayal on that scale must have just about killed you.'

I smiled ruefully before answering.

'You're right, it did, but I can't allow myself to give in to it, otherwise he will have won.'

'Have you ever thought about *really* getting even and making him pay for what he's done to you?'

'All the time!' I laughed. 'Our divorce hearing is coming up soon and my solicitor seems pretty optimistic, so I guess he'll get what's coming to him and be made to pay then.'

'Maybe, but that's only money. That's not really what I meant.'

I looked at him quizzically, wondering what he was talking about and why the hell he was being so cryptic after a few drinks. Spike worked in finance in the city but was ex-Navy and a tough cookie underneath.

'I'm just saying that, if you ever wanted him to be taught a serious lesson, I could put you in touch with people who would be happy to help you.'

'What do you mean? Order a hit on him? Oh come on, do hitmen really exist outside of James Bond movies?' I laughed again.

'You'd be surprised. A couple of my old Navy mates do just that for a side-line these days. A bit of a kicking, a roughing up...or worse, depending on how strong your stomach is and how far you're prepared to go.'

'You're actually serious, aren't you?' I said, instinctively lowering my voice.

'Deadly. I know if I were in your shoes, I'd want him punishing the good old-fashioned way. I certainly wouldn't be leaving it to the whim of the Courts.'

'Bloody hell Spike, I wouldn't dare do anything like that. What if they got caught? It'd all come back on me and I'd be the one that'd end up in prison, I bet.'

'It doesn't work like that. They're professionals. They don't get caught and, even if they did, they have a code of conduct. They'd never name you. Absolutely no chance.'

This was not a conversation I had ever anticipated having, but I could not help feeling intrigued about the dark underworld that apparently existed behind the comforting scenes of everyday respectable life. God, I was naïve. No wonder Daniel had played me for a fool all these years. I needed to wise up. Spike continued.

'The guys I'm talking about…they are pretty choosy about the jobs they take on. They like to think of themselves as 'avengers' if you like. It's not all about the money. They only go after people who have done stuff to hurt others and got away with it. Their ethos is to put things straight by righting wrongs and restoring the correct order in the world if you see what I mean.'

'That all sounds very admirable, but I'd still be nervous about involving anybody else like that. I've developed a fair few trust issues, to be honest, and, if I was going to do anything to Daniel, I'd probably feel I had to do it myself.'

'You say that, but could you *really* do it yourself? Like I said before, these guys are professionals,' he added, holding my gaze.

I suddenly burst out laughing and shook my head.

'God, I can't believe we're having this conversation. How much have we had to drink again?'

'Not nearly enough. Here, take this.' He pressed a black and gold business card into my hand.

'You may feel differently after the court case, especially if things don't go your way. If you do decide to call, make sure you mention my name.'

I stuffed the card hastily into my purse as Rob returned from the bar with our drinks.

Never say never, I told myself, deciding that it would be prudent to keep an open mind.

The time capsule

The truth has the power to set you free, but the little white lies will make sure you kick ass along the way.

Grace

I stared at the laptop screen in front of me. It had been a week since Charles' funeral and already life was continuing as before.

'We all think we're indispensable and the world will stop turning when we die, but of course it doesn't,' he had once said.

As I stared at the screen absent-mindedly, thinking about Charles, I began to focus on four little words on the menu at the left-hand side: *time capsule shared device*. It wasn't the first time I had noticed them, but suddenly something clicked in my mind and they took on a whole new significance.

I remembered my visit to Lorraine all those weeks ago and how she told me she had hacked into Daniel's iPhone and Apple time capsule, the backup device for his computer. She also told me she was sure there was a second-time capsule somewhere, possibly up at our house, which may have more information on it. At the time, I had no idea what she was talking about and had never heard of a 'time capsule', other than in the context of a box containing memorabilia, that people bury in the ground to be dug up many years and possibly many centuries down the line. I promptly forgot all about it after I met her, but as I sat there daydreaming in the kitchen, something stirred in the back of my memory and another piece of the jigsaw suddenly slotted into place.

My Macbook Air laptop had been Daniel's in a previous life before he upgraded to a more powerful version and donated the old one to me. The machine, obviously, still remembered the backup device he had used, the time capsule, and kept trying to link up to it.

- Why did I not think of this before?

I snapped the lid shut and raced up the stairs to the office, laptop in hand. The desk was clear apart from the monitor, but there was still a pile of stuff on the windowsill. It looked like junk, which was exactly why I had shown no interest in it until now. An old radio, a lamp that didn't work, desktop speakers, an assortment of books and some headphones. My heart sank, but something inside my head repeated insistently that the device would not show up on my laptop unless it was actually there in the house. I moved the curtain to one side and sure enough, nestled there amongst the jumbled mess was a shiny white box, the size of a small box of chocolates, with the unmistakable silver apple logo on the top. I punched the air in elation.

'Yes! Come to Mama, you little beauty,' I screamed out loud.

I could not believe my luck that somehow, in his initial hurried confusion to clear out the office, my darling husband had missed this little gem and seemed to have forgotten all about it in the ensuing chaos. Or maybe he was just so arrogant he thought it didn't matter, as I was too thick to know what it was anyway.

I carefully removed it from the windowsill and avoided the unpredictability of the WiFi by plugging the USB cable into my own laptop, only to be greeted by the inevitable message: *Enter password.* For the next ten minutes or so I tried every combination of letters and numbers I could imagine Daniel using, but none of them worked. I was fighting a losing battle and was beginning to fret about how many attempts it would allow me to make before locking me out. Undoubtedly not many.

Think! - I admonished myself, determined not to be outdone.

People forgot passwords all the time. I certainly did. There had to be a way to reset everything when that happened. I opened Safari and searched 'how to reset the password on an apple time capsule', praying that it would not involve sending a link to an email I had no way of accessing. I opted for a short Youtube video, which talked me through the process step by step. To my sheer and utter amazement, it turned out to be so simple a five-year-old could have done it. All I had to do was locate a tiny hole at the back of the device, stick a pen tip in it for five seconds and lo and behold the password was wiped. I stared in awe and disbelief as the folder entitled Daniel's Macbook Air flashed up on the screen of my laptop.

I always thought Daniel just used the iCloud, but apparently not. There were literally thousands of documents suddenly at my disposal, all neatly filed and organised, unlike their paper cousins. As I scrolled rapidly through the list, the ones called Cars and Vett (presumably short for Vettriano) caught my attention immediately.

I tried the Vett file first, but it turned out to be disappointingly sparse, containing nothing more than some background information on the painter and a couple of invitations to auctions. I had heard of Jack Vettriano but knew nothing about him, so I was intrigued to read that he was described by some critics as a 'purveyor of soft porn' and a 'painter of dim erotica'. That sounded right up Daniel's street, I thought to myself. I did a search of his paintings that had been sold recently and found one called Scarlett Ribbons that had gone for £32,000, apparently. The painting was of a woman, naked except for a white bra and suspender belt with black stockings, dark pubic hair on full display. She was standing up straight with her arms slightly out to the side and bound by red ribbons to a frame. Her head was thrown back, exposing her neck but her face was obscured. There was certainly no denying the eroticism. I wondered whether that was one of the paintings Daniel had bought but had to content myself with printing off general information for the moment.

I turned my attention to the Cars folder, clicking on it to reveal a separate file within for each car. There, in the one called Ferrari, was the original bill of sale, dated several weeks earlier with Daniel's name and signature on it, no mention of The Whale anywhere. That would prove the bastards were lying about *her* owning it for a start. I pressed 'print' triumphantly, then sat back and waited, knowing that, at last, I had found the goose that would lay me some golden eggs.

I tried to ignore the nagging little voice in my head, urging caution and telling me that it was not quite that simple. My solicitor had warned me on more than one occasion that I had to be very careful about how I obtained any of the documents I was intending to provide to the Court, her suspicions having been aroused when I suddenly produced the insurance schedule for the cars. I remembered our last conversation very clearly, as I had been made to feel like a naughty schoolgirl, summoned to the Head's office for a telling off.

'The Court is very strict about this Grace,' she said sternly. 'People, even Daniel, have a right to privacy and if you obtain information by means that infringe that right, then I'm afraid it will simply not be admissible in court.'

'That's ridiculous,' I retorted angrily. 'If the documents exist and prove that Daniel is doing things that are at best underhand and at worst *illegal*, surely it doesn't matter how the hell I got hold of them?'

'I'm afraid it does,' she replied curtly. 'As I said, anything obtained by hacking someone's computer, opening mail addressed to them, stealing mail addressed to them, stuff like that...simply won't be allowed. That's the law.'

She looked at me pointedly.

'Well, the law stinks. And it clearly exists to protect the wrong people. I thought you were supposed to be on my side,' I added sulkily.

'Believe me, Grace, I am, but you simply cannot afford to be anything other than lily-white here.'

I felt bitter and let down by the system. Daniel was lying through his back teeth to everyone, including the Courts, and it seemed to me that there was a very good chance he would just get away with doing so. Nobody seemed to be prepared to stand up to him.

I tried to keep calm and think things through logically. Maybe I was going about it all the wrong way.

From what my solicitor was saying, there was only a problem if I hacked into his computer or back up device. If I could prove I had legitimate access to the time capsule and had simply forgotten the password, then I was doing nothing wrong. A plan began to form in my mind and I smiled to myself as I thought how impressed Daniel was going to be with my new IT skills, given that he had always thought I was something of a dunce in that department.

First, I opened the Finder screen on my laptop and took a screenshot of it, clearly showing the all-important words *time capsule shared device*. It was the word 'shared' that had given me the idea and was the key to everything.

Next, I set about copying the contents of my own laptop over to the time capsule, saved the folder and named it appropriately, smiling as it appeared on the screen exactly as I wanted it to:

Daniel's Macbook Air
Grace's Macbook Air

I immediately took a screenshot of the two folders, which proved, in my opinion, that the device was indeed 'shared' and we both had access to it.

Finally, I copied the entirety of the Daniel folder over to my own Maxtor hard drive and I was done. Simple as that. I had the information I wanted and I had the proof to present to the Court that I had obtained it legitimately.

I yanked out the leads of the time capsule, wrapped the wires around it and promptly hid it in my special place between the mattress and base of my bed in the spare room. I would get it out of the house later so that there was no chance of it being subjected to any kind of forensic examination when Daniel found out about it.

I reminded myself once again that I was not the main suspect in a murder case.

Settling down to business in the kitchen, I knew that time was of the essence. I had two days to go through all the files before the meeting with my solicitor to finalise my witness statement for court and I urgently needed evidence to support every claim I was making about Daniel's ownership of assets.

The time capsule treasure chest of files did not disappoint.

When I arrived at Eleanor's office for our meeting I was carrying a large box full of documents I had printed off and files of evidence I had laboriously prepared. I could hardly contain my excitement as I presented her with the original bill of sale for the Ferrari, in Daniel's name of course, together with the amended one in The Whale's name that I had found in Stainsford.

'Just look at that,' I announced, slapping the bill of sale down on the desk in front of her. 'I told you they're obviously in cahoots together and this proves it. She must be so desperate she's prepared to put up with anything to keep him. Well, she's welcome to him, but there's no way on earth she's getting to keep that car, I'm going to make sure of that.'

'I admit this is good, Grace, and I hate to rain on your parade, but I *am* a little concerned about how you got hold of it. Questions will be asked you know.'

'I know that,' I snapped caustically. 'You explained already. The thing is I found the fake documents in the office in the house. He must have left them there by mistake at some point. Obviously, these are just copies; I left the originals on the desk for him. They disappeared, so I assume he took them when he was sneaking around on one of his visits to the house when I was out. So I haven't done anything wrong, have I?' I asked, challengingly.

I looked her straight in the eye and waited for a response. I took particular care not to look to the right, as my research on lying had told me that normal right-handed people always look to the right when they are telling lies.

'Okay, go on,' she continued. 'Tell me about the time capsule you found.'

Without hesitation, I trotted out the pre-prepared story I had come up with.

'The time capsule was a shared back up device that we both used.'

I handed her the screenshot I had printed out and helpfully pointed out the words *shared device*.

'Daniel was always telling me to keep my stuff backed up the way he did, he had once lost a load of stuff when a computer crashed. When everything was thrown up in the air by the email, there was total mayhem as you know and I think we both forgot all about the time capsule. To be honest I think he started using the Cloud for everything instead, as he thought it was more secure. For some reason, I suddenly thought about the time capsule a few days ago and realised that Daniel would potentially have access to all my files, so I decided to erase my stuff from it, as a precaution. Unfortunately, the password didn't work, so I thought I had either forgotten it or Daniel had changed it without telling me the new one. I eventually managed to reset the password and get my files off it, but as I was doing that, I couldn't help seeing some of Daniel's files for the cars and other stuff on there. I presumed there was nothing confidential, as he had left the time capsule in the house, knowing full well I had access to it and used it regularly.'

I looked at my solicitor defiantly, daring her to say something to contradict my story, but she didn't. She accepted my version of events. Just as I expected the judge to do.

'Right, I see. Good. I don't see the judge having any objection to that. So, where is the time capsule now?'

'I don't know. It's disappeared, so I assume Daniel took it. I know he comes in and out of the house all the time when I'm not there. Obviously, I left it on the desk for him so he could take it once I had erased my own files.'

'Okay. Great. Well, I guess we better crack on with this final witness statement. We don't want to miss any court deadlines. You need to appear whiter than white, as I've already said. The more Daniel refuses to comply, the more damage he is doing to his case. I have to say, Grace, I take my hat off to you. Most women who found themselves in your position would just curl up in a corner and give up. When I first met you I wasn't sure you had it in you, but I was wrong. You have a tough streak and appear to have discovered nerves of steel from somewhere. I wish more of my clients were like you. I really mean that.'

There was a look of genuine admiration on her face as she spoke.

'Wow, thanks Eleanor,' I said in surprise. 'At the end of the day though, I had no choice. The only other option was to lie down and die, which was never going to happen.'

It took us a full three hours to put my statement together. I baulked at the mounting cost of it all, at over £300 an hour for Eleanor's time, but I was finally satisfied that it was good and it was comprehensive. In the end, there were two lever-arch files of exhibits for Judge Barraclough to wade through. It was to be the poor man's last case before retirement, apparently. I suspected he would remember it for a very long time.

As I lay in bed that night, I was kept awake by my anger at the injustice of the British legal system I found myself trapped in. Daniel had shown utter contempt for the whole process (although why that surprised me, I had no idea), refusing to attend any of the initial hearings and failing to provide any of the required financial documents. There were warnings about the consequences of perjury and failure to comply with Court Orders but, to my increasing frustration, nothing ever happened to him. He was laughing at them all.

Of course, I had no choice at that stage but to remain on the relentless hamster wheel of justice, but it was becoming increasingly obvious to me that the only way to deal effectively with Daniel was to take matters into my own hands and play as dirty as him. People like him simply had no respect for the law. My thoughts returned to the black business card with the gold writing on it that Spike had given me at Charles' funeral. Nicholas Barrington. Nice name. Maybe I would give him a call, just for a chat.

Whatever the outcome in court, I was determined to make Daniel rue the day he underestimated me. Two could play at the lying game. It was turning out to be surprisingly simple and actually quite a lot of fun, now that I finally understood the rules.

A courtroom battle

Never confuse justice with law. Justice is an ideal,
seldom attained by the tools of the law.

Grace

I stood tall in front of the full-length mirror, pulled back my
shoulders and took a deep breath. This was it. The day to settle the
score.

I was wearing a grey fitted dress from French Connection, knee-
length and demure neckline, bought specially for the occasion. Plain
black, suede court shoes and sheer, flesh-coloured tights, together
with my favourite black, Mulberry handbag, added the finishing
touches to my outfit. I had opted for minimal makeup, just a bit of
blusher, mascara and a new nude lipstick. My hair was piled up in a
neat bun, secured with a pearl clasp to match my pearl earrings and
necklace. I took a deep breath and exhaled slowly, confident that I
was portraying exactly the right image for the judge. I slipped on
my timeless, Jaeger, camel coat, picked up the car keys and set off
for court. There was no Lola to worry about, as my friend Sue was
looking after her for the day. She would need to have her tomorrow
as well if things dragged on as expected.

My phone pinged and there was a message from my brother.

Good luck for today. I'm sure everything will be fine. Text me when you get out.

There was a string of other messages wishing me luck on WhatsApp. I had spent most of the previous evening on the phone to my Mum and various other close friends, but there was nothing more I could do. My fate was now in the hands of one man, the illustrious Judge Barraclough. I was trying hard to remain optimistic, but I had heard a particularly irritating phrase rather too often from my solicitor recently:

'There are no guarantees in litigation.'

In my opinion, that wasn't strictly true. There was one cast-iron guarantee in litigation, namely that the whole entourage of solicitors and barristers would get their hefty fee, no matter whether I was hung out to dry or not. I prayed they were worth it.

Eleanor was waiting for me outside the court so that we could go in together. Safety in numbers. Anthony, my barrister, was already there in the little office assigned to us, doing his final preparations. He smiled reassuringly as I entered.

'Don't worry. You have a very good case and I intend to do everything in my power to get a good result for you. Judge Barraclough is a fair man with a lot of experience under his belt. I don't believe he will tolerate any nonsense from Mr Callaghan today. It'll be his turn for cross-examination first, so you don't have to worry about going on the stand until this afternoon, maybe even tomorrow.'

My stomach was churning and I still felt anything but reassured.

'Okay,' I said nervously. 'Let's just hope he doesn't spring any nasty surprises on us in there.'

The court clerk called us in bang on time and I was glad to be walking down the corridor flanked by my two 'bodyguards'. Daniel appeared from another room and walked in behind us, far too close for my liking. I could feel his glare burning into the back of my head. My mouth was dry and my palms were clammy.

Anthony sat down on the front row next to Daniel, who had chosen to represent himself, apparently unable to afford a barrister of his own. Eleanor and I sat on the row behind. I looked around me and noted the witness stand over to one side and the judge's desk at the front, set imposingly on a raised platform, presumably designed to intimidate.

Judge Barraclough did not keep us waiting. We all rose to our feet respectfully as he strode into his courtroom (even Daniel, who must have decided to work on his image) and my first comforting impression was that he looked like a kind man, not dissimilar to Santa Claus, with grey hair and steel-rimmed spectacles. He motioned to us all to be seated, but before he could speak, Daniel launched in, firmly establishing himself in everyone's eyes as an arrogant arse.

'Your Honour, could I just say, I don't actually know why we're here. I don't even *want* a divorce. I have offered to go to mediation, but she has refused. This could all have been sorted amicably without the need for coming to court and wasting your time.'

Santa looked nonplussed but was firm in his response.

'Mr Callaghan, I think it's gone a little beyond that, don't you? There is no question of this divorce not happening, so please sit down and let's get on with the proceedings.'

Daniel, confident as ever, was not to be deterred.

'Actually, Your Honour, there is something else. These proceedings should *not* be allowed to go ahead. She has hacked my time capsule, which is a computer back up device, as I'm sure you know,' he added patronisingly. 'She has stolen documents from it. I have done some research and I believe that evidence obtained in such a way is *illegal* and therefore *inadmissible* in this courtroom. I'm pretty sure she's tracking me somehow as well, which is also illegal.'

Daniel paused and turned to look at me with a smug grin on his face. I noticed he was wearing glasses, which I had never seen him wear before, possibly in an attempt to make himself look more scholarly and barrister-like.

I refused to make eye contact with him and stared straight ahead at the judge, who spoke calmly, despite his obvious annoyance.

'Mr Callaghan,' he began patiently. 'Perhaps I should remind you that this is *my* courtroom. Firstly, I would ask you as a matter of courtesy to please refer to your wife by her name and not simply *she*. Secondly, the problem, as I see it, is that the only evidence we have here today is that which has been provided by *Mrs* Callaghan. Your own response to repeated requests for documentation has been woefully inadequate. I presume you are not disputing the content of the documents your wife has provided, merely the way in which she obtained them. Is my understanding correct?'

'Well, yes, I suppose so, but...,'

The judge cut him off before he could continue. *Go, Santa!* I liked this man more each minute.

'So I shall simply ask Mrs Callaghan herself to explain how she obtained the various exhibits she has provided, in particular, the ones from your computer back up device that you are so concerned about.'

Judge Barraclough looked at me and smiled encouragingly, waiting for an explanation. I had prepared for this moment and was almost looking forward to it. I looked the judge straight in the eye and told him all about the shared device (big emphasis on the *shared* of course) that had been kept in the office at home and how I had had to reset the password in order to access my own files, etc, etc. Daniel looked as if he were about to spontaneously combust and interrupted rudely,

'That's a lie, Your Honour. She never knew the password and never had access to that device. It's all lies!' he shouted indignantly.

Oh, the irony.

Unfortunately, the problem for Daniel was that he had told so many lies, nobody was ever going to believe him anymore, even when he was actually telling the truth. The little boy who cried wolf. I, on the other hand, had maintained my credibility and integrity throughout and therefore would be believed without question.

The judge did not attempt to hide the fact that he was irritated by Daniel already.

'Mr Callaghan, please refrain from raising your voice in my courtroom. Mrs Callaghan's explanation seems perfectly reasonable to me and I am prepared to accept what she has told me. As I mentioned before, we have very little else to work with in this case. As for your concerns about her having used some sort of tracking device, I believe that it is a fairly common practice in cases of adultery such as this, but it is *not* a matter for this court. We are here to deal with finances. Now, let's stop wasting time and get on. There is an awful lot to deal with here.'

Ha! Me one, Daniel nil - I thought to myself, fist-pumping the air and doing a little victory dance in my imagination, while my face remained resolutely impassive.

Daniel let out an exaggerated sigh and shook his head, muttering something under his breath about the whole thing being a farce and a stitch-up, endearing himself to the judge even more. I sat back in my chair and crossed my legs, maintaining a neutral expression with just a hint of the tragic heroine.

I was starting to enjoy this.

The opening gambit from my barrister as Daniel took the stand was priceless. Daniel's response even more so.

'So, Mr Callaghan, on a scale of one to ten, ten being the highest, how would you score yourself in terms of honesty?'

'Ten of course,' came the reply from the stand, without a moment's hesitation.

I let out a muffled snort, as my barrister raised his eyebrows questioningly and the judge looked up abruptly in disbelief. Daniel noted the unanimous reaction and decided it may be appropriate to amend his reply.

'Well okay, I admit I've been a bit of a naughty boy…eight and a half then.'

If he was hoping to get the judge on his side with his laddish quips and unrealistic perception of his own charm, he was sorely mistaken. Judge Barraclough took notes without commenting, but the look on his face was one of ill-disguised contempt. This was going better than I had dared hope.

Having established a clear picture of Daniel's character for the judge, my barrister set about dissecting and analysing every piece of evidence in my two hefty ring binders. The process was made all the more tedious by Daniel's evasive answers and Anthony's absolute refusal to let him off the hook. I loved watching him sweat as he came out with more and more pathetic attempts to talk his way out of things.

Contradiction after contradiction, lie after lie.

Anthony missed nothing and was effectively tying him in knots, but still Daniel refused to deviate from his web of increasingly implausible lies. In a nutshell, Daniel was claiming that he earned a salary of around £30k a year and merely worked for a big American company these days, Jupiter Holdings, who had bought out his small packaging company a year or so earlier. According to him, the directors of Jupiter Holdings were entrepreneurial businessmen and had apparently chosen to buy numerous assets as investments, including a race yacht, a helicopter, several cars and motorbikes, all of which they had inexplicably exported from the USA and Europe to the UK and made available for Daniel's personal use 'as a bit of a perk'. Daniel himself owned nothing of course. He merely procured and managed the assets on behalf of the company.

Everyone in the courtroom knew that was utter nonsense. Everyone except Daniel, who frighteningly appeared to be totally convinced by his own ridiculous story. Thanks to my extensive PI work over the last few months, there was plenty for my barrister to get his teeth into and he grilled Daniel mercilessly, keeping him on the stand for the entire day.

The only uncomfortable moment for me came when Daniel tried to create a red herring and accused me of 'stalking' his partner and her daughter. He actually had the cheek to say they had been so scared they had talked to the police about getting a restraining order against me.

Seriously? - I thought, offended.

'Stalking' was a bit dramatic. All I had done was check out where The Whale lived when I first found out about her. Admittedly I had gone there on a few different occasions to stake the place out and take photos, but I was pretty sure she had done the same to me.

His accusation was bad enough but what really got to me was the insulting reference he then made to them having clocked me hanging around outside the house in a 'badly fitting blonde wig'. I glared angrily at Daniel, remembering how I had bought the wig to do an ABBA tribute with my friend Eva at a school charity concert we had put on a few years ago. I thought I looked quite good in that wig actually and lots of people had said I should go blonde after that. Anyway, what had that got to do with anything here?

The judge was clearly of the same opinion and moved things on. By the time 5 pm came, the poor man was ready for a rest. I looked at Daniel's drained expression and hunched back and almost felt sorry for him. Almost, but not quite. After a full day on the stand, he had failed spectacularly to offer up any credible information or evidence to refute the fact that he personally owned all of the cars on the insurance schedule I found and that he and Jupiter Holdings LLC were, in fact, one entity. He had floundered repeatedly in the face of an onslaught of difficult questions regarding his bank accounts, both business and personal. In particular, he was questioned about several large payments going out to Jane and Anita, the 'mothers of his children'.

'Why are you making what you claim to be payments for child maintenance from your business account Mr Callaghan?' demanded my barrister.

Tricky, that one.

I smirked, but Daniel stuck to his story heroically.

'As I've already said, they did work for the company from time to time, hence the payments,' he replied curtly.

'But surely child support is an entirely different matter, is it not Mr Callaghan? It all seems a little unorthodox to me.'

My barrister had explained to me before the court day that our game plan was all about raising doubt and discrediting Daniel in the eyes of the judge. The more he lied with his implausible answers, the more his credibility was called into question. That could only work in my favour. Anthony changed the subject abruptly, catching him off guard with his next question.

'Why have you failed to declare the monies in your numerous American bank accounts, which contain not insignificant amounts, from what we have seen on the statements Mrs Callaghan found?'

'I've told you already, she hacked my computer and none of this should be relevant,' he snapped, avoiding answering.

The judge intervened sharply.

'And I have told *you*, Mr Callaghan, that this court intends to review all of the evidence submitted by Mrs Callaghan. I will decide what is relevant and what is not. Now please respond to the questions.'

'Of course, I apologise, Your Honour,' he said tersely, clearly not meaning it. 'Those accounts are empty. I closed them months ago. Why does nobody believe me when I say I'm in serious trouble financially?'

My barrister's reply was delivered with an ironic smile:

'I wonder why indeed, Mr Callaghan.'

He turned to address the judge.

'I think that's all for today from me, Sir.'

The judge looked palpably relieved and quickly rounded up proceedings for the day.

'Thank you Counsel. Thank you Mr Callaghan. We will reconvene 9.30 am tomorrow.'

He addressed Daniel with one last parting shot.

'I shall expect to see up to date bank statements for all the accounts in question Mr Callaghan, as well as documentation to support your claims that the various assets listed for consideration in these proceedings belong to other people, namely the directors of Jupiter Holdings. I will need *full* details of *all* directors of the company. If you fail to produce the relevant documentation, you may be held in contempt of court, which could result in serious consequences for you. Good afternoon.'

With that Judge Barraclough rose to his feet and left the courtroom, undoubtedly heading for a stiff gin and a much-needed nap.

Daniel turned to me with a venomous glare and hissed under his breath:

'You lying cow. Don't for a second think this is over. You're going to get nothing, you do realise that, don't you?'

I refused to engage, which made him all the more furious, letting my barrister take the lead. After all, I was paying him enough.

'Please refrain from talking to my client and using abusive language Mr Callaghan. You need to leave the courtroom now or I will have to call security.'

We remained in the room for twenty minutes or so after Daniel had stormed out in a flurry of papers and mutterings, to give him time to get well away and avoid any further confrontation.

'So what do you think?' I asked Anthony tentatively.

'I'm very happy with the way things went today and I think you definitely have the judge's sympathy. But, as I told you before, this hearing is all about money and assets. Daniel's conduct in your marriage, however appalling and distasteful, has little bearing on the outcome here and the judge cannot be seen to punish him for it in the financial settlement. It will all come down to how much value the judge believes there is in the various bank accounts and assets, balanced against how much of a debt he believes is owed to HMRC and all the other creditors Daniel has dragged out of the woodwork.

Whatever the final amount comes to will effectively be split 50:50 between you in the interests of fairness,' he concluded.

'*Fairness.* You're joking aren't you?' I asked bitterly. 'I just hope to God there is something left for me when all the calculations are done.'

'I'm certainly optimistic. The thing I am aiming to establish is that all the assets Daniel claims are owned by third parties are, in fact, owned entirely by him and, as such, should be in the marital pot for division between the two of you. At the same time, we need to be mindful of the threat of bankruptcy, although we still don't know how true that all is. He is due a bit more of a grilling tomorrow morning and then it will be your turn on the stand. Daniel will, of course, have the opportunity to cross-examine you about your evidence, but it's important you try to stay calm and don't let him rile you. Just tell the truth and explain things as clearly as possible.'

Easier said than done - I thought to myself.

I was dreading the impending showdown. Daniel would know exactly what buttons to press and I would have to be careful not to lose my temper and spoil my 'whiter than white' image.

*****

Day two came around all too soon and, as Daniel took the stand for the second time, it was clear he was employing a change of tactics. Judge Barraclough was reading through a document he had been handed on arrival. He put the piece of paper down on the desk, sighed and turned to Daniel.

'Mr Callaghan, what exactly is this?' he asked wearily. 'You have given me a letter, supposedly from a medical professional, making assertions about your current state of mind and questioning your mental fitness to cope with these proceedings. I understand from this that you are seeking a postponement of the hearing on medical grounds. Is that correct?'

'That is correct Your Honour. My therapist says I have a schizophrenic personality disorder. That means I compartmentalise different elements of my life and it explains how I got myself into such a mess with so many different relationships. Unfortunately, all the stress recently has taken its toll on my mental health and I am being treated by the doctor for depression. It's got so bad that I even have thoughts about taking my own life. I really don't feel I can cope with all this at the moment.'

Therapist? Since when did he have a therapist? - I thought angrily, wondering where this was all heading.

Daniel even managed to give a half-decent impression of someone who was honestly contrite and upset, but to my relief Judge Barraclough could see right through him. He pushed the letter to one side in disgust.

'That may well be true Mr Callaghan, but I have no intention of accepting this letter in court as evidence of anything. The letter is not signed, there is no name of the 'therapist' anywhere on it, nor is it written on headed paper, as would be expected if it was indeed from a medical professional. In short, you could have typed this up yourself last night. We shall continue with the proceedings as planned. Thank you, Counsel,' he said, dismissively.

- Oh, Daniel, when will you ever learn?

I could barely conceal my delight as I recognised the resigned look of a condemned man on his face.

Daniel's cross-examination dragged on for the rest of the morning and when we finally broke for lunch, he was beginning to look decidedly grey around the gills as he trudged off in the direction of Costa. The Ferrari debate over the amended bill of sale in The Whale's name resulted in an important victory for me, although I had to admit I had become obsessive about the Ferrari, embarking on a personal vendetta to ensure that The Whale did not get her hands on it. Surely no one could blame me for feeling like that?

When we returned for the afternoon session, it was my turn to take the stand and face my soon to be ex-husband. He rose to his feet and made a point of shuffling through his notes before clearing his throat and preparing to address me. I steeled myself.

'So Grace. May we look at your Form E first of all, your declaration of finances. Anthony has submitted this on your behalf….'

He turned to my barrister as an afterthought.

'May I call you Anthony?'

'No.'

The reply was short, sweet and very much to the point.

'As I said, Anthony…,' Daniel continued, oblivious, forcing Judge Barraclough to interject crossly.

'Mr Callaghan, I believe Counsel would prefer you to address him formally as Counsel or Mr Porterhouse.'

I suppressed a little snort of amusement at this latest blunder. I felt like I had been transported onto the set of a low-budget TV courtroom drama. Daniel had clearly been brushing up on his skills by watching Judge Rinder, although if his current performance was anything to go by, he needed to watch a lot more episodes.

'I apologise, Your Honour. What I am trying to show here though is that Grace lied on her Form E. She failed to disclose her car, her horse and her baby grand piano,' he announced with a flourish, clearly delighted to bring this astounding revelation about my hidden wealth to the attention of the Court. The judge looked at me questioningly with a slightly bored expression. I addressed him directly and contritely.

'I didn't lie, sir. The piano was a gift from my parents to me when I was a child. The car and the horse were birthday gifts to me from my husband. I was told by my solicitor that I could omit them, as gifts would remain outside the overall settlement.'

'So you admit you lied!' Daniel cut in, leaning forward with his hands on the desk.

'No, I…,'

'You *lied*!' he shouted again before I could finish.

This was turning into some kind of ridiculous pantomime. What the hell was Daniel trying to prove here? Apart from anything else, the disputed values were totally insignificant in the grand scheme of things. The judge was clearly thinking about getting home at some point that evening and abruptly put a stop to the farce playing out before his eyes.

'*Mr* Callaghan, I really don't think we need to pursue this any further. *Mrs* Callaghan, he is right that you should, in fact, have declared those assets, so for the sake of all our sanity, I will put a total value on them of fifteen thousand pounds and that's the end of the discussion.'

I nodded in agreement and attempted to look repentant.

Judge Barraclough did not hide the fact that he was unimpressed by Daniel's attempts to turn his courtroom into a circus. Over and over again, Daniel insisted on reverting to his arguments about how I had hacked his computer, stolen documents addressed to him, etc, etc. Time and again the judge interrupted him and shut down his line of questioning. After about two hours of the painful and cringe-worthy process, everyone in there was losing the will to live and I was finally released from the witness stand, as the judge announced with a sigh that there would be a short break while he retired to consider the evidence.

I hoped Judge Barraclough had some of the character traits of Santa Claus as well as the appearance.

A judgement

---

*All men are free to choose, but no man is free from
the consequences of his choices.*

Grace

Judge Barraclough loathed Daniel. That much was obvious. On
the flip side, I got the distinct impression that he liked me, or at the
very least, sympathised with me. All of that meant nothing in the
end though and would have no bearing on his final judgement. It
came down to a simple exercise in mathematics.

I realised I was completely drained, both emotionally and
physically. For the last two days I had been forced to sit in silence in
the courtroom and endure the humiliation of Daniel's lies. Every
aspect of our life together had been picked apart, not just his
financial dealings but also the most intimate details of our marriage.
I had listened to him telling the judge our marriage had been over
for years and that he believed I always knew about his other
relationships. He spoke passionately about his love for his two
children, stressing his sense of responsibility and how desperately
he wanted to be a good father to them and support them. There was
no doubt in my mind that he would know just how much it hurt me
to hear that, but I refused to give him the satisfaction of seeing it on
my face. He laid it on thick about his depression and his

psychological issues, which he said had led him to spin his elaborate web of lies. Apparently, he just couldn't bring himself to hurt anyone, which is how he, unfortunately, ended up with such a collection of women.

Unfortunate indeed. The most unfortunate thing so far as I could see was that Lorraine had blown the whistle a few months too soon for him because before that, he had been well on the way to implementing his creative business plan for securing his own future. He had invested a lot of time and effort into putting everything well and truly out of reach of the grasping fingers of the tax man (and the divorce lawyers), but he had not quite managed to complete it all. I supposed I should really be thanking Lorraine for that.

The American umbrella company, which owned several smaller companies in the UK was based in the state of Delaware, a 'notoriously sexy location', as the forensic accountant I went to see described it. When I asked him what that was supposed to mean, he explained that it was practically impossible to get any information about companies or bank accounts out of Delaware. It was the state of choice for anyone wanting to dodge UK taxes, apparently. Nothing actually *illegal* about it, he had told me with a wry smile, but a business practice generally regarded as sailing very close to the wind. I explained about the cars and bikes that were being imported from the States and Europe, and he nodded his head knowingly, saying it sounded to him like something known as 'carousel fraud'. A cunning way of avoiding paying tax on the assets apparently, but very difficult to prove, whereby goods are passed around between companies in a similar way to how a carousel revolves. I thought of Daniel's substantial debt to HMRC and the long string of subsidiary companies he had recently set up. I remembered how he used to brag to our friends that he was able to run rings round the taxman.

I had to hand it to him; Daniel had almost pulled it off. 'Almost' being the operative word. Because the whole plan had come to a grinding halt the day Lorraine sent the infamous email.

Not one to be put off or give in easily, for two whole days Daniel looked the judge straight in the eye and stuck to his sob story about no longer owning any of his assets and struggling to make ends meet on his lowly salary from the American company who employed him. He had told the lie for so long and repeated it so many times I was certain he now truly believed it, but I doubted very much the judge did.

It was a long hour before he was ready for us all again and, in spite of my earlier optimism, I found it hard to fight back a sense of impending doom as I re-entered the courtroom to hear the judgement. It felt like everything had been taken out of my hands, as though I was not of sound mind to deal with my own affairs.

We sat obediently in silence, bracing ourselves, as Judge Barraclough looked over the top of his glasses, put his hands on the table either side of his papers and began to speak, in an undisputed tone of authority.

'This is an application brought by Mrs Grace Callaghan for a financial order arising from the divorce between her and her former husband, Mr Daniel Callaghan. Mr Callaghan has rightly referred to Section 25 of the Matrimonial Causes Act, which states that it is the duty of the Court to give first consideration to the welfare of minor children of the family.'

He paused and my heart thumped hard in my chest as I began to panic. Daniel was smiling happily and nodding in agreement. He had warned me his kids would take precedence over me. I had to force myself to focus and listen as the judge began to speak again.

'Well, there are no minor children of the family in this case, although Mr Callaghan has two other children outside the family for whom he clearly has concerns and responsibilities. I am satisfied that Mr Callaghan has sufficient earning capacity and other financial resources to provide for those children. How exactly he does that will be a matter for him moving forward, but it need not impact on my judgement today.

I breathed a sigh of relief.

Strike one to me.

Daniel sat up abruptly and began to bluster.

'What? But I thought you just said...I have to look after my children and that's not cheap these days.'

'Mr Callaghan, please do not interrupt me while I am giving my judgement. This is no longer a forum for discussion.'

Daniel shook his head and muttered something under his breath about the whole thing being a joke. Judge Barraclough continued with his less than complimentary analysis of Daniel's conduct, because of which he intended to draw 'adverse inferences'. I wasn't sure what that meant, but it didn't sound particularly good for Daniel.

'It is correct that there should not be a punitive financial order because of Mr Callaghan's conduct in leading a multiple faceted life. However, for pretty much the entirety of his marriage, he has practised a significant deception, maintained households in both this country and in America and has fathered two children to two separate ladies during that period, all to the ignorance of the applicant wife.'

I baulked inwardly at his use of the word 'ladies', thinking I would have preferred 'slappers', but I made sure my face did not give me away.

'His conduct gives rise to what I might describe as a credibility issue, in that a man who can practise such successful deception for such a period of time has to have what he says viewed with a degree of circumspection. There are also adverse inferences to be drawn from the fact that more than one domestic establishment has been maintained, to the detriment of the marital establishment with which we are dealing today.'

Daniel appeared to have learned his lesson about interrupting and limited himself to rubbing his hand across his face and sighing loudly. My palms were sweating, but outwardly I fought to maintain a neutral expression of calm serenity, as I held the judge's gaze and ignored Daniel's furious glances in my direction.

'Mr Callaghan wanted to make out in cross-examination that Mrs Callaghan's Form E was full of deliberate lies. I do not take that view. When you compare her small omissions with what I can only describe as the cavalier attitude that Mr Callaghan has displayed towards his own Form E, then her inadequacies pale into insignificance and I have to say that it is more likely that I am going to believe Mrs Callaghan in this courtroom. Having heard her give evidence and having examined her documentation, I do not believe it is based on 'Hell having no fury like a woman scorned'. Nor do I regard her as a woman driven by jealousy to exaggerate matters. There were far too many inconsistencies in Mr Callaghan's evidence, with all of it tainted by a remarkable arrogance. He would try and tell me that this marriage effectively broke up after a couple of years and that therefore what has gone on since is of no great consequence and everybody has been comfortable with the arrangement. That is utter nonsense.'

There were certainly no flies on Judge Barraclough. He was summing up Daniel with alarming accuracy, given the relatively short amount of time he had been given to get to grips with all the complexities of the case.

I dared to see a flicker of hope on the horizon as he continued.

'It is instructive to read the report, apparently given by Mr Callaghan's therapist, a certified hypnotherapist and life coach, although there is some doubt surrounding the authenticity of the report. It does, however, sum up how his life has been lived in very clearly defined compartments and it was only when one of those compartments leaked big-time that everything went wrong.'

I lost concentration at that point, hearing only the term *life coach*. The Whale called herself a life coach. Suddenly it all made sense.

Daniel didn't have a *therapist*. It was yet another fabrication, cooked up by the two of them to enable him to somehow wriggle off the hook. I half opened my mouth to protest, but instantly closed it again, remembering the judge's thoughts about interruptions and realising that it made no difference now anyway. I would do better to concentrate on what he was saying.

'It is unimpressive for a businessman who tells me he is dealing in multi-million-pound contracts with a limited company to be conducting more than one account in either his own name or the name of a girlfriend, in an entirely *un*-business like way. This conduct is much more consistent with someone trying to confuse anybody who is going to look at their financial affairs than it is consistent with good business practice. It is a highly devious way of conducting business and that deviousness does not stop at the confusion regarding the company Jupiter Holdings. Every time he cannot answer a question he puts it down to Jupiter Holdings, yet I have not been favoured with even the slightest evidence of their existence, let alone any information about the relationship he has with them.'

The judge appeared to be warming to his theme and I lost count of how many times I had heard the word 'devious'. I was starting to enjoy the entertainment, which was turning out to be a total character assassination of Daniel.

I couldn't have done better myself.

'His devious business practices continue with the issue of child support, paid by the company rather than from his own pocket, in the form of wages for the two women who are the mothers of the children concerned. Unimpressive indeed and certainly there is little evidence to support his claims that they carry out any form of proper work for the company, or that it is anything other than a ruse on his part to make the company, rather than him personally, pay for his parental responsibilities. He tells me there are significant financial difficulties yet, as part of the arrogance of his evidence, he says he has a triple-A credit rating and can borrow money very easily. That does not sit well with what he has told me about his general finances or those of the company.'

This was priceless. I tried to take note of the juiciest comments to report back to everyone later, but I was struggling to keep up. The onslaught continued.

'So far as the cars, bikes and various other things are concerned, I need to make a discreet finding. I regard the bills of sale and all that I have been told about these cars being shifted to Jupiter Holdings or any of Mr Callaghan's lady friends as just poppycock.'

I sniggered at the word 'poppycock', quickly masking it by clearing my throat and looking down.

What a great word that was. I quickly wrote it down on my notepad and double-underlined it to make sure I didn't forget.

'I do not regard those bills of sale as in any way reliable. They are at the very least self-serving and if I were pressed, I would say they had been produced for the purpose of these proceedings and no other reason. The monies that are said to have been paid are monies that have come from an account over which Mr Callaghan had complete control. I do not think these assets have gone any way out of his ownership. That is pure fiction. I regard them all as being wholly his property and therefore part of the matrimonial pot.'

Boom!

This was getting better and better. I wondered for a moment whether Daniel had done enough for someone to actually put him behind bars. Everyone said perjury was a serious offence. And I really should make an effort to shop him to HMRC about the 'carousel fraud' thing. That would be the icing on the cake.

'So where do all these failures on Mr Callaghan's part take us?' Judge Barraclough continued. 'The law is quite clear. There is an obligation to disclose. Not only has he failed to disclose, he has made deliberate efforts to cover things up. I am concerned that this is because he thought that what he might get away with by being occasionally disbelieved in a few minor aspects would be less painful than what might be the case if the full and true picture were known. What I have to do is decide on the capital assets more than anything else in this case and how they should be divided in a broadly equal way, being fair to both parties.'

- Whoa, just a minute. Why do we need to be 'fair' to Daniel? When was he ever fair to me?

I took a deep breath and tried to take myself mentally to my happy place and remain calm as the judge pressed on.

'However, I have to err on the side of making sure that the failure to disclose does not produce an injustice to *Mrs* Callaghan when it is balanced up. *Mr* Callaghan loves to mix the business and the private, the work with the pleasure and it really makes things very difficult to unravel, but if I err on the side of unfairness it must be on *his* side rather than on Mrs Callaghan's side.'

- Ok, that's more like it.

I relaxed as I heard the judge's last sentence, breathing a sigh of relief at his comforting words. We were back on track.

Now we were down to the nitty-gritty. Time for the calculations. Maths was never my strong point and I was quickly lost. All I could do was home in on the assets that were being thrown into the pot. They included both houses, all the cars and bikes, the helicopter and the J125 race boat, although Daniel was still insisting that most of them were 'owned' by either the directors of Jupiter or The Whale. Added to that were the sums of money in the numerous bank accounts I had found statements for. The Swan had been left out of the calculations, to my intense irritation, as had the Vettriano paintings, as Daniel vehemently refused to admit he had ever bought them and, despite my best efforts, I had been unable to find a shred of evidence to the contrary. I heard the judge state a final figure of 1.6 million, give or take a few thousand. I was under no illusions that Daniel had a whole lot more stashed away, probably in the States, but I had been advised by the forensic accountant that I would almost certainly never get my hands on it and would run the risk of bankrupting myself in the process of trying. I did not need to be greedy and knew I had to let it go. Half of the sum the judge was quoting would enable me to start again and make a new life for myself, free of financial worries.

I was happy with that, I decided as he continued.

'However...,'

- Uh-oh. My heart sank.

'there is also a substantial debt of £690,000 due to the Inland Revenue, which is clearly going to have to be paid. I can only suspect that if he has dealt with HMRC in the same cavalier way as he has dealt with these proceedings, they will have had no hesitation in issuing bigger and bigger penalties. When Mr Callaghan is questioned about the bankruptcy proceedings he answers that he knows nothing about them. Yet we have seen paperwork which gives the exact reference of the accounts. I, therefore, have a debt to take into account which may be about to torpedo a lot of his finances if it indeed leads to bankruptcy. On the other hand, he tells me with a degree of confidence that the debt can be settled for 25 percent. Well, so be it. I will take him at his word and calculate the debt accordingly.'

Daniel went to speak, but the judge silenced him with a raised hand. Daniel had always been quite fond of using that 'talk to the hand' thing, infuriating my friend Sara on the boat, and I knew she would find it as hilarious as I did that he was now on the receiving end of it from the judge. I thought of her recent suggestion that we should hoist Daniel's favourite pink bloomers to the top of the mast for all to see, then send all the halyards up there as well, so that he would have no way of getting them down other than shinning up the mast himself. Given Daniel's level of athleticism, that was a feat well beyond his capabilities. A smile played on my lips as I forced myself to concentrate on the business in hand.

There were further calculations concerning my pension and the helicopter before Judge Barraclough came up with the only real figure I was interested in.

'I am as content as I can be, having regard to the paucity of evidence, that I have got as near to a fair figure as I can do.'

He looked over the top of his spectacles at Daniel and addressed him directly before he delivered the death blow.

'The Order is that you make an adjusting payment to Mrs Callaghan of £487, 500 and she will retain the house in Conway, her car, her horse and her baby grand piano.'

Daniel stared back at him in disbelief. He was unused to people seeing through him and clearly did not like it.

'Where am I supposed to get that from?' he demanded, defiantly.

'Well, you have a choice of either selling some of your assets or using the monies in your various bank accounts. There is, of course, the question of your pending bankruptcy and, whether or not it goes ahead, Mrs Callaghan is entitled to be protected. For that reason, the assets I have mentioned will be charged to her with immediate effect and sold by her if you fail to pay the debt. The cars must not be moved by you, but Mrs Callaghan may wish to arrange alternative storage. That is a matter for her to decide.'

To my amazement, Daniel seemed to see a glimmer of hope and visibly cheered up.

'Yes, Your Honour, that is actually fine. I would be quite happy to sell the house and other things to pay the debt, working on a time scale of say three to five years....'

'Mr Callaghan, let me stop you there. We are not talking about three to five years. You have fourteen days to pay the debt, otherwise Mrs Callaghan will have the right to sell the assets herself to recover that debt.'

Daniel leapt to his feet, bright red in the face and leaned his hands on the desk. He was shouting again, in a slow and patronising tone, as though making allowances for the fact that the judge had learning difficulties.

'The assets. Are. Not. Mine. This is a real issue. Why won't you listen to me? I'm telling you, I'm going to have a real problem getting hold of the cars, as I don't even know where most of them are. I am going to have to negotiate with the directors of Jupiter Holdings over in the States and I strongly suspect they will put a third party claim in. I am absolutely certain that Jane will also be putting in a claim against Grace.'

He paused in his rant to look back at me with an expression of pure hatred that sent a shiver down my spine. Judge Barraclough stepped in to take control of the situation.

'Sit down please, Mr Callaghan. You need to act very sharpish to try and work out, either from memory or enquiry, exactly where those cars are. The same applies to all the other assets. Believe me when I say that this situation can only get a whole lot worse for you if you fail to deal with it as a matter of urgency.'

'And where exactly am I supposed to live if my house is sold?'

'As I understand it there is a bedsit in Stainsford that you are currently renting and I am sure that will be perfectly adequate, at least on a temporary basis,' replied the judge, helpfully.

I bit my lip as the unwelcome vision of Daniel's bedsit in Stainsford and all I had found in it came into my mind. Poor Santa would be even more traumatised if he knew about that.

Daniel was now a desperate man, pleading pathetically with the judge.

'I do not understand the maths, Your Honour. What do I get out of all this? Have I got *any* assets left? You seem to be assessing me on things that do not exist.'

He actually looked like he might start to cry, but I noted happily that it did not wash with Judge Barraclough, whose tone and expression remained as cold as steel.

'I have dealt with things which certainly *did* exist and for which there is no satisfactory explanation as to what you have done with them. That is the whole point of the adverse inferences that I drew and which I set out very carefully at the beginning of my judgement. That is my final say on the matter. Counsel, will you please draft an Order for me in the terms I have set out?'

The poor man had clearly reached the end of his tether with this case and would almost certainly need a therapist himself.

'I will, Sir,' replied my barrister.

And with that, the proceedings were over.

Judge Barraclough left the room and within seconds Daniel erupted, metaphorically throwing his dummy, closely followed by all his toys, out of his pram. He was crimson in the face as he stormed towards the back of the room, hurling abuse and accusations at both me and Anthony. He stopped just short of the door and leaned back against the wall, eyes rolling wildly in his head, his breathing loud and far too rapid. He appeared to be hyperventilating. To my amusement, a court official came over and provided him with a paper bag to breathe into, while we stood back and waited for him to calm down.

What a drama queen - I thought to myself.

I desperately wanted to laugh but realised it might be seen as inappropriate and managed to control myself.

In my eyes and, apparently, also in Daniel's, I had won. I would have given anything to be a fly on the wall when he informed The Whale that they would have to hand over the Ferrari to me. At last, it was all over and I was finally going to be able to draw a line under this whole disastrous episode of my life.

If only crystal balls really worked and I could have looked into the future, I would have known then that the real nightmare was only just beginning.

A Friendly Warning

Jane

As soon as Matthew walked through the door Jane knew there was a problem. She stared at him with eyes narrowed and arms folded.

'So what happened?'

'Let me get through the door, for Christ's sake. I need a drink.'

Matthew flung his briefcase on the floor and flopped down onto the sofa, running his hand through his hair.

'That conniving fucking bitch sat there like butter wouldn't melt and lied about everything. You should have seen the stuff she got away with. The worst of it is, the thick fucker of a judge believed every word she said! I'm apparently supposed to hand over the best part of half a million to her in fourteen days, or else she gets to sell everything from under me. I just can't believe this is actually happening. Where the fuck am I supposed to get that kind of money from?'

Jane sat down opposite him. She despised him for the mess he had made of everything, but she couldn't let him see that just yet. There were still too many loose ends to tie up. Thank goodness she had arranged for Aaron to have a sleepover at a friend's house. It was going to be a very long night.

'We both know you can get your hands on the money if you really wanted to Matthew, but it's all about priorities. You'll obviously be fine, given your American 'interests', so as I see it, your main priority now has to be to make sure we, as in Aaron and I, do not suffer. You need to make sure that our assets are protected, including all the new ones.'

'Well, there's a problem with that for a start, because the judge has ruled that all the cars are mine, including the ones in your name, and therefore part of the divorce pot. He pretty much gave her every fucking thing I own.'

'Oh for God's sake, get a grip. They don't even know where the cars are. We stay calm and we move them all tomorrow to different locations. We have all the paperwork for them and we stick to our story. Nobody can seize things if they can't find them.'

'You're right,' he said, feeling a little calmer. 'We'll move the lot. Then we draft a third party claim from both you and the directors of Jupiter about the cars. I'm going to make her life hell! And after her performance today, I'm going to make sure she gets nothing off me. Not a fucking thing.'

That was more like the attitude Jane wanted to hear. At last, he appeared to be getting with the programme.

By 7 am next morning, they were on the road, with the car trailer hitched up to Daniel's Range Rover. The unit where most of the cars were stored was about an hour away, in an insalubrious area of Dunston, near Wolverhampton. The process of moving one car at a time was going to be a tedious but necessary one. Jane had rented a unit of her own for the Ferrari and the two other cars she now 'owned'. Everything else would be scattered far and wide in many separate locations, making it impossible for that bitch to track them down.

By the time Jane looked at her watch, she saw to her intense irritation that it was already 1 pm and they had only managed to move two cars. She phoned her friend Tracy and asked her to pick up Aaron from school and keep him until she called that evening. The sooner she could get Daniel to commit to paying for boarding school the better as far as she was concerned. She loved her son of course, but a child was a massive inconvenience at times.

When they arrived at the unit for the third time there was another car parked there, a black Range Rover Sport with blacked-out windows. Matthew looked instantly concerned.

'Who the fuck is that?'

As they pulled up outside the roller shutter doors, a burly, thick-set man in a black polo shirt and tattoos up both arms got out of the car and came towards them. His pal got out of the passenger side and looked every bit as much of a thug. Matthew got out to meet them with a last-minute attempt at chivalry.

'Stay in the car and lock the doors.'

Matthew was not small by any means, but the two thugs dwarfed him. Intimidation was clearly their business and, from the look of them, they were pretty good at it. They stood side by side and spoke quietly, but loud enough for Jane to hear.

'We believe you are moving cars which you have no right to move, Sir. Our client has asked us to collect five cars on her behalf and we have the authority to move them to alternative storage facilities.'

'Who the fuck do you think you are? You're not taking those cars anywhere. They're mine and the only person moving them will be me,' Daniel stated, with reckless bravado.

Jane observed the action from the safety of the car. She was unsure about the wisdom of Matthew raising his voice and adopting such an aggressive tone with the henchmen. She noticed they were careful not to lay a hand on him, but they blocked his path every time he moved towards the entrance of the unit. Jane could no longer hear what they were saying, but she could see that the expression on Matthew's face had changed from one of arrogant annoyance to fear. They were standing far too close to him and the one who had got out of the driver's side kept holding out his hand as if asking Matthew to give him something. Matthew took a step backwards and looked around him with an air of desperation, but they moved with him. The driver was speaking again, leaning his face in towards Matthew and gesturing towards her and Matthew's own car. She checked the doors were locked and looked at the keys in the ignition. It crossed her mind to swap seats and drive off, leaving him to his fate but decided against it for the moment.

The argument continued for a good fifteen minutes after which Matthew, apparently, gave in and opened the door of the unit. Thug number one disappeared inside with Matthew, while Thug number two took out his mobile and rang someone.

Half an hour later Jane and Matthew watched helplessly as the remaining cars were loaded onto the multi-car transporter that had miraculously turned up shortly after the phone call. Before they drove off after the transporter, the thugs handed Matthew a business card and held out a hand for him to shake.

'Fuck you!' he shouted and banged on the window for her to open the door. He was ashen-faced and shaking as he got in and slammed the door shut, but Jane was not letting him off the hook lightly after the charade she had just witnessed.

'Why the hell did you open the unit for them? I can't believe you let them take the bloody cars.'

'Are you for fucking real? Did you see them? You've no idea what they were threatening me with. That bitch Grace is behind this and I'm telling you she's gone too far this time. If she wants to play rough, she's going to find out she's messing with the wrong person. What the fuck is she playing at, getting involved with low life scum like that?'

Grace was actually going up in Jane's estimation. She had to admit she was proving to be more of an adversary than she had initially anticipated. Jane wondered just for a moment whether she might be more useful as an ally than an enemy, but she put that thought quickly out of her mind. That would never happen.

'You need to calm down and get your act together,' she snapped at Matthew. 'At the end of the day, all she's managed to do is get Dumb and Dumber to move a few of the cars, but we already got the Ferrari and the Beamer out of there. First thing tomorrow we need to put a claim into the Courts for the other stuff and play it by the book for once, as we planned. We've put a lot of effort into modifying all the paperwork and there's no way she can prove anything. We just have to be patient and let the Courts take everything back off her.'

'I'm sick of the whole bloody business now,' Daniel whined, looking hassled. 'I was supposed to be going over to the States again this week.'

Jane's face darkened at the implications of that. She didn't entirely trust him not to just bugger off to America and stay there, shacked up with that tramp and her kid. That was why she needed to protect her own interests over here. It was about damage limitation now. Even she was realistic enough to see that. So long as he stayed in the UK she was okay. She had already screwed private school fees out of him, on the grounds that their son was being bullied in the local school. It should be easy to move that on to the next stage of boarding school. She knew there was plenty of money around, despite what some of the many accounts showed, and their business arrangement for milking the company in lieu of child support payments could continue. So long as he didn't abscond.

She had already threatened him with whistleblowing to the taxman, but again, that would only work if he stayed in the country. They would have a job to pin him down if he ran off to the States. As would she. She was walking a tight rope and would have to be careful not to push him too far. Right now he was in a blind rage and did not seem to be capable of thinking or acting rationally. It was actually a bit unnerving.

Maybe it would be best if she dealt with Grace herself rather than leaving it to him. Ex-wifey was certainly flexing her muscles and clearly thought she was holding all the cards now. Perhaps it was time to disabuse her of that thought.

What Jane did not know, however, was that Matthew was already one step ahead of her on that score.

Shifting goalposts

When someone pulls the rug from under you, you need to learn how to dance on a moving carpet.

Grace

I felt the soft, buttery leather of the All Saints jackets on the rail in Harvey Nichols and put down my bags, containing a new pair of grey suede ankle boots and a dress from Reiss, eager to try it on. I felt justified in treating myself, now that I had finally stopped haemorrhaging money on solicitor's fees. This was the start of my new life and I had to dress for the part. The last couple of weeks since the court case had not been easy and Daniel had done everything to put obstacles in my way, but the fact remained that I now had a signed and sealed Court Order stating exactly what he owed me. Of course, I had to be realistic about the fact that he had absolutely no intention of paying me a penny, so I had to get as many of the assets as possible sold. I had managed, with the help of the tracker, to get my hands on most of the cars and motorbikes and I had rented a specialist storage unit for them in Leeds. It had not been cheap to move them but, hopefully, it would only be for a short time.

Daniel and The Whale had got one over on me with the Ferrari, but my solicitor had said I just had to bide my time and wait for the court process to take its course. No judge was ever going to believe the story they had concocted, especially not the bit about her paying him for the car in cash with a pile of fifty-pound notes she had found in a tin box under the floorboards of her father's house after he died.

Everyone involved in the storage of the assets had been served with the Court Order and warned that they were not allowed to let anything be moved by Daniel. I was certainly not going to let the grass grow under my feet and intended to get the cars to auction as fast as possible. Some of the other stuff, like the helicopter, was trickier to get my hands on, so I was concentrating on the cars, the bikes and the house for the moment.

My phone buzzed in my bag and I scrabbled to get it out and check the screen. Eleanor. My mood changed abruptly, as it always did when her name came up, and I wondered what the hell she wanted. She didn't usually ring with good news.

'Grace, are you okay to talk?'

'Yes, I'm in a shop, but its fine. What's happened?'

'I don't want you to panic, but I have just had news from the Court that they have received third party claims from Jane Sutcliffe and the directors of Jupiter Holdings about the various assets, including the Ferrari of course.'

'Shit, what does that mean? I don't understand…there *are* no other directors of Jupiter Holdings apart from Daniel.'

'As I said, there is no need to panic. It wasn't entirely unexpected. We just have to deal with it and hopefully it can all be sorted out of court. There should be sufficient evidence on our side to get the claims thrown out, but if they are prepared to force the issue and stick to the lies, we may need to go to a hearing.'

'Oh Christ, just what I need. I really thought I was free of all this.'

'I know and I'm sorry, but as I said, we thought he would probably do this.'

She paused and I sensed there was more.

'There was one other thing. I found out today that Daniel has been declared personally bankrupt.'

'Bloody hell. I didn't expect that. I really thought he would do a deal with them like he said he was going to. Serves him right if you ask me. I'm still okay though, aren't I? You said if I had a Court Order I would be protected.'

Again, the hesitation.

'Well, yes, I believe so. I've been speaking to Phil, the head of our insolvency team and he says that, even in the worst-case scenario, you would still be entitled to half of all the assets outside of the bankruptcy. So yes, you should be ok,' she concluded.

The word 'should' did not fill me with confidence.

'You don't sound convinced to me.'

'Look, Grace, there is no point in jumping to conclusions at this stage. I need to make some more enquiries and find out the facts. I intend to speak to the Official Receiver assigned to Daniel's case today and I'll contact you again after that. Please try to stay calm about this. It's not the news we wanted, but I'm sure you'll be okay.'

Given with one hand, taken away with the other. It seemed to be the story of my life. What was it Eleanor was so fond of saying?

'No guarantees in litigation.'

My mood had plummeted and I felt unspeakably glum as I trudged back to the car park, minus the All Saints leather jacket I had coveted. This latest development had opened the flood gates for the start of a whole new legal battle. I had not dared to add up the financial cost of ridding myself of Daniel, but I had a pretty good idea it was already in excess of fifty grand. I had taken a gamble. Speculate to accumulate. I had put my trust in the legal system and hoped I would come out on top, banking on the fact that I would be leaving my marriage with significantly more than the legal fees I had to pay out. After my day in court, it actually looked like the gamble had paid off, but that was before Life threw me a curveball. Suddenly everything was up in the air again and my solicitor sounded less than positive about a good outcome for me. It looked like we were back on the carousel, but this time an insolvency lawyer and an insolvency barrister were joining us at the fair. I could almost hear the cash tills rattling.

I could not face going straight home, so I opted for the place that had become my safe haven over the last few months. As I let myself in through the kitchen of the hotel, Sylvie was in there preparing the staff meals. I could not hold back the tears and she instantly stopped what she was doing and came over.

'What's wrong darling?' she asked with a concerned look on her face.

'There's been a new development. You're not going to believe this...Daniel's been made bankrupt and Eleanor's really not sure where I stand now.'

'Oh my God! I *never* believed he'd actually go bankrupt. Look, try not to panic. You've got your Court Order, so they won't be able to touch any of the stuff the judge gave you. Go straight through to the bar. Adam's in there with Andrew. I just need to finish this quickly and I'll come and join you.'

Adam took one look at my face and poured me a large glass of red.

'Sit down and tell us all about it. What's Knob Head done now?'

I laughed despite myself, grateful for the way his calm, relaxed manner and dry sense of humour always seemed to lighten the mood.

'He's been made bankrupt. Both the company *and* him personally. Eleanor just rang to tell me and she sounded worried. I'm so scared that everything's going to go wrong for me all over again, just when I thought I was finally sorted.'

'But she said you'd be okay if you got the Court Order before the bankruptcy, didn't she?' Andrew queried.

'Well yes, she did and that's what I thought, but apparently there seems to be some sort of grey area she wasn't aware of.'

Adam poured himself and his father a drink and sat down opposite me.

'I warned you about the Courts,' Andrew said wryly. 'The legal, above-board route just doesn't work with people like Daniel and the only ones that win in the end are the lawyers.'

'The man is an absolute tosser,' Adam stated. It's obvious he's got a load of money stashed away in America and yet he's determined to shaft you completely. And Dad's right, you can't trust the solicitors either. If you want my advice, tell them as little as possible and sell everything you can as fast as you can, especially the stuff no-one knows about, cash transactions wherever possible. Hide the things you can't sell straight away and remember you've always got the Stainsford Secret to hold over Daniel. If I were you, I wouldn't be ruling out blackmail when this all dies down.'

I sighed deeply and took a large gulp of wine before responding.

'How the hell did my life come to this? I honestly don't know how much more I can take. No matter what I do, I just can't get ahead. I wonder if this is what it was like for Julia? Maybe this is what she felt like in the end.'

Sylvie walked in and caught the tail end of the conversation.

'Oh darling, please don't talk like that. It really upsets me and I hate to think of what he did to poor Julia, but you're not her. You have come so far and handled everything so well, I'm sure you're going to be okay. You have a Court Order, signed by a judge, for God's sake. There's nothing anyone can do to change that or take anything away from you, surely. Eleanor is just being over-cautious. Typical solicitor. Stay strong.'

'I hope you're right,' I said, unconvinced, as she hugged me tightly.

I wanted to believe it, but I had learned the hard way not to take anything for granted. Suddenly I wanted to go home and wallow in self-pity on my own.

'Anyway, thanks for listening guys and thanks for the wine pick me up. I don't know what I'd do without you. I need to go now, as

I've got a load of stuff to do in the house. Catch you tomorrow and I'll let you know if I hear anything more from Eleanor.'

Sylvie hugged me again.

'Anytime, darling. You know you're always welcome here.'

Andrew came to the door with me.

'Have you changed the locks at home yet? It's bloody ridiculous that he's allowed to come and go as he pleases. I don't like it at all, especially now he's obviously furious with you. He's dangerous and unpredictable in my opinion. I've told you before, I think he had more of a hand in his first wife's death than was ever reported.'

'Yeah, I know all that and believe me, I'm not exactly happy about the situation, but I've been told by the Court that I'm not allowed to change the locks or deny him access, as it is still technically his house. I can't move out either, as I need to protect my claim to it. There's certainly nothing of mine of any value there anymore and I can assure you I am very careful when he's around.'

'I still think you should maybe apply for a restraining order against him. Say you're afraid of him. That's what Lorraine did isn't it?'

'Yes she did, but they won't entertain the idea without some concrete proof. In her case it was easy. He shot himself in the foot by being abusive and violent to both her and the police.'

'True. I think it's worth a try though.'

'Maybe, but with any luck, this will all be over soon and the house will be sold. I'm applying to the Court for the right to sell the house at auction to make sure it goes quickly. Daniel's objecting of course, but Eleanor reckons the Court will permit me and then he won't be involved or able to interfere anymore. I'm just a bit worried about how his bankruptcy will affect things now.'

'I suppose you just have to wait until she gets back to you on that one. In the meantime take care and remember you can call us anytime if there's a problem.'

I gave him a quick hug and left. They were all right of course. I had to stop letting things derail me so easily. I would wait to hear from Eleanor and deal with things when I knew the full facts.

Lola pounced on me excitedly as I opened the back door at home. The room felt cold and uninviting, which was strange, as the AGA always kept the kitchen warm. I walked over to the big stone fireplace and was surprised to feel cold metal. Daniel had changed the AGA over to electric a couple of years before to avoid any issues with burners or running out of oil. It was more expensive, but way more reliable and had never caused a problem before. I opened the little fuse box on the wall and found the fuse had been removed, then when I went to check the display on the electrical control unit, concealed at the side of the AGA, the whole thing was gone. Daniel. So that was the way he was going to play things. I flew into a temper, sending the poor dog scuttling to her basket.

'Fucking, arse-hole bastard!' I yelled in frustration.

He had got one over on me yet again. I bent down and cuddled Lola, my tone softening.

'It's okay, baby. It's not your fault, it's not you.'

She lifted a paw and looked at me, ever hopeful of a treat in consolation. I laughed and gave her a little handful of her biscuits. Inside I was seething and already racking my brains for ways of revenge. He was threatening me. Showing me he could snoop around the house when I wasn't there and mess with things. I shuddered at the memory of the fire in the house all those years ago and what Kieran had told me. Daniel was an electrical engineer by trade and was more than capable of creating a 'wiring fault'. I began to worry about what else he might have been up to in my absence.

My thoughts were interrupted by the buzzing of my phone and I saw from the display it was Eleanor again. Great. Undoubtedly that meant more good news.

'Hi Grace. I just wanted to let you know that I have spoken at length to the Official Receiver in charge of Daniel's bankruptcy. He was very nice and helpful and seems to be confident that you have nothing to worry about, as you already have a financial settlement and a Court Order. They are now in the process of appointing a Trustee in Bankruptcy to administer things and they will be in touch with us shortly. In the meantime, I suggest we continue as planned, selling the assets to realise your money.'

'Right,' I said, taken aback and hardly daring to believe what I was hearing. 'I wasn't expecting that. It sounds positive then.'

I told her about the latest fun and games with the heating at the house and naturally, she was furious on my behalf.

'What? How dare he. He has no right to do that to you. I have already submitted the application to put the house up for auction and I will bring this up at the same time. It should help our case, to be honest. I've asked for an urgent hearing so we will hopefully have a date in a couple of weeks.'

She hesitated, then added,

'I'm worried about your safety, Grace. We need to push for you to be able to change the locks after this. Are you going to be okay in the house by yourself?'

'Yes, I'll be careful. There's no way I'm moving out until everything is settled.'

I still had the tracker, which meant I could at least keep an eye on Daniel's movements. In theory, anyway. In practice, I was starting to feel slightly uneasy about the tracker these days, as I had recently noticed *Daniel 1* remaining stationary for days at a time, which was not normal practice for him at all. I had a sneaking suspicion he was using another car to thwart me, probably The Whale's. That made things a lot trickier and a lot less safe.

As I lay in bed that night, with Lola snoring beside me, I thought how utterly disheartening it was that the sand always seemed to be shifting beneath my feet.

A surprise party

If you are left behind, run faster to catch up. Never give in and when Life knocks you down, make sure you throw the first punch next time.

Grace

The hearing about putting the house up for auction was indeed dealt with as a matter of urgency and within four weeks we all trooped back into court. Judge Barraclough had decided to hear the third party claims from Jane and Jupiter Holdings at the same time, clearly anxious to get the whole thing out of the way at once before he had a nervous breakdown. I suspected he was as curious as I was to find out what Daniel had cooked up about the 'directors' of Jupiter Holdings.

As I walked into the large waiting room with Eleanor I noticed it was a busy day in court and there were a lot of people already there. I wondered briefly what all their stories were. My eyes lighted on Daniel over in one corner with The Whale in tow. She was wearing a voluminous smock top over a pair of black leggings and I immediately noticed how her puffy feet spilled out over the straps of her unfashionable sandals. I avoided eye contact and sat down with Eleanor, crossing my legs slowly and deliberately to make sure that The Whale could not miss the red soles of my Louboutins. Five minutes later the clerk appeared and called us into Judge Barraclough's room, but to my utter confusion, practically everyone else in the room stood up at the same time and began to follow us.

'What the hell is going on?' I hissed to Eleanor. 'Who are all this lot and why are they coming into our hearing?'

Eleanor looked as baffled as me.

'I have no idea Grace. Let's just get in and we'll find out what's happening.'

There was a tense note in her voice, which did nothing to boost my confidence.

'It's the bankruptcy lot, isn't it? It can't be anything else,' I snapped furiously.

'I'm very much afraid you're right, but I have no idea what they are doing here. I should have had some sort of notification. This really is totally unacceptable.'

Judge Barraclough himself looked as surprised as we were at the number of people filing into his little room. He even had to send the clerk out for more chairs and two of the entourage had to sit at the side as there was no more room around the table. I was positioned opposite The Whale, with Daniel at the head of the table, looking pompous and full of his own self-importance, as he casually shuffled a pile of papers around. The Whale was flanked on either side by two women, who were every bit as large as she was and I thought for a moment that it must be a Weight Watchers outing, but before I could helpfully point out that the WW meetings were held in the building next door, they introduced themselves as her solicitor and her barrister. I felt instantly outnumbered.

-Why didn't I have a barrister?

Daniel had an irritating, smug look on his face that made me want to punch him. I waited with trepidation for the others to reveal their identity.

'Natasha Remington, solicitor for the Trustee in Bankruptcy in the case of Daniel Matthew John Callaghan and my trainee Victoria Bates.'

'Vanessa Harding from Miller Laidlaw, Trustee in Bankruptcy in the insolvency of Daniel Matthew John Callaghan. This is my assistant Jonathan Carter.'

'Corinne Burns, barrister appointed by the Trustee in Bankruptcy.'

A grand total of eleven people, most of whom had no need to be meddling in my business as far as I could see.

The judge was keen to get things moving and the lovely Ms Burns was quick to jump in and suggest she begin by explaining the Trustee's position.

I sat in a dazed stupor, trying desperately to understand what was going on, while Eleanor scribbled notes furiously beside me.

'I would like to draw everyone's attention to Section 284 of the Insolvency Act 1986, referring to the disposal of assets.'

There was a pause while we all found the appropriate document to look at in the substantial bundle we had been handed on arrival.

'Section 284 essentially states that no party can be given preference over the disposal of assets in insolvency. All assets of the Bankrupt must be dealt with by the Trustee in Bankruptcy and divided equally among the creditors of the estate. Effectively, what that means here is that Mrs Callaghan should not have been given any of her husband's assets as part of her financial settlement. All of those assets will need to be handed over to the Trustee immediately. If any of them have already been sold, she will need to surrender the money received for them. She is then, of course, more than welcome to submit her claim to the Trustee and stand in line with the other creditors,' she concluded, dismissively.

Her voice had an annoying nasal twang and was grating on me already. What I had thought was a routine hearing was rapidly turning into my worst nightmare. If what she said was true, I was about to have everything taken off me, and then some. Eleanor interrupted.

'Judge Barraclough, I really must object to the fact that I have had no notification of this intervention at all and so have had no opportunity to prepare. This is the first I have heard of any of it. Grace has a Court Order as you know, having signed it yourself, setting out the terms of her financial settlement following her divorce. Surely that Court Order stands, despite her ex-husband's subsequent bankruptcy?'

Corinne reminded me of a nasty tempered, yappy Jack Russell. She stared at Eleanor with her beady little eyes and began again.

'I'm afraid that is not the case and you have been misinformed,' she barked. 'In cases such as this, the Insolvency Court takes precedence over the Family Court and we have the right to backdate things to when the petition for bankruptcy was first issued. That was, in fact, four months before your Court Order. Any assets owned by the Bankrupt at that time are deemed to be assets of the bankruptcy estate now. That includes all the assets listed here in the Order.'

Corinne tapped a neatly manicured finger disdainfully on my Court Order in front of her. Apparently, it was not worth the paper it was written on. Daniel was clearly enjoying my misery and chose that moment to pipe up.

'Excuse me, Your Honour, presumably that does not include the assets owned by other people? I am referring of course to the third party claims from both my partner Jane here and the directors of the company I work for.'

- Oh, here we go!

Judge Barraclough glowered at him and did not attempt to hide his contempt when he replied.

'Mr Callaghan, my findings about those assets stand. If the 'third parties' have any real evidence to prove otherwise, they will, of course, be given the opportunity to present it to the Court. For the moment, I suggest we all need time to take stock of the situation and propose we reconvene for a hearing to consider the evidence properly in two weeks. In the meantime I am giving a ruling that no further assets be dealt with by *any* of the parties,' he declared sternly, looking around at the faces in the room over the rim of his spectacles. 'That includes the marital home. And Mr Callaghan, as I have already warned you, if the directors of Jupiter Holdings wish to present a third party claim, they must supply their full contact details and proof of identity as a matter of urgency.'

Eleanor looked shell-shocked and was clearly out of her depth as the Trustee and her entourage swept out of the stuffy little room, closely followed by The Whale and her two buddies. Daniel waited until the end and followed Eleanor and I out, no doubt anxious not to waste an opportunity to gloat.

'Gosh, you've put weight on Grace.'

There was so much he could have said and yet that was the line he chose.

Hilarious.

My only consolation in this whole sorry mess was that he had saddled himself with The Whale of Willowmede and I was sure he would be getting nothing but grief from her over everything.

Eleanor led me hurriedly to a little side room to discuss the situation and closed the door. She was struggling to maintain her composure.

'Right, let's just sit down for a minute and talk this through.'

'Well, it doesn't look good, does it?' I snapped at her. 'You've been telling me all along I was fine because I had a Court Order and now it transpires that the whole process has been a complete waste of time and money. I'm going to lose everything and there's not a damn thing we can do about it, according to that bitch of a barrister.'

'Look, I really think you're jumping the gun a bit,' said Eleanor, in an attempt to placate me. 'Let's wait until we've spoken to our insolvency team again and done some research on this. We've got a couple of weeks to catch our breath and at least now we know what we're dealing with. Let's see what Daniel comes up with regarding the directors of Jupiter Holdings. My guess is he can't provide contact details for *anyone*, let alone proof of identity. Jane's witness statement about the cars should be interesting too.'

I found it difficult to share her apparent optimism, feeling let down and betrayed all over again by the people I had trusted. At the end of the day, this was just another job for her, whereas in my case, it was my whole life at stake and suddenly it was spiralling wildly out of control.

I was beginning to think Daniel was right when he told me all those months ago that this would end in tears. Except back then, I had been certain they would be his tears, not mine.

A meeting with an insolvency barrister was hurriedly scheduled for the end of the week. It would be limited to two hours maximum, which, at his exorbitant fee of £950 per hour, would still net him a nice little bonus for the weekend. I had a growing sense of impending doom about the whole thing, not least because I was once again shelling out ridiculous amounts of money that I simply did not have. As I feared, he confirmed the fact that Section 284 of the Insolvency Act 1986 did indeed apply in my case.

Of course it did.

Not one to give in without a fight, I clung to the hope I had been given by my own insolvency lawyers that I was entitled, as Daniel's wife, to half of the assets anyway, outside of the bankruptcy. Wrong again apparently. Not unless I could prove that those assets were paid for either wholly or partly by me.

'Who the hell can prove things like that? Do you keep receipts for things you bought ten, maybe fifteen years ago?' I demanded, then continued immediately without allowing him to respond. 'It's all just so unfair and to be honest, makes a complete mockery of our legal system. And what about the cars I already sold? I've paid that money into my mortgage now and I won't be able to get it back out. Why should I *have* to pay it back anyway, when I was given the assets by a judge and told I could sell them?'

I might as well have been banging my head against a brick wall.

'I do understand your frustration Mrs Callaghan and I sympathise that you have been caught up in all this through no fault of your own but, unfortunately, all I can do is tell you how the law works. The insolvency court takes precedence over the family court here.'

Basically, what he was saying was that neither he nor the law of the land could give a shit about me. I was wasting my time and money. I felt suddenly claustrophobic and needed to get out of there. Standing up abruptly, I held out my hand and thanked him curtly for his time and advice, bristling at the fact of how much I had paid for the privilege.

It was raining outside, which seemed fitting for the general mood of the occasion. I thought of my dad and wished for the hundredth time he was still here to help me through this. He would have known what to do; he always did. He was the most positive, determined and stubborn person I had ever known. I heard his words in my head:

There's no such word as can't. Never give up and remember that every problem has a solution. You have to keep trying your hardest, no matter what happens.

Letting him down was not an option. He would never have given in and so I had no choice but to pick myself up and keep fighting.

As I drove through the gate to the house, Daniel's car was on the drive. Typical. He was the last person I wanted to deal with, given that he had obviously come to gloat. He was sitting at the kitchen table when I walked in, a cup of coffee in one hand, stroking Lola with the other. I knew I was being childish, but I couldn't help feeling annoyed at my dog's lack of loyalty. I spoke sharply to her.

'Lola, come here! Get in your basket.'

Her ears drooped as she obediently headed for the basket, wondering what the hell she had done wrong. I instantly regretted my harsh tone and gave her a biscuit, a sure way to win her over.

'Good girl. I'm sorry, it's not your fault.'

I turned to Daniel.

'Just leave her alone. Don't even touch her,' I said, petulantly. 'I suppose you're proud of that little performance in court?'

He sighed and shook his head sadly, as though he had the weight of the world on his shoulders. He really should have gone into acting.

'Not at all. I was as shocked as you were by what they were saying. But I did warn you about the bankruptcy. They're like vultures and it looks like they're going to get the lot now. I just wish you'd listened to me at the beginning and let me help you. I told you I didn't want you to end up with nothing like this.'

'You lying bastard,' I exploded. 'That's all you ever wanted. All you want to do is make sure *you're* alright and protect the interests of that fat lump you're shacked up with in Willowmede. You know, that's what I really don't get. I mean, seriously, she's gross.'

'She is the mother of my child, Grace,' he goaded me, with a saintly expression on his face. 'I have to make sure both she and my son are properly provided for.'

It was almost as if he enjoyed twisting the knife.

'Don't call her that, you bastard,' I screamed at him. 'Besides, I know it's all lies about her buying the cars from you and I can prove it.'

I knew I sounded like a fishwife, but he was pushing all my buttons and I just couldn't keep my temper.

'I'm sorry, Grace, really I am, but everything I've said is true. Look, I don't want to argue with you. Believe it or not, I still love you.'

'Shut the fuck up, you bloody liar! How can you say you love me after all you've done?'

'Because it's true. You know I never wanted a divorce. I wanted us to find a way to work this out. I'm just sad you couldn't bring yourself to feel the same. It's all that bloody Lorraine's fault. What a lying, treacherous bitch she turned out to be. Just another few months. That was all I needed and I would have had everything sorted.'

He paused again for dramatic effect and sighed resignedly, as though he were the victim in all this, before continuing.

'Anyway, I'm only here to take some of my stuff. If I were you I'd do the same, before they repossess the house.'

'They can't do that, because I have rights to it as the marital home,' I spat.

But I was far less sure of my facts than I sounded, given the events of the last few days. He laughed quietly.

'Well, good luck with that one. I think you'll find they can do *exactly* what they want. The worst of it is that you've gone and made it a whole lot easier for them with that court case you insisted on. Thanks to you, they now have chapter and verse on everything I own and where it is stored. I spent years putting everything in place and now this whole divorce fiasco has ruined everything. I only hope they believe me about the assets owned by the guys at Jupiter Holdings, because if not, I've got big problems with my bosses.'

I looked at him incredulously.

'You lying piece of shit. Even now you still won't be straight with me. Don't give me all that crap about Jupiter Holdings and your 'bosses'. You and I both know there is no one else involved in that company except you. It's just another way for you to get away with keeping stuff for yourself. Well, I'm telling you now, if I can't have it, I'll make bloody sure you can't either. Oh and by the way, what's the idea with the AGA? Great way to show you care.'

'I had to do that because I can't afford to pay the electricity and heating bills you were racking up.'

'I don't believe you. It's just another way of making my life more unpleasant. Who needs hot water and electricity, eh? Anyway, don't let me keep you. Isn't it time you were off now? I really don't want you hanging around here and I'm sure The Whale is expecting you.'

I stood looking at him, my arms folded in defiance. To my surprise, he got up without a fight and put on his leather jacket, sighing dramatically.

'What a waste of both our lives. Just think about that when you're sitting on your own in a crappy little bedsit somewhere, unable to afford the heating. It's no fun being lonely you know and don't think you'll find it easy to meet someone else. Julia found that out the hard way. All the men your age are looking for younger women and time is not on your side, is it Grace? You need to think seriously about what you're doing with your life.'

'You just can't resist another dig, can you? Why don't you crawl back under your stone and leave me alone. I can't wait until you're out of my life for good and I never have to see you again.'

He stood in the doorway about to leave, adding as an afterthought:

'Your car looks good, by the way. Very clean and tidy. Glad to see you're looking after it.'

- What is wrong with him?

'What the hell has that got to do with anything?' I yelled at him furiously.

To my intense annoyance, he just gave a little laugh and walked out.

I slammed the door behind him and locked it, leaving the key in the lock.

I sat down at the kitchen table, visibly shaken, and took out the glossy, black business card Spike had given me at the funeral, turning it over and over in my hand. The clock was ticking now and I had to move fast.

I could fight dirty when I needed to. I had learned from a master after all.

Girl on fire

---

*It is only when you have looked death in the face
that you can ever feel truly alive.*

Grace

As I tramped across the fields with Lola the day after Daniel's last visit, I had time to myself. Time to think things through and try to come to terms with the ever-changing situation. It was glaringly obvious to me that I was standing on the edge of a precipice and the most ironic thing about it all was that Daniel was right. I had made it all so easy for the bankruptcy thieves to plunder everything. Left to their own devices, they would never in a million years have found the things I found. They would have been bumbling around forever and a day, trying to track down the assets Daniel had hidden. The Trustee must have thought all her birthdays and Christmases had come at once when she saw my Court Order, listing everything so meticulously, and realised I had done her job for her. Extremely efficiently, I might add. Maybe I should send her an invoice. All she had to do was collect the assets I was now being forced to hand over to her.

I quickly came to the bitter conclusion that I despised her and her scavenging entourage even more than I despised Daniel, and that was saying something.

If I was really lucky I might be able to hang onto *my* house, the solicitors had told me. They were throwing me under the bus, I thought angrily and, now that they could see the money tree wilting, their interest was most definitely waning as well. I had trusted in my lawyers and the Great British legal system, believing that justice would be served, Right would triumph over Wrong.

What a mistake that had been.

I put Lola in the kitchen and had a quick shower before heading out again. I was meeting Frieda in town for a coffee and I was running late as usual. Realising I had left my car keys in my other bag upstairs, I decided to take the spare keys to save time. I went straight to the little pot at the back of the dresser, where I always left them but, to my consternation, I found only the spare door keys. I couldn't understand it, as I never moved them and had virtually never used them. I cursed myself for having put them somewhere else, in a 'safe place' I no longer had any recollection of, but I did not have time to search. I ran back upstairs and grabbed the main set out of my bag, pausing as I hurried out of the door to salute a lone magpie in the garden. I was not particularly superstitious, but I was taking no chances of incurring any further bad luck.

One for sorrow….

As I drove out of the gate and headed down the hill I knew almost immediately something was wrong. The car seemed to be lacking in power and to my horror, I could see smoke coming through the air vents in the dashboard and rising up from under the bonnet. I pulled over immediately to the side of the road and slammed on the brakes, but before I could get out of the seatbelt, I saw flames leaping out from under the bonnet and smoke rising up from the passenger side foot well.

'Shit, shit, shit!' I screamed as I fumbled with the seatbelt.

I grabbed my bag from the passenger seat and pulled the door handle to get out.

There was no familiar click and the door didn't move.

I tugged at it frantically and pressed the central locking button on and off over and over again, but nothing happened. Panic overcame me as I felt the heat under my feet and the smoke began to engulf the interior of the car, making it difficult to breathe or see. I could actually see flames in the passenger side foot well.

I jabbed at the steering wheel with the heel of my hand to sound the horn, but again there was nothing. I was trapped like a sardine in a tin can, being burned alive, while the world outside remained oblivious to my plight. I screamed and screamed for help, knowing I didn't have much time, then squirmed around desperately in the bucket seat of the Porsche to free my legs from under the steering wheel and began to kick wildly at the window in a futile attempt to smash it.

I did not want to die. Not like this. Please God, not like this.

I coughed and spluttered as the toxic smoke filled my lungs, but I managed to twist my legs around further, pushing my feet up against the soft top of the car and again kicked as hard as I could. Still nothing. The dashboard was in flames and I could no longer see out of the windows. It was all happening so quickly. I was utterly terrified, as I suddenly realised that I was not going to get out of there.

Nothing mattered anymore. The fighting and bitching with Daniel, the court battle, the scrabble for money and assets...it all seemed suddenly so unimportant. What was the point in any of it now? They say it is only when you have stared Death in the face that you truly appreciate the value of Life. I thought in desperation that I really, really appreciated my Life and I was not ready to give it up, but my strength was fading.

Suddenly there was a loud banging on the window next to me and I could make out the shape of someone yelling at me to duck down. There was a ripping noise above my head and I could see daylight.

Two men were hacking at the material roof of the car and ripping it back from the framework. They were shouting all the time.

'It's okay love, don't panic. We'll get you out of there.'

I was already scrambling to stand up on the seat as they reached in and grabbed hold of my arms, dragging me up and out through the roof. Another man had a fire extinguisher and was attempting to put out the flames, which were by now consuming the whole front of the car. Somebody else was yelling at him to stand back, as the car could blow. I was half dragged, half carried to the other side of the road, still choking as I took in big gulps of the clean air I thought I would never breathe again. I could hardly believe I had escaped, literally snatched from the jaws of Death.

'Thank you, thank you, thank you,' I sobbed through my tears of gratitude and shock.

One of the men put a big coat around me and hugged me comfortingly. I could see blood running down my leg, where the frame of the roof had torn through my jeans and put a gash in my right thigh. I didn't care. I was alive. My Guardian Angel was looking after me and I vowed that I would never again take my life for granted.

I watched dumbstruck as my beautiful car burned. It did not, in fact, explode, but by the time the fire brigade arrived, there was not much left of it. The police had arrived first and had taken my details, but quickly realised I was in no fit state to shed any real light on what exactly had happened. I was bundled into the back of an ambulance, wrapped in warm blankets and given an oxygen mask, while one of the paramedics began to dress the wound on my leg. The whole thing felt like some kind of weird, out of body experience, as if I were watching it all happen to someone else.

There was no time to properly thank my saviours, who were talking to the police by the side of a lorry. I felt something vibrate in my pocket. My phone. At least I still had that, but everything else was gone, including my bag and purse. I reminded myself that it was just stuff, all of it was replaceable. The paramedic spoke kindly to reassure me as he worked and assessed me for further injuries.

'You are a lucky lady. This cut on your leg is superficial and the breathing will start to get easier now with the oxygen. Just try to relax. It must have been terrifying for you in there. I've seen how quickly those car fires can get a hold.'

The horror of the moment I realised I was trapped and believed I was about to die came rushing back to me. Tears were streaming down my face and I was shaking uncontrollably.

'I just don't understand it. The car is not even that old. It's not long had its MOT and it's been running fine, no problems at all. It doesn't make any sense that the doors and windows wouldn't open,' I sobbed.

'My guess is it was some sort of electrical fault which caused the central locking system to fail, but the accident investigation team will find out the details. Don't you worry about any of that. Right now we need to get you to hospital for a proper check-up, just to be on the safe side. The police will no doubt come and see you in there. Is there anyone you'd like to call?'

I got him to call Frieda for me. There were already several missed calls from her and naturally she was worried, as I hadn't shown up for our meeting. She was in town and by the time I got to the hospital she was already there waiting for me. I was taken to a little side room in A&E and told a doctor would be in to see me shortly. Frieda was allowed in to wait with me.

'Oh my God, Grace, what happened? I couldn't believe it when you told me you were being taken to hospital.'

'I know. It still doesn't feel real to me. The car literally just set on fire. It happened so quickly and I just couldn't get out. I tried everything, I really did, but the doors wouldn't open. I swear to God I thought that was it. If those guys hadn't turned up....'

'Don't even think about it. You're safe now, that's the main thing. It's just so weird that it set on fire like that...but the police will find out what caused it.'

'Yeah, I suppose so.'

I looked at her, debating whether to say out loud what I was really thinking.

'Frieda...there was something else. This is all going to sound far-fetched, but the spare car keys were missing when I wanted to use them this morning. I know exactly where they should have been and they just weren't there. The more I think about it, the more I think Daniel must have taken them. He's always snooping around in the house when I'm not there. What if he did something to the car? He was acting really weird last time I saw him, saying the car looked good and he was glad I was looking after it. Like he knew something I didn't.'

She looked at me doubtfully.

'Well, we all know he's a lying, cheating arse-hole...but do you really think he would go to the lengths of sabotaging your car, knowing you could be seriously hurt, or even killed?'

'Yes. I do. He blames me for everything. Everything he's lost in the divorce...the bankruptcy...the lot. He says that if it wasn't for me and all my 'meddling', he wouldn't be in this mess. And something else has been bothering me...hear me out, because I've been thinking about this a lot. What if he did have hidden cameras in the bedsit in Stainsford and we missed them? What if he's known all along I was in there?'

I hesitated.

'I'm scared, Frieda. Really scared of him. I honestly think he might hate me enough to want me dead.'

The one that got away

Daniel

Daniel took a sip of his coffee and put down the paper with the headline facing upwards.

Local woman escapes car fire horror

Not the headline he had been expecting to read.

He kicked the table leg in frustration. She was like a cat with nine fucking lives, that one. Everything was going wrong for him at the moment and he was majorly pissed off about it.

Women. It all came down to them. They were the cause of all his current troubles. Fucking bunch of manipulative witches, the lot of them. If he could just wind the clock back, he would never have got involved with any of them. They were all the same at the end of the day. It was always great at the beginning when they were trying their hardest to please him with sex, doing whatever he wanted, dressing up in suspenders and stockings, just like the whores they really were underneath. He despised their pathetic eagerness to satisfy him with their mediocre blow jobs and role play games.

That fat bitch, Jane, was the worst of the lot. She was happy to take it any which way if she thought there was something in it for her, he thought to himself, sniggering as he remembered all the home videos bearing testament to that fact. He certainly did not need pills to get it up when he was allowed a bit of peace and quiet to watch the videos on his own in the flat. It never failed to turn him on seeing just how far he'd been able to go. In fact, he noticed with a smirk, he was getting hard just thinking about it. Jane would be out for at least another hour and he thought briefly about indulging in a little light relief there and then, but decided against it. There were more pressing issues to be addressed. He picked up his mobile, scrolled through his contacts and selected the number listed as BSS. A woman's voice answered after three rings.

'Well hello, stranger,' she drawled, with the gravelly voice of one who smoked forty a day. 'I was wondering when we were going to hear from you again.'

'I've been somewhat preoccupied, as you well know.'

'Yes, indeed. How are your 'troubles'?'

The woman's sarcastic tone did nothing to improve his foul mood.

'I'm working on it. In the meantime perhaps you'd like to remember who pays your wages.'

'Oooh, easy tiger,' she mocked. 'I assume you're calling about this weekend?'

'Is everything in place?'

'Of course. All sorted. Twelve of our regulars on the guest list and twelve of our escorts signed up and ready to deliver. Will you be there yourself?'

'Probably. I could certainly do with the distraction.'

'Well I'm sure we can help with that,' she said with a low chuckle.

The woman looked around her at the various outfits and paraphernalia on display in Stainsford's Big Sexy Superstore. Their customers were primarily men, who perhaps felt that the plus size women's lingerie section in Debenhams was not quite for them, and they prided themselves on their extensive selection of sex toys, outfits and aids, but more importantly on their discretion. The man she knew only as Mr D, had set up the store initially to feed his own habit, she assumed, but it was doing a roaring trade and there was now the added spin-off of the little soirees he had come up with the idea for. Invitations to the parties were always in high demand, offering a select clientele the opportunity to indulge freely in whatever fantasies they wanted, with no inhibitions and no boundaries. By putting a strict limit on numbers, they had created a ferocious demand for invitations, which in turn allowed them to drive up the price of tickets. She had to hand it to him; it was a sound business model.

'Oh, by the way,' she suddenly remembered, 'I meant to tell you last week. There's been a woman hanging around here a couple of times now, taking pictures outside. She even came into the store once, looking completely out of place. All seemed a bit weird. Tall, blonde hair...obviously a cheap wig. She said she had been recommended by you, which sounded odd to me, especially as she didn't seem to know what she wanted. Wouldn't leave a name. Obviously, I told her nothing.'

Daniel clenched his fist and felt the rage bubbling up inside him.

'Call me immediately if she shows up again. And have the cash ready for me at 6 pm on Friday.'

He ended the call abruptly, having no intention of engaging in small talk with her.

The 'blonde' woman was obviously Grace, snooping around again in that ridiculous attempt at a disguise she persisted in wearing. Who the fuck did she think she was? More importantly, how the hell had she found out about his latest business interest? He was more certain than ever that she was tracking him and made a mental note to drive Jane's Audi Q7 regularly for the moment; his money had paid for the damn thing after all.

He already suspected Grace of having been in the flat. Nothing he could put his finger on, but call it intuition. The thing that puzzled him, and made him uneasy, was that she had never said anything about it to him and it was most unlike her not to go shooting her mouth off, especially if she thought she had got one over on him.

She was like a dog with a bone, always had been, which was why she had to go. It had been the same with Julia, snooping around to catch him out in the beginning, then hiring a bloody private detective to follow him. Grace had obviously gone for the cheaper

DIY option, but it was no less irritating and he would need to monitor the situation very carefully to find out just how much she did actually know. Then he would deal with her.

Daniel opened his laptop and clicked on an encrypted file. The last dinner party had been a great success and most of the guests were now regulars. It had all started out as a bit of a hobby but had turned into an unexpectedly lucrative, little business. He had been meticulous in his research and it had taken a good while to build up the niche group of clients on his list. Some of them were business contacts, but the majority had been recruited due to their frequent visits to the shop. All of them had a penchant for doing things a little 'differently' and all of them had succumbed to the good old honey trap. Incriminating photographic evidence, gathered from the parties, ensured their continued loyalty.

Not that he would ever blackmail them of course; that would be illegal.

He had actually been surprised how easy it all was to manage. Like taking candy from a baby. At a grand a head for each evening they hosted, his targets were all well-heeled; in fact, that was the main selection criteria for securing an invitation. He smiled to himself as he calculated his profits for the planned evening's work. Good luck to HMRC trying to pin him down on that one. They hadn't got a clue.

Daniel opened a file named Gallery and clicked on a video, silently congratulating himself for having hit on such a winning formula. He licked his lips in anticipation, as the camera panned around the room. Ever the opportunist, he casually unzipped his flies and slipped his hand inside his chinos, caressing himself through the material of the silk slip he had taken to wearing underneath his clothes these days.

A huge table was set lavishly for twelve guests, with white-linen table cloths reaching down to the floor. The diners seated around it were a mixed bunch, all wearing black tie and chatting happily. Some of the men were there with their wives or partners, while others had come alone. So long as they paid up, he didn't really give a toss. The 'hosts' had been recruited carefully for their youth, agility, good looks and legal invisibility. He had left that side of things to his assistant in the shop. Some were male, some female and some he referred to as 'lady boys', not being one to adhere to political correctness. Their job description was simple: mix things up and do whatever the guests wanted. He had to admit, the new age of gender fluidity was certainly working to his advantage and the evenings often degenerated into a mass of writhing bodies, almost indistinguishable as individuals, moving seamlessly from one to another in their insatiable quest for sexual gratification.

Daniel watched, increasingly aroused, as the hosts circled around the table, serving food and pouring wine without saying a word, blending perfectly into the background. Some of the girls wore black skirts, short enough to reveal suspenders and no knickers, with peephole bras allowing their nipples to poke out above their low-cut tops. The boys who were clothed wore tight-fitting shirts and trousers, the bulging crotches of which left nothing to the imagination. Several hosts of both sexes were wandering around stark naked, their lithe bodies tanned and oiled. Almost imperceptibly, one at a time, they glided to the end of the table, bent down and slipped under the long white tablecloth. Six of them disappeared discreetly below the table, while six remained above to serve dinner. Daniel clenched his teeth in excitement and felt his erection grow in his hand as he stared avidly at the screen. The scene switched to below the table, where the action was being recorded by several different, strategically placed cameras. The emphasis here was firmly on the unexpected. Silent and cat-like, the hosts crept along the length of the table on all fours, carefully avoiding the feet and legs of the diners, until they arrived at their pre-selected targets.

Daniel chuckled as one of the girls deftly parted the legs of a female diner, pulled her panties aside and began probing and stroking with her fingers, before burying her face in the woman's crotch and setting to work expertly with her tongue. The camera, operated remotely, zoomed in on the action. Staring avidly at his laptop, Daniel loved how the woman's eyes widened and she squirmed on her chair as she desperately tried to continue her conversation with her husband. She was undoubtedly imagining one of the fit young men she had been ogling earlier between her legs, but she was in for a shock.

Further along, one of the 'lady boys' had unzipped the flies of a man Daniel recognised as a business customer, liberating an unimpressively small, but hard cock. The man shuddered with pleasure and groaned, in between debating the current state of the stock market with his neighbour.

The absolute triumph of it was that none of them had any clue at all as to who was working on them below the table. Daniel got the biggest kick out of seeing their faces when the truth was revealed. The expressions of the ones who claimed to be totally heterosexual were always the best, because the camera didn't lie, showing them writhing around in blissful ignorance. Despite their initial protestations of shock, they were only too happy to trot off to the private rooms with their escorts afterwards, often several of them at once. Daniel had a little office, where he could sit pleasuring himself while enjoying the variety of activities going on in all areas of the venue on the monitors. It seemed that the average populace of Stainsford and the surrounding area were rather more liberated than one might originally have thought.

The escorts were good at their job, considering the pitiful amount they earned, but in Daniel's opinion, that was the price you paid if you were in the country illegally. Throughout the evening, they moved silently amongst the clients in the dimly lit rooms, creating a wonderful atmosphere of 'anything goes', happy to do as they were told and adapt where necessary.

Daniel closed the file and shut the lid on his laptop. He was pleased with his editing, which meant that the video alternated between the scenes above and below the table. He had installed cameras and two-way mirrors everywhere, including the bedrooms and the bathrooms. Guests could purchase a copy of the dinner video and their own private sessions at great cost if they so wished and many of them did. It seemed he was not the only one that liked to watch. His clients were given assurance that all videos and photos would be destroyed 24 hours after the event, but obviously he lied about that and kept the ones he liked best for his own private collection. He had even nicked a few ideas from some of his more inventive clients and tried them out with Jane, Lorraine and a few of his other 'special friends'. Grace and Anita had always been too uptight for any of that stuff.

Daniel's mood soured again as he thought about Lorraine and what she had started. The poisonous bitch had pretty much vanished from the face of the earth, along with a considerable amount of his money and personal effects, not to mention that bloody house she had kept her paws on. She had even got a restraining order against him by lying about his so-called 'violent' behaviour. Fucking psychopathic slut.

And as for Jane. She would be home soon and would no doubt start on him about money again. She would not be happy he had screwed up the other business with Grace either. Not that it was anything to do with her really. He honestly didn't know how much longer he could stand living with her in that house and told himself he was going to have to do something about the situation, sooner rather than later.

Daniel sat back and rubbed his hand across his face in irritation, asking himself for the hundredth time where the hell it had all gone so terribly wrong? He was not a bad person, he told himself in all sincerity. He never set out to hurt anyone. All he ever wanted was to enjoy the life he deserved and he had put a lot of bloody effort into setting himself up, with the nice house, the cars, the boats, the holidays…. He was a respected local businessman, well-liked in the community and everyone thought he had married the ideal woman in Grace. To be fair, the arrangement had suited him perfectly for a while. Back in the day, when she behaved herself.

In short, he loved the respectable image of himself that the world saw.

That was all anyone was ever *supposed* to see.

He insisted to himself that it was not his fault if he wanted more. Life was too short, so why make it boring? Why limit yourself to one woman? In fact, why limit yourself to just women? There really was no need.

Everything in life was a game to Daniel and he always played to win. He had run rings round the taxman for years and when that became boringly easy, he had been forced to look elsewhere for his adrenaline rush. His other lives aside from Grace, the ones with Jane, Lorraine, Anita and, of course, his alter ego in Stainsford, were simply a way of allowing him to indulge in his fantasies like all men really wanted to do, in his opinion. He had continued to push the boundaries ever further over the years, for no real reason other than that he could. He wasn't doing anyone any harm, so far as he could see.

Yet now here he was, being portrayed as the villain of the piece. Grace was slagging him off right, left and centre to all their friends, who had immediately taken her side and stabbed him in the back, practically cutting him off. Even the ones he had known since they were all teenagers, long before Grace was on the scene: Frieda and James, Neil and Gwen...treacherous bastards, all of them. No loyalty at all.

She had somehow managed to pull the wool over the judge's eyes as well and shaft him in the divorce, although that had obviously backfired on the stupid bitch in the end. To cap it all, he now had the Trustee in Bankruptcy and her Rottweiler lawyer trying to take everything off him, including his bloody house. That had most definitely not been part of the plan.

It was so fucking unfair. Why couldn't everyone see that *he* was the real victim in all this? The victim of a bunch of vindictive, stupid, manipulative whores.

It had started all those years ago with Julia. Another one who refused to do as she was told and could never just let things go. Look how that all ended.

Daniel's increasingly dark thoughts were interrupted by the rattle of the letterbox and he quickly rose to his feet, smoothing his slip down under his jeans and zipping up his flies. The envelope had clearly been delivered in person, as there was no stamp on it. It had his name on the front, written by hand in capital letters. He opened the door and looked suspiciously up and down the street, but there was no sign of anyone. Back inside the house he tore open the envelope and found a single sheet of paper with a short typed message:

You know what you are and I will make sure everyone else does as well. I know everything and I mean 'everything'. You're a con artist, a liar and a thief. You are pure evil and your soul is beyond redemption, if you even have a soul that is. You can't be saved and you can't be reformed. You truly believe what happened to you is all someone else's fault and you are determined to make them pay.

I'm telling you, you will die trying.
And you will die alone.

Daniel laughed out loud as he screwed up the piece of paper and promptly deposited it in the bin. Grace. Had to be. His wife (ex-wife, he reminded himself), with her cryptic messages and overdramatic threats, was turning out to be the worst of the lot.

A change of tack was needed where she was concerned.

Letting go

---

*If you want to fly and be free you must first find a
way to let go of all the things that are weighing
you down.*

Grace

I sat in resigned silence and stared at my brother across his kitchen
table. Phoebe was making coffee behind us. She brought the three
mugs over and sat down beside him as he read the tediously long
email, setting out the position of the Trustee in Bankruptcy with
regard to the estate of my ex-husband.

'I honestly don't think I can take much more of this,' I began,
tearfully. 'That email arrived just before 5 pm on Friday. It seems to
be standard practice to send a shitty, threatening email at the end of
the day on a Friday, giving you no time to respond before Monday
and ruining your weekend sweating about it. I've had enough of
lawyers and courts to last me a lifetime and I'm telling you our legal
system is a complete joke. I've shouted it from the rooftops until I'm
blue in the face that he's lying about Jupiter Holdings and the
'directors', but nobody seems to be prepared to force him to tell the
truth. I've even given them proof, so I honestly don't know what
else I can do. Even my own bloody solicitor now refers to me as 'the

point of least resistance'. In other words, it's easier for the Trustee to get stuff off me than Daniel, so he just gets away with it all, like he has done for years, while they put the screws on me.'

'I still can't believe there were no repercussions for him after all that business with your poor mum,' interrupted Phoebe, angrily.

'Oh God, don't get me started about that,' I said, smarting as I remembered the look of fear on Mum's face as she read the email from Bernard Tolstenn, director of Jupiter Holdings, aka Daniel.

When I first found out about the bankruptcy, I had done as Adam suggested and acted quickly, taking a leaf out of Daniel's book and 'selling' Mum one of the more valuable cars, a 1977 E-type Jaguar, listed at £50k on the insurance certificate. Within a matter of days, it was tucked up safely in her garage, possession being nine-tenths of the law and, of course, I had made sure that all the necessary paperwork pre-dated the bankruptcy petition. Two could play at that game. I had to admit though, even I was surprised at the depths Daniel was prepared to sink to, when he began sending threatening emails to my eighty-five-year-old mother, knowing she was in poor health, from the fictitious persona of Bernard Tolstenn:

Mrs King,

It has come to our intention that you are in possession of one of our assets, namely and E-type Jaguar car. This asset was part of a Court Order that has now been made void and we want our asset returning forthwith.

If you have any more of our assets in your possession, we will also require these returning.

If this asset is not returned to us or made available for collection before 4 pm Friday UK time this week we will instruct our attorney to instigate court proceedings, this will be at the High Court in London.

Yours,
Bernard Tolstenn
Senior VP Jupiter Holdings LLC

When Mum showed me the email on her iPad, hands trembling and face white as a sheet, the first thing I noticed was the errors. *'Intention'* instead of *'attention'*; *'and'* instead of *'a'*; the use of a comma instead of a full stop after *'proceedings'* (particularly offensive to me as a teacher); the scribbled, illegible signature; the unrealistic legal deadline of four days....

I put my arms around her and gave her a comforting hug.

'Mum, seriously, please don't worry. This is obviously Daniel. It's got him written all over it. There *is* no Bernard Tolstenn, I promise you. Nobody's arresting you or taking you anywhere. I'll get that bastard for this. How dare he terrorise you!'

Mum clearly had visions of the police hammering on the door, cuffing her and carting her off in the back of the paddy waggon to await trial in the High Court of London. I was already fuming, but the 'friendly' email from Daniel to me, less than five minutes later, only served to fan the flames:

Hi Grace,

The guys from America are getting really heavy with me and chasing some of their assets. I haven't told them anything, but you need to be aware of them. They are threatening me with all sorts! I want to help you if I can. I don't want you to loose out.

Love, Daniel xx

Words failed me completely. Had he never heard of a spell checker? *'Loose'* instead of *'lose'*, I noted angrily.

Employing my new found skills as a PI over the last few months, a quick search on Google confirmed there was no such living person as Bernard Tolstenn. Of course, there wasn't. A further check of the IP addresses for the emails showed that they were, in fact, sent from the same computer. I imagined Daniel doing several quick costume changes and having board meetings with himself, reaffirming in my mind that he was indeed a psychopath with multiple personalities. The parallel with Norman Bates in the film Psycho, where Norman sits in his mother's rocking chair at the end, wearing her shawl and mimicking her voice, was not lost on me. I shuddered at the thought that I had actually been married to him for twenty years.

Not wasting any more time, I copied the emails, together with all the information about Bernard Tolstenn (or the lack of him), screenshotted the IP address details, and promptly sent it all off to my solicitor and the Trustee's solicitor, Natasha Remington, confident that I was putting the final nail in the coffin so far as Daniel's lies about Jupiter Holdings were concerned.

To my consternation Natasha replied, thanking me for my email and informing me that she was currently attempting to verify the details Daniel had supplied for a *third* director of Jupiter Holdings, a Mr Patrick Salenden. I knew that name. It took me a few minutes, but it finally came to me. Amongst the hundreds of files I had scrutinised on the infamous time capsule, there had been one entitled Scam, which had naturally intrigued me. To my great amusement at the time, it contained documents pertaining to a scam Daniel himself had been the victim of, whereby a certain Patrick Salenden had relieved him of forty thousand dollars in exchange for a car that never materialised. Salenden had provided fake photographic ID and a statement notarised by a bogus solicitor. Daniel actually had the brass neck to be using the scammer's details and ID for his own self-serving purposes, in a last-ditch attempt to convince the Courts that the directors of Jupiter Holdings really did exist. As I fired an email back to Natasha, giving her chapter and verse on Mr Salenden, I wondered excitedly whether Daniel might have done enough this time to end up behind bars for fraud.

But, of course, he hadn't. As usual, nobody listened. Nobody cared.

I took a sip of coffee and reached for the comforting chocolate biscuits in front of me, looking at Phoebe and shrugging my shoulders, as she sighed and shook her head.

'It's an absolute disgrace. I honestly just can't believe he's not been banged up in jail.'

'Ha, I wish. He's like Teflon; nothing sticks. The only small satisfaction I get is that he has lost his precious house and I know for certain he didn't want that to happen. It's a status symbol for him, playing lord of the manor in the big house in the country.'

'Pompous twat,' Phoebe interjected, with conviction.

'Not that it's done me any good in the end though,' I said, bitterly. 'The Trustee has control of the sale and she's already agreed to let it go for far less than its worth, just to get rid of it quickly. I have to be out by next week, they've told me. I also have to hand over all the cars and the paperwork, having struggled for months to find them all. In the end, I have just done their job for them. For free, as Daniel was only too happy to point out the last time I saw him. According to him, now that they have all the information I 'dug up', he has been left completely broke.'

My brother looked up from his laptop and interrupted.

'Grace, listen to me. I know it's shit, but I honestly think you have no choice but to sign the agreement. I don't want to sound harsh, but you're going to have to give this up and move on, because if you don't, it'll ruin your life and drive you mad.'

I stared at him sulkily.

'Easy enough for you to say. You're not the one being left with nothing.'

'As I said, it's shit, but if you carry on and try to fight this in court, you could end up bankrupting yourself and *really* losing everything. You can't afford to risk it; it's as simple as that. At least by signing this settlement, you get to walk away with your head held high and keep your house.'

'Yeah right. *And* its mortgage, the one that I *doubled* to supposedly bail his company out.'

He sighed again.

'I don't know what else to say. Mum has said she will lend you the money to pay them off until you can sell that car. Sign this, pay them and then you're free. Seriously, you have no choice. What goes around comes around and he will get what's coming to him one way or another. Believe me, I know how much it will hurt to do this, but I also know that you will feel like a weight has been lifted from your shoulders afterwards.'

Phoebe pulled a face and muttered under her breath.

'He should have died in that helicopter crash. He would have been doing the whole world a favour. Couldn't you arrange for him to have an 'accident' now? I'm sure some people actually do that sort of thing. I'd certainly chip in to pay for a hit on him; in fact, I think there'd be a queue.'

I smiled as my brother raised his eyebrows in exaggerated surprise.

'And who do you think you are? The Godfather?'

The mood was lightened, but my thoughts had been drawn back to the little, black card in my pocket. I carried it around with me all the time these days, like a sort of comfort blanket, or good luck charm. Somehow it made me feel like I had choices, like I was in control. I had eventually plucked up the courage to call Nicholas Barrington and we had had a long, but non-committal chat on the phone. He had a nice voice and I was beginning to wonder what the face behind the name looked like. Maybe I should just do it and arrange to meet the guy. Where was the harm in that? I thought for a moment, then on an impulse, I took out the card, ripped it in half and threw it in the bin. That was not the way forward. I had to stand on my own two feet.

I grudgingly had to admit that Jeremy was right and I had to sign the damn settlement. It was the only way to get the Trustee in Bankruptcy off my back once and for all.

Phoebe began again, undeterred.

'There's still the option of blackmail if you ask me. You've got plenty on him, what with all his dirty, little secrets in Stainsford. And you've got all the photos you took when you got into the flat. It seems a pity not to put them to good use.... He's a total pervert,' she concluded, pulling a face.

Jeremy as always was the voice of reason.

'Yes, and then who'd end up in jail? Anyway, Daniel in his Stainsford gear is an image I'd rather not have in my head. I mean, he's not exactly 'lady boy' of Bangkok is he? Can you imagine what he must look like, all six foot two of him in his bronze sparkly stilettos, frilly bloomers and false tits?'

'Ewww!'

I spluttered with laughter in spite of myself, as he stood up and minced around the kitchen on tiptoes, doing an exaggerated impersonation of Daniel, to everyone's great amusement. At least by ridiculing him, I could tell myself I had the upper hand. Phoebe looked at me and grinned, shrugging her shoulders.

'Sod the coffee, let's have a gin.'

'Good call! Alcohol is just about the only thing that keeps me going these days.'

My brother sat down again and looked at me with a straight face.

'On a serious note though, just remember you have no idea who Daniel really is. Or what he is really capable of. None of us do. A psychopath essentially fears two things: losing control and being exposed. I don't need to spell it out, do I? He's already lost control of the bankruptcy, which he is furious about and blames you for. In addition to that, although he may not be sure, he certainly suspects that you know enough to expose his biggest secret to the whole world. He *is* a psychopath, don't doubt it for a second. My advice to you is to get the settlement signed and then cut all connections with him. Make sure he gets the hell out of your life. For good.'

I heard what he was saying loud and clear, but my thoughts drifted as I focused on the words *losing control*.

For a moment I was back in the pretty Norman church of St Agnes in our village, saying my wedding vows to Daniel in front of God, our friends and my family.

'To love, cherish and obey. Till death do us part.'

Obey.

I remembered how Daniel had insisted on that part, despite it generally being omitted from modern marriage vows. Even the vicar had said I should think very carefully about it, reminding me sternly that I would be saying my vows in front of God and must ensure I did not make a promise I could not keep. He advised us that the modern clergy took the view that marriage should be a partnership of equals and offered alternative wordings. Daniel was having none of it and in the end, I acquiesced, against my better judgement.

In hindsight Daniel should have concentrated on modifying his own vows:

'To love, honour and betray....'

Dangerous Lies

When you choose to make a deal with the Devil,
remember that he always comes to collect.

Grace

Two days later, I was back home and packing up the last remnants of my life from the house that had once held so many possibilities and been so full of hope. I had resentfully signed the financially crippling agreement with the Trustee first thing on Monday before I could change my mind. I stood on the stone patio and looked around me at the hundreds of trees we had planted the first year we were married and thought of how barren and stark it had seemed the first day I went there. I saw the wooden swing seat my parents had given us for our first anniversary, where we had once sat contentedly wrapped in each other's arms, looking out over the valley below. I remembered my dad coming down to stay with us, working tirelessly to fit my new kitchen, sanding the oak beams by hand and loving every minute of it. I thought of all our plans for the house, our dreams for the future. The house that would have been so perfect for a family. I had totally bought into the illusion of the life I had there, but over the last few months, I had been forced to watch it all evaporate into the ether without a trace, powerless to hold onto the tiniest part of it. A crushing and unexpected sadness engulfed me.

- Why hadn't I been enough for him? How did everything go so horribly wrong?

My thoughts were interrupted by my phone vibrating in my pocket. I looked at the display and saw Daniel's name. I usually ignored him these days, but after a brief hesitation, I decided to answer. There were still one or two loose ends to tie up before I severed all ties completely.

'What do you want?' I snapped, defensively.

'Don't be like that. Are you okay?' he asked, apparently concerned. 'I was worried about you after I got an email about the house from the Trustee. I tried to stop them selling, but there's really nothing more I can do.'

'Like you care. You caused all this, remember?'

'Of course I care. I still love you. I will always love you,' he declared dramatically, in a pained voice.

He paused and I could almost hear the violins. I wondered whether he realised he was quoting from The Bodyguard.

'I know you don't believe me, but it's true, Grace. I can't just erase you from my life. Nor do I want to.'

'Daniel, seriously, don't do this. I'm not Julia. I know the mind games you played with her after you split up, but there's no going back for us. I've changed. I'm not the naïve girl you married anymore and I will never forgive you for what you've done to me.'

'I know that. I don't expect you to, at least not straight away, but please let me help you. I want to help you.'

'What's that supposed to mean? How can you possibly help me?'

'I've thought of a way we can salvage at least something from all this, but we would need to work together. Just hear me out, please? Can I come round to the house now? We can't do this on the phone.'

'Do what you want,' I said, dismissively. 'I'm only here for another hour or so anyway. I've almost finished.'

'Okay, I'll be there in ten minutes.'

I ended the call and wondered what the hell he was up to now. I didn't trust him for a second but, at the same time, I could not deny the fact that the thought of keeping anything from the grubby paws of the Trustee and her bitch of a solicitor was immediately attractive to me.

When Daniel arrived, I was in the kitchen, boxing up my cookery books and the coffee machine my parents had bought us one Christmas, the last remnants of my old life.

'Hi,' he paused. 'How are you?'

'How the hell do you think I am?' I retorted angrily.

He took a step towards me and I instinctively moved to the other side of the kitchen table. He looked hurt.

'Please don't look at me like that.'

'Like what?'

'I don't know, like you're scared of me or something. I'd never hurt you. Surely you know that.'

I thought of the car fire incident and wondered whether he could possibly be telling the truth. He certainly seemed different. Softer somehow.

'Look, Daniel, I haven't got long, so why don't you just tell me what this great plan of yours is and how it benefits me. I'm warning you, it had better be good.'

'Well, it's not much, but I think we can get away with hiding the boats from them.'

'Boats *plural*. As in the Swan you never bought?' I demanded furiously.

'Yes, well I might have told a little white lie there...,' he smirked.

'I knew it. You bastard! It really doesn't matter anymore though, does it? They've got the house, they've got the cars, they've got the bloody lot. I'm left high and dry with nothing, which is exactly what you intended to happen all along.'

'Oh come on, Grace. I'm not the enemy here anymore. The point is they have more than enough to be going on with for the moment with the cars you so kindly handed them, and the house. The boats are a different matter though. They are unfamiliar territory for them and far more tricky to pin down. They have no idea where they are for a start and no idea how to find any paperwork for them. They can't prove anything about the Swan, so it's safe in Ireland and I moved the race boat to a small marina on the Isle of Wight. When they asked me about it, I said *you* must have moved it. When they asked you, you said *I* must have moved it. And so the confusion goes on....'

'So it does,' I said sarcastically. 'Except I was telling the truth. Whereas you, surprise surprise, were lying again.'

'The thing is Hun, you have to know how to deal with these people. There is no point in being honest and telling the truth, as you've found out the hard way.'

I had to admit he had a point there, but I resented the patronising tone.

'I've told you before, don't call me *Hun*. Anyway, what's to stop me telling the Trustee about all this? How do you know I won't just drop you in it with her?'

'Because you're not completely stupid. And because if you did, you'd be guaranteed to get absolutely nothing out of it.'

His tone hardened as he continued.

'All I'm asking you to do is help me move the boat over to Ireland, to where the Swan is on the west coast. We'll sell them both from there and you can have half the money, I promise. That should at least pay off your mortgage. I really do want to help you. Just trust me, please.'

Trust him. Hilarious. Did he realise how ridiculous that statement was? I almost laughed out loud as an image of Kaa singing Trust in Me from The Jungle Book came into my head. I could not help drawing a parallel with the spiralling eyes of the cartoon snake as he hypnotised his prey and brought them under his spell.

'Why does it have to be me?' I demanded. 'Plenty of people could help you move the boat.'

'Because we always were the best team. You know that.'

Daniel was a master in the art of manipulation and he also knew that, if my first Achilles heel was children, my second was, undoubtedly, the boat.

I was well aware of how treacherous he was. And yet, inexplicably, I was tempted by his ridiculous idea. I knew I was striking a deal with the Devil, but I simply couldn't help myself. Or maybe I just couldn't be bothered to fight with him anymore.

He stepped towards me again and this time I didn't move away. Time stood still and I stared at him, mesmerized, as he spoke again.

'I'll never forgive myself for hurting you. I would give anything to turn back time,' he said tenderly.

It was the old Daniel speaking. The one I fell in love with all those years ago. He was so plausible, so convincing and I wanted so much to believe him.

A thousand memories raced through my brain and I felt the pain of the last few months disappearing as I was transported back to our first date. I let him hold me, while he stroked my hair and I rested my head on his shoulder. I let him kiss me goodbye, holding my face in his hands. I wondered fleetingly what my life would be like now if I had decided to just sweep all the horrors of my recent discoveries under the carpet, but then I reminded myself that the most dangerous liars of all are the ones who actually think they are telling the truth. The ones who believe their own lies.

None of it was real. I knew that. I also knew that a life devoid of all traces of self-respect was totally out of the question. Every part of my being screamed that I deserved better.

I watched Daniel go through the door and up the stone steps to the car park, and then I turned away, wiping the back of my hand roughly across my mouth to erase any trace of him from my lips.

Moving as if in a dream, I loaded the last of my personal things into the car and stood for a moment in the kitchen. I wondered to myself why we all set such store by owning our houses? I remembered how Charles used to say we were all just custodians of the buildings, for the duration of our all too brief time on the planet.

I was already no more than a ghost from a time gone by, rapidly fading, soon to be forgotten, as the house prepared to welcome its new custodians.

I closed the door and locked it for the last time, knowing I was saying goodbye to my past.

Day of reckoning

The Devil whispered in my ear, 'You are not strong enough to withstand the storm' . Today I whispered in the Devil's ear, 'I am the storm'.

Grace

I stood on the pontoon, bow line in one hand, stern line in the other, ready to cast off. It was 3.30 am and it was already getting light. We would be sailing non-stop from East Cowes on the Isle of Wight round to Dingle on the southwest coast of Ireland.

Just Daniel and me.

The breeze was due to build later to around 18 to 20 knots and, if the forecast held, it would be behind us or on the beam most of the way. A fast passage, which suited me fine. We had opted for the small delivery main with a reef in it and the number 3 jib, given that it was just the two of us.

I stood looking at the name Mistress on the side of the boat, with the accompanying graphics of a topless woman in suspenders and stockings, long, black, high-heeled boots and carrying a whip. It had been a bit of a laugh at the time but now made me cringe. Daniel used to warn me jokingly that his boat was his 'first mistress'. Unfortunately, I had no idea there were so many others.

Daniel whistled to get my attention and held out his hand to catch the rope.

'Okay, let's go. Chuck me the stern line and jump on.'

He began to reverse slowly out of the berth and I walked along the pontoon to make sure the bow did not touch, before catching hold of the forestay and stepping lightly aboard.

No going back now.

As we slipped quietly out of the harbour and into the familiar waters of the Solent I looked down at the mooring buoys we passed. There was hardly any tide at all as we set off and it would be turning in our favour soon, remaining with us for the next few hours. Once in the open water, Daniel cut the revs on the engine and headed up into the wind to allow me to hoist the mainsail and unfurl the jib, before bearing away onto our westerly course. We would start a watch system of 3 hours on, 3 hours off later in the day. I went down below to boil the kettle for a much-needed coffee, while Daniel remained on deck and began to set up the autohelm to steer the boat. I preferred to steer myself to be honest, as it gave me something to focus on and generally made the time go more quickly. I plugged a USB cable into my phone and selected a random playlist of rock ballads that I knew Daniel wouldn't object to. A quick look out of the hatch confirmed he was oblivious to anything I was doing, then I switched on the deck speakers for the stereo and sat at the chart table, looking at the information on the plotter. Calmly I picked up the VHF and called up the Coast Guard on channel 16. When they answered, they immediately told me to switch to channel 10, standard practice in order to keep channel 16 open and free for emergencies. I wanted to make sure they knew our movements. Just in case.

'Good morning. This is yacht Mistress calling to advise you of our passage from East Cowes to Dingle. Two persons on board, both wearing life jackets and lines, carrying a life raft. ETA approximately 3 days from now. Over.'

'Good morning Mistress. I can see we already have your passage logged, but we were told there was only one person on board. Please confirm, over.'

'I confirm there are definitely two of us, one male, one female, over.'

'Roger that. Thank you. Have a safe trip. Solent Coastguard out.'

'Thank you. Mistress out.'

I replaced the receiver and sat back. Daniel had never informed the Coast Guard of anything in his life and yet, for some inexplicable reason, he had decided to do so on this occasion. And he had chosen to do it at a time when I was out of the way, probably up at the marina washrooms before we left.

One person on board.

There was only one possible explanation. He wanted to make sure there was no record of me being on the boat for this trip. He didn't want anyone to know I was on board. That way it would be so much easier for me to simply disappear. My head felt as if it was being crushed in a vice and I struggled to suppress the rising panic.

- How could I have been so stupid? Again!

The rational part of my brain told me sharply to get a grip, but I couldn't dispel the growing feeling of unease at my recklessness in embarking on such a crazy venture. I asked myself why I hadn't at least told someone where I was going, but the answer to that one was easy. There was no way I could admit to any of my friends or family that I was within a hundred miles of Daniel, let alone on a boat with him, heading across the Irish Sea. It had to be our secret and besides, it suited me that way. I looked at my mobile. No signal.

My thoughts were interrupted by Daniel, shouting to me from the deck.

'Hurry up with that coffee, will you? And pass me a sandwich as well, Hun.'

Hun. The very word set my teeth on edge and I took a deep breath before responding.

'I'm just waiting for the kettle. Chicken sandwich okay?'

'Anything. I'm starving.'

I leaned out and flung the pre-packaged sandwich along the cockpit floor towards him. A few minutes later I emerged with two mugs of coffee to join him on deck, hunkering down on the floor with my back against the bulkhead to shelter from the morning wind, still chilly despite it being the height of the British summer. Daniel smiled at me happily.

'Just like old times. Just you and me.'

'Hmm. Except it isn't really though, is it? There never was a 'just you and me'.'

'Come on Grace, I'm trying here. When you stand back and look at things objectively, the real cause of the problem was everybody else interfering in our business; your family, all our friends.... I still believe that, if you hadn't gone around telling everybody, if you'd just given me a chance to explain properly, we might have been able to get through this.'

I cut him off with a barbed laugh.

'Oh, I'm sorry. And there was me thinking the cause of the problem was you shagging anything that had a pulse and lying to me throughout our entire marriage.'

He must have been practising the ridiculous, hurt expression he had on his face because we both knew that he didn't really give a shit. And we both knew that he was intent on getting his revenge on this trip.

All part of the game.

'But it's not like you're completely innocent though, is it?' he continued.

I looked at him incredulously.

'What the hell is that supposed to mean?'

'Jason?'

His eyebrows were raised questioningly as he waited for me to respond.

- Oh. Jason.

The name hung in the air as I was transported back in time.

Jason had been one of the crew on the boat in the early days. He was our main sheet trimmer and it was true we had always enjoyed a bit of a flirt and a laugh together, but it had never been anything more than that.

Not really.

'That was one drunken, bloody kiss,' I said indignantly in my defence. 'It meant nothing and you know it. It pales into insignificance compared to what you've done in the grand scheme of things.'

'How do I know it was just one kiss?' he taunted. 'You could have been lying to me for years.'

'Well, it was. And I wasn't.'

'I suppose I just thought that, if you were playing around, it didn't matter if I did the same.'

'Don't you fucking dare,' I spat at him. 'I was not 'playing around' and you know it. Do *not* try to blame me for what you did.'

I looked at him defiantly. How come I was suddenly the one having to defend myself and justify something and nothing from years ago? How dare he look at me with that smug, self-satisfied look on his face?

He was referring to the barbecue at Cookie's parents' house one summer when we had been married for about three years. They had a fabulous place on the headland with a garden that ended in a little pathway and a set of stone steps leading right down to the beach. We had gone there in the RIB as it was quicker than driving and we would both be able to have a drink. We took the anchor ashore with us as the tide was out and set it in the sand, before walking the five minutes up to the house through the garden. Daniel and I had had a stupid row before coming out and I was furious with him for totally refusing to listen to my point of view. Because of that, I was drinking far more than was good for me, given that I did not hold my drink well and I was busy helping myself to another glass in the kitchen when Jason came over to me.

'You might want to check the anchor on the RIB, as the tide is coming in quite fast. I'll come down with you now if you want. Come on.'

He started walking down the garden and I trotted unsteadily after him, eager to get away from the party for a bit. As soon as we were out of sight of the others he grabbed my hand and started running, pulling me along behind him and onto the little strip of beach that remained. We stopped abruptly and stared out to sea, then burst out laughing. The tide had come right in and the RIB now seemed an awfully long way out, with the anchor rope leading straight down and pulled taught.

'Uh oh. I guess we'll have to swim for it. We don't want to get our clothes wet though....'

I looked suggestively at Jason and began to walk slowly towards the water.

'Go on then, after you,' he said, clearly waiting for me to make the first move.

It was a warm summer evening and I was wearing a loose strappy top and a stretch mini skirt. In a couple of quick movements, I removed all entrapments of clothing and stood for a moment, emboldened by alcohol, hoping he appreciated what he saw, before running into the sea and daring him to join me, gasping and squealing as the cold water hit me. He was quick to follow, but I was a good swimmer and reached the RIB first, diving down to retrieve the little anchor from the sea bed and holding onto the side of the boat to catch my breath. Jason had his arm around me, pulling my body into his. I could feel how much he wanted me and there was no denying it was intoxicating, but the cold water quickly killed any chance of a meaningful passionate encounter. Together we swam back to the shore, towing the RIB with us. We put the anchor at the top of the beach, just above the tide line of seaweed and hurriedly got dressed, shivering and giggling like kids. As we did the walk of shame back up to the house through the garden, both of us with dripping wet hair and damp clothes, I could not help noticing Daniel's furious stare. I felt ridiculously pleased with myself. I had wanted to wind him up and it looked like I had managed it.

I walked straight past him and into the house to get another drink, a provocative smirk on my face. As I emerged back into the hallway, Prosecco in hand, Jason was blocking my way. He took the glass from me and put it on the side, then in a split second move, he entwined his fingers in mine, raised my arm above my head and forced me back against the wall, pinning me there with his lithe, muscly body, which I already knew far better than I should. His mouth was all over me; my lips, my neck and down to my breasts, while he caressed my body with his free hand. The body he had already seen every inch of. I threw my head back and arched into him, forgetting where I was.

Or maybe that was the attraction.

His breathing came in short rasps and the raw, urgent passion I was guiltily surrendering to was something I had not experienced for a long time. He stopped for a moment and looked me straight in the eyes, his lips almost touching mine.

'Why don't you leave him? He doesn't treat you right. You know how I feel about you. I'll wait for you. I mean it. However long it takes.'

Reality check. I laughed nervously. I was flattered of course, given that he was younger than me and had most of the yacht racing girls swooning at his feet, but I loved Daniel and he was my husband. This was just a wind-up, because I was mad at him. It didn't mean anything. I could never hurt him, never betray him. Before Jason could say anything else, Cookie appeared.

'Well hello, you two water babies,' he joked to diffuse the situation, putting his arm around Jason and pulling him away from me. He flashed me a warning look and shoved a beer into Jason's hand.

'There are clean towels in the bathroom, Grace, and Tina has put some dry clothes out for you to borrow. She reckons you're about the same size.'

'Ok, thanks,' I mumbled, feeling suddenly foolish and unable to meet his eye, as I ambled off in the direction of the bathroom.

And that was that. Nothing had happened, but I could not deny I had briefly wanted it to, caught up in the moment. I wondered whether adulterous thoughts and intentions could actually count as cheating. I decided not.

Jason finished the season with us but then went sailing on another boat the following year, citing a clash of personalities as the reason for the change.

It was all such a long time ago. Another life. Another me.

I gave Daniel a withering look and reiterated my original point.

'As I said, it was just a stupid kiss to wind you up because you were being a twat with me. And it was years ago. Why the hell would you bring that up now? Hardly comparable to your years of scheming and lying. Please don't try to make out that we were both somehow equally to blame in all this because nothing could be further from the truth. It's bullshit and you know it. I'm going below now. I'm freezing.'

'Okay, okay, I'm sorry,' he apologised, no doubt not meaning a word of it. 'I just wanted you to see how easily things can get out of hand.'

'But things don't just 'get out of hand' though, do they? You made conscious decisions over and over again to pick up women on the internet to cheat on me with.'

'I really am sorry you know,' he continued, thoughtfully. 'I guess you never know what you have until you lose it.'

'More bullshit. You knew exactly what you had. You just never believed for a moment you would actually lose it.'

I had to get away from him then, so I made it clear the pointless conversation was over and disappeared into the cabin. A huge sadness enveloped me again and I felt suddenly crushed under the weight of it. A thousand 'what ifs' and 'if onlys' were racing through my thoughts, as I imagined a different life. Maybe I would have been happy with Jason. I knew he was married now, with three beautiful daughters. A different decision all those years ago and that could have been me. As I reflected on my own life, I was devastated by the thought that I had wasted most of it, blundering from one disaster to the next, making wrong decision after wrong decision.

I abruptly pushed all thoughts of the past to the back of my mind, where they belonged. I refused to allow myself to dwell on things like that. One thing I knew with absolute certainty was that regret was a wasted emotion, and one that had the potential to destroy all chance of future happiness if it was allowed free rein.

Alone in the cabin, I kept my boots and outer layer of waterproofs on, in case I was needed on deck, and tried to lose myself in a book. How dare he bring all that stuff up and make out that I was somehow a guilty party! My thoughts turned yet again to poor Julia. Everyone said Daniel had messed with her head until she practically went mad by all accounts. I had no intention of going down that route, but I totally understood how it had happened.

I looked at the chart plotter periodically and alternated with Daniel to keep watch on deck. The wind had picked up a little, but it remained on our stern and we were eating up the miles. By nightfall, we were passing Lizard Point and heading into the open waters of the southern Irish Sea. I had taken it upon myself to make all drinks and food on the trip, determined not to give Daniel any opportunity to drug me or poison me. Not that food involved anything more than cup-a-soups and pot noodles, given the feeble, two-burner, meth stove the boat was equipped with. She was a race boat through and through and had been built for speed, not comfort, with no unnecessary weight allowed on board to slow her down. I made sure I slipped Daniel the odd Amitriptyline in his coffee, from my emergency supply, just to take the edge off his reactions and make me feel safer.

Memories of happier times were all around me. I would miss the boat and the camaraderie of the crew, but those days were behind me. There was no way I could fund a race yacht on my own, so no matter how much I resented it, she had to go, leaving yet another gaping hole in my future.

I volunteered to do the first proper watch as darkness fell, Daniel feeling understandably drowsy. We checked the chart plotter and agreed to stay on the same course for the next few hours, but we would almost certainly need to gybe at some point, as the wind was swinging around. I settled into as comfortable a position as possible, given the absence of any cushions and focused on fascinating pastimes such as counting the stars and scanning the horizon for any other lights.

So far Daniel had not made any attempt to shove me over the side, stab me, throttle me or bludgeon me to death and I was beginning to wonder if I was being overly paranoid, as I watched him disappear down below to sleep. He even seemed to be mindful of my safety with his parting shot:

'Shout if you need me or if the wind changes direction any more. And make sure you stay clipped on.'

'Obviously,' I replied sarcastically, showing him my lifeline. I thought of the Fastnet Race of 1979, when five yachts sank, twenty-four crews abandoned ship and fifteen souls were lost. So many lessons about safety had been learned from that tragedy. I looked at the chart plotter, churning out a constant stream of information for me and wondered what it must have been like for the sailors in that race, without recourse to any of the sophisticated navigational equipment we now benefit from. What unspeakable terror must they have endured that night, knowing they were at the mercy of Nature at its most vicious, cruel and uncompromising?

I looked around me at the waves rising and falling rhythmically in the darkness, with nothing to do except think. I imagined falling into the water and watching, helpless, as the boat sailed away from me and disappeared. People said drowning was a peaceful death and you saw your whole life flash before you as you drifted into oblivion. I didn't believe that for a moment. I knew for certain that I would be fighting until my very last breath, fighting to stay alive, despite the searing pain that the water entering my lungs would undoubtedly cause.

The loud squelch noise from the VHF snapped me back into reality as the weather forecast began and my dark thoughts vanished.

Daniel's face appeared in the companionway after the agreed three hours.

'How's it going?'

'The wind's dropped a bit, but we're still making good headway and you can catch some good waves to surf down if you want to steer.'

He clipped his lifeline to the jackstay before climbing up on deck and stretching.

'I need a pee,' he announced, as he made his way clumsily to the back of the boat, bracing himself against the rear guard rails and holding onto the taut lifeline and the backstay for balance.

Maybe if he'd just kept his treacherous mouth shut for once, I might have changed my mind and things might have ended differently, but he had to push it. He yawned and picked up the thread from an earlier conversation.

'I meant what I said about wanting you to meet my kids you know. You'd love them. I've already started teaching Aaron to sail and he's a natural. He'd have loved this trip. You always wanted kids so badly...it'd be like a ready-made family for you, without the pain of childbirth. Don't close any doors, Grace, that's all I'm saying.'

He just loved to twist the knife. Sadistic and cruel to the end. Couldn't help himself. I knew at that moment he would always be there, lurking in the background, drawing me back in and looking for an opportunity to torture me, just like he did with Julia. Making me fear for my life one moment and telling me he loved me the next. Mind games, which had already driven one woman to an early grave. I would not allow him to do the same to me.

In the end, it was easy.

The wind was coming from behind us over the starboard quarter of the boat. Without warning I altered course, bearing away sharply and setting in motion the chain of events that would ultimately set me free. The boom, with the full weight of the wind now on the wrong side of the mainsail, sliced across the boat with ferocious speed and slammed out on the other side in a crash gybe. I knew exactly what would happen and braced myself with my foot as the boat rounded up sharply into the wind, sails flapping and rigging shuddering violently.

Behind me, I heard a frantic scrabbling, a thud and a startled shout as the boat heeled over at an alarmingly steep angle. Daniel, totally unprepared, found himself thrown off balance down to the leeward side and then, to his horror, dumped unceremoniously into the water. The lifeline pulled tautly and he must have believed for a moment, as he was dragged coughing and spluttering through the water behind the boat, that I would soon be desperately trying to help him scramble back aboard.

That was never going to happen.

I stared steadfastly ahead, ignoring what was going on behind me and concentrating on getting the boat back under control. Priorities. Leaning forward, I released the jib sheet and pulled it in on the new side. I took hold of the wheel and adjusted my course until the wind began to fill the sails.

I refused to look behind.

Don't look back. You're not going that way.

The words on the card Neil and Gwen had sent me when the shit first hit the fan all those months ago.

Sound advice.

I switched on the autohelm to steer the boat for me and moved forward as if in a trance to release the mainsail halyard, then up to the mast to pull the sail down, securing it against the boom with sail ties and thanking God it was only the small delivery main. It was no mean feat on my own, but I persevered and the boat would be much easier to handle under jib alone, now that it was just me.

Only then did I steal a furtive glance behind me, peering into the darkness.

Nothing but the relentless march of the waves, rising and falling.

Daniel was gone.

It was as if he never really existed.

Lost at sea. A fitting end.

I felt a strange sense of calm wash over me, as I concentrated on the one thing I now had full control over, sailing the boat to safety. I looked up and saw the sky, covered in a myriad of stars, with the full moon lighting a pathway on the water. It was beautiful.

I did not kill Daniel.

I am not a cold-blooded murderer.

I simply made a split-second decision to provide Fate with the opportunity to dole out her own form of justice and restore the natural order of things: Good prevailing over Evil, Right over Wrong.

In a fleeting moment of benevolence, I hoped I had been wrong in my theories about drowning. About the pain at least. I imagined Daniel's confusion, as he watched his only hope of salvation sailing away from him into the night, the little white stern light growing dimmer and dimmer. The point at which he realised the inevitability of his fate must have come quickly I decided, and I told myself that, if his life really had flashed before him at the end, at least his final moments would have been entertaining. I hoped for the sake of his soul that he felt some remorse as he was finally forced to confront his own mortality and give himself up to the eternity of the sea.

I stared at the rear guard rail wires trailing behind in the water and reached down to pull them back into the boat. The two sets of taut wires, stretched horizontally across the stern of the boat, were there to help prevent anyone falling overboard. They were normally secured with shackles, which were then wrapped in insulation tape to ensure the pins could not work loose and fall out.

I felt in my jacket pocket and pulled out the pins I had removed earlier, before taping back over the fixings. The treacherous arrangement had appeared normal, as I knew it would, but there had been no chance at all of it holding under any real pressure, certainly not the pressure of a ninety-eight kilo, six foot two man lurching against it. I thought of Daniel, clutching frantically at anything that might give him a firm handhold in the crash gybe. I imagined his utter disbelief as the guard rails went loose in his hands, leaving the back of the boat completely open and exposed.

I tossed the pins into the water and secured the guard rails properly this time with new shackles and several wrappings of PVC tape. In fact, I went all around the boat, replacing the tape everywhere, so it all looked the same. I turned my attention to the jackstays, the long pieces of webbing stretched along the length of the deck from front to back on both sides so that the crew could clip their lifelines on and move around the deck freely, safely attached to the boat at all times. At least, that was the idea. I saw Daniel's face in my mind's eye, the relief as his lifeline held fast, changing to incredulity and fear as it came loose from the webbing straps and he was left floundering.

Poor Daniel.

How could he ever have suspected what would happen?

I made sure the jackstays were secured properly, in the same way as the guard rails, before attaching my own lifeline to them. It would be plain silly to risk falling overboard myself.

Finally, I felt in my other pocket and fished out the automatic inflation canister that belonged in the lifejacket I had handed Daniel to wear when we set off. He was never one for checking the safety equipment. At least I had given him a life jacket. And there was always the option of blowing it up manually, which would have bought him a bit of time, although probably not much in all likelihood. As I understood it, the chances of surviving longer than about half an hour in the water were slim, due to the low temperatures, even though we were in the middle of one of the warmest summers for years. I consigned the canister to the murky depths of the Irish Sea to join the shackle pins, confident in the knowledge that there was absolutely nothing to suggest this was anything other than a tragic freak accident.

Three hours later I checked the plotter and saw that I had covered about twenty-five miles. It was time.

I threw the yellow lifebuoy over the side of the boat into the water, then pressed the MOB button on the plotter, setting a loud alarm off. I switched on the engine and furled the jib to make life easier for myself as I began to circle randomly as if trying to recover the lifebuoy. The chart plotter would be checked and it was important for them to see I had at least attempted to search for Daniel. I put the engine into neutral, to remain in more or less the same area.

There was just one more thing I needed to do.

I stood on the deck behind the wheel, keeping a watchful eye out for any other vessels. I picked up the VHF transmitter and took a deep breath, steeling myself, before making the channel 16 call that no sailor ever wants to have to make.

'Mayday, Mayday, Mayday. This is yacht Mistress, Mistress, Mistress. Man overboard, urgent assistance required, over.'

There was a brief pause and the squelch crackled, then came the reply. Calm. Assured. On my side. Someone else was in charge now. All I had to do was comply and follow instructions.

I was confident I had injected just the right amount of hysteria into my voice as I gave the details of my position and of the person who had fallen overboard.

But of course, that wasn't going to be much use to anyone.

****

Several hours later I was on dry land once again, sipping the hot chocolate laced with rum that Brandon, the harbourmaster of Cork, had given me. I huddled on a chair in his office upstairs, my feet tucked under me, pulling the blanket tighter around me. Everyone was being so kind to me.

They all mistook my indifference for shock and I was more than happy to let them.

A full SAR operation had been launched to try to rescue Daniel initially, but latterly the focus had changed to recovering Daniel's body.

Still, they had found nothing.

Twenty-four hours later, they regretted to inform me that they had been forced to call off the search, as there was no longer any chance of him being found alive.

It was over.

Questions were asked of course. Lots of them. A man had died at the end of the day. Reports had to be filed, there had to be an inquest and reasonable conclusions had to be drawn, given the lack of a body.

I told the truth. At least, my version of it.

He came up on deck for his turn on watch and went to the back of the boat for a pee. Yes, he was wearing a life jacket and yes, he attached his lifeline to the jackstay. Or at least...I thought he did. I couldn't be sure. I was steering the boat when a rogue wave caught me off guard and made me lose my balance. We only veered off course for a moment, but it was enough to cause a crash gybe and that must have been when Daniel fell over the back of the boat (loud gulp). I didn't realise at first. I was too busy trying to look after myself and get the boat back under control. I still don't understand how it could have happened. He was an experienced sailor. By the time I regained my balance and looked around, he was gone. Vanished. Not a sign of him anywhere (tears). I can only assume his lifeline mustn't have been attached properly. I know for sure he was wearing a lifejacket – I gave it to him myself. Even if there was a problem and it didn't inflate, he could always have blown it up manually. He would have known that. Unless maybe he banged his head and knocked himself out....

Of course, I tried to search for him, but manoeuvring a boat like that on my own was not easy. Oh God, poor Daniel (accept offer of tissues).

I did my best.

I did everything I possibly could, but he had simply disappeared (more tears).

Of course, I left out a few details here and there, but I felt happy that I had given a pretty accurate version of events. There was even the added bonus that the press were all over it and it seemed I would be able to sell my heart-wrenching story to the highest bidder.

Every cloud.

The real icing on the cake however, was what the unfortunate tragedy meant as far as Jane, Anita and their kids were concerned. As Daniel's body had not been recovered, there would be no death certificate before a minimum of seven years had passed. Until then, all his assets and bank accounts would be frozen, including the ones in America. Even after seven years, I learned he would not automatically be presumed dead. There would still be a lot of hoops to jump through to get a death certificate and release funds. And of course, there was the Trustee in Bankruptcy, prowling around in the shadows like a hyena, waiting to scavenge whatever she could from the carcass and having all the time in the world to make both Jane and Anita's lives a misery.

It was one hell of a mess, I thought to myself, unable to resist a little smile of satisfaction.

A mess I no longer had any part in. Finally, I was free of all the lies, the deception, the humiliation.

I learned the hard way that none of us can ever know what we are truly capable of until we are pushed to our limits.

Everyone has a breaking point. Mine turned out to be the door to my future.

Epilogue

Monsters really do exist. They move amongst us, disguised as one of us. We can never truly get rid of them. That is why they are so dangerous.

The little yacht, Talina, bobbed around in the waves, sails flapping gently. There was almost no wind and the two men on board were in no hurry. They were about fifty miles off Falmouth, but they had no intention of actually going into the port. Not with the twenty kilos of cocaine they were carrying, stashed in the bilges. The older of the two was at the helm, smoking a cigarette, while the younger one chose to pass the time playing games on his iPhone. Neither of them showed any interest in making conversation.

The young man looked up abruptly from his phone.

'Did you feel that?'

'What the feck are you talking about?'

'We hit something in the water just now. I felt it. There it is again.'

He reached into his pocket and leaned over the side to shine a torch down into the water along the length of the hull. It had been almost imperceptible, but he had definitely felt something knock against the fibreglass of the boat. He gave a startled little cry of shock and instinctively moved back.

'Holy fuck, there's someone in the water! Quick, help me!' he shouted.

The light had picked up the reflective strip of a partially inflated lifejacket. The thing knocking against the hull was the man's head, barely above water.

'Leave him, I say. The last thing we need is anything to draw attention to ourselves. He's most likely dead anyway. The water's feckin' freezing.'

'Fuck man, we can't just leave him. No way. I'm not having that on my conscience. Come on, for fuck's sake! Help me get him on the boat.'

The older man muttered something incomprehensible under his breath, tossed his cigarette into the water and, against his better judgement, reluctantly went over to lend a hand.

The man in the water was not small and, with his sodden clothes weighing him down even further, it was a mammoth task for the two men to drag him aboard. In the end, they had to winch him in with the help of an improvised sling made from one of the halyards. He was unconscious and frozen to the touch, but further checks confirmed that he was, by some miraculous form of divine intervention, alive. Half carrying, half dragging him down below, the two men set about removing his lifejacket and outer layers of clothing and wrapping him up in anything they could find, in an attempt to raise his body temperature to something closer to normal. After about half an hour, they decided they had done all they could and left his fate in the hands of the gods, while they went back on deck to discuss the implications of this new situation for them. They were a couple of hours early for the rendezvous, so they had a bit of breathing space, but neither of them was under any illusion that this new 'complication' would not go down well with the boss man. The older of the two, whose name was Vincent, lit another cigarette, clearly rattled.

'Where the fuck did he come from anyway? There's not another vessel in sight for fuck's sake. How the hell is he even alive?'

A low moan from the cabin reaffirmed that the stranger had indeed lived to tell the tale of his ordeal, whatever it may have been. The younger man, Darragh, moved to go down and check on him, but Vincent gripped his arm sharply to stop him.

'Put your balaclava on,' he hissed. 'We can't risk him seeing our faces or I swear we'll have to finish him off ourselves.'

Darragh looked at him, unsure whether or not he was serious, but he knew better than to question and did as he was told. The man was barely conscious but had begun to shiver violently. A good sign, if the bits of information he had gleaned about hypothermia over the years were true. He searched around in the cabin and found an old sleeping bag someone had left in the back of the boat. After a bit of a struggle, he managed to manoeuvre the man into it and zip it up to keep any remaining scraps of body heat from escaping. It seemed to do the trick and the shivering subsided a little.

Vincent looked around as he drew on his cigarette and saw a white steaming light heading their way.

'For fuck's sake, they're here already.'

An hour later their highly valuable and totally illegal cargo had been swiftly and efficiently exchanged for a bulky envelope of cash. Faces were concealed at all times. There were no names and no pleasantries, just a simple, no-nonsense business transaction and the two boats disappeared in opposite directions. Nothing had been said about the additional crew member, but as they headed back home to the southwest coast of Ireland, they realised they had to decide quickly what the hell they were going to do with him.

In the end, they had plenty of time to come up with a plan because it was a good five hours before their 'problem' was awake and able to talk. The men had by then decided on a course of action that would enable them to get rid of him, but also keep their consciences clear, given the fact that informing the authorities of the incident was completely out of the question. They would pull into a secluded bay they knew of on the south coast and take him ashore in the dinghy. They would dump him there on the beach but, after that, he would be on his own. He would find himself miles from anywhere, but that was his problem. At least he would be alive and on dry land, with significantly improved chances of survival. He would never have seen their faces and the boat bore no identifying name on the hull or stern. She was as anonymous as they were. It was the best plan they could come up with and they were as happy with it as they could be, given the circumstances.

Darragh was the one to break the news to the man as they approached the bay. He expected the stranger to plead with them to take him safely to a port, beg them to get him back to his home and his family, but to Darragh's amazement, there was only relief on his face and just a hint of a smile.

'Thank you,' he whispered, closing his eyes for a moment before continuing.

'That suits me fine. Being 'dead' is a particularly attractive option for me right now.'

THE END

Printed in Great Britain
by Amazon

44882494R00236